Circ

Simon Fairbanks
Maria Mankin
Yasmin Ali
Jason Holloway
Livia Akstein Vioto
Luke Beddow
Danielle Bentley
William Thirsk-Gaskill
Sue Barsby
Giselle Thompson

Pigeon Park Press

Paperback ISBN: 978-0-9927034-6-2
Ebook ISBN: 978-0-9927034-7-9

Published by Pigeon Park Press

www.pigeonparkpress.com
info@pigeonparkpress.com

Cover artwork created by and copyright © Mike Watts – www.bigbeano.co.uk

<u>Acknowledgements</u>

The authors and editor would like to offer their thanks to those people who helped make this book possible.

To the Ten To One judges, James Brogden, Mike Chinn, Max Patrick Schlienger, Martin Tomlinson and Kit de Waal for their monthly scores and comments on the fresh chapters.

To the 700+ Facebookers who voted for their favourite chapters each month and offered the writers so much encouragement and support.

To our most helpful beta-readers, Matty Millard and Maren Tirabassi, who truly helped shape the final novel with their insightful views and perspectives.

To Daniela Horsley for her help with the Romanian dialogue (although all errors regarding Romanian language, history and culture in the novel are ours).

And, finally, to our Crowdfunder supporters (Helen Allan, Julia Becker, Richard Castell, Pilar Esteban, Scott Franklin, Berni Sorga-Millwood, Harriet Undery, Jolly Demon Productions, drunkenrocker, paulmchale, sarahknitting, lets_do_it, nonievmcd) who gave their money and support to this novel project.

Thank you, thank you, thank you...

Foreword

The circus elephant

Circ is a story set in a tacky seaside resort on the generally flat, cold and bleak east coast of England. It is also a story about circuses or, more accurately, it is partly about circus folk who have lost their circus. It just so happens that the first circus I ever went to was on the generally flat, cold and bleak east coast of England.

It would have been at some time in the early 1980s. I don't recall the name of the circus company or many of the acts. What I do recall is how disappointed I was, specifically by how much the performance – See the woman with her performing poodle (singular)! See the world's most indifferent clowns! – failed to live up to the bright, bold and dynamic promise of the circus poster. I could swear blind that there was an elephant on that poster. There was no elephant in that circus. Poodles (sorry, poodle, singular) do not equal elephants in any child's imaginations.

But what did it matter? The poster had served its purpose. It convinced my dad to part with his cash and we were suckered in, sat on hard benches beneath a not very big top in some damp fenland field. Posters, book covers and advertisements do that. They exist to draw us inside and, frequently, we don't get what we expected and, sometimes, we feel cheated.

Circ came out of a writing project called Ten To One, which I started in late 2012. The basic concept was of a novel written by ten authors who would, in the style of X-Factor or Strictly Come Dancing or Insert-reality-TV-show-here, be voted out of the novel one by one as the story progressed. I pitched the project to the global writing community as a fight to the death with pens instead of guns and knives, as a cutthroat competition in which those who could not stand the heat would be rapidly expelled from the kitchen. The project was even going to be called Write Or Die (until I realised that name had already been taken by a very successful website).

In my imagination, this literary equivalent of *The Hunger Games* or *Battle Royale* would produce a story that was... well, like *The Hunger Games* or *Battle Royale*, a story of violence and cruelty and a rapidly diminishing roll-call of characters. In fact, my personal secret touchstone for the story was going to be Agatha Christie's *And Then There Were None*, a story that could easily have been written by such a project.

That was my pitch. That was my advertisement. That was my enticement.

And once I had my ten intrepid volunteer writers selected from the list of applicants, once they were brought *inside* and the project began in earnest, was that what happened?

No, of course not.

The Ten To One authors devised much, if not all, of the novel through collaborative discussion. Given that none of them had met each other before the project began, that seven of them were based in the UK, two in the US and one in Brazil, we should be grateful that we live in an age of instant communication and cloud-based document sharing or else their discussions would have taken years rather than months.

Their discussions and internal democracy determined the setting of the novel and the original plot (albeit one that was for a long time no more complex than "There is an old man and he has a secret"). Characters were formed, character relationships were discovered and, more importantly, the writers forged relationships with one another and they went from being competitors to being teammates, collaborators.

And so, once the project got underway and authors began writing chapters for votes of a social media audience and the approval of five literary judges, we saw something that was certainly not a literary fight to the death, was nothing like *Battle Royale* or *The Hunger Games*. There was a degree of competition but it was competition to be the best team. The authors assisted one another, shared plot development suggestions rather than hoarded them, drew from one another the best possible story. Even once the voting started and the writers and their characters were evicted from the story one by one, to my surprise they stayed on the 'team', as story advisors and editors.

Ten To One became a project unlike the one original envisaged or advertised. Once the ten authors were inside the circus tent, it was they who changed it into something else.

The blind men and the elephant

There is the old Indian story about a group of blind men who come across an elephant in the forest. Once seizes its rough and gnarly leg and declares he has found a tree. Another takes hold of the elephant's tail and pronounces it to be a length of rope. The trunk is a snake, the tusk a pipe, the elephant's side a wall. Each of the men discovers a piece of the picture, a nugget of truth, but none of them has apprehended the entire elephant.

The Ten To One project was a surprising inversion of this fable. The ten authors started out with a vision of their story - they already knew they were dealing with an elephant – but, through the eyes of their ten characters, they had to approach the story from different points and perspectives. In terms of the metaphor, one of them had to start out with the feet, another with the tail, another with the trunk.

Picture it as a drawing exercise. Get a piece of paper and some pencils. Get some friends. Draw an elephant. A single elephant. All of you. Simultaneously.

You'll end up with something like an elephant but not the elephant any of you intended. Does your elephant have four legs? Or two or six? Is it more of a hippopotamus than an elephant? Has it transformed into some strange and fantastical beast? I'm sure it's beautiful, whatever it is.

Circ, as a novel, is not the elephant anyone imagined it would be. Looking back on the piece with distance and an objective eye, I would say its major themes are circuses, fires and lost childhoods. None of that was in the original agreed brief or the early planning documents. These were parts of the whole story that neither the writers or I expected to find as we explored this fantastical beast of a novel.

The elephant statue

According to an apocryphal quote attributed to any number of sculptors, when asked how he was able to carve a perfect statue of an elephant, the sculptor replied that you started with a block of marble and chipped away anything that didn't look like an elephant. Once *Circ* was finished, it was certainly not the elephant we had intended to make and, though that isn't a problem per se, it wasn't really the elephant we needed either. That's not the fault of the authors. Every novel needs editing - don't let anyone suggest otherwise – and it is inevitable that some of the prose needs trimming and shaping.

With ten authors, the issue of editing becomes a slightly different one. If our collaboratively produced elephant ended up with two trunks then one of the trunks would have to go, even if both of them were perfectly formed. Our elephant's eyes can't be looking in two different directions, no matter what they are looking at. Our elephant has to have at least one foot on the ground.

What I'm saying is that some genuinely magical prose had to go. Some brilliant plot developments had to be removed. There are spin-off stories that are just begging to be written. What happened to Nell's husband? What threads link Shaun, Gracie, Harry and the Brotherhood of the Stars? And what exactly is the deal with Bobby and Marcus?

There are loose ends but, here, they are not a bad thing.

I believe, the joy of working on *Circ* and of reading *Circ* is in following the journeys of our ten protagonists, knowing that each of them is managed by a different author with a different authorial voice and knowing that the judges and the public have determined who will leave the narrative and who will stay.

So, join Anastasia the artist, Bobby the small-town gangster, Flic the social worker, Gracie the fairytale dreamer, Mungo the drunken clown, Nell the American widow, Sabina the sword-swallowing waitress, Shaun the cult survivor, Tim the young carer and Valerie the scheming actress. Watch them as they go round and round, crossing paths and slipping from the story one by one. Watch this fantastical beast. It's not what you expected but you won't feel cheated.

Iain Grant
Editor

PROLOGUE

Gracie

Drip, drip, drip.

"Mister Pop, what's that sound?" Gracie asked.

"Hm? What's what?"

"That sound."

"Ah," the old man smiled in that strange rumbly voice he called an Accent, "it is Bau-bau knocking to be let in. He is a creature from my country. Like your English bogeyman."

"That's not knocking," the girl argued. "It's water."

"Bau-bau has many ways of knocking, little one." He glanced across the small, dark flat scattered with vibrant, exotic objects to the kitchen door and then back to his young friend. "But do you know why he knocks?"

"To be let in!" she said.

"Yes, but why?"

Drip, drip, drip. The noise no longer sounded like a leaky tap. Mister Pop's mischievous smile and that strange name bursting from his lips like a bubble of magic – Bau-bau – turned the beats into a rhythmic chant. *Drip, drip, drip. Let, me, in.*

"He sounds wet," Gracie suggested. "Does he need to borrow a towel?"

Mister Pop shook his head. "He wants to steal children like you, and put fairies in their place so nobody will know they are missing."

"But I don't want to be stolen!" Gracie said.

"Stolen. Don't you worry. Only a grown-up can let him in, if a little one has been bad."

"But I've been good."

"Very good. And you had better be good for your mother and father as well, or they might decide to hand you over to Bau-bau themselves."

Gracie frowned. "Sarah and Arthur won't give me to him," she declared. "They want to be my mummy and daddy so they won't. But they're not my real mummy and daddy. And Laura can't give

9

me to Bau-bau either, even if she wants to, because she's not a grown-up."

Mister Pop's wrinkly face wrinkled up just a bit more and he sat straighter in his armchair. "Be grateful that you have kind people who want to take care of you," he said. "Would you want to go back to where you were before? With the other children? No. You want to be in a family. It is good to have a family."

"I don't remember what it was like," she growled as she folded her arms. "But I bet it wasn't like here. I bet you can do what you want in a care home."

Drip, drip, drip. The sound strained between them now as Mister Pop tried to look Gracie in the eye and she stared at her feet. Her knees did not reach the lip of the chair.

"When Bau-bau takes children," she said, "where does he take them?"

The dripping would not stop. Bau-bau must really want to get in, she thought, probably because he could smell her in here. Even though she knew that he could not get in, it frightened her to think that he was right there inside the tap, waiting for an invitation that would never come. Would he want to drag her into the pipes? She imagined a dark, cold, wet prison where her chest was squeezed so tightly that she could hardly breathe, and shivered.

"He takes them to the Forest," replied Mister Pop. "It is called the Other Realm and it is where all of the fairies live. It is a very hard place to get to. Only Bau-bau and the fairies know the way, because it is hidden in the gaps in our world and people cannot see it. In some ways it is just like our forests. In other ways it is much greater, and full of impossible things. Some people would call it a frightening place. Some people would call it beautiful."

"What do you think?"

"I think it is both."

"I don't want Bau-bau to get me," she mumbled as she cast another look at the kitchen door. "Tell him to go away. Tell him I'm good."

"He will not listen to me, little one. I am just an old man."

"What does Bau-bau look like?"

"Like any man. A bad man."

"How will I know if he is trying to get me?"

"He will knock for you. That is how you can always tell."

There was a short silence, interrupted only by the *drip, drip, drip* of the tap in the kitchen. Mister Pop gazed at the carpet, as though he was seeing something that wasn't there.

"Tell me a story," she demanded abruptly. "Please."

"About Bau-bau?"

"No. An exciting story. About somewhere far away and long ago."

"Would you like socată while you listen?"

Gracie nodded, and as Mister Pop disappeared into the kitchen his voice crept through the walls like a ghost's, and all the clay and wood and glass objects around the flat seemed to lean in and listen. A red mask on the wall looked down at her with its great white mane billowing about it and its horns glinting in the dim light.

"In a far green country beside the sea," Mister Pop began, "there was once a kingdom. Its people were rich and happy, and its great city was always loud and bright with celebrations. The King who lived in this city was loved by his subjects. Under his rule they never went a day without fine food, finer wine and some grand entertainment. It was a city of laughter at the heart of a joyful kingdom."

The old man emerged from the kitchen and handed Gracie her mug of hot socată, easing himself into his armchair. She had forgotten about the dripping tap.

"Go on," she commanded.

Mister Pop chuckled. "Though the King was very kind, he was not very wise, and while the Kingdom enjoyed the best of everything they were not prepared for any of the terrors that life holds in store for us all. On this day, as they chatted in their public houses and watched their travelling shows, a great terror was already flying towards them from out of a brilliant blue sky. It was a gigantic thing hidden in smoke and fire, protected by scales so hard that diamonds would have broken against them. It roared with a force that shook the mountains and rattled the very ground of the Kingdom, and far below, the people cried out in surprise and fright."

"Eeeeee," said Gracie, adding her own vocal effects.

"Yes, like that. The shock came rumbling through the floor and opened a crack in the very tiles of the great hall where the King sat on his throne. The King's guard burst in through the doors and knelt down before him.

"'Your majesty,' their captain cried, 'Balaur has come! He is setting the city on fire with his-'"

"What's Balaur?" asked Gracie.

"The most terrible of all the dragons, child," said Mister Pop. "Don't interrupt. The captain of the guard said, 'He is burning the city with his breath and crushing the houses with his claws. Will you ride with us and face the monster?'

"The King sat frozen with fear but said, 'I will ride.' As the guards left the great hall, a crowd of the King's servants and maids swarmed in, panicking and screaming. They threw themselves at his feet.

"'Your majesty!' they wailed. 'Balaur is here! He is roasting people in their homes! His three heads keep watch over the whole city! Will you ride out and protect us from his anger?'"

"Three heads?" said Gracie.

"Of course he has three heads," said Mister Pop. "He was Balaur after all. 'I will ride,' the King said to them. The servants and maids shed tears of happiness and ran from the hall. As they disappeared, the King noticed a small boy standing in front of the doors waiting to be received. The King called him in, and the child walked up to the throne and bowed low. He was the son of one of the noble lords.

"'Please, your majesty,' the young boy said, 'my father has gone to fight Balaur. I do not know if he will live or die. Will you ride out with him, and tell him that his son is waiting in the castle? Tell him that I am proud to have such a brave father.'

"The King was very pale. 'I will ride,' he told the child.

"'Thank you, your majesty,' said the boy and, with another bow, was gone. The King sent out an order for his horse to be saddled. He jumped up onto the animal's back without his sword and rode as fast as he could around the city towards its gates, which were wide open. Then he turned away from the burning houses and rode away as quickly as the horse could carry him. He would rather let his whole Kingdom burn to the ground and let all of his people die than face Balaur the dragon in battle."

"What?" said Gracie. "He can't do that."

"He can," said Mr Pop. "And he did."

"What happens next?"

"Ah, no," the old man said. "I do believe it is time for your dinner."

Sure enough, at that moment she heard Sarah calling from across the hallway.

CHAPTER ONE

Mungo Joey

Mungo Joey awoke on his usual bench on the pier. His bloodshot eyes met a cloudy spring sky. He could hear the waves and the seagulls but no people. Once again, he had slept through most of the morning but, sure enough, there was a healthy pile of coins in the floppy clown hat in front of his bench.

It still astounded Mungo that people got any enjoyment from a lazy, grotesque clown sprawled on a bench. He didn't do anything worthy of their attention. He just lay there in full clown garb, eating junk food, drinking Wonky Donkey and ignoring the passers-by. Yet, the crowds seem to think it was an ironic performance and the coins kept coming.

Along the pier he saw a peculiar sight. There was a red-headed woman sketching a dead seagull. Could it be...?

"Spitfire!" Mungo cried and leapt from his bench.

The red-headed woman jerked with surprise and took a step back upon seeing a dishevelled clown bundling across the pier towards her.

Mungo dropped to his knees by the dead bird and began inspecting the corpse: lifting its wings with his gloved hands and checking its lifeless head for markings.

"Hey!" the woman tapped Mungo with her sketchbook. "I was sketching that!"

"Forgive me," Mungo replied, his voice thick with Wonky Donkey. "I have been terrorised by a feathered Fury known as Spitfire for a long time. The beast steals my food and paints my bench with excrement but this is not him. I was mistaken."

Mungo bowed his head and removed his curly green wig as a sign of respect for the deceased. The redhead raised her eyebrows.

"Well, there goes my sketch," she sighed. "You've repositioned the wings. I'll have to take this home and finish it there." She produced a plastic bag and stuffed the dead gull inside. Now it was Mungo's turn to be shocked. His mouth dropped open.

"Are you going to eat that?"

"Eat it? Christ, no! I plan to turn this creature into art."

"You do?"

"Of course," she said. "I am Anastasia Boty."

Mungo shrugged.

"Perhaps my name does not carry much recognition in the circus community," Anastasia said. "I have a following in London. I was short-listed for the Turner Prize."

"Well, you're a long way from London," Mungo said. "Maybe you should leave the bird here."

"So its carcass can be picked over by its friends? My plans for its remains will be a lot more fitting. Anyway, you have yet to tell me your name."

Mungo felt the need to justify himself. After all, he was an artist of sorts and felt an ego rising under his face paint. "I am Mungo Joey, classically-trained clown and resident attraction on the pier."

Anastasia smiled politely.

"I have a following in Skegness," Mungo added.

"I don't doubt it." Anastasia said and pocketed her charcoals. "Well, good to talk but now I have work to do."

She started to leave, plastic bag in hand, but then stopped. She fixed Mungo with an intense stare, one that only an observational artist could conjure.

Mungo winced as she looked him up and down, taking in every aspect of his appearance: the donut crumbs on his spotted jacket, the make-up cracked around his crow-footed eyes, the receding hair underneath his threadbare wig and the sad, world-weary eyes.

"People normally throw some coins in my hat when they stare for that long."

Anastasia looked thoughtful and edged towards him.

"Sorry, it's just, I specialise in decay and despair. Maybe I should sketch *you*."

Mungo blinked. "Pardon?"

"A beautiful concept: a clown – usually a figure of joy and energy – wasting away on a splintering bench against a grey, forlorn seascape. Alone and lost and sorrowful, receiving cruel laughs or loose coins depending on the crowd, but no spotlight, no applause, no love."

Mungo shrivelled at the autopsy of his character. Of course, she had captured him perfectly. Anyone that comfortable with a dead bird was always going to be well-practised at sticking in the scalpel and dissecting a life.

However, his hurt was outweighed by the fear of being the centre of an art project. He didn't want widespread recognition. His curious brand of popularity on the pier was one thing. It earned him enough coins for candy and chips and that was all he needed. But this award-winning artist might make him a media sensation. Didn't she say something about the Turner Prize? He couldn't go back to the spotlight. How could he be a circus of one if people were flooding into his Big Top to see the clown from the paintings?

Anastasia edged closer, reaching for her charcoals once more.

"Please..." Mungo began.

But then a blue light on the beach caught his attention. There were several police vehicles parked on the sand and a white-suited forensic team had just arrived. Mungo had seen a much bigger version of this scene twelve years ago, when Circus Romero burned down. He knew what it meant: a dead body.

Anastasia's attention had also been redirected. A dead body apparently held more fascination than a dead bird or an over-the-hill clown. She walked down towards the beach, the sketchbook poised in her hands and the plastic bag dangling from her arm. The forgotten cadaver of the gull bumped against her side with each step.

Mungo breathed a sigh of relief. He was left alone on the pier. Loneliness had been his blanket for the past twelve years and it was comforting. He had no intention of going near that crime scene. He kept his curiosity to a minimum and that kept people out of his life. The crowd would drift back to the pier eventually and his Third Life would resume, as if nothing had happened.

It was then that he heard the bird's cry.

Mungo turned and there sat Spitfire on his bench, mocking him. "No! Get away foul beast!"

He started sprinting back to his bench, slapping the boards of the pier with his big clown feet and waving his wig like a battle flag. Spitfire remained unfazed by this charge and instead focussed on Mungo's half-eaten bag of donuts.

"Don't you dare!" But it was too late. The gull snatched up the bag and flew into the air with the remainder of Mungo's afternoon snack.

Mungo waved a gloved fist in the air. "I hope you choke on them!"

He slumped defeated onto his bench. Sadly, Mungo found himself sitting in the unpleasant surprise that Spitfire had left splattered on his bench.

Mungo sighed. "This isn't over."

Anastasia

The elegant stillness of the central figure displayed on the beach contrasted with the frantic activity all around. The body's pose was classical, a martyr, almost a Christ. His wounds stigmata, agony splayed for all to see. Attending to this figure were ghosts, or angels, in the white paper jumpsuits of forensic services. Beyond them, fanning out across the stretch of beach, were the lumbering, monochrome shapes of the police officers, bulky in their anti-stab vests, sealing the perimeter of the scene, holding back the rapidly growing crowd, who were gallows happy at this public display.

Anastasia's pencil flew across the pages of her small sketchbook, capturing the essence of what she saw. Racing through her mind were shapes, colours, allusions to religious art from ancient icons, to renaissance saints, to Falun Gong kitsch. What a productive day.

As the SOCO people began to erect a white tent to preserve the scene, Anastasia folded away her sketchbook, and reached down to pick up the carrier bag containing the corpse she had found earlier. How she would love to have that other cadaver in her possession, too. She envied Gunther von Hagens and his plastinated figures; human bodies skinned and posed, familiar and strange. Whoever the unfortunate man on the beach had been, surely his dignity would be better served, his immortality assured, by the ministrations of a Turner Prize shortlisted artist, rather than by a butchering pathologist? Such were Anastasia's thoughts as she began to walk along the promenade, heading in the direction of Castleton Boulevard.

She spotted a familiar figure just ahead of her.

"Shaun?" said Anastasia.

The caretaker of the flats on Castleton Boulevard turned at his name. He was a little shorter than Anastasia, a boyish figure.

"Ms Boty, isn't it?"

She clearly hadn't been resident long enough for him to be certain.

She scuttled forward to keep pace with him. "Has my parcel arrived?"

"No," said Shaun. He hesitated, before continuing. "Why are you carrying a seagull?"

At this, Anastasia stopped. "Why are you carrying a tube of silicone sealant?" she said. Shaun paused, too, but whereas Anastasia's disambulation had seemed a decisive act, Shaun's tentative halting motion was accompanied by foot shuffling, and the redirection of his gaze from Anastasia, to the seagull, to the tube in his hand, as if he had suddenly been overcome by the meaningless of it all. "Well?" Anastasia prompted, gesturing in the direction of the tube of Geocel.

"The tap in number seventeen's been leaking," said Shaun. "I usually do minor repairs like that."

"A wide skill set, then," said Anastasia. "Excellent. You could be useful. Tell me, how would I go about accelerating the decomposition of a sea bird?" With this, Anastasia set down the gull on the ground between them, as though challenging Shaun to begin the process at once. The bird's insolent orange feet stood proud of the top of the bag.

"I guess you'd have to pluck it first," said Shaun, eying the creature warily. "But why? I mean, what do you want it for?"

"Well, taxidermy's too kitsch, and obviously formaldehyde is out of the question," said Anastasia.

"Obviously?" said Shaun.

"I'm sorry," said Anastasia. "There's no reason why you should know. I'm an artist. Some work I'm doing at the moment. I need a skeleton, and this bird contains one. Any idea how I get it out, cleanly and fast?"

"Bath of bleach, maybe?" ventured Shaun. "I don't know. There's an abattoir on the industrial estate. The chicken factory. They might be able to help. Are you really an artist?"

Anastasia bent to pick up the handles of the plastic bag, disentangling them from the webbed feet.

"Yes, of course I'm an artist," said Anastasia, almost amused at the novel thought that she might be anything else.

"Like a painter?" said Shaun, searching for a name that was not 'and decorator'. "Like Picasso?"

"I've never been compared to Picasso before," said Anastasia with a wide smile. "I don't usually paint. I mostly make 3D work. Installations, sculpture, sometimes video. I work with concepts, ideas. It's all about capturing the strangeness of the world. Though I have actually been doing some painting, too. I've got a show coming up."

"Really? At the Hildred Centre? Or the Embassy?" said Shaun.

"Er, no," said Anastasia, as they approached Sammy's Snacks, the greasy spoon cafe. "The show's at the White Space Gallery in Shoreditch. Look, if you're interested, drop in to my studio some time. I'll show you my work. I can do it now, if you like?"

"I'd like that," said Shaun. "But not now. I'm trying to avoid someone."

"Not Valerie, by any chance?" said Anastasia, "the old luvvie?"

"How did you know?" said Shaun.

"That she's an actress?" said Anastasia.

"That I was avoiding her," said Shaun

"We're all avoiding her," said Anastasia. "Good luck hiding. But the invitation stands. Call by my studio any time."

"Thanks," said Shaun, "I will."

"And thank you," said Anastasia, "for the suggestion about the poultry processor. I'd better get home and stash this gull in the freezer until I can work out what to do with it."

Nell

Nell grabbed the chair nearest her and began the process of brushing off the worst of the spilled breakfast. Sammy's Snacks had been packed all morning, but the rush had finally died down. A few customers from the Wa'shum and Dry might pop in for a quick bite, but other than that, the café wouldn't see much action on a day like this. Easter was still two weeks away. Down North Parade to the pier, in the tacky heart of Skegness, most businesses would still be closed, or on reduced winter hours, although the arcade would fill up after school let out. Some of the kids would stop in to ruin their supper with a bag of chips on the way home, but Nell would be long gone by then.

She turned back toward the kitchen with a tray of salt and peppers to refill. Sabina was taking advantage of the break to sort cutlery and have a chat with one their regulars, Shaun. He came in a few times a week to play chess, though Nell couldn't understand why here, of all places.

"Oi, Nell, look sharp," Sabina said.

Nell glanced up. A bear of a man, stood in the doorway and letting in cold air, was bleeding from at least three places she could see. Shaun had faded further back into his corner than seemed possible, his chin tucked as he trained his gaze on the board in front of him. Nell wracked her brain for a name and came up with *Lewis*.

He took a step toward her but she held her ground. "Bobby sent me," he grunted. "Said you've helped his guys out before."

"You got cash?" Nell asked.

"Christ, he's bleeding," said Sabina.

"I can see that," said Nell.

"Bobby's covering me," said Lewis.

Nell narrowed her eyes. "Cash up front's the deal. He knows that."

"Take it up with him," Lewis said. He wiped at a gash across his face with a dirty sleeve.

She took a more careful inventory of his injuries then turned to the other waitress. "Will you be alright in here if I take my break?"

"Maybe we should just call an ambulance. Or the cops," Sabina said.

"Fuck that," said Lewis.

Nell shook her head. "I can handle him." She reached around the counter and grabbed her bag.

21

"Really?" Sabina didn't bother to hide her scepticism.

"I think so. I know who's holding his leash at least. Let me know if it gets busy again. Oh, and hey," she turned at the door, "if my aunt shows up, try to keep her out front, okay? She doesn't exactly know about this..." She waved a hand in Lewis' general direction.

"Second job? She'd kill you if she found out."

Nell snorted. "Yeah." She swung the counter up and gestured for the man to follow her into the back.

"I've seen you somewhere." Lewis said. "You train over at Studio Gym?"

"Yeah." She pushed him ahead of her into a large storage closet and gestured for him to take a seat on the stepladder.

"Take off your coat." She pulled out a pair of nitrile gloves and studied the deepest wound on his arm. Grabbing his chin, she tilted his head back so that she could get a better look at the cut on his cheek. "What the hell happened? These are knife wounds."

"Something like that."

"Hate to see the other guy," she said.

He grunted in agreement. "Yeah. You would."

In the confines of the closet, she couldn't escape the cloying scent of liquored sweat. He must be a heavy drinker, but he seemed sober enough at the moment. He'd glazed over once he was off his feet. In shock, maybe. Nell left him examining his bloodied knuckles as she ducked into the kitchen to grab clean towels and a pitcher of water. A small, reasonable part of her considered phoning the police but Lewis worked for Bobby "The Baron" Thomas and Nell wasn't about to draw *his* fury down on her own head.

Nell had started to stitch and fix at the bare knuckle boxing matches Bobby presided over. Nell kept her head down and her hands busy since the gig paid well and she needed the cash. It also meant she could actually make use of the paramedic training she'd received back home in Virginia.

It took longer than expected to clean and bandage Lewis up, and she scowled when she caught sight of the clock. She finished wrapping the last cut across his forearm and stood, pulling the gloves off with a practiced snap.

"I need to get back," she said. "If you keep the bandages clean, you should be fine."

Lewis pushed himself up, and it was clear now that the adrenaline had left his system, he was hurting. "You got anything for the pain, doc?" he asked.

"I don't do pills," she replied curtly. "There's a pharmacy up the road."

He squinted down at her. "You got a fiver then?"

"You owe me, not the other way round."

"You think Bobby shirks on his debts? Man runs this town, with my help."

"With your help, huh?"

"If he says he'll pay, he'll pay."

Sabina poked her head through the door from the kitchen. "Nell, I need some help out here."

"Coming," Nell called, taking advantage of the opportunity to shove Lewis toward the door. He groaned as she edged him out and slammed the door soundly in his face.

Valerie

Valerie Manning had been trying the effect of a scarf over her hair. The biting wind off the sea played havoc with her usual neat style but she had a sneaking suspicion that she hadn't the right shaped face to pull off a headscarf. Less 50s starlet and more sexless frump. Perhaps if she teamed it with red lipstick? Leaning into the mirror, she applied the makeup, pressing her lips together and blotting with care.

A movement outside caught her eye. Shaun was returning from the cafe. He didn't seem to hear her earlier as she called to him, talking to that lovely artist. Anastasia Boty.

Valerie had watched Anastasia these last months, just as she watched everyone. Anastasia Boty was an exotic flower among the stout blue rinses and mobility scooter brigade of Skegness, and she was easily the whitest person Valerie had ever seen. Her skin was pale to the point of translucence, her hair tumbling about her face in wild copper waves.

Valerie had seen Anastasia at night, raiding refuse bags, sorting through skips. By day she'd sometimes opened up the doors on the workshop across the road, and she'd glimpsed her in overalls, wearing a mask, protective goggles, wielding throbbing, whirring, sparking power tools. Valerie had originally assumed she was a mechanic of some sort, not an artist.There hadn't been a chance to talk yet but Valerie was certain they'd have a lot in common. She hadn't moved quickly enough this morning and had lost her chance for introductions. She'd thought about following Shaun into the cafe for a chat but the smell of grease and the possibility of being overheard stopped her. No, in hindsight, it was best to talk to him privately.

She pulled the scarf from her head, used it to remove the lipstick, and left the flat.

"Shaun dear, I wonder if I might have a word? I have a teensy maintenance issue," she said.

He didn't look pleased to see her, of course, but she expected that. She smiled at him, a practised reassuring look that some of her past clients would have recognised. Poised like a tigress in the long grass. He smiled back, still nervous. She gestured towards the stairs that led down to Shaun's basement. Downstairs, he fumbled with the lock and they went inside. It was gloomy and there was a faint musty smell that combined damp socks and tinned beans.

Shaun closed the kitchen door though not before Valerie had glimpsed a plain room, cup, bowl and spoon washed and sat on the draining board. Closing the door cut off a source of light, rendering the room even gloomier.

"What was your maintenance issue?" Shaun asked.

"What?" she smiled sweetly. "Oh, nothing. Unless you count a loose splinter on the bedroom door frame I keep catching sleeves on. I just wanted a word in private."

She could see by his face that he'd been dreading her saying this, that he hadn't really believed she needed legitimate help. She turned and prowled round the room.

"Heavens aren't you neat? Everything in its place." She poked a few papers with her finger and her long shiny nails managed to catch the remainder of the light.

"I'd rather you didn't touch those if you don't mind," he said.

"Or what?" she fixed him with a clear stare. "Now darling, do you have anything for me?"

He shook his head as she turned her attention back to the letters.

"Oh dear. That is a shame. You don't seem to have taken me seriously."

"No I have, I..." Shaun ran his hand over his hair and looked nervous.

"Oh Shaun, I can't imagine all these good people here would be happy to let you into their flats if they knew about your past."

"I'm not ashamed of my past."

"Really? Are you sure? Your susceptibility to... dark forces?"

Replacing the letters on the side she continued to pad around the flat, picked up a book and flicked through it, put it back down again and looked at a picture he had in a frame, holding it up to the skylight for a better view. Like any good actress she knew when to wait, when silence was more potent than dialogue. It was a technique that had worked well in the past, some of her weaker clients lasted only a few seconds before promising payments – sometimes cash but often something more, an introduction or a role, access, in short, to the kinds of social circles that Valerie's acting career hadn't quite allowed. She had thought about giving it all up when she fled up here but it was all too much fun to stop. And when there was such an easy target as Shaun it seemed too good an opportunity to miss.

"Please don't say anything," he said. She stopped and smiled at him again.

"It's just that I'm not really sure what it is that you want."

"Whatever I can get dear. Since you don't have any money or opportunities for me, I'll have to take something else. Your knowledge, for example. Tell me about Anastasia."

He looked confused.

"That is her name isn't it? You were speaking to her earlier, outside the cafe."

"Yes, yes, Anastasia. I know her. She's an artist, she does conceptual stuff. Famous I think."

"Fascinating. I used to sit for a painter for a while at the beginning of my career. Dreadful pictures of course, never went

25

anywhere, stoned half the time, which didn't help. Fun while it lasted. Where does she paint? Anastasia I mean. She has a studio, doesn't she?"

"On Cavendish Road."

"Right. And she's interested in conceptual art?"

"Yes. She looks at the world differently, finds meaning in it. You know, stuff like that."

"Oh don't they all? Well, that'll do for now." She walked to the door. "I'll be back of course. Do try and find out some more about her, sharpish, or I might be inclined to spill the beans. Don't look so worried, darling, I'm not a monster! But remember, I know all about you!" She blew him a kiss and let herself out of the flat.

Valerie didn't go back upstairs to her flat yet but trotted along the road to the corner shop. The inert silhouette of the owner, Mr McNair, sat in the window while the neon Budweiser and Lotto signs shone like a welcoming beacon in the cloudy gloom of the day. It was a false comfort. The shop itself was unpalatable and Valerie often felt the urge to wash her hands after a visit. Still, needs must.

"Good day, Mr McNair," she called as she entered.

"Now then, Val," he replied. "How's your day been?"

Valerie bristled. She'd always hated being referred to as *Val* and was certain she'd mentioned this to Mr McNair before. A charitable person might say he'd forgotten but it was more likely he didn't care.

"I just had to pop in, I've run low on coffee and the supermarket seems to have left that out of my delivery this week. Such a pain." She turned a corner and bumped into the shop boy, Tim, who was arranging tins of beans on a shelf.

"Oh I am sorry, darling, how clumsy of me," she said. Tim took a hasty step back out of her way, and stared at his trainers. His t-shirt, a stranger to the ironing board, hung off his skinny frame, its once bold logo faded and ineffectual

"Do you have ground coffee for a cafetiere?" she asked. He shook his head and a few flakes of dandruff drifted between them both.

"There's instant," he said and pointed.

"Thank you," she said, glad to turn away.

"You done there, lad?" said Mr McNair. "You've still got stock to sort out before you're done."

Tim scuttled out the back of the shop.

"He seems a little fragile," said Valerie, handing over a five pound note. "Is he all right?"

"He's fine, just a bit slow," said Mr McNair who hardly looked speedy himself. Valerie wondered if he ever managed to get out from behind the desk, wedged in by his stomach as he was.

Tim

Tim could smell his own pubescent sweat as he shoved the curry sauce mix onto the top shelf in the stock room. There were three more boxes to go, and then he was finished for the day. He tossed each of the remaining boxes in turn into the air and caught it, just because he knew he could, before doing a clean and jerk to get it onto the shelf. He had worked three hours less than the previous day, but had shifted more stock and had to deal with more difficult customers. Just for once, he felt ready to go home while it was still daylight and while his mother might still be awake.

Mr McNair had told him, as usual, to take something for his supper, and something for his mother. He took a 3-litre bottle of white cider, a packet of Holman's pork butcher's sausages, some microwave chips, three tins of sweetcorn, and a copy of yesterday's Times (today's having sold out). It felt good to resist the urge to take a packet of fillet steak for himself and a bottle of Glenfiddich for his mother. He did not want to have to do too much cooking when he got home, and the one bottle of white cider a day had been keeping his mother more stable than she had been for a long time. It was now a hundred and two days since anyone had been to the flat to complain about her behaviour.

Tim locked down the computers before he left. He had all the codes and passwords for the alarm system, the EPOS system and the shop's broadband account, in his head. Mr McNair knew sod all about IT. He had given the whole job of making it work smoothly to Tim, who had already cut down the size of the shop's outstanding debt by means of a spreadsheet which showed customers in red who owed money for more than two weeks' worth of orders. Mr

McNair had given him an extra twenty quid for setting that up. That twenty pound note was now in Tim's secret stash of money, in a place where no-one would ever find it. Mr McNair would probably not want to mess about with the computer while Tim was away, but he liked to make sure by locking it.

As he headed out and crossed the street onto Lincoln Road, Tim almost worried that his life might be getting too easy. His mother was stable. He had income, and he had more opportunities than he had ever had in his life. He had access to the internet, which his mother could never interfere with. And Mr McNair believed everything Tim told him.

Tim took longer and longer strides. The two 'Support Your Local Shop' carrier bags he held in each hand bounced more and more at his sides. His mother would be still awake when he got home, but, today, he felt his head was as full of nonsense as hers. He would give her the cider. He would cook. He would eat. He would read or do a sudoku while his mother fell asleep on the sofa. She would not piss herself or throw up. He would not have to put on any rubber gloves or dilute any bleach in lukewarm water. He would go to bed, and he would awake refreshed the next day.

"You're the boy from the corner shop, aren't you?"

Tim stopped. It was that woman again. The one with spiky hair who had stared at him when she had been in the shop the other day. The one he had ducked down behind an aisle shelf to hide from. This time she was in jogging gear. She was breathless and looked pissed off. She was holding one of those oval, plastic water-containers with a hole in the middle.

"Why aren't you in school?" she said.

"It's evening," he replied.

The woman rolled her eyes.

"Don't try to be clever with me, young man. I mean, why are you never in school? Why aren't you in school during the day?"

"I'm seventeen."

"I say again: why aren't you in school?"

"I've left school."

"Among all the developed nations, only in the United Kingdom is it considered acceptable to have young people working

28

in shops when they should be extending their education and developing their experience."

Tim said nothing.

"How old are you?" she said.

"I just told you, I'm seventeen."

"Which school should you be going to?"

"I told you. I've left school."

"Where was your last school?"

"Sand du Plessis High School, Bloemfontein."

"Brum-fountain? Where's that?"

"Bloemfontein. South Africa."

"South Africa. I see. What was the headmaster's name?"

"Er. Mr Morkel."

"What was the dialling code for the school's phone number?"

Tim strode away. He heard the woman start to speak again, and he jogged, then sprinted. The bags he was carrying got in his way.

"I know where you work. I'm going to find out where you live and whether you're at risk. I want to help you. I really do. You think I'm out to get you, but I'm not."

Tim kept running all the way until he turned the corner on Lyndhurst Avenue.

The door of the flat was ajar when he got to it. He stopped for a moment and listened. Just as he was thinking about entering, a figure in a pink towelling dressing gown stormed up the stairs and barged past him. It was his mother. Tim followed her. He put his shopping down and observed his mother's procession around the living room. Her balance was okay. She was babbling, but not slurring. She was dressed in a manner which, while strange, would not have got her arrested. Tim did not bother to imagine what she might have been up to.

Tim's mother noticed he was there, and fixed her gaze on him.

"And upon her forehead was a name written," she said. "Mystery, Babylon the great, mother of harlots and abominations of the earth!"

Tim considered this, and hoped that his mother had not been looking at the magazines that he kept under the carpet in the corner of his bedroom. He placed the bottle of white cider and a plastic beaker on the coffee table, next to the Bible and the I-Ching, and went into the kitchen to prepare supper.

Flic

A cold breeze ruffled the long breakers that sighed halfway up the beach and sucked wearily back down again, small particles skittering in the receding sheets of water. A few thick raindrops from a dark grey sky coined discs in the sand.

The body lay where the high water line was a wiggle of whitish sea froth, littered with seaweed and discarded plastic. The forensics tent had been erected squarely across the line. Acres of sand had been cordoned off by the police. The beachside path was closed as far as Sea View Road.

Flic ran with her head down, shoulders strained forwards, feet, in trainers heavy with sea water, clomping on the packed sand. Her ears were plugged in to her waistpack with a white cable. She stopped at the barrier tape.

POLICE LINE, in blue capitals, stretched across the white nylon tape that quivered in the wind, along a row of orange cones. Beyond it was another line of cones, and tape in red and white. Someone in a white hooded scene suit, facemask and overshoes operated an SLR camera with blue-gloved hands. A policeman guarding the cordon approached Flic.

"What is it? What's happened?" she asked him, pulling out her earphones.

"There's been an incident, madam," said the policeman. He was a solid, middle-aged man. A sideways twitch of his head was his signal to Flic that she should move on, guided by the tape barrier, up the beach towards the town.

Instead Flic ran back along the beach, pounding her feet into her own footprints. She then crossed the car park by the pier, settling into rhythm along North Parade, with seafront hotels on one side and lawns on the other. Loops of coloured lightbulbs strung between lampposts were redundant in the late afternoon sun that edged under a heavy grey layer of sky. She turned the corner into Castleton Boulevard, passing traffic queuing to get out, the exhaust fumes and cigarette smoke mingling with the chip fat smell from Sammy's Snacks, and ran on, eyes narrowed against the glare, passing flats and guesthouses in the broad tree-lined avenue with parked cars either side.

McNair's was the corner shop, its window patched with ads for international money transfers, mobile phone top-ups and soft drinks. An election placard adorned with a St George's cross urged support for a far-right candidate. At the counter, a black man was talking in a low voice to the shopkeeper. Flic hesitated, then sidled past him and stared into a glass-topped freezer of convenience food. The man's voice grew louder.

"OK, McNair, it's payday. Comes around all too fast, especially for maggots like you. Even faster if you display racist posters in your shop window."

"They're not racist. They're a legitimate political party." McNair was starting to sweat.

"Whatever, it's payday, McNair." The man was thickset and filled his tailored black suit. His head was shaved. He wore a diamond stud in one ear.

"I don't owe no one nothing," said McNair, his small grey eyes watery, his lower lids hanging loose showing the red. His mouth shut tight between his jowls.

"Yeah, well," the man leaned across the counter and closed his fist around McNair's collar. He wore a gold sovereign ring and a fat gold watch. McNair's flesh complied, his stomach spreading itself over the counter top as the arm drew him slowly forward. Their faces were breath to breath. "You know what happens. I'll cut that flab off you, and mince you up so small that I'll be able to package you into your own trays of convenience food."

Then he followed McNair's gaze along the lines of shelves to Flic, who was standing by the freezer, her face expressionless.

"What you fucking looking at?" His voice was deadpan. His dark eyes glared out from under heavy eyebrows.

"Nothing," she said.

"Fucking mind your own business, right?" he said softly.

"What d'you think I'm doing?" Flic sized him up. A heavy, strong man, but unfit. She had her self-defence training. She stood side-on, ready to block him, but looking down, sliding open the glass lid of the freezer. In her peripheral vision she saw the man release McNair, and advance between the shelves and fridges, hands loosely by his sides.

"Bobby. Chrissakes," said McNair.

"I know where you live," said Bobby to Flic. He grinned. "I've seen you out running. You just watch yourself, OK? So easy to trip on a badly maintained surface, and find you're under the wheels of a car."

Then he turned and walked past McNair. "I'll give you to the end of the week, McNair." The shop door clicked shut behind him.

Flic went to the counter and put a frozen lasagne down.

"You OK?" she asked.

"Yeah, yeah. Tim - my lad'll be back in a minute. I'll be fine. It's OK. Some people, you know, just trying it on. I ain't done nothing to him." McNair's ugly face glistened sweatily in the light from the street. He scanned the lasagne, the till beeped, he pushed a button. "That's just two pounds ninety nine then," he said, opening a carrier bag.

"Your shop boy," said Flic, as she paid, "I've seen him, he delivers to my flats, doesn't he? Castleton Court."

"Tim? Yeah, yeah, he delivers to the flats. He'll be back in a bit." He held out her change, nicotine-stained fingers with overlong nails trembling faintly. "Thank you."

"How old is he?" asked Flic. The lasagne lay in its white plastic bag on the counter top. *Buy British at McNair's Convenience Stores* was underlined by a Union Jack.

"Oh, he's only doing a Saturday job, it's nothing," said McNair. "Thank you." He was still holding out her change.

"It's Monday," said Flic.

"Thank you," repeated McNair, his hand, with the change still outstretched, still trembling.

"So, how old is Tim?" Flic jutted out her jaw, hands on hips.

"Eighteen," said McNair, putting the change down on the counter top and wiping his palms on his stomach.

"If he's eighteen why did you say it was a Saturday job, when it's Monday?"

"I never said that, I don't remember saying that." McNair gave Flic a smile, which she did not return.

"Who's after you then?" she asked. "What have you done?"

"Thank you. Bye now." McNair pushed the change across the counter top.

Flic took the money and the *Buy British* shopping bag, and left.

Shaun

As he climbed the stairs, Shaun listed the residents on each floor. It had taken months to remember all of their names. Some of them even remembered his now. There was something comforting about reciting them. Before long, Valerie would be knocking on his door again, and he wasn't sure he would have anything to tell her. He swept a sweaty hand across his hair as his tools crashed around in his holdall. By now, he had reached the top floor. He pushed through the green fire-doors and rapped Mr Popescu's letter box.

The door swung open, and Shaun realised this was the first time he had spoken to the old man without a chessboard between them.

"I've come to look at your er..." Shaun trailed off. The old man stared at him.

"Yes! Yes!" he said suddenly. "Come in."

Shaun stepped into the flat. His trainers pattered on the plastic runner as he followed Mr Popescu through the living room. The armchair looked as though it had been covered with old hotel curtains, and a polished, wooden chess set sat on a small table in the corner.

"Can I get you a drink?" Popescu asked as they entered the kitchen.

"Tea please," Shaun responded. "Two sugars."

"Suit yourself."

Mr Popescu hit the switch on the kettle, then took a bottle of single malt whisky from a cupboard and poured some into a small tumbler. Shaun looked around the kitchen. There was a pan of cold water and peeled potatoes on the side. At the sink, a thin line of water trickled from the tap into the washing up bowl. The old man handed Shaun a mug of dark, reddish tea. It was strong and bitter, and the sugar only made it sickly. When Popescu left the room,

Shaun put the mug back on the side and opened the cupboard under the sink. He pushed aside the cleaning fluids to find the water meter, then turned the stopcock and listened as the tap dripped into silence.

Laying his tools out on the sideboard, he eyed a stack of open letters. Shaun liked to think of himself as an honourable individual, a professional caretaker who could be trusted and relied upon by the residents of his flats. But then there was Valerie and her needs, her incessant demands and so he took one last look through the kitchen door before picking up the pile of letters. He shifted through them quickly, hoping for some small titbit to pass to Valerie, something to appease the dragon of a woman.

A water bill, a bank statement, a sheet of vouchers for the nearest Morrisons, and then an envelope with a foreign stamp. There was a neat tear across the top. A few photographs fell on the floor as he removed the letter. It was handwritten in a language he didn't understand, but stapled to the back was a dark photocopy of a map, a town called Mangalia, wedged between the sea and a vast forest, where someone had pencilled crosses and notes. Shaun picked up the photos. A circle of trees. A patch of ground. It meant nothing. He slotted the envelope back into the stack.

"You're from Romania, aren't you?" Shaun called into the other room. "You know, originally?"

"Yes," the old man called back, "why?"

"Just thinking." Shaun knew nothing about Romania, except that it was where Dracula came from. "Do you miss it?"

"No. Not what it has become."

Shaun took a flat-head screwdriver from one of his lunchboxes and used it to prise the top off the leaky tap.

"How about you?" asked Popescu. "You don't seem like a local."

"Doesn't matter. This is my home now," replied Shaun.

"Is it? With the rides and the arcades? The tourists who get drunk behind the crazy golf shack then throw up under my window at two in the morning? This town wasn't built for people like us."

"What do you mean 'people like us?'" Shaun called back, searching for the right Phillips head screwdriver. He swore under his breath; the screwdriver was missing. Shaun never misplaced his tools. He thought about using the next size down, but he didn't want to damage the screw. When he was a child, Shaun's mother used to keep her tools in the bottom kitchen drawer. He looked at the drawers in Popescu's kitchen and shrugged. He'd already read the man's mail. Opening the bottom drawer slightly, he slid his hand under the papers and the takeaway menus.

"We're survivors," said the old man. "Out here without family, without friends."

"I have friends..." Shaun broke off. He had grasped something heavy, metallic, and he pulled it from the drawer. He was clutching a gun. His instinct was to pull away as though it burned, but fear kept it in his grip. Slowly, he laid it on the chopping board. It was like something from a spy film – dark rubber and bright metal. Even resting, there was a menace to it.

Shaun realised he hadn't spoken for a long time. "I have friends." He tried to sound normal. "A few anyway. I like it here." Five minutes earlier, that had been true.

He waited till he had packed away his tools then picked the gun up carefully. It was heavier than he had first thought. He adjusted his grip, kept his fingers far from the trigger as he placed it back in the drawer, trying hard to remember how he had found it.

"All done," Shaun said as he walked back through the living room.

By the time he heard the old man's 'thank you' he was out of the front door.

Sabina

Sabina turned spoon after spoon of sugar into her cup while the kettle boiled. *Just because life is bitter doesn't mean tea has to be.*

Her shift at Sammy's Snacks was over, the café empty and clean but she still needed to wind down, tidy away the emotions and the events of the day. Today, she mostly wondered what kind of trouble Nell was getting herself into with that bloodied man who had stumbled into the cafe.

Nell and Sabina were not exactly friends, however Sabina still worried about her, even if she didn't mean to. She couldn't help it.

Nell and her Spartan act. Eyes that resembled a storm brewing or a calm yet clouded sky – depending on the mood Nell was in – had become familiar to Sabina. After years on the wind, with no roots or anything else to anchor her, she didn't take familiar lightly.

Immersed in thoughts as she was, Sabina missed the kettle handle, touching the hot metal with her palm instead. A searing pain spread through her left hand, causing an older pain to surface.

Fragments of memory, the screams, the smell of smoke. The flames roared mercilessly, like the wrath of God. The big top of Circus Romero was engulfed in flames and smoke. Horror-struck and paralysed, Sabina was a helpless witness, as everything she ever knew and loved burned.

She stood on the wet kitchen floor, wide-eyed as the child she had been back then.

"Stupid," she said to herself.

She fetched her purse and hurried out of the kitchen, not bothering to clean up the mess she had made. She crossed the café and stepped out into the cool air.

Once locked up, her feet took her to North Parade instead of home, because thinking of the fire always made her think of him.

Mungo Joey. The clown was one of the few survivors of the fire and the closest thing to a family she had. Mungo was in bad shape and in a bad place. He drank too much and did little else. He was on a downward spiral of alcohol and seaside junk food.

She pressed on against the cold wind, past coin-operated rides and fish and chips stalls. Sabina usually had a quick-pace, swinging her hip from side to side as she walked, but today she was moving even faster.

As she spotted Mungo on his regular bench on the pier, she kissed the little medal she always carried around her neck – the only gift she had left from her mother – a silent prayer to the patron saint of lost causes. *Saint Jude has his work cut out for him with this one,* she thought as she looked at the clown.

"Hey, there," she couldn't help but smile at him. *He looks more like a tramp than an auguste clown these days.*

He looked up at her, moving the least that he could.

"You again." He sounded disgruntled. "Hello, I guess."

"May I sit for a moment?"

He started to move, slowly, making room for her.

"For a moment," he said, raising his finger, more of a plea than a warning.

"I've been worried about you."

"You are always worried. You should try worrying about yourself," he replied leaning to fetch his hat, "I'm fine as always, whether you worry or not."

He started to count all the coins and notes sticking out of the hat with one hand while reaching for his cider with another.

As he gulped his cider, his green curly wig nearly falling off his head, Sabina remembered Don Quixote. Her father would tell her all sorts of stories, and the tramp sitting next to her brought the Ingenious Gentleman to Sabina's mind. There was something noble about him, despite the grunting, something chivalrous.

"This guy showed at the café today, all covered in blood. He'd been in a fight. God only knows the state of the other guy."

"And you thought of poor ol' defenceless me?"

"Not quite. I burned my hand. I..."

"Who would mess with a clown?"

He cracked a bittersweet smile.

"Nobody messes with this clown," he answered his own question, the smile still hanging on his face like a crooked portrait on a wall.

That smile brought back the lyrics and melody of Vesti la Giubba, one of the ringmaster's favourite arias, to Sabina's head. The ringmaster that had been a father to Mungo. A shadow crossed her face as she looked at the broken clown next to her.

"All the cider in the world won't make you forget..."

"And coming here won't bring anything back," he retorted.

Sabina's eyes started burning, tears wanting to come.

Mungo turned and stared into her eyes, speaking softly now.

"Would you just give up on me, please?"

But he knew the answer already, and it didn't falter.

"Never," and that little word carried all her determination with it.

He sighed, resigned.

"Would you leave me alone, at least?"

She smiled, getting up.

"For now," she said, walking away. "Be safe."

He grunted, returning to his default position, lying on his back.

"I'm sure your blood-soaked thug is going to be leaving me alone. He's probably getting his just desserts right now."

Bobby

This. Bobby thought as he plunged the gore covered pencil into Lewis' eye for the third time, *isn't likely to reinforce the image of reassuring stability I'd hoped to project.*

When Lewis walked had through his office doors minutes earlier, Robert "The Baron" Thomas had had every intention of maintaining his carefully constructed demeanour of rationality and thoughtful consideration. Anxiety bordering on open fear was worming its way through his organisation. Bobby needed to show that he had everything under control. Changes might be in the air, but Bobby The Baron was still captain, mate, and master of Skegness – all Skegness, not just the Coin Fountain amusement arcade, the garage, the gym above it and a protection racket cum loan shark operation that stretched up to Mablethorpe and down to the Wash. Those who sheltered under his protection or relied on him for their daily bread need not fret. All would be well.

First, though, it would cost Lewis. Lewis would serve as an example that the order Bobby imposed upon Skegness' underworld remained intact.

From behind his desk, Bobby gave Lewis a head-to-toe assessment calculated for maximum insult. Lewis was a big man. Hell, he was a bruiser, no getting around it, and he knew how to handle himself, too. An undeniably menacing piece of work, Bobby concluded. The patched up wounds on his head and body only added to his threatening demeanour.

This will need a delicate touch, Bobby thought. *The man is on edge. Tact is the key.*

"You cock-sucking inbred yellow-belly motherfucker," said Bobby simply.

"What?" said Lewis. "He came at *me*."

The big man gestured to the cuts on his face and upper arm. Bobby dismissed it all with a flick of his hand.

"A man comes at you and so you leave his fucking corpse on the beach like some oversized donkey turd?" he said. "My fucking beach? And what do turds bring, Lewis?"

Lewis's face twitched.

"Flies," said Bobby. "You want the cops to come sniffing at my door?"

"Hey!" snapped Lewis. "A man comes at you – a foreign bastard comes at you – with a weapon, you kill him."

"And I'll kill you!" Bobby screamed in a sudden enveloping fury at the stupidity of the man. Rage coursed through him, stealing his self-awareness as it had so many times in his life. He could no more stop it than he could stop the world spinning on its axis. When it let him go Lewis laid still on the floor with a pencil lodged into what was formerly his right eye and Bobby's carefully laid plans and best intentions had more or less turned to shit.

"Stability isn't really my bag," said Bobby wearily. "Not my bag at all."

He looked down at the mess he had made on the floor of his office.

"Shit, Lewis," he said softly. "You make things hard, boy."

Lewis, not dead as presumed, seemed to take this as some sort of instruction.

He gained his feet and pushed Bobby hard enough to send him sprawling on his back and bouncing the back of his head off the floor.

"Fuck."

Lewis even seemed to be getting something like a second wind, now staggering around the office, very much alive despite Bobby's certainty he'd pierced the idiot's brain with a piece of wood. *Lewis the Lobotomized*, Bobby thought to himself. *A Loud Lobotomized Lewis. Likely of interest to the Law. He's making more noise than someone who's been…. Alright, maybe he's making an appropriate amount of noise given his current situation. I can't say I wouldn't make a fuss myself if I were in his place. The difference is that I'd be well on my way out of here instead of stumbling around the office breaking expensive objets d'art. Or, I'd go after the cunt who had just destroyed my depth perception.*

Lewis suddenly arrived at the same conclusion.

He came at Bobby in a berserker rage, the wreckage of Bobby's tastefully, and expensively, decorated office in his wake. Bobby, his own rage sated with a bit of eyeball stabbing, retreated and looked for an opening, either to flee or get in a shot to Lewis' throat or kidney. He mused briefly on trying for Lewis' remaining eye but thought it unlikely he'd get the opportunity. He was out of pencils, anyway.

"Marcus!" Bobby yelled. "Where the fuck are you, you fidgety weasel?"

Out of nowhere, Marcus crept up on the insanely enraged Lewis and firmly inserted four inches of a knife into the base of his skull. As the life went from Lewis and his dying legs gave way, Bobby ripped the pencil from Lewis' eye socket and brought it down in an incredible overhead smash, making it a permanent fixture of Lewis' skull.

Lewis slumped and rolled, spraying the skirting boards with eyeball jelly.

"It's called aqueous humour," said Marcus.

"Where," gasped Bobby, "in the fuck have you been, you worthless little maggot?"

The neatly dressed little man shrugged with, what Bobby considered exaggerated nonchalance. "I was taking a piss when I heard the screaming from your office. I went downstairs and closed the arcade. No one was there, anyway. It's a shitty business."

"Once I catch my breath I'm going to cut off both your hands and put you in charge of making change for the punters who frequent that shitty business. You ever see it when it's busy? Kids screaming at parents, parents screaming at kids, flashing lights and enough godawful racket from the machines that you'd pray to be struck deaf. It's hellish. I hope you're not epileptic, Marcus No-Hands. If you are you'll want to see your doctor about getting stronger medication before you start down there."

Marcus put his foot on Lewis' corpse and pulled his knife out of it.

"I'll have to get rid of this," he sighed.

"Lewis, too," said Bobby. "You murdered him after all. In a very callous manner, I might add."

Marcus shrugged. "Someone was bound to kill him sooner or later."

The two men stared at each other in silence.

"Yours is an unsettling nature, Marcus," Bobby said after a few minutes of mutual consideration. "I'll get you a new knife. Ditch your knife along with the dearly departed. You'll need muscle you can trust to move him. We'll roll him in that rug. It's ruined anyway. He bled all over it when he fell on that pencil. Clumsy fucker. There's lime in the store cupboard. Use it generously."

"I won't need it."

Bobby raised an eyebrow, but said nothing.

"I want it done yesterday, understand? Take him out the delivery access in the back. You can park in the alley and slide him right into the boot. I shouldn't have to tell you any of this, right?"

"Right."

"Then you call my mobile, say 'Job's done' and not one more fucking word. You getting all this?"

"We're throwing out an old rug, right?

"You're a weasel but you do have some capacity for abstract thought. I've forgotten why we fell out."

"You have a temper, Baron. A nasty one."

"True. You'll see it if you don't tell me you have someone looking for the man who put the beating on our beloved Lewis. He mentioned the guy was an immigrant."

"What kind of immigrant? Polish? Chinese?"

"He didn't have time to say."

"You were too busy turning him into a desk tidy?"

"Christ, what I wouldn't do for a nice, sharp pencil right now."

"That's why you want a propelling pencil," said Marcus. "Always sharp. Better chance of penetrating the sclera and getting into the brain."

"You're an insightful psychopath, I'll give you that," said Bobby. "Go ahead and tell me what else I want."

"You want new furniture by tomorrow morning. I can get you a desk and chairs. Upscale stuff but not the quality of what Lewis broke. You want the arcade open. I'll have it running after breakfast."

"What happened to Lewis?" said Bobby to himself. "When did he become such a liability? Oh, who fucking cares? He made life miserable for everyone inside and outside the organisation. He was a bully and a thief."

"And he was your number two," said Marcus.

Bobby straightened up. Age weighed on him.

"Then congratulations on your promotion, Captain Marcus."

Marcus turned on his heel and walked out of the office and, watching Marcus go, Bobby felt reassured. He needed reassurances. Change was coming and a wise man would keep his pencils sharpened and close to hand.

CHAPTER TWO

"But I don't want to go back there! I already went yesterday!"

"Now, sweetheart, everybody has to go to school," Sarah Greenwood said as she tried to put the toothbrush into Gracie's mouth.

The girl shook her head and shut her lips tight because if she didn't brush her teeth then they couldn't leave the house.

"We need to be off in ten minutes and I haven't packed your bag," said Sarah. "I'll make a deal with you, okay? If you let me brush those teeth, I promise to put some chocolate in your lunchbox."

Gracie opened her mouth straight away.

Sarah smiled and began to brush. "We have to look after our pearly whites, don't we?"

"Yesh," she said through the toothpaste.

"Yes what?"

Gracie knew that Sarah wanted her to say *Yes Mummy*, but she wouldn't ever because Sarah was making her go to school and it wasn't the truth anyway. As soon as the toothbrush was back in the pot she started to moan again.

"But they tell you off for running," she protested, "and we don't go outside enough because they make us do boring work, and when we do go outside the girls only want to make looms and play families, and the boys won't let me join in knights and horses. And Miss Long is nasty to me, and Charlotte, because she says I'm strange. I want to see Mister Pop."

Sarah pulled on a cardigan and made Gracie put hers on too. She gathered up their bags and took Gracie's hand in hers as they left the flat. All the way down the corridor and the stairs Gracie dragged her feet and made them stomp, squeezing up her face in a sour pout.

"Now," Sarah turned around suddenly as they were about to step out into the street. She bent to look at Gracie properly and when her face came closer there were little purple bruises under her eyes that hadn't been there a few weeks ago. "You have to stop that. Stop sulking. Do you think the people walking on this road will look at you and see a lovely well-behaved girl, or a bad-tempered one? Hm?"

Gracie stuck out her chin.

"They will see a sad girl."

Sarah blinked, and then quickly stood up and started walking again without taking Gracie's hand. Gracie had to take big steps to keep up with her foster mother. A naughty idea came to her as she puffed along behind the woman's tall slim frame, and she almost decided to carry it out as they came closer to the school gates. How sorry Sarah would be if she turned around and Gracie was simply gone. But they were hurrying onto the playground now amongst the other children and their parents, and her pretend mum slowed to a standstill in the middle of them all like she had forgotten what she was meant to be doing, just looking at them. They were saying their goodbyes and reminding one another about after school clubs and kissing each other on the cheek and smiling. Gracie looked at Sarah. She was not smiling. She was doing the exact opposite.

"Please can we go home?" the seven-year-old tried for the last time.

But already her foster mother was telling her to be good and have fun and make some friends today. Gracie found her flowery backpack and pink water bottle being pushed into her hands, and stood watching as Sarah made a swift departure without stopping to chat with any of the other mums and dads.

Shaun put his bowl down next to the monitor and threw on a hoodie as he walked across the room. He didn't like strangers to see his flat. He kept it in good order just as he had learned at Starhaven, but he felt that his space here in the basement rooms, marked him as 'not normal', and he had tried so hard to be normal. Through the peephole, the two figures looked distant and warped. He slid out the security chain, turned the lock, and opened the door.

"Hello," the woman spoke first, showing her badge. "I'm Detective Sergeant Young, this is my colleague, DC Castell."

"Yeah," Shaun said, "we spoke on the, er..." He gestured toward the monitor and intercom.

"Oh. You're the concierge?" She looked surprised.

"Caretaker. Janitor. My name's Shaun."

"Okay, Shaun. We're investigating an incident that took place on Monday. We'd just like to come in and ask a few questions, if that's alright?"

"Is it about the body on the beach?" Shaun asked. Sabina had been talking about it in the café yesterday.

"Yes," said Young, "can we come in?" She looked too nice to be a detective, Shaun thought. She reminded him of Sky.

"Sure," Shaun said, stepping aside. "I don't know if I'll be much help, though." He thought of Popescu's gun. So far, nobody had been able to tell him how the man had died.

"Were you anywhere near the promenade or Tower Gardens on Monday?" Castell asked. *He* looked like a detective – two days' worth of stubble and an open necked shirt.

"Yeah, I went to get some sealant from Homebase. I walked back along the front. I saw the crowd and the tent on the beach, but I don't know any more than that. Sorry."

The detectives settled into the old leather sofa. Shaun hovered by the coffee table, hoping they wouldn't notice the duct-tape holding in the stuffing.

"That's fine," Young reassured him, "we're really just hoping for some information about the victim. Nobody has been able to identify him yet."

"I'd like to help," said Shaun, "but I don't know many people round here. Can I get you anything?"

"A black coffee would be nice, thank you." When DS Young smiled, her eyes lit up behind her glasses.

While the kettle boiled, Shaun took the opportunity to hide a half-smoked spliff in a drawer by the oven, just in case. He walked back to the sofa and set the mug on a coaster next to the *Fortean Times*.

"Thank you," Young said, smiling at him again.

Shaun pulled the office chair across and sat down.

"We'd like you to take a look at a photograph of the deceased and see if you recognise him," said Castell, handing him a picture. "It's a little unsettling."

The man in the picture had been beaten badly, but there was no sign of a gunshot. The area around one eye was black and

45

swollen and his jaw had been knocked off centre. The left side of his skull had been caved in. Shaun ran his hand through his hair, lingering where the man's wounds would be. The tattoo on the man's neck was obscured slightly by the angle of the photograph, but Shaun could just make out a blue eye looking up at him. The Eye of Horus.

He thought about his own tattoo - a star-map of Orion, hidden in the Nazca spider. He kept it covered since he left the Brotherhood of the Stars. You never knew who might see it. Some of the Brotherhood had this eye symbol among their tattoos.

"Do you recognise him?" asked DS Young.

"No, but this tattoo – the Eye of Horus – it's an avatar of Wedjat, the snake-headed goddess."

"The what what?" said Castell.

"She protects people who make journeys over the sea," said Shaun.

"Well, that didn't work out too well for this poor fellow," said Castell.

"She protects the dead too," Shaun replied. "You really have no idea who he was?"

"We had a few people come forward," DS Young replied, "said they'd seen him with another male earlier in the day, but nothing more substantial than that. We believe they were both eastern European. We spent yesterday questioning labourers on the farms, but nobody claimed to recognise him."

Shaun knew little about the way the police were structured, and he was only just beginning to realise that Young was in charge. She was younger than Castell, perhaps not much older than himself, but there was a sense of certainty about her which made him feel like a child

"Lukasz, the chef at Sammy's, is from somewhere over that way," he said. "Some twats from the holiday park got kicked out of the cafe for mouthing-off about it the other week. Maybe it was a race thing?"

"Could be," said Castell.

"Sorry I couldn't be more help. I usually stay close to the flats. On call, you know?"

"It's quite all right," said Young, "Is it just you down here?"

"Yes," Shaun replied, "just me."

DS Young and DC Castell looked at each other. Young shuffled herself closer to Shaun.

"It's quite dark in here."

"No windows," he said, "I try to keep it tidy, though."

"I can see that." She smiled again. It was an official sort of smile, but Shaun still smiled back.

"Have you lived here long?" she asked.

"About a year."

"How old are you, mate?" asked Castell.

"Twenty-three, why?"

"Just wondered." He looked around. "I think this is better than where I was living at your age."

"That's a lot of UFO books," Young nodded towards a bookshelf loaded with books about ancient aliens and paranormal phenomena. "Do you like science-fiction?"

Shaun recognised the concerned tone of her voice. When his father had used it, he used to respond with sarcasm, but Young seemed nice. It felt good that someone like her might be worried about him.

"Not really, I'm more into history," he said.

"I studied history at Norwich," she replied.

"You're familiar with ancient astronaut theory then?"

"I'm not sure..."

"Von Däniken and them? The Annunaki? Did you do much about the Nazca lines?" Shaun asked. "Or the secret chamber in the great pyramid? It's compelling stuff. The evidence is everywhere."

He had thought the Watchers – the civilisation who had raised mankind from apes – were Brotherhood doctrine, but since he left, he'd found mention of them in other places.

Young glanced at Castell. "I did more modern British history, really," she said.

"Oh, I see," said Shaun.

"We should get going," said Young, standing. "Lots of calls to make."

"I understand."

"But thanks for your time, Shaun," said Castell.

"And thanks again for the coffee," added Young.

"No problem," Shaun replied, walking them to the door. Before he could stop himself, he added: "Come back anytime."

The door closed behind them. Shaun's hands were shaking. He placed the cups neatly by the sink and returned to his congealing cereal. The flat suddenly felt small.

"Hello, Gracie. Why are you playing on your own?"

In the middle of cutting off the third of Balaur's heads, Gracie paused at the sound of that familiar voice. Immediately her sword turned back into a stick, the great dragon faded into thin air, and the playground was once again a dull and chilly place completely devoid of mortal peril. Gracie dropped her useless weapon.

"Oh," she said and took a step back from the man standing on the other side of the criss-cross fence.

He bent down on one knee so that he was Gracie's height and showed her a wide smile, smoothing back his tufts of brown hair. Gracie looked about for a teacher, but nobody was this far out on the playground. Nobody could even see him because there was an overgrown hedge joined to the fence that hid him from view of the school. It was thick and evergreen and hadn't been trimmed for a while. Gracie noticed that it only merged with the fence because there was so much of it – there was a gap beside the metal edge of the fence, concealed by loose branches that could be pushed through easily. Her tummy did a little jump.

"It's me. Harry. Your old care worker." The man nodded reassuringly. "I've just come over to see how you're doing."

"Uh-huh," she said.

"I thought it might be nice to catch up, you and me. It's very quiet with you gone." His smile wavered a little in the face of her stubborn silence. "What were you playing? It looked very exciting."

"Dragons," Gracie mumbled with her face turned down and away from him, hands gripping each other behind her back as she pointed one of her feet towards the tarmac and twisted it left and right, left and right.

"You weren't fighting dragons the last time I saw you. Have your mum and dad been reading you fairy tales?"

"You know they're not."

"Not what?"

48

"Not my real mum and dad."

"I know they're not yet, but that is what they want to be. And they will be, soon, if you give them a chance. Unless you're unhappy here." His green eyes flickered back and forth as he searched her face, and for the first time she really looked at him.

"I'm not happy," she snapped. "I don't like it here. I hate school. I don't like Laura and I don't like the way Sarah and Arthur talk to me. Like they're scared of me."

"They aren't scared of you. They're scared for you." Harry frowned in a way that wasn't angry. "But you know that you can always come back to Haven House if you really feel like you aren't fitting in. You must try a bit harder with your foster parents, because we want you to settle in and have a nice time with them. But all you have to do is ask, and you can leave their flat and come and live with us again."

A strange, cold shudder ran from the bottom of Gracie's spine all the way to the top. "No," she said. "I don't want to go back. I don't remember that place."

"Don't remember?"

"I don't remember and I don't want to go back with you."

"Of course you remember," he told her in a soothing voice. "You lived at Haven House for two years, Gracie. Don't tell me that you can't remember your own care workers. You know me. You know Tammy and Sky. And you know your friends. Katharine and Samantha and Thomas."

"I don't remember," Gracie said more firmly as she began to back away from him. In her mind she reached out desperately for those names, trying to force herself to recognise them. She was met with a blank fog that covered everything, everything before she had come to Skegness, everything before her foster parents and Laura and Mister Pop. "I only remember you because you came with me in the car, when Sarah and Arthur were bringing me here."

Harry stopped trying to talk to her and just stared instead, his eyes like dense stones putting their heaviness onto Gracie so she couldn't move away. Still she tried to do what he asked and break through the fog. There was nothing. No faces, no voices, no places. The whistle would go soon, she hoped, and it would break the awful spell, and she could go back to forgetting what it was she couldn't remember.

"All right," Harry said at last. "You don't remember. So we'll stop talking about that. Have you made any friends at all while you've been here?"

"Yes," she breathed. "Mister Pop."

"And who is he?"

"He lives across the hall. He's an old man. He tells me stories."

Harry nodded in a thoughtful way, but he didn't say anything about Mister Pop. In the middle of that silence the bell went, and Gracie shrugged Harry off suddenly like he was any stranger and ran to line up. For once she was glad about the school rules.

Anastasia pushed up the visor on her safety mask and peered at Shaun as he stood awkwardly in the doorway. With a jerk of the head she indicated for him to follow her through into the studio. "Don't touch anything. I need to kill the power."

"Have the police been to see you?" said Shaun.

"No," said Anastasia.

Shaun looked about him. It wasn't his idea of an artist's studio. Anastasia herself was dressed for a shift in a steelworks. Heavy duty power tools hung from the walls. Large vats bore the names of industrial chemicals. Gas cylinders were stacked in one corner.

"The murder," said Shaun. "The body on the beach. The police came to see me."

"Did you kill the man?" said Anastasia. She was removing safety masks, gloves, ear muffs, as she spoke.

"I don't know anything about him," said Shaun, his voice a little shrill. Anastasia lifted her head and smiled. Shaun might have felt foolish for failing to catch her teasing tone, but he was distracted by the sight of a group of mannequins, life sized figures of the sort used in shops.

"Do you like my girls?" said Anastasia, as she unzipped the shapeless overall. She walked across to the bald forms.

"Well, they're..." said Shaun.

"I know what you're going to say," said Anastasia. "It's all a bit Anthony Gormley."

"No," said Shaun, immediately regretting it. Perhaps he was meant to say yes? He tried to cover his confusion by scrutinising the mannequins as though they were exhibits in a museum. Close up the figures were slightly disturbing. They lacked the joints that normal mannequins possess, and there was something about their texture that provoked unease. The surface was suggestive of pores, and hair follicles. Their female forms had small, pert breasts, but with their narrow, bony hips, concave stomachs, and sharp clavicles they looked more like starvelings than runway models.

"Getting the mould made was a bore," said Anastasia, "but they're turned out well. I'll use some as they are, and I might do some amputations or dismemberment on the others." The artist's animation was in contrast to the immobility of the figures, her wild red curls a rebuke to their smooth scalps. Nevertheless, as Shaun's gaze moved uneasily between the woman and her handiwork, there came the slow realisation that these forms were casts of Anastasia's own naked body.

"What else have you made?" said Shaun quickly.

"Gracie Greenwood, go and put your name on the red band right now!"

They had been back in the classroom for five seconds and she was already in trouble. Charlotte and Emily had tried to stop her lining up between them in her right alphabetical place – they had pinched her and pulled her arm silently to get her out of the line. So she had done what a brave knight would have done: she chopped at Charlotte's neck in the hope that her head would come right off and that would be the end of it. She had chopped pretty hard but it was no good, and now Charlotte was crying and Miss Long was very angry.

Gracie rushed to the behaviour chart with her eyes stinging hot and her chest clenching up with angry breathlessness, wondering if she would ever manage to get along with anybody and why nobody was fair to her, and why they thought they could boss her about anyway. She wasn't used to being in trouble. Her hand shook with rage as she pulled her name from the green band and moved it down to the red one. And then – the most terrifying thing that she could ever think of happened.

Knock, knock, knock.

"Bau-bau," Gracie whispered.

"Hang on!" called Miss Long as she herded the other children into their places on the carpet. She was going to open the door. Bau-bau had come for Gracie just when she was moving her name down to the red band where the naughty children were, and now Miss Long was going to invite him in, and she would let Bau-bau take her away through a cold dark place to that big scary forest called the Other Realm. It was all coming true, just like Mister Pop said.

Blind panic swallowed Gracie up like a dragon's gaping jaws, and all she could think about was that hole between the hedge and the fence, and the other door between playground and classroom, which Miss Long hadn't shut yet because they had only just got in from break.

Gracie stood transfixed with horror as her teacher walked away from her, towards the door where Bau-bau was waiting. Miss Long turned the handle and peeked out into the corridor, and another voice answered her.

The voice asked for Gracie by name.

It was Harry.

Her tummy felt like she'd been spinning too much and her hands felt cold and there was a tingly feeling crawling all over her back.

She forgot to breathe all the way across the school yard, so that by the time she reached the hedge her legs felt stiff from the frantic running and her head span a bit, but the grown-ups hadn't even moved inside the classroom which meant they didn't know she was gone, and she might just be able to get away without being seen at all. The evergreen leaves gave way under her hands, just like it seemed they would. She wriggled and huffed and suddenly she was free, like Peter Rabbit scraping under Mister McGregor's garden gate. It didn't matter which way she ran, as long as she ran fast and didn't look back.

"Come over here, and you can see what I'm working on," said Anastasia.

She led Shaun back to the rear of the workshop. It was brighter there, with natural daylight pooling in from high windows and a large skylight. There were tables covered with papers, and piles of sketchbooks and photographs.

"The police showed me a photo of the body. It nearly made me throw up," said Shaun.

"I think it's beautiful," said Anastasia.

"Beautiful? The poor guy's dead," said Shaun.

"Look," said Anastasia. She opened up a small sketch book. The first sketch bore some resemblance to the shape of the body on the beach, but it was also a series of delicate, elegant lines. The following sketches were variations on the theme, some more abstract, or decorative, others more realistic, but none of them was gruesome.

"They are beautiful," said Shaun. "You're good, aren't you?"

"Here," said Anastasia. She was pulling a large piece of paper from a folio. "This is probably closest to what I'll do for the final piece." If Shaun had not seen the sketches Anastasia had made from death on the beach, he would not have recognised this piece as a version of the dead man. It was intricate, but also a little more stylised than the sketches. The man's tattoo was remade here as the design on a robe. There was something about the colour, the pattern, the use of gilt, that struck Shaun as familiar.

"I've seen something like this before," said Shaun.

"Of course you have," said Anastasia. "I've got one here." She opened a drawer and pulled out a small rectangle of rough wood, and turned it for Shaun to see.

"Mr Popescu has got one just like that," said Shaun.

"The old man?" said Anastasia. "I suppose he would. This one's Serbian, but icons are found wherever there are Orthodox Christians. This is St. Matthew. What's Popescu got?"

"I don't know," said Shaun. "But he's got a lot of weird stuff. He's got loads of odd pictures of kids."

"That doesn't sound good," said Anastasia.

"I mean, the pictures are innocent enough, but there's so many of them," said Shaun. "And he's got loads of documents, papers. And he's got a gun."

"A gun?" said Anastasia. "What would he need with a gun?"

"It looks old. He was a policeman in Romania," said Shaun.

"That would explain it, I expect," said Anastasia.

"I don't know," said Shaun. "I mean, are things just coincidences? Maybe I'm a bit spooked, what with everyone asking questions. I don't like it."

"Who's asking questions?" said Anastasia.

"Well, the police, for one thing," said Shaun.

"That's their job," said Anastasia.

"And Valerie," said Shaun.

"That unpleasant woman?" said Anastasia. "I wouldn't take her seriously. Got too much time on her hands."

"She's...," said Shaun.

"She's what?" said Anastasia.

"No," said Shaun. "It's nothing."

"It's obviously something," said Anastasia.

"She makes me tell her things," said Shaun. "I had to tell her about the gun."

"Small town nosy parker," said Anastasia. "Tell her lies. Make it all up."

"She's asking questions about you," said Shaun.

"She can read about me on Wikipedia. It's all true, apart from the thing about doing trials for the Arsenal Ladies team," said Anastasia. "I have no secrets."

"Everyone has secrets," said Shaun.

"Secrets are a pain in the arse," said Anastasia. "I need a fag break." Anastasia walked across to the side door of the workshop, Shaun trailing behind. He followed her into the narrow alleyway that led down to the street. As Anastasia lit up, they heard light, urgent footsteps in the street. They turned towards the sound and saw a small girl run by, her arms and legs pumping.

"That's Gracie Greenwood," said Shaun.

"Yes," said Anastasia, "she's a curious little thing. I've got some sketches, but ideally I'd like to draw her sleeping."

"Do you draw everyone?" said Shaun.

"I've got a few of you. The poison thesp is interesting, too. All that face powder. She morphs into the clown on the beach," said Anastasia, drawing deeply on her cigarette.

"Can I see them? Those drawings," said Shaun, "I've never seen myself through an artist's eyes."

"And you won't now, either. When I sketch you in one of my notebooks, I'm not making a representation of you," said Anastasia. "If that's all I was doing, I'd be no better than one of those people on the prom doing bad charcoal drawings of tourists." She threw the remainder of her cigarette down and ground it out with a heavily booted foot. "I'll show you my Castleton Boulevard book."

Shaun followed Anastasia through the studio once more, taking in again the cluster of life sized nude Anastasias. What had at first seemed chaotic was now beginning to take on a feeling of order, although to what skewed logic it conformed was beyond Shaun's understanding.

"So why do you draw people?" said Shaun. "Why do you make copies of yourself?"

Anastasia was looking through a set of sketchbooks. She laid two on the table.

"You mean," said Anastasia, "What is art?"

"I don't know what I mean," said Shaun. "I don't know what you mean. Sometimes I worry that I don't understand anything at all."

"You can do general maintenance, which is more than most people can manage," said Anastasia. "Now here's a sequence with the child." She showed a series of sketches of the little girl talking to the old man. "I want two things from these. Their hands, and their eyes." The following sketches were of hands and eyes. The old man's hands, emerging from a threadbare sleeve. The child's plump, perfect skin, like the hand of a Raphael cherub. The eyes, Popescu's hooded, heavy, almost lashless; Gracie's round, clear, indecently lashed, and somehow knowing.

"These are beautiful, Anastasia," said Shaun.

"These are the nuts and bolts," said Anastasia. "Now this is what I do with them." Anastasia picked out a larger drawing. "Eventually they'll be part of the triptych."

"Will I be part of it?" said Shaun,

"I don't know, yet," said Anastasia. "Here's a few of you. I might use that one. I like the shape."

"These look more like us than the photographs do," said Shaun. "How do you do that? It's like you can see our souls."

"It's worse than that, Shaun," said Anastasia. "I can do what I like with your souls."

Flic stared at the monitor screen as her fingernails skittered across the keyboard. The council's information systems were ridiculous, she had to log on every five minutes it seemed. As if she had time to do all this, with her safeguarding caseload. She opened her calendar on the screen. Seven meetings to schedule in the next three days, some of them overlapping. An electronic referral, concerns from a school about neglect, family non-English speakers. A hundred and twenty eight unanswered emails. Damaged children, anxious schoolteachers, neighbours reporting screaming. Kids trapped in the toxic trio: substance abuse, domestic violence, mental health problems. And if she had to speak to one more crazy Eastern European through an interpreter, she was going to end up deranged herself. It was worse than being in London. *Only a few more days*, she thought.

Another referral. Care worker trying to contact a previous client at her school, child now missing, police involved. Another case to get dragged into. How would she find the time? She picked up the phone and was halfway through dialling the number when she changed her mind and put the receiver down.

She decided to do something else for a few minutes.

That boy at McNair's. Tim. How old was he? He looked about fifteen at the most. Tim Walker. If he was on the systems, she'd find him. She logged in to another system. This recorded children who had been referred to social services in the past, active cases, closed cases. Nothing. Okay, she thought. The school database. It would show her any child in a local school, past or present. There were four Timothy Walkers, but three lived a long way out in Lincolnshire, and the fourth was only eight years old.

She had a couple of extra logins the people in the council tax department had given her. It wasn't totally above board, but it saved her ringing every time. Council tenants, council tax, housing benefit. Anyone who had their rubbish collected by the council had their name on this system. Walker, 52c Lyndhurst Avenue. Sasha Walker. Number of children under 18 living at this property: 1.

Flic scrolled through her contacts and dialed a number in Glasgow. Sure enough, there he was on the Benefits Agency database. Sasha Walker was claiming Child Benefit for him. She was also receiving a disability allowance due to mental health problems. Tim Walker was fifteen. And he was not on any school roll. He was completely invisible to the local agencies.

Flic began to feel that she was getting somewhere. She would park that information until she had a chance to get more detail. She was still trying to summon up the strength to ring the police about the missing child. A few minutes, dealing with a few of the simpler emails, and then she picked up the phone again.

The child's name was Gracie Greenwood. DI Vivienne Scott needed the social services files on the foster parents, and any background information about Harry Mason, from Gracie's care home. Flic got his records up on the screen, and frowned.

"His record's empty," she said. "There's a mobile number, that's all. I'll have to speak to HR and see if they've anything on paper. The care home's contracted out to a private provider, and the information's probably with the contractors. We haven't even got his CRB check on file."

"Can you look in to that and get back to me, then," said Scott. Flic suppressed the urge to rant about the privatisation of public services. She dialled Harry's mobile number.

When he answered the phone, it sounded as though he was speaking from the seafront. The signal kept breaking up, and as he realised who Flic was and started pleading with her to help him, she could hear the wind blustering into the phone and the whine and bleep of the amusement machines.

"I knew she wasn't happy," he was saying. "I saw her all alone in the playground, so isolated, miserable. I just wanted to speak to her teacher, you see, but she just ran out of school. She's a very disturbed little girl."

"I don't understand why you went to the school like that," said Flic. "Why didn't you make an appointment to see her teacher?"

He seemed not to understand her question.

"Did you hear me?" she said, her irritation nagging again, and repeated it, raising her voice over the sounds from the seafront. The noise bounced back at her from the concrete walls of her office.

"I just had a feeling," said Harry. "I knew something was wrong. We were very close to each other at Haven House, I knew she would be missing me and she wasn't happy. I just had to go there and try and get her to speak to me. No good talking to the professionals, they just fob you off and they don't really know what they're talking about anyway. No offence, miss."

"That's not good enough," said Flic. She was not in the mood to indulge the self - opinionated bastard. Her voice turned cold. "You have to maintain a professional attitude and avoid over-involvement with these children."

"Avoid over-involvement?" said Harry. "That's why these children go from one foster home to another, month after month. Some children have four or five different homes in the space of a year. They don't know who's looking after them, they never form secure relationships. Don't talk to me about over-involvement."

"You need to report to DI Vivienne Scott, at the police station," snarled Flic, and banged down the phone.

Mungo sighed. Audiences used to have much higher standards. There was a time when people used to gather for gravity-defying gymnastics, women being sawn in half and blokes going head-to-head with a lion armed with nothing but a foot stool.

Now all it took was a dead body.

Since the arrival and departure of the SOCO tent on the beach there had been a surge of activity on the pier. The crowds started on the beach but soon realised that the best shots could be captured from above so they relocated to the pier, desperate to snap a photo of incriminating footprints that had long since faded in the sand.

The crime scene junkies were a diverse group. There was the local media, eager to capitalise on the biggest news story to hit Skegness since the beach bagged its Blue Flag. There were the locals who wanted a nosey, mostly out of fear that they were missing out on something, and, of course, there were the tourists who couldn't believe their luck. Any holiday-makers disappointed that they couldn't afford Benidorm this year now had a murder to write home about. Theories on a postcard!

Yet, despite this increased footfall, Mungo's hat was emptier than usual. A drunken clown was evidently not as appealing as a dead body.

Well, he certainly wasn't going to start performing. He had made a fair share of coins from sitting on his backside for a good twelve years. Why break the habit? He would just have to make cut-backs, that was all. Perhaps he would forego the mushy peas when ordering his fish tonight.

Mungo closed his eyes and daydreamed of candyfloss.

"Are you supposed to be a clown?"

There was a little girl standing by his bench. Mungo grunted and chose to roll over, hoping that she would go away.

"Because you *look* like a clown," she said.

Mungo honked his nose by way of response. "What gave me away?"

"If you're a clown, where is your circus?" the girl asked.

"I had one once," he said, and took a swig of Wonky Donkey from a plastic bottle the size of a fire extinguisher.

"Where is it?"

"Gone. Poof! The circus doesn't stop here anymore."

"Do you live on that bench?" the girl asked.

"No, this is my office. Now go away, I'm trying to work."

Mungo returned to his default position: lying on his back with his hands on his stomach and his eyes shut to the outside world. His curly green wig provided an ample pillow.

"You don't look like you're working. You look like you're sleeping."

"Then maybe you should keep the noise down."

The girl went quiet for a second but only a second.

"You should learn how to juggle."

Mungo groaned.

"You would get more money if you learned how to juggle," the girl persisted. "Blind Man Hugh juggles on the promenade and he gets loads of money. I once saw someone give him a fiver."

"Good for him. He can see through that blindfold of his, you know."

"What about magic? Clowns are supposed to know magic tricks. Can *you* make things disappear?"

"I can make this donut disappear." Mungo presented a deep-fried donut from his paper bag and sent it swiftly vanishing down his gullet. Crisp on the outside, soft on the inside and coated in delicious sugar. *Whoever said Paris was the culinary capital of the world had never been to Skegness*, Mungo considered and not for the first time.

"My mummy says donuts are bad for you," the girl said but Mungo detected the longing in her voice.

"You better stick to couscous then," Mungo replied, licking his fingers.

"So you can't make anything disappear?"

"I'll make *you* disappear over those railings in a minute."

"You're very grumpy. I thought clowns were supposed to be happy."

"And I thought children were supposed to be scared of clowns. Look, what do you want from me? I'm trying to put my feet up. I've been hard at work all day."

"I'm hiding from my friend Harry," the girl said. "Have you seen him?"

"No, I'm relieved to say. I'm not sure I could endure interrogation from another child."

"Harry isn't a child."

Mungo frowned. He didn't want to get involved but he heard himself say, "No?"

"No, Harry is a grown-up. He used to be my care worker and my friend. He took me on long walks in the woods and gave me piggy-back rides if the ground was too muddy but lately he's been acting really strange."

"Oh?" Mungo was fully awake now.

"He came to see me at the school fence."

Mungo stared at the girl, sobering up quite quickly.

"And then Harry knocked on my classroom door to fetch me from school but I was scared so I ran away."

Mungo was sitting up by this point, red clown lips hanging open.

"Do your parents know that you're out here?"

The girl shook her head. "No, I crawled under the school fence."

"Bloody hell."

The girl gasped. "You're not supposed to say that."

Mungo raised his eyebrows. "And little girls aren't supposed to run away from school."

"But I had to. The teachers wouldn't understand. No one listens to anything I say. Everyone treats me like a baby but I'm seven years old! I wish Harry wasn't acting so odd. At least Harry treats me like a grown-up."

I bet he does, thought Mungo.

"Look, little girl – "

"Gracie."

"What?"

"Gracie Greenwood. That's my name."

"Seriously? It sounds like a stage name. Maybe *you* should try clowning."

Gracie folded her arms.

"Anyway, Gracie, you need to listen to your parents and teachers. You shouldn't run away from school. If I hadn't overslept, I would be at First Plaice right now –"

– ordering delicious fried fish, he fantasised, *coated in crunchy batter and sat atop a heap of soft golden chips –*

"– and the rest of this pier is far too preoccupied to notice you. No one would help if Harry found you here. You'll be safer with your teachers. They won't let Harry take you without your parents' consent. You need to head back to school."

"*No!* I'm never going back there! You're as bad as everyone else! Sarah and Arthur made me come to this place and leave all my old friends and teachers behind and I hate it!" Gracie stamped her foot on the pier. *THUD!* Her face was red and she was out of breath. She had begun shouting and her eyes were full of hot, angry tears.

Mungo shrank back into the grooves of his bench as far as possible. He had unconsciously grabbed his polka dot briefcase and clutched it to his chest like a shield. His mouth hung open like the cod he had planned to purchase with his hatful of spare change. Underneath his green curly wig, his brain scrabbled around for a suitable response. He settled on –

"Here. Have a donut."

Gracie was confused. "But... my mummy says..."

"Look, do you want the donut or not?"

Gracie nodded and wiped her eyes on her sleeve. She selected a donut from the bag and sat herself on Mungo's bench to eat it.

Being a well-mannered host, Mungo did not want his guest to eat alone so he helped himself to a donut and the two chewed thoughtfully in silence for quite some time. When Gracie finished the first donut, Mungo thrust the bag at her again to prolong the silence for a little longer.

As they ate, Mungo noticed a figure walking amongst the crowds of crime scene junkies. It was a man and he appeared to be looking for someone. He wandered the crowds for quite some time, spinning on the spot and scratching his head. Eventually he swore and strode off, back towards the promenade. The man never thought to glance over at the drunken clown sharing donuts with his new companion.

Not today Harry, thought Mungo.

And then Mungo was vaguely aware that something strange was happening. He was smiling. Not just a smile of red face-paint but an actual smile. He felt a zephyr of good feeling breeze through his chest. This was a long-forgotten emotion. What was going on? And then he realised what was happening. He was happy.

Mungo had helped a little girl and it had made him feel good. It was the first time he had felt joy about anything other than fried food or extra-strength cider since his final bow at the circus. It was nice. It was also incredibly unnerving.

There goes my solo act.

Tim found the photos of the children while putting away Mr Popescu's groceries.

He had deliberately left a tin of loose tea, a box of sugar lumps, and two jars of anchovies out on the kitchen counter, as if he was still busy. He had then quietly opened every cupboard in the kitchen, but found nothing new. He knew the kinds of things Mr Popescu ordered from McNair's.

He'd tried one of the drawers, opened it slowly, so that Mr Popescu and the talkative, posh-sounding woman he was having a conversation with in the next room would not hear him. The woman was asking the old man about his time as a policeman in Romania. Tim imagined Mr Popescu as a plainclothes detective, in a trench coat and a hat, rather than just a constable who directed traffic. It was annoying that the woman's voice was much louder than Mr Popescu's. He could hear all the questions clearly enough, but he only caught bits and pieces of the answers. The contents of the drawer had been the usual, boring stuff: cutlery in a dirty plastic tray, a box of matches, an apple-corer, two corkscrews, a bottle-opener with the word URSUS in red enamel on it. Tim had gently pulled the drawer all the way open. At the back there had been some string, old biros, a bottle of blue-black fountain-pen ink, and a rusty tin with a picture of a lady in an old-fashioned hat and dress on it.

Tim opened the tin. The inside smelt of dust, like Mr Popescu's flat. It contained a set of black and white photographs, held together with an elastic band. The corners of most of the photographs were bent, because the tin was slightly too small for them. Tim removed the elastic band, and it broke with age. The photographs were of children: boys and girls, who mostly looked about eight or nine. The boys had very short hair. They all looked miserable. Each photo was about the size of a postcard, and had twelve pictures on it, with a white border between them. Under each picture was an eight-digit number, apparently not in any sequence. There were about fifty photos. They looked almost like they were for playing some horrible, Communist era card game.

The kitchen door creaked, and Tim put the photos down on the counter so they were hidden by his body. The woman came in.

"Are you having some kind of problem, young man?"

"No. I'm fine, thanks."

"Why are you taking such a long time?"

"I've nearly finished, but I noticed that the hinges on this cupboard are loose. I was looking to see if Mr Popescu had a screwdriver so that I could tighten them."

"So you have finished?"

"Nearly."

"Well, get a move on, please."

"Yes, miss." The woman gave him a sideways look, but Tim's face was blank.

Tim said goodbye to Mr Popescu on his way out with the empty trays, but got no reaction. The old man looked as if his mind was in another place and time. The sun went behind a cloud and the colour seemed to fade from him, as if he was turning into an old photograph.

Outside the flat, Tim placed the trays gently on the floor and stood with his ear close to the door. Mr Popescu was speaking more clearly, now, and was describing how the Romanian Communist Party and someone called Ceausescu had lost control of the country. Tim listened and waited for the conversation to drift back to Mr Popescu's own life, and what he had seen and done when he was a detective.

"Oi, you." Tim lurched round to see a tall girl with dyed red hair and a nose-stud. Tim put his finger up to his lips.

"Are you ear-wigging?" the girl continued, at the same volume. "And don't shush me. This isn't a bloody library, you know."

"I know, but I'm trying to hear what they are saying," whispered Tim. "It might get interesting again in a minute." The girl moved next to Tim, and joined him in listening.

"Did you hear that?" she whispered. "He said, 'Securitate'. I bet that's the Romanian secret police."

"It is," said Tim.

"Mr Popescu wasn't in the secret police."

"I know. He was in the ordinary police."

"He gets parcels from Romania from time-to-time."

"How do you know?"

"Because the postman asks us to look after them if doesn't get an answer from Mr Popescu's."

"No, I mean how do you know they are from Romania?"

"Because they've got a Romanian postmark, you dick-brain. You need a stronger deodorant, by the way. Lifeguard is a good one."

Tim frowned. He could feel his cheeks starting to get hot.

"At least you don't soak yourself in aftershave like most boys. I remember where I've seen you, now. You work at McNair's, don't you? I thought there was something about you which reminded me of bog roll and Tampax."

Tim looked round desperately for some means of getting the girl to shut up. He did want to speak to her, but not here, not while he was trying to concentrate on Mr Popescu's conversation with the posh woman, and not while she was doing her best to make him blush. She was wearing a skinny T-shirt with a wide neck. Tim could see one of her bra-straps. The T-shirt was white but the bra strap was greyish-blue, and looked as it if had been put through the wrong wash.

"I think we'd better move, before someone notices us," said Tim, picking up the trays.

"Why are you so interested in Mr Popescu?"

"I've just got a funny feeling about him."

"I see. My name's Laura. This is our flat, opposite."

Tim took the photograph he had removed from the rusty tin out of his pocket, and showed it to Laura.

"I found this. There were about fifty others like it. I want to know what it means and why Mr Popescu has it."

Laura stared with rapt attention, and stroked her fingertips slowly over the photograph.

"Wow. That looks scary. Is it something to do with the war?"

"I don't know."

"Who are all those children? What happened to them?"

"I don't know. That's what I want to find out."

Tim walked along the corridor and, as he descended the stairs, realised that Laura was following him.

"You're a bit shy, aren't you, whatever your name is?"

Not again, thought Tim.

"Haven't you got something better to do?" he said.

"No. My folks are out. My little sister, Gracie, she's kicked off at school or something and they've gone off to act all hysterical. Have you got a girlfriend?"

"Not at the moment."

"Does that mean you've never had a girlfriend?"

65

Tim said nothing.

"Ah, I see," said Laura. "How old are you?"

"Seventeen."

"You don't look it. Do you work full time?"

"Yes."

"What's Mr McNair like to work for?"

"All right."

"Good. He always looks at me as if he thinks I'm going to steal something, and I've noticed him perving at my tits sometimes." Laura opened her mouth and pretended to stick a finger down her throat. Tim noticed that she had very white teeth and a brace on both jaws. "What time do you knock off work today?"

"I'm not sure. That was the last delivery for today."

"Great. You can take me for a coffee, then."

Laura laughed her head off when she saw Tim's tricycle.

Valerie felt as if they were making progress. Yes, the boy's intrusion had been irritating, but on reflection, she'd have needed some time to soften the old man up anyway. She'd been in here an hour now and it was time to move on from this pleasant chit chat.

She'd dressed carefully, as if for a performance. Soft lilac cashmere jumper, black trousers and black suede ankle boots. Her hair, dyed an auburn-chestnut colour, was in its habitual fat doughnut bun but shone in the pale light coming through the net curtains. She knew she looked good, a shot of glamour contrasting against the dingy surroundings of the old man's flat. They were on first name terms soon enough, she rather enjoyed rolling his name around her tongue. *Razvan.*

She'd done a spot of reconnaissance on Popescu since Shaun had spilled the beans about what he'd found in the flat. Poor boy, she'd really had to press him before he came out with all of it. Thinking he could just get away with telling her about a few letters, silly thing! Clearly that was never going to be enough. She could tell he was hiding something. She didn't let up. The number of times he'd run his hand over his hair! Eventually he'd told her all of it. She'd leave him be for a while now, he'd served his purpose. There were more interesting folk to find out about.

Her eyes strayed to the kitchen drawers. The knowledge that the gun was there was quite distracting. It wasn't as if she needed to see it. She mustn't keep staring out there.

Razvan stood up.

"Could I get you another drink?" he asked. He looked towards the front door, frowning at the voices outside.

"Another coffee would be lovely," said Valerie.

"I was wondering if you wanted something stronger?" Razvan brandished a bottle and couple of shot glasses. "I think I'll have one myself, it's getting to be an indulgence in my old age, so if you'd care to join me?"

"Don't mind if I do," smiled Valerie. They clinked the glasses together.

"Chin, chin," she said. She downed it in one and placed the glass on the table. The old man looked a little surprised.

"Sorry, it's from my early days in theatre," she explained. "You learn to drink hard." He nodded.

"I must say, I didn't expect someone from your country to be a whiskey drinker," said Valerie, sitting back and crossing one slim leg over the other. "No, I always thought you all knocked back vodka. Of course I've never been to that part of the world myself. You do hear stories though don't you, in the media and so forth. I got the impression it was quite dangerous over there? Is that actually the case?"

"Perhaps you are thinking of organised crime," said Razvan. "It gives my country such a bad name. These stories slip out because it sounds so..." he paused.

"Sordid? But interesting." She supplied. "Everyone's fascinated by the idea of gangsters aren't they? Capone, Bonnie and Clyde, all those movies. Even if reality is different. I suppose you'll have seen a different side of things, being a policeman?"

"Yes, the reality is a lot less noble than the fantasy," he replied. "Coppola and Brando have much to answer for."

"Indeed," said Valerie. "Whereabouts in Romania was this?"

"Mangalia. Believe me, I saw nothing noble about the crime by those people. It was all fear and power. Mess and blood. Trying to get rich quick on the back of others. Nothing noble at all."

Valerie made sympathetic noises. This had potential.

"Terrible. I imagine whole families were affected?"

"Yes."

"And how was that to manage? For the police?"

"Very difficult. You're fighting corruption *within* at the same time as you're fighting criminals *without*. There was a lot of bribery, a lot of collaboration."

"You knew the gangsters? Worked with them?"

At this he put his glass down on the table. There was something in his eyes, a cold flinty look, and she felt a shudder go through her. She was glad she was no longer holding her glass.

"I had ways of doing my job," was all he said. He continued to stare at her. The stare, one of suppressed fury, reminded her very much of her last confrontation at home, the one that had made her seek refuge in this remote place. She couldn't help it, she knew she shouldn't but her eyes slipped past him to glance at the kitchen drawers again. His eyes narrowed. Did he, could he, know that she knew about the gun? She started to panic a little.

He poured himself a second drink, waved the bottle at her. She shook her head.

This is silly, she told herself. Calm down. She forced herself to do a breathing technique she learned years ago when she needed to overcome stage fright. She smiled at him. Change the subject. Find a way to get out of there without raising any more suspicion.

"How do you find it here? It must be quite different for you in this out of the way town."

"Yes, it's quieter obviously. But there's a lot going on when you take time to watch people, yes? You must see this too, I think."

"I do find others fascinating, I must say. It's par for the course, I think, in acting, being interested in people."

"There's quite a mix of people here, more than you'd expect. And yet you stand out. With your appearance and the car. I often see you when I'm on my way to play chess at the cafe."

"Ah yes the Figaro. Sweet little thing." She shifted in her chair. "It's useful to have for when I need to get away, for work. I still have a few irons in the fire, I don't see myself staying here forever."

"I would think not." He smiled back at her and the hard look had completely disappeared. Had she imagined it altogether?

Just then there was the sound of angry voices outside the door.

"I can't imagine what you were thinking, Gracie," a plaintive female tone said. "Why do something so silly? It's really disappointing."

"We've gone to all this fuss," said a man's voice. "I'm afraid school's something you've got to deal with but if you're unhappy you should come to us and talk about it. Running away isn't going to solve anything."

"Oh dear," said Razvan. "My little friend from across the hall sounds like she's in trouble."

Valerie raised an enquiring eyebrow.

"Gracie," he explained. "She lives in number eight. They're not her parents. Adopted. She's a nice little thing, often comes over to hear my stories. I am telling her of the defeat of Balaur the dragon."

"How imaginative," said Valerie.

"I like children," he said. He ran one hand over his trousers and looked towards the door again as the sound of Gracie's parents faded behind their closed door. "Do you have any?" he asked.

"We did try for several years," said Valerie. "No luck though. After a while we gave up. Of course Eric had a daughter from his first marriage, my step-daughter Jeannie, but we've never really hit it off. I think the divorce probably affected her – she was only eight when it happened – and she's never warmed to me. It would have been lovely to have children though, if only to have someone now. I'm all alone."

She stopped, she'd gone further than she'd intended. It was the earlier panic, making her babble and not pay her usual careful attention to what she was saying.

"What about you?" she said, trying to gain back some ground. "Do you have any children?"

"No, no, we couldn't have any. Not after..."

There was a knock at the door. Popescu got to his feet, emitting a slight grunt as his knees cricked. His soft-soled shoes made a shushing noise as he shuffled over to the door and opened it.

"Good afternoon," said the young woman standing outside. She flashed a badge at them both. "I'm DS Young, Lincolnshire

Police. I wonder if I might ask you a few questions about an incident on the beach?"

71

CHAPTER THREE

The first bout of the night in the Studio Gym was everything Bobby had hoped to avoid.

Although he never quite figured out which fighter was White and which was Evans, he could say with great certainty that either White or Evans plastered the ring with his opponent in an unrelenting torrent of raw brutality. The spectators showed their appreciation by heaping verbal abuse upon both fighters in correlation with the win-loss ratio of their wagers. It was old hat to Bobby. Hell, it was old hat to anyone who had ever placed a bet. The only consistent winners were the bookmakers, but he'd never met a gambler that would believe it. A bookie's odds weren't reflective of the likelihood an event would occur. They were incentives to make bad bets to offset money riding on favourites. Bookies were the MBAs of the underworld. They profited on the artificial margins they created and the ten percent juice from losing bets. Most gamblers knew they were being set up. They didn't care. They had systems, tips from the stables, divine inspirations. Any justification would do. The rush was all that mattered.

His irritation was devolving into general disgust. If he left now he could avoid the spectacle of another bloodbath in the ring. The ubiquity of tracksuits and trainers in the crowd was getting under his skin, too. Grown men without the vaguest sense of decorum....

"You're glaring at the crowd, Baron. It's not being well received."

Bobby bared his teeth at Marcus.

"They started it."

"They're admiring your suit, Bobby."

"It's right off the rack, if you can believe it. I'm drunker than I think I am, Marcus. Tell me I'm not surrounded by members of the EDL."

"Most days, you couldn't throw a stone in this town without it bouncing off some BNP or Combat 18 motherfucker. But these guys are just badly dressed locals. Baron, you scare the living shit out of most of them, and scared people do stupid things, especially in groups. You're working your temper up over nothing. Last time this happened I got a promotion."

"Bless your evil, twisted heart," said Bobby and laughed despite himself.

Bobby looked around the Studio Gym for what he decided was going to be the last time. After more than twenty years, he could barely stand the stench of it, a combination of stale sweat, mildewed paintwork and the oil smell of the repair garage he also owned on the ground floor. It was a place devoted to celebrating failure in all guises. Failed boxers were only the expression of a deeper, more fundamental failure of people devoid of humanity. It was a place that had never known a moment of compassion.

Lewis had loved it.

"It's yours if you want it, Marcus," said Bobby.

"What?"

"This."

"The gym?" said Marcus.

"I can't say I think you should take it. People like you and me...well, we're just barely holding on, if you know what I mean."

Marcus shot him an odd glance and seemed on the verge of chastising him, then said quietly, "No, I don't want anything to do with it. Give it to Tom. So, are we downsizing our operations, Baron?"

"Consolidating our assets," said Bobby. "War is coming."

"We can't win a war with any of the Eastern European or Russian boys. Our organisation isn't built for that kind of thing."

"No," Bobby said.

"It could be," said Marcus lightly. "The freelance muscle we use for bouncers and security could be taken on full time."

"Marcus, this is Skegness and I'm not much more than a jumped up loan shark. I'm not looking to re-enact 'The Godfather'."

Marcus grunted.

"Someone's staring at you," he said, nodding across the way. "The lady doctor, Nell Harrison, the one propping up that wall."

"That's not unusual," said Bobby. "I'm strikingly handsome with exotic features. Am I concerned with her staring?"

"Concerned? No. Even if you were, I'd have your back."

"I'm starting to find you tolerable again," said Bobby.

"Same here, Baron. Shall I send Tom Collins over so you can give him the good news?"

Bobby sighed the sigh of the deeply weary.

Nell leaned against the concrete wall, half an eye on the action in front of her. The gym wasn't nearly full, although Evans and White were putting on a good show tonight. Most of her attention was focused on the group of men watching the fight. Bobby had come in earlier than usual, although Lewis was nowhere in sight. Usually they were attached at the hip at these local fights, where the bets were lower and Bobby didn't have to entertain out of town "guests." Nell ground her teeth. If Lewis planned to stiff her after the shit he pulled, he'd better think again.

The thump of fist on flesh had a numbing effect. She could watch the blows land with professional curiosity, and when the fight ended, offer whatever assistance was needed. Some of the regulars preferred to take care of themselves, or to let their managers clean up and ice the worst of their injuries. The ones who knew her would find their way over before the night was done.

Men with families were most likely to seek her out. They didn't like turning up at home bloodied or ending up answering awkward questions in Accident and Emergency. It was easier to hang onto a piece of the action when they could get bandaged up and sent back to their wives with minimal fuss. The quasi-professionals – fighters who made the rounds and only stopped in Skegness when the money was sweet – viewed her with suspicion.

They usually arrived in pairs, throwing punches with hostile desperation. Those fights got ugly; the more money they had on the line, the worse it got. The locals fought hard, but the knowledge that they were neighbours kept things civil enough. Nell was happiest when the out-of-towners ignored her. It was the ones with a predatory air who reminded her to pull on a bulky sweatshirt and long pants when she stayed late. She fingered the Swiss Army knife in her pocket. It had been a parting gift from her husband before his last tour and just about all she'd kept when she sold the house in Virginia after his death.

"Harrison!" Nell's head snapped up. White was still laying into Evans. She glanced around and saw Danny Collins waving her

74

over. He spent all his spare time at the gym, although he didn't get many fights, which she suspected was due to the fact that his daughter had Downs. He wasn't great in the ring, and most of the guys felt terrible taking money out of his pocket.

At least his brother, Tom, managed to keep his own finances in order and all his bones in place. Danny was lucky to have a brother like Tom.

At the moment, Tom was deep in conversation with the very person Nell needed to see tonight. Of course, in this light, Bobby Thomas looked even less like a man she wanted to tap for money.

Bobby had probably seven stone on her and fairly towered over the Collins brothers. Bobby Thomas also had the distinction of being the darkest-skinned man, by a considerable margin, she'd seen in Skegness. He seemed accustomed to being noticed and appreciated. His own beauty obviously pleased him, and it put Nell on her guard. In her experience, beautiful men were dangerous, vain and easily angered. She straightened up.

"Where are you, Lewis?" she muttered to herself.

"You wanted to see me," said Tom Collins.

Bobby gazed thoughtfully at the man.

"We've known each other a long time, Tom," Bobby said.

"I remember when you came to Skegness, Baron. You were good to old man O'Grady. You ran all the little crews out of town and bought the ones that didn't run. I remember you saying that the police never stopped a single crime, they only showed up after to take their reports. When O'Grady retired, you were a natural successor."

"You remember that?" Bobby asked.

"Like it was yesterday, Baron. You'd only been discharged from the Paras about a year, I think. Those were special days."

"None of it really worked out, did it?" Bobby breathed deeply and shook his head. "I'm done with boxing, Tom. Done with boxing, done with the gym, done with the people. I'm fifty four years old and if I don't save myself now I never will."

Tom nodded slowly.

"I'm giving you our stakes in the boxers and the gym," said Bobby.

75

"Shit. Really, Baron?"

"It's your turn now, Tom. I don't care what you do with it as long as you kick up my monthly cut. After I walk out of here tonight, I don't plan on ever coming back. Do we have an understanding?"

"Sure, Baron, sure," said Tom. "But..."

"What is it, man?"

"I need to know one thing."

"I'll tell you anything you want to know," Bobby replied, with the sudden largesse and comfort of a man who had just shucked off a heavy load.

"Are you running from something?" Tom asked.

Bobby blinked.

"What we're all running from, I guess. Change. Time. Bad decisions. This world I built for a Black man in a White town. I'm weary. It shows, yeah?"

"How do these look, Doc?" Danny Collins asked as soon as Nell stepped close enough to have a hand thrust into her face.

The fingers were still taped, but the swelling had gone down. "You've been icing them every night?"

"Just like you said."

"I can tell. They look better," she said, putting gentle pressure on them.

"Jesus!" Collins snatched his hand back.

"You're out of commission for a while yet." He groaned dramatically and Nell grinned. "Susan still giving you trouble?"

"You'd think I'd gone and died with how useless she makes me out to be."

Danny's expression suddenly shifted. Nell turned. Bobby Thomas gave Danny a single look and he skedaddled.

"Bobby," said Nell.

"So, *Doc*," Bobby drawled, "how are you enjoying the festivities this evening?"

He had turned to see the latest bout, and she followed his gaze. Evans had retired for the evening, but White had stayed in to take on a man Nell had only heard referred to as Smalls. Predictably, he was the size of a barge.

She focused on the thud of landed punches.

"I was looking for Lewis actually," she said. "Haven't seen him around tonight."

"What do you need with him?"

"Thought you knew," Nell glanced at Bobby. "He had me do some work."

"Work?"

"Stitching and patching up."

"Is that right?"

"Said you sent him."

"Did he?" Bobby shifted, and she was immediately aware of how he controlled his strength. He reminded her of rattlesnakes she came across growing up. His tone was a warning to tread carefully.

"That's what he said," she said.

"Is that all?"

Nell felt Bobby's gaze move from the fight to her face.

"No," she replied. "He also said you'd pay."

There was a long pause. Nell forced herself to wait him out.

"And how much do I owe for this expert attention?" said Bobby.

"Forty."

"Seems steep for an unqualified Yank," he said.

"I have a license. I was a paramedic back in the States."

He grunted. "Doubt that means much here."

"You didn't seem overly concerned when I started bandaging up your fighters a month ago," she said.

"Maybe I've changed my mind."

"Maybe I don't like you sending thugs to my aunt's place of business," she snapped.

"Watch your tone." Bobby's voice lost its edge of amicability. The gaze he dropped on her now was an unchecked warning. He pulled out his wallet and handed Nell a tenner.

"Do we have an understanding, Ms Harrison?"

She clenched the cash.

"I'll look Lewis up for the rest then," Nell said.

"Let me know how that works out for you," smiled Bobby.

"He assured me you always pay your debts."

"Did he?" Bobby tapped the side of his nose and winked at her. "He would know."

Nell held his gaze for as long as she could bear before turning away. She felt his eyes follow her as paused to scoop up her bag. As soon as she was down the stairs and the door slammed shut behind her, she broke into a run.

Sabina started this Thursday night show the same way she always started practice, by swallowing a wire coat hanger. That's how one learns how to swallow a sword, practicing with the flexible coat hanger before attempting the inflexible blade of a sword.

She stood on the stage of the Sand Castle, her back straight and her head tilted backwards, ready to finish the first part of her act by suddenly bringing her head forward, causing the coat hanger to bend inside her throat.

Sabina brought her head forward and bowed for the applause that didn't come, removing the bent coat hanger and displaying it to the uncaring crowd.

As she put the coat hanger down and picked up the three stiletto daggers she would use in the next part of her act, Sabina wondered why she even bothered performing.

She returned to the centre of the stage in her off-the-shoulder black and red leotard. Black, stiletto-heeled court shoes and fishnet tights worn under striped, black and white stockings completed her stage look tonight.

She extended her arms forward, displaying the daggers to the audience. *This is a sad place,* Sabina thought, as she looked around.

The Sand Castle looked like an actual castle from the outside, crenulated walls and stone cladding. The inside felt like a warehouse someone decided to decorate with cheap looking medieval props. There were as many unicorn and lion embroidered banners, stuffed stag heads, iron-wrought chandeliers, and fake torches as there were tables in the Sand Castle.

Sabina straightened her back and bent her head backwards, going into her swallowing stance, and inserted the first dagger down her throat. She paused for a moment and proceeded to swallow the second, and then the third. With the hilts of the three daggers coming out of her mouth, she bowed again.

She removed the daggers from her throat, one after the other, and sighed. Even though Sabina didn't perform for the applause, she still wanted it. Any performer who tells you they don't care about it is lying.

It had taken Sabina over two years to learn how to manipulate fire, four years to be able to swallow a sword and she didn't even know how much time she had spent learning how to care for and perform with snakes. All this effort not only went unappreciated tonight – it went entirely unnoticed.

The dying art of sword swallowing, which Sabina helped preserve, was a dangerous and unpleasant one. It took focus and dedication. It took love. *It is supposed to show people what one can do when one puts their heart and mind to it*, Sabina thought, *it is supposed to bring awe and amazement to ordinary lives.*

She put the daggers down and picked up the sword for the final part of her act. Making sure she was in the centre of the stage she looked at the small, indifferent crowd at the Sand Castle – holidaymakers looking for a cheap lager and a nice carvery and locals looking for a drink, some company, or an escape from their wives or routines – and sighed once more.

Assuming her swallowing stance, she brought the sword up and licked the blade, then started sliding it down.

Most sword swallowers don't actually swallow the sword, but rather relax the throat enough to allow the blade to slide down all the way to the stomach.

The blade goes into the mouth, behind the epiglottis, past the hyoid bone and the pharynx, behind the larynx, and down the oesophagus through the upper oesophageal sphincter. Once past the sphincter the sword passes swiftly with the aid of gravity, straightening the flexible oesophagus on its way down.

The sword passes between the lungs, only millimetres away from the heart and the aorta, and past the liver in its path to the stomach. Each step must be done correctly and precisely, for one slightly wrong move could cause a scrape, a cut, or a puncture.

Sabina had performed every step with accuracy, and stood on the stage with seventeen inches of metal within her.

She bit hard on the blade and removed the hilt of the sword, a dangerous move designed to demonstrate that the sword wasn't retractable. Without the protection of the hilt, only Sabina's teeth prevented the sword from sliding all the way down, killing her in the process.

One... Two... Three, Sabina counted the seconds before reattaching the hilt and removing the sword with a flourish. One last bow out of habit – and for the integrity of the performance – and she would be done.

That's when something unexpected happened: somebody applauded.

Sabina looked around, startled, trying and failing to locate the source of the applause. *It is probably Nell*, Sabina thought with both affection and disappointment as she gathered her things and prepared to leave the stage.

Nell sometimes stopped by the Sand Castle on Thursdays to support Sabina and bitch about work over a couple of drinks. *There is always something to complain about when you work serving people*. Sabina smirked and made her way backstage to change.

As she replaced her costume with a long-sleeved black dress, Sabina hoped no creeps would try to pick her up tonight. *Even when they don't notice my act they always seem to notice my arse*. She grabbed her things and headed to the bar.

Walking assertively, easily finding her way past the pool table and around the many chairs and tables of the Sand Castle, she sat on one of the empty stools by the bar.

"Hey, Dan!"

"Sabina, good show," the bartender greeted her and placed a drink in front of her.

"Say, Dan," she paused to take a sip, "have you seen Nell?"

"The Yank? No, haven't seen her tonight."

Sabina was surprised.

"I thought she'd be here. I sure could use some venting. This week has been a drag."

Dan leaned sympathetically on the counter.

"Come on," he said encouragingly, "get it off your chest."

"Oh, I'll bitch about it to Buto and Foc later."

"Who?"

"My snakes."

"Right," he said, giving her a deliberately weird stare.

Sabina smiled.

"Oh, you know, Dan. It's just your usual uncaring crowd here."

She moved her head around the room. He nodded understandingly.

"Plus," she continued, "there was the whole harassment of that man coming by Sammy's injured and what not..."

She drank and leaned slightly over the counter.

"Mind you, that didn't put Shaun and Mr Popescu off their chess game," she giggled.

Dan smiled back at her and turned to look at the man who had sidled over and sat on the stool next to Sabina.

Sabina's smile disappeared as she noticed the man was looking intently at her. *Great, just what I didn't want!*

"Could I have another one?"

The man asked with a strong accent, pointing to his glass, and then turned his attention back to Sabina.

"I couldn't help but hear you saying Popescu, that's a Romanian surname, a fine surname."

"I suppose it is," she answered. "It has a nice ring to it."

Dan served the man his drink and made himself scarce.

"Allow me to introduce myself," he extended a hand. "Mihai Radu."

Sabina extended her own hand to shake his, and was surprised when he kissed it instead.

"It is a pleasure to meet someone who practises the ancient art of sword swallowing," he said.

Sabina smiled. There was something so formal and old-fashioned about this man's way of speaking and moving – it was almost theatrical. Yet somehow, at the same time, he looked just so open and vulnerable, that Sabina couldn't help but to feel an instant fondness for him.

"I grew up in a circus," she said simply. "I'm Sabina."

He nodded and took a sip from his glass. There was a sadness about this man that pulled her in. But there was an edge there, too.

"I am Romanian," he paused for a moment waiting for a reaction. She nodded and smiled, unsurprised. His accent had given him away.

81

"You said you grew up in a circus, my people practically invented the circus. Circ Romane."

"Is that so?"

"Yes. The circus life is a noble one, bringing wonder and magic to – how do you say? – to the day-to-day of people."

"That is it," said Sabina with a smile. "That is it precisely."

He took a long swig of his drink and looked at her quite pointedly.

"Tell me," he said, "who is this friend of yours, Popescu?"

Nell turned to cut through between the darkened houses on Edward Rd, picking up speed as a dog's sharp yelps followed her onto Victoria Rd. Her heart was thudding in her ears, but she pushed harder even as she felt the muscles in her shins protest.

Nell slowed to let a van pull into the hospital's drive. It had been a mistake to approach Bobby tonight. She should have waited until Lewis showed up and demanded he get the money himself. Now she'd put herself on his radar. Her adrenaline surged and she sprinted through the roundabout toward Scarborough Avenue. Nell forced herself to slow to a walk as she neared the entrance to the Sand Castle. She wiped away the worst of the sweat with her sleeve and shook her hair out before ducking inside.

It was obvious she'd missed Sabina's act. Nell sagged in the doorway. She just wanted to grab a drink with the kind of company that could make her forget the fear curled around her spine. She headed to the bar.

"Hey," she said, as the bartender looked up. "You haven't seen Sabina tonight, have you?"

"Sure," his name tag read *Daniel*.

"Since the show, I mean?"

"She grabbed a drink right after she wrapped up, but she left with a guy a while ago," he said.

"You know him?" Nell asked, tugging his sleeve as he started to turn away.

"No," he replied, staring pointedly at the fingers creasing his cuff. "Had an accent though." He looked up. "Think he said he was Romanian."

"You know a guy named Popescu, by any chance?"

Daniel twitched his shirt sleeve from her grasp and shook his head. Nell pushed away from the bar; she couldn't afford to drink at an over-priced tourist trap, not without Sabina as an excuse. She resigned herself to a bottle of her aunt's cheap red and a double-locked door, and headed home.

CHAPTER FOUR

Snap. Snap. Snap.

The supporting ropes of the tent burnt through and the flaming canopy began to fall.

The sirens were wailing but it was all over now. Sabina stood by the scorched ground, soot and tears on her face, hearing all the late sirens in the distance: ambulance, police cars, the fire engine...

Her knees gave out and she collapsed to the ground, feeling its roughness against her skin. Then all stopped. All the sirens went silent. The whole world: silent.

Everything was still. Everything but a clown, running, far away.

She just knelt there, looking. Feeling the anguish one feels when the whole world comes crashing down.

Then she heard it, the wild roaring of the fire. Sabina couldn't understand, she thought it was over. She looked up as the flames built over her like a giant wave.

Sabina sat naked on her bed.

"Are you all right?"

Mihai was sitting shirtless on her sofa, watching her, her dress and his shirt folded neatly next to him.

She nodded without conviction.

"Did you sleep well?"

Mihai had told Sabina about his own sleepless nights, thinking about his lost younger brother, the one he hoped Popescu could help him find. Lost family – that was something she could understand.

"I haven't slept this well in a long time," he smiled suggestively.

She smiled back, watching him stretch. He looked like a feline about to pounce, and she wondered if he danced or fenced. Looking at his bare arms, she remembered how surprised she had been at his strength; he looked so slender overall. Her eyes focused on a tattoo on the back of his hand, a blue stylised eye of Horus.

"That's pretty," she said.

He followed her gaze.

"That's from long ago."

"Does it mean anything?"

"Protection, just like that," he pointed at the medal around her neck, "it is supposed to keep safe lost souls in their journeys." He changed the subject. "It doesn't look like you slept well."

"Just a nightmare. Who doesn't have them?"

She walked the few feet separating her from Mihai. She put on her dress and carried out her morning routine: bathroom, incense, coffee.

"Want some coffee?"

"Coffee would be great." He moved to one of the two chairs around Sabina's small table.

Sabina's studio flat looked like a circus caravan. It was small and packed with mismatched old furniture. Rugs and carpets covered the floor and a good portion of the walls. An old circus poster hung above the bed, and there were candles everywhere. Swords and daggers, beaded curtains and trunks. Two tanks containing snakes completed the unintentionally bohemian look.

"Do you perform with snakes?" asked Mihai.

"Every now and then," she answered, filling the cups in the kitchenette. "This," she pointed at the biggest tank, "is Buto, a ball python. When I do perform, it is with her. And this one," she tilted her head to one side and pointed at the other tank, where a twenty inch grey viper, with a black zigzag pattern running through its back, watched, "is Foc. He's an Ursini's viper, and a treacherous little thing at times. But I love him all the same."

Mihai moved a heavy book to make space for the tray she brought over and looked curiously at its cover.

"Interested in anatomy?"

"Yes." She dumped two sugar cubes into her cup. "A professional curiosity. I need to know where my organs are to avoid them."

He chuckled.

"That's good. We wouldn't want you getting hurt, now would we?"

"That's the idea."

Sabina leaned back on her chair, enjoying coffee and company alike.

"Do you have nightmares often?" he said.

Sabina looked at him, realising just how much Mihai's tone resembled that of Pablo, the horse trainer. There was something both soothing and commanding in it.

"The nightmares are fine. They are just smoke that fades away when you wake up. Now, life..." She shrugged the rest of the sentence off.

"But where there is smoke..." Mihai started.

"Fire. Sure."

She put the cup down, got up and walked towards one of the trunks. Mihai drank his coffee, watching as Sabina fetched a tin and sat cross-legged on a particularly faded rug.

"I told you I grew up in a circus," said Sabina.

"You did."

"But I didn't tell you what happened to it."

"What happened?"

"It burnt."

"How come?"

"Nobody really knows. The police could never figure out who did it or why."

Sitting next to her, he got her hand into his own and pressed it encouragingly.

"Circus Romero. It was dress rehearsal, and everyone was under the big top."

She realised she was talking the way people do in therapy or confession. It was a role, an act, but one that she found easy to stay in.

"I was in my mum's caravan – Rózsi was a dancer and a snake-charmer. I was there whenever I could, with the snakes. These two were hers." She looked tenderly at her snakes.

"I hid them before the police got there. Thumper kept them for me until I could care for them."

She bit her lip and lowered her voice.

"I was in the caravan when I heard it. I didn't know fire could roar. Loud and wild like a beast. My mother was caught inside and my father too."

"Sabina, I'm sorry."

"What are you gonna do, right?" The smile was back on her face, like a bad habit. "The show must go on."

"That it does," he agreed.

Regaining control of herself, she removed the tin's lid and turned it upside down. Promo shots, Polaroid shots, and newspaper clippings rained on the rug. "It's not much but they are all I have to hold on to."

Mihai took a photograph from the pile.

"Is that you?" He pointed at a small girl standing by a beautiful woman who was wearing little else other than a python around her neck.

"Yeah, I was ten. I used to help my dad with his act. He was a magician. Thoros was his stage name." She pointed at the woman. "This is my mother and this is Buto around her neck."

She picked up a promo shot.

"This is Mungo Joey, one of the best auguste clowns I've ever seen."

"High praise, that is. Who's that with him? He looks like some pirate."

"That's Ringmaster Romero," she said, the smile fading from her face. "He was a great man. Always had a lollipop for me."

She sighed, thinking of Mungo now. He would probably be lying on his favourite bench by the pier, drunk or on his way there.

"One of them is dead and, the other, broken."

"You care for him, for this clown," said Mihai.

"Yeah, I do. Sometimes I think he would rather I didn't."

"I don't believe that."

"That's because you haven't met Mungo yet."

"Were there many survivors?" He asked suddenly.

"Only five," she replied, showing him a promo shot of a big man lifting a barbell above his head. "Thumper here was one of them."

"And you and this Mungo... your parents?"

She shook her head. Mihai nodded solemnly, looking at the pile on the rug. He picked up another photograph.

"Is that you again?"

"Yes, I was fifteen or sixteen," she replied. "Dress rehearsals."

"Who is that behind you?"

"That's my mother, she-"

"No, on the other side, the man."

She took a closer look and the world started spinning.

"In the background, I've never noticed him there. It must be the only shot of him without his turban! What was his name? Something the Magnificent, they were all magnificent, or grand, or something. Marku! Marku the Magnificent!"

"Sabina, slow down," Mihai pleaded.

"He was Marku the Magnificent, a mentalist with Circus Romero. I thought he was dead," she explained. "But he is alive."

"How do you know?" Mihai asked; his tone suddenly cold.

This change didn't go unnoticed. Sabina started placing the photos back in the tin, thinking Mihai was like a matryoshka doll – kind and charming on the surface, cold and menacing underneath. She got up, Marku's photo in one hand and the tin in the other.

"I've seen him," she finally answered.

"Where, where have you seen him?"

"In the café, he often goes to Sammy's to play chess with Shaun," she answered absent-mindedly while putting the tin back in its place. "He lives in some flats on Castleton Boulevard, near the Sand Castle."

"This mentalist," he said slowly, "is Popescu?"

"Yeah," she replied, grabbing her jacket and two sets of keys. Sabina knew what she needed to do – she needed to tell Mungo.

"Mihai, I'm so sorry, but I've got to go," she said, sliding into her shoes. "Let yourself out when you're ready." She placed one of the sets on his shirt. "You can keep my spare key for now. Lock up when you go, please."

Mihai was staring out of the window. His reply, one single word, was barely audible.

"Step right up! Step right up!"

Mungo Joey had his blank white stare fixed on his nemesis, the Punch and Judy Man. Spitfire the seagull – the food-stealing rat with wings – was circling overhead in the grey overcast sky but Spitfire could wait. Mungo's vendetta with the Punch and Judy Man took precedence.

The Punchman had appeared on the pier earlier that day, dragging his mobile puppet-box behind his tricycle. That blasted trike creaked and lurched under its heavy load. He was attracting a good-sized audience. Never one to miss an opportunity, the Punchman had ditched his spot on the promenade and returned to the pier to cash-in on the crime-scene junkies still lingering four days after the body was found. After all, they had kids too.

"Come one! Come all!" the Punchman yelled in his high-pitched voice. "Come and marvel at the adventures of Mr Punch!"

More and more families gathered around the striped puppet-box, like druids around a red-and-white monolith.

The Punchman rubbed his hands greedily. He was always rubbing those hands. Not in anticipation of the performance but rather in anticipation of the money he would collect afterwards. Look at those fingers! Great, long digits like the Grinch.

The most disturbing thing about the Punchman was the likeness he shared with his titular puppet, Mr Punch. Both had huge grins carved across their rosy faces, both seemed to be in a perpetual state of self-satisfaction and both had hooked noses and jutting jaws that almost met in the middle. He even styled the remains of his hair into a well-oiled point, reminiscent of Punch's sugarloaf hat.

Perhaps all performers began to look like their creations over time. Mungo's real nose was certainly the same red as his clown nose these days.

Either way, the Punchman's face gave Mungo the creeps and he was relieved when it finally ducked under the canopy of the puppet-box, like a vampire returning to its casket.

Mungo crunched his breakfast toffee apple with malice. He liked to get his five-a-day but right now he was just glad to have something to grind his teeth against.

It was showtime.

"*HELLO BOYS AND GIRLS!*" shrieked Mr Punch in his trademark kazoo-style voice.

And so it began.

Mungo watched in horror as Judy left Punch to look after their baby whilst she popped out. Punch immediately sat on the baby in a misguided attempt at 'baby-sitting'. He then proceeded to throw the poor thing down a flight of stairs when it wouldn't stop crying. As a last resort, Punch decided to shove the baby through a sausage-making machine. As ever, the audience squealed in delight at this flagrant display of child abuse.

Of course, then Judy returned home and the sticks came out. The dreaded slapstick. Judy started the ruckus – in fairness, she *had* just found her husband shredding their new-born into mincemeat – but Punch soon gained the upper-hand. He swiftly beat her to death. Spousal abuse and domestic violence, always a winning formula for children's entertainment.

Now for the infamous line: "*THAT'S THE WAY TO DO IT!*"

That bloody line. That vile, heinous line. Mungo knew it had been Punch's catchphrase for four-hundred years but the world had moved on since the seventeenth century. They still hunted witches back then, for God's sake. These were modern times. People deserved better entertainment.

What's worse, what *really* drove Mungo's vendetta against the Punchman was the inclusion of another line, an ad-libbed line of the Punchman's own design and that line was, "*SHE HAD IT COMING! SHE HAD IT COMING!*"

Mungo couldn't forgive that line. His father had favoured that line. He found himself raising an arm to throw the remains of his toffee-apple.

"I suppose it's because she's adopted. I wish she would get over it, and not use it as an excuse to be the centre of attention every bloody minute of every bloody day. Tim, this is Laura, here. This is space-station Laura calling planet Tim. Do you read me? Over."

"What?" Tim was facing the window of the pier café. Beyond the glass, he could see a Punch and Judy show playing to a dozen spectators, all with hoods up, and some of them blowing repeatedly into their cupped hands. The pier's resident drunken clown stood at a short distance, glowering at the performance, a half-eaten toffee apple in his hand.

"Actually," said Laura, "I think what I am going to do is have a big liquidy dump, and then rub it with meticulous attention into your chest-hair, if you have any."

"What?" said Tim, abruptly focussing on her.

"There he is! How was it?"

"Was what?"

"Wherever you were. What were you thinking about, Tim?"

"Domestic violence, a crocodile, and sausages," said Tim.

Laura, who was facing the counter, was lost.

"What the actual...?"

"The Punch and Judy show."

"Aah. Of course. I'm starting to get it now."

"I was thinking that the sausages on that string are huge in comparison to the size of the puppet of the crocodile. Each one would be as big as a whole salami."

"Why don't you go over and buy me a drink, and I'll sit here and contemplate the size of your sausage?" she said.

"Mungo! I need to talk to you!"

Mungo dropped the apple. He dragged his glare away from the puppet-box and saw Sabina hurrying along the pier.

"Can't you see I'm busy?" Mungo scowled, turning back to the carnage across the pier.

Sabina noticed the puppet-box. "Oh, were you watching the show?"

"No, my dear, I was watching a man murder his wife and child."

"The crowd seem to be enjoying themselves," Sabina observed.

"Of course they are," Mungo sighed. "Skegness is hardly known for good taste. This is a town that chose a fat fisherman as its mascot, after all."

"Don't be so mean," she said. "These people give you money every day."

"That's their business. I don't ask them for money."

"Then why do you put your hat in front of the bench?"

"I have to put it somewhere!"

Joey the Clown had just made its appearance on the little stage. Mungo often wondered if Ringmaster Romero was aware of the Punch and Judy association when he gave Mungo his clown name all those years ago.

"If you don't want their money, why do you perform out here?" said Sabina.

Mungo was offended. "I don't perform! I just sit here minding my own business."

"You *do* perform," Sabina laughed. "In your own way. Why else would you put on your face paint every day?"

"Because a clown puts on his face paint every day. The circus doesn't stop here anymore but we're still here."

"It's the circus I wanted to talk to you about."

"Circus Romero is nothing but a scorch mark at North End," he said. "The Big Top is dust. The troupe, I'm sorry to say, are ashes."

"Not all of them," said Sabina.

"What?"

For the first time, he drew his attention away from Punch's killing spree.

"Remember Marku the Magnificent?" said Sabina.

"The psychic guy? From Bulgaria?"

"Romania. Well, wait till you hear this. I'm pretty sure he's alive."

Mungo froze. Sabina beamed at him in excitement but Mungo suspected he didn't give her the response she hoped for.

"No, no," he said. "There were only five survivors that night."

"I thought so too."

Mungo kept quiet. Luck had nothing to do with his survival. Cowardice would be a better word.

"Well, now I think there was one more who survived that fire."

Sabina shoved the photo in Mungo's face. He squinted. "What am I looking at here? This is just a photo of you at a dress rehearsal."

"No, in the background." She tapped the photo. "That's Marku. It's the only shot I have of him without the turban."

"So?"

"Don't you think he looks like that old man in the café?"

Mungo gave her a look. "Sabina, when was the last time you saw me in the cafe? I don't get off this bench for anything except candy floss and cider. What old man?"

"His name is Popescu," she explained. "He plays chess with a young lad every day. The old man looks exactly like Marku and he is *Romanian*."

Mungo groaned. "Sabina, it's not unthinkable that two Romanians have been to Skegness over the years."

Sabina gave him a look. "But I *know* Popescu is Marku. I can feel it."

"Sabina, why are you telling me this? If you're so sure then why don't you just go and talk to this Popescu?"

Sabina looked confused. "Don't you want to come with me?"

"Even if he is Marku, why would I want to talk to him?"

Sabina frowned. "Another circus survivor is living here in Skegness! He is one of us. We could reunite for a show!"

Mungo sighed. "Do I look like someone who wants to form a circus troupe?"

Sabina raised an eyebrow at Mungo, dressed like a clown.

"Okay, don't answer that. But come on. You can't be serious. No one wants to see three circus has-beens stumbling around on stage. Even the Sand Castle would turn us away."

She was beginning to get upset. "But –"

"No Sabina! Give it up. The circus is gone. I know you miss it. I miss it too. There, I said it. But this miraculous survivor theory is just fantasy."

The rainclouds above the pier gave a deep rumble. The downpour began.

Sabina glared. "You think I'm crazy?"

"No, I just think that you desperately miss the circus and now you're looking for things which aren't there."

"So you *do* think I'm crazy!"

Mungo rubbed his face in frustration. "Sabina –"

"Look, just forget it! I don't know why I even bothered coming here. The old man *is* Marku. You just don't want to see it! If you want to forget our glory days then fine. Just sit there on your bench and rot." She shoved the photo back into her pocket. "Enjoy the show." And with that she stormed off.

But the show was over. The rain had seen to that.

The Punchman finished on his usual skin-crawling note: *"THAT'S THE WAY TO DO IT! THEY ALL HAD IT COMING!"* Mungo clenched his fists.

Judging from the pile of dead puppets on stage, it looked like Punch had managed to bludgeon a few more puppets before his fun was stopped by the weather. The Doctor, the Skeleton and Jack Ketch the Hangman were lying lifeless on stage.

The rain was really coming down now. Rather than get up, Mungo popped open his pink umbrella. He watched as the Punchman scrambled around the crowd with his bottle, collecting what he could before the spectators ran for cover. Moments later, the Punchman cycled after them himself to find shelter.

Mungo was left alone on the pier. As he listened to the pitter-patter of rain against his umbrella, he thought of his father, he thought of the fire and he thought he might have just sent away his only friend.

Tim considered that cappuccino was outrageously expensive in comparison to its volume or nutritional value, but he placed the cup in front of Laura trying to give the impression that this was a routine experience for him. Having carried the cup and saucer with both hands, he went back to the counter and brought over his own drink.

"What's that – Pimm's?" asked Laura.

"Orange and lemonade," said Tim.

Laura smirked.

"Awww, little Timmy-boy," she said, and tried to ruffle Tim's hair. Tim felt himself colouring again. He wondered if he was ever going to be able to enjoy this girl's company for more than five minutes at a time. He dodged Laura's hand, and so she jabbed him in the ribs with the other. It tickled, and he struggled to suppress his reaction. He could not let this girl know any of his weaknesses.

"Is he ticklish? Is little Timmy-boy ticklish? Doesn't he like being tickled, little Timmy-boy?" A fat lady in a tweed coat and an old man in a flat cap looked up from their newspapers and frowned.

"Get OFF!" said Tim, much louder than he intended. Laura stopped, and regarded him contemplatively. The sky had darkened and rain was beating against the glass front of the café.

"Okay," she said. "Okay." She placed her hands flat on the table. They sat in silence for a while. Tim hoped that Laura would not notice that he was on the verge of crying. Laura looked at him again with intense curiosity, as if he were a rare South American moth that had landed on the back of the chair in the café.

"Tim –"

"What?"

Tim started to panic, afraid that she would tell he was close to crying.

"You aren't seventeen, are you?"

"I am. I can prove it." He controlled his voice. He was grateful to Laura for having given him the chance to go into one of his rehearsed routines. He nonchalantly reached inside his coat pocket and pulled out his driving licence. He held it up for a second and then put it away again.

"So fake," said Laura. "Fake. Fake. Fake." She put her fists out in front of her and started a gyrating motion with her hips and her arms as she sat in her chair. "Look. This is me doing my fake-spotting dance."

"But you didn't inspect it."

"I don't need to. So fake, yeah. So fake, yeah. So fake, yeah. So..."

"How do you work that out?"

"Obvious."

Tim wished he had a fire-extinguisher to spray this girl with. Something non-lethal but powerful to shut her up.

"So how come Mr McNair lets me drive the van?" he said.

"Because Scary McNairy is a little, baldy, pointless, goth-hating, tit-perving twat who would not know a fake driving licence if it was rolled up tightly and anally inserted."

She looked at him askance.

"Eeeew!" she exclaimed, at her own words.

Another pause. The wind shook the building, and blew more rain against the glass. Tim could see bits of moss and black stuff scattering out of the over-loaded guttering above the shop-front. He felt cold and weak. He wondered what wind velocity would be required to destroy the building they were sitting in.

"Where do you live? Actually, who do you live with?" asked Laura.

"My mother." It sounded to both of them like an admission of defeat. Laura was determined that it would not be the end of the conversation.

"Is that difficult for you?"

"She's mad."

"In what way?"

Tim said nothing, looking down at his lap. He was thinking, and re-living, and trying to process experiences. Laura reached out and held Tim's hand.

"Tim. Tim. You can always talk to me. I'm here for you. Tim? Are you hearing me?" He glanced towards her.

"Poor kid," she said. "I guess this means that my original plan's out the window. I was going to get us both a bit pissed in the pub, let you cop off with me and then persuade you to drive me to an interview at Holman and Sons in two days' time."

Laura sighed and squeezed his hand.

"She's completely mad," said Tim. "She never gives me a moment's peace. I don't know how much more I can take."

"Oh, Tim."

Tim hunched over and gave way, quietly but too noisily for the other café patrons to ignore, to sobbing. With a scraping of chair-legs, Laura moved towards him. She hugged him. She took out a clean tissue and she dried Tim's tears. "You just let it out."

He stopped being a retail assistant and IT expert. He stopped being a van-driver. He stopped being everything he had built up over the previous months, and he reverted to being a frightened, naked child in the dark who, for the first time, had been shown a light and offered a dignified way to safety. He cried onto Laura's shoulder. He did not want the shoulder ever to be taken away. He wanted Laura to hold onto him more tightly. Laura did hold onto him more tightly.

A man in a grubby apron came out of from behind the counter.

"Is he all right?"

"Yes, he's fine."

"Is he a bit mental? Is he not all there?"

"He's my boyfriend, and yes, he is definitely all there."

"Well, can you try to keep it down? You know what I mean?" The man returned to his place behind the counter. Laura wiggled her little finger at his retreating back, while she stroked Tim and wondered what to do next.

"Tim. Tim. Look at me. I know you are in a depleted state, but is there somewhere we can go? I can drive if need be. Tim? Can you hear me?"

"Yes."

"Is there somewhere we can go?"

"The back of the van."

"Won't that be cold and uncomfortable?"

"There's a mattress. I sleep on it sometimes, and blankets."

"Are the blankets nice and dry?"

Tim nodded slowly.

Laura dragged Tim by the hand as they walked back to the van. She felt in his pockets for the key, opened the back doors, arranged the mattress and blankets, and laid Tim down. As soon as he was lying down she undressed him. His modesty was covered by plenty of blankets, and the driving rain deterred onlookers. She lay down and undressed herself, under the covers. Laura hugged Tim and shushed softly in his ear. He made low, murmuring noises in reply as the rain drummed rhythmically off the roof.

As he was drifting off to sleep, Laura laughed suddenly.

"What?" he said.

"Nothing," she cooed. "Just thinking. You might be the sanest potential boyfriend I've ever met."

"Boyfriend?"

"Shush, baby."

She hugged him tighter. She stroked his back. She stroked his hair. She took one of Tim's hands, and moved it between her legs. He could feel her pubic hairs between his fingers but did nothing.

A sudden sense of the passage of time settled on Tim and he sat up.

"I've got to get to work."

"Oh, behave."

"No, I mean it. I might get sacked. I've got to get to work." Tim turned on a torch and began to look frantically for his clothes. The fact that he was naked did not seem to bother him.

By the time Tim was fully dressed, Laura was still looking for her bra. Tim opened the back doors, allowing a spray of cold rain to make goose-bumps all over Laura's upper body, got out, slammed the doors again, and got into the driver's seat. Laura was pitched from side to side as Tim drove back to McNair's.

"Can you give me a lift home?"

"I've got to get to work. I've got to get to work."

"I know, darling, but can you give me a lift home, first?"

"I've got to get to work." They drew up in McNair's yard. Laura was still virtually naked. Tim closed the driver's door and locked her in the van. He began the ritual of opening the shop, to begin his shift. Tim's pay-as-you-go mobile pinged with a message.

"Hello. This is Laura. Can you unlock the van, please, and let me drive myself home, since you didn't take me to the pub and I am completely stone cold sober? You can walk over in the morning and pick it up. X"

A minute later it pinged again.

"I can't find my shoe. Let me out of the van now."

Nell came out from the kitchen of Sammy's Snacks and was surprised to see her aunt standing outside the front of the café under the umbrella of a man a few years her junior. The foul rain had not let up all day. Nell saw him flash some sort of ID, and she took an instinctive step back towards the kitchen.

The bell over the door chimed as the man held it open for her aunt. He carefully shook his umbrella outside before leaning it against the window.

Rachel waved her hand in a general line between the stranger and Nell across the otherwise empty café.

"Nell, this is Detective Constable Castell. This is my niece, Nell Harrison."

"Ms Harrison," said Castell. "Your aunt's been telling me all about you."

"Oh?" Nell smiled automatically. "Only good things I hope."

"Would you like tea?" Rachel asked, already in the process of grabbing a cup for him from the stack on the counter.

"Only if it's no trouble," he said.

"None at all," she said and disappeared through the swinging door.

Castell's gaze swung to Nell.

"I'm sure you've heard we've had a couple of unfortunate incidents recently?"

"A body washed up on the beach, right?"

He nodded and then pulled out a seat to sit down. Nell sat opposite.

"I should warn you," said Nell, "My aunt's tea is terrible."

"Oh?"

"Rachel may have lost her Yankee edge after two decades, but she brews tea like she moved here yesterday."

Castell took out a little notebook and flipped the cover open. He clicked his pen against his bottom lip a few times as he studied his notes.

"This unfortunate business on the beach. I imagine you hear a lot of gossip working here."

She shrugged. "A friend of mine, a guy I train with, he said he heard it was an immigrant."

"You work out?"

Nell froze. "What?"

"You ever been to Studio Gym on Scarborough Road? Ugly place," said Castell. "Sits above a garage in one of the industrial units."

"I know the one."

"Bobby Thomas runs it."

"I heard he sold the place just a few days ago." She mentally edged back from any conversation involving Thomas. Castell waited. "But, yeah. That's where I go," she said.

"You know, we've gotten calls about illegal gambling there, and fights. It's not really the kind of place you want to get comfortable."

"It's the only place in town to box," Nell said.

"You like to fight?"

"I like to box."

99

He studied her face. "Ever met Lewis Marshall?"

Nell straightened, bumping Castell's knee in the process.

"A couple of people I've spoken to saw him here," said Castell.

"I helped him out once."

"You gave him medical attention?"

"Yeah. I mean, I guess." Nell folded her hands together to keep them from shaking.

"You do know this country has free healthcare?"

"I've heard. Very nice," she said.

"So why would he come to you instead of checking himself into the hospital? Do you have credentials I should be aware of?"

"I have a visa," Nell said.

"I was thinking of medical credentials, but in fact, I do need to make a note of your status," he said, gesturing for her to continue.

"I have a British Ancestry Visa," she said. "My grandparents - Rachel's parents, and my mother, Rebecca's - they were born here, so I was able to apply for a five year stay. Apparently, there's an option to extend it, but I haven't really looked into that, seeing as I've only been here...well, not even a year."

"And your medical qualifications?"

"I was an EMT before I moved here. I have a license in the States, and it's valid."

"Sorry? EMT?"

"Emergency Medical Technician. A paramedic, you know?"

Castell nodded minutely in response to this. When he finished writing, he allowed the silence to hang between them. Nell was familiar with this technique though. Her husband's ability to play out a pause had bordered on pathological.

The pause was broken by Rachel returning from the kitchen with a steaming mug of tea. She placed it in front of Castell, gave him the little smile she always gave to cute, young men and, without a word, retreated back into the kitchen.

"One of the bodies we found," said Castell, not touching the tea. "He was badly beaten. However, he also had a few recent injuries that had been tended to quite expertly."

"Lewis is dead?" Nell asked, knuckling her thighs under the table. "But he's - he was fine when he left."

"We don't know for certain that Marshall and this body are one and the same, but if they're not, and I find that you've been...assisting other men like him..."

"Lewis asked for help, and I gave it to him. That's all."

"In return for?"

"Nothing."

He eyed her sceptically.

"Really," she said. "He didn't pay me. I doubt he ever intended to."

"Did you ask him for money?" Castell asked.

Nell shook her head, biting down on the lie. "I haven't seen him since."

"You knew him from the gym though?" he pushed.

"I didn't recognise him at first. He looked like hell, but he said he'd seen me there before."

Castell pushed a picture toward her. "What about this man? Have you seen him before?"

She dragged the photo closer with tips of her fingers. The dead man's face was turned toward her, his eyes wide. "No."

"Do any of his wounds look similar to what you saw on Lewis Marshall?"

Nell leaned forward, her fingers twisting into the cuffs of her shirt. "I can't tell. All the swelling, you know? But whoever got the jump on Lewis had a knife, if that helps."

"It might." He dropped the pen and pad into his jacket pocket and held out his hand for her to shake. "Thank you for your time. If you think of anything else, do get in touch."

He took a sip of the tea before he stood up and pulled a face.

"How do you stay in business charging for that?" he asked, nudging the cup as far away as possible.

"Pity, I suspect," said Nell. "Also, we only let Rachel make it first thing in the morning. The rest of the day, we keep her away from hot beverages all together."

"Smart," he said.

Valerie was curled, catlike, on her sofa. She sipped her camomile tea, listened to the rain and scrolled through the tablet on her lap.

The policewoman who had interrupted their little tête-à-tête yesterday had asked only routine questions of herself and Popescu. Valerie left the flat at the same time as the sergeant, making small talk with her as they clopped down the stairs. It reminded her of her appearance on The Bill, back at the height of her TV career. How she would have relished playing a smart sexy detective. Instead she'd got a few episodes as a minor love interest and petty criminal. It was about par for her career. Still, it paid the rent.

She couldn't get thoughts of Popescu out of her head. She'd lain awake for hours running over it in her mind. She resolved to stick to the facts. That's what Eric would have advised. So far she knew this: Popescu had a gun; he was from Mangalia in Romania; and he used to be a policeman. It wasn't much, was it? And not enough for even the mildest forms of blackmail. Not yet.

"Stick to your instincts darling," she told herself. "There's something shifty there. You'll just have to do a bit more digging."

So this afternoon she'd settled down with her tablet to do a spot of research. She had a weakness for gadgets and this was lovely, her scarlet fingernails made a satisfying tap against the screen as she scrolled and pinched and doubled clicked.

She started off with a search for Mangalia. A coastal city, port and seaside resort, it appeared rather dull though she noted the weather reports with some envy. The golden sand, blue sea and bikinis; it was Skegness with added sunshine and European style.

She made more tea and spread a couple of Ryvita with cream cheese before continuing her search.

A couple of blog posts by travellers were well written enough to offer a whiff of life in Romania, or at least the rural side of it though they were sanitised to suit the romantic tendencies of the authors. She moved onto searches for Ceausescu and life under communism. Most of the sites concerned themselves with the fall of the regime, his execution and the transition. Accounts of the orphanages were interesting. Appalling, even now. She delved deeper, wiping away a genuine tear as she looked at the pictures and descriptions of the conditions.

She shifted in her seat, suddenly stiff and looked at the clock. She realised she'd been reading for several hours and needed to stretch her legs. A bit of fresh air, she thought, she'd go for a walk, maybe get a coffee at the cafe and see who was around to chat to. She clicked just one more link.

The coffee and walk were immediately forgotten as she read. The piece was part of a series written by a pair of journalists, one Romanian, one American.

The charred remains of the orphanage still scar the landscape near a farm just outside Mangalia. As I walk around the site I can make out the blackened stumps of walls and rooms, softened by grass and vines but still visible. You can imagine the cramped conditions, the lack of space for children to run around, you can see the blank walls of their rooms and the fight for adequate food. But this building, as poor as it was, was devastated in a fire that swept the beds, the rags, the walls aside.

January, 1990. A cold night only a few weeks after the execution of the man responsible for so much terror and misery in Romania. The fire swept through the building and destroyed it completely. Situated some ten miles outside the port city of Mangalia, the orphanage was too far for the fire service to access quickly. We managed to track down a farm worker living there at the time and he overcame his reluctance and initial wariness to talk to us about that night.

"I woke to a smell of smoke," he says. "I slept in a barn outhouse at the time and the fumes made my nostrils itch. The orphanage was a huge blaze. It had been burning for some time. I cried out to wake everybody at the farm and we alerted the authorities. But everything was in chaos and it took them a long time to come. We ran over to the orphanage to see if we could help but there was nothing we could do. The fire destroyed it all. It was terrible, terrible."

Estimates place between 150-200 children and up to 20 staff at the orphanage at the time. The farmhand says there was no one standing outside the building when he got to the fire site.

"We couldn't get close, the heat was too strong. But I saw no one there. I thought they must all have been killed."

Looking at pictures from similar orphanages of the time, seeing the cramped conditions and layout of the rooms, it seems likely that many children would have been killed. If they woke it may have been hard to find their way out in the smoke and the confusion. And it seems likely that many would have suffocated from the fumes before the flames reached them.

Which of course makes it strange that no bodies were recovered from the fire. Official records are patchy but what we have been able to find contains no mention of bodies or survivors.

The farmhand passes on one further detail:

"I was seeing a girl who worked at the orphanage," he says. "We used to manage a few nights together once in a while. After the fire she disappeared. I never saw her again. I inquired at the hospitals, with the council, I even tried to find her family but there was no trace of her. There were no bodies and we never saw anyone from the orphanage again."

He shakes his head and refuses to talk to us further, his mind perhaps still on the girl he loved and lost.

Valerie sat back on her sofa. Her imagination was working overtime, picturing the confusion of the fire, the heat against the cold night, the smoke, the crackling noise and roar of the flames, the onlookers standing uselessly at the side. The article was illustrated with a few grainy photographs. She peered closer.

One was the orphanage site as it was today, ghostly black lumps protruding from the ground. There was an official state photo of the building before it burnt down and then there was a black and white picture, possibly reproduced from a newspaper. The quality was quite poor and yet, what was that?

The picture showed a group of people gathered close to the burnt orphanage, a few wisps of smoke still rising from the charred remains. The picture didn't say who the onlookers were but police were trying to move them along. One had his hand resting on a stick in his belt. The quality may have been poor but Valerie immediately recognised this policeman as the man who had kissed her hand and made her coffee yesterday. It was Popescu.

"Well, well, Razvan," she smiled.

She plugged the USB connector into the tablet and switched the printer on. The piece didn't take long to print and she checked her appearance before she collected the sheets. She'd take these up to show him. She wanted to talk some more about this, about the mystery of the bodies and what he knew. There was definitely a screenplay in this, she thought to herself. Could she pitch something to ITV? It sounded like a possible Sunday night drama. She'd need more information. And a starring role of course.

She wouldn't tell Razvan about the television possibility, she'd just sympathise with him about how awful it must have been. She thought back to what he'd said about the corruption and devastation wrought in the country by crime and poverty. Surely he wouldn't mind a sympathetic ear?

She walked up the stairs to his door and found it was ajar. Perhaps he'd just come in? Or was going out. She pushed it a little and opened her mouth to say hello. Perhaps there was a frog in her throat or something, no sound came out. She was about to try again when she heard a noise from the kitchen. She walked a little further inside.

The squirrel, Anastasia reluctantly concluded, had been a mistake. She stood on the flat roof of her studio, ignoring the lightening rain and surveying the sorry evidence of her experiments. Anastasia had constructed a bed for the non-native rodent with pallets lined with tough black polythene, filling it with a mixture of John Innes potting compost and fresh horse manure. To haul the materials onto the roof she had rigged up a makeshift hoist, a Heath Robinson contraption with a handle rescued from an industrial mincer. But the project had not gone to plan. The grey squirrel still looked like a soft toy abandoned in the rain; a small bundle of flattened, ragged fur squashed into the rich brown loam. Admittedly the eyes had now gone, replaced by a squirm of larvae, but otherwise the flesh seemed stubbornly resistant to the imperative to return to dust.

One last photograph, thought Anastasia, before she adjusted the surgical mask over her face, and reached for the garden tool. She lowered the spade, easing it carefully into the soil. The remains were fragile now. To scoop up the corpse she had to probe under the animal. As the blade disturbed the soil, a cloud of flies rose into the air. Flesh and maggots crumbled from the remains of Anastasia's roadkill find. Balancing the spade with care, Anastasia crossed the roof, trailing bluebottles in her wake, lifted the top of a small plastic chest, and dropped the squirrelly mulch down into the maw of the wormery.

Decomposition was a science hitherto unknown to the artist. Her early attempt with the squirrel, in a home-made raised bed, had been slow and insanitary. Another experiment had involved dropping dead rats into a wormery; a box full of tiny white worms that ingested animal and vegetable matter and turned it into compost. Anastasia had hoped to rescue the rats' remains at the point at which the fur and flesh had been removed, yet the bones remained. Alas, the worms were too efficient, turning everything, including the bones, to slurry in record time. For the seagull, now defrosting comfortably in the sun on a small hammock, she would commission expert help.

The phone pulsed in her pocket. Nate, her assistant in London.

"Any news?" said Anastasia.

"Sebastian's been round. Thinks he's got a rich Russian who wants to be your patron," said Nate.

"The guy who bought the Zoroastrian stuff?" said Anastasia.

"Yeah," said Nate, "Kaletsky. Sebastian wants an update on how the White Space stuff's coming along?"

"Slowly," said Anastasia. "Too damned slow. I was hoping you'd phoned with a lead on the skeleton business."

"I tried every master butcher in Lincolnshire," said Nate's voice. "Same story each time."

"Health and safety, yeah, I know," said Anastasia.

"They can't use their premises to prepare a carcass, if it wasn't killed in a registered abattoir," said Nate.

"So what now?" said Anastasia.

"The vets were more helpful. They know where to buy small animal skeletons," said Nate. "They use them for teaching students."

"No," said Anastasia, "that's not how I work. I need this bird. I know where it comes from."

"Well, the meat processor you mentioned? I've tracked it down," said Nate, "Holman and Sons. But it'll probably be the butcher problem all over again."

"Leave it, Nate. I'll do it myself," said Anastasia. "The personal touch might work better."

"Mrs Manning came to see me yesterday," Popescu said. "I don't know what she wanted."

Shaun knew exactly why she had been there. "She was probably just trying to get to know her neighbours," he said.

Shaun picked at the peeling edge of the board as he waited for Mr Popescu to make his move. Before the two men had begun their daily ritual, the chess set at Sammy's Snacks had sat, boxed and unnoticed, next to a stand of tourist information leaflets. There was a stain on the lid, and dust stuck to it in clumps.

Popescu advanced one of his knights, putting pressure on Shaun's bishop. Already, both men had castled, hiding their kings in the relative safety of the board's far corners.

Shaun immediately tucked his bishop back behind the row of pawns. His father always used to say he played too cautiously. 'If you don't take risks,' he used to say, 'then you'll never surprise anyone." He made a living taking risks in the courtroom. They rarely spoke after Shaun had come to live with him in London, and when he rolled in at midnight, seventeen and high, they played out their arguments in silence across a polished chessboard. It was an argument Shaun rarely won. He smiled grimly; he bet his father had been surprised when he ran off to Wiltshire with the Brotherhood.

Popescu brought his own bishop further into no-man's land. Outside the window, a couple of pensioners in socks and sandals stood under the awning and smoked in the afternoon drizzle. Shaun looked into the old man's eyes. They were narrow and icy, like the tattoo on the dead man's neck. The Brotherhood of the Stars had taught him that all things were connected, and he knew it could not be a coincidence that he had discovered Popescu's gun on the same day the body turned up on the beach. He decided it was time to take a risk.

"Did the police speak to you yesterday?" he asked, pushing a pawn into the old man's sights.

"Yes, they arrived as Mrs Manning – Valerie - was leaving. It's funny, I'd just been telling her about my own time as a policeman."

Shaun nodded. Popescu had never told Shaun much about his past; they usually stuck to talking about the weather or the bad street lighting on Rutland Road, but this made sense. Popescu had taken the bait. The old man's bishop captured Shaun's pawn and sprung the trap. Shaun's queen leapt forwards, taking the old man's piece off the board.

According to the Brotherhood, most of life's patterns were reflected in the movements of the stars. Shaun tried to decide where Popescu fitted. Law was governed by Jupiter, but so was growth and good fortune. That didn't seem to fit with Popescu's tiny flat, his exile on this grey coast.

Pressing his advantage, Shaun pushed a rook towards the centre of the board. In Wiltshire he used to help make chessboards to sell at the commune's shop, and David had told him once that each of the pieces was linked to a planet in astrology. Rooks were Saturn, moving ponderously along the board's ranks and files. That was Popescu: bound by discipline and duty, melancholic. The old man took another pawn out of its starting position, advancing his line but exposing his king in the process. Perhaps Popescu had something of the king about him, too. It wasn't authority exactly, not anymore. It was more a feeling that he was somehow at the centre of things, like the sun, while all the other planets danced around the edges.

Shaun lifted a knight and placed it along the left flank. At some point, somebody had stuffed the piece with blu-tack to add weight to the cheap plastic. Knights, of course, were Mars – impulsive and warlike. Since leaving the commune, Shaun had read all sorts of reasons why astrology shouldn't work, but it still made sense to him. He didn't know if the Watchers had taught early man to read the patterns in the sky, as the Brotherhood claimed, but it seemed like a more dignified way for them to communicate than sending psychic messages to seven men in the south of England.

"We'll be seeing more of the detectives, I think," said Popescu.

"What makes you say that?"

"That body was right in the middle of the beach where anybody could see it. In my experience, that means someone was trying to send a message, or someone got clumsy. Either way, there are going to be repercussions."

Shaun shook his head. He had come to Skegness hoping for a sanctuary. He struck his knight into the old man's line. It was a bad move – Popescu took his piece without even blinking. Shaun brought his bishop into play, hoping to secure the centre files and rectify his mistake.

"You think there'll be more bodies?" he asked.

Popescu shrugged. "When there are gangs, these things happen occasionally. They usually blow over."

"Gangs?"

Popescu pushed forwards with his rook, capturing Shaun's bishop and taking control of the middle of the board.

"Perhaps, you are scared?" he asked. "You've never lived in a place where there is real danger."

Once again, Shaun thought about the girl he'd left behind at Starhaven. Sky's father was on the Council of Seven, and she had been raised there. But after she had come back from her outreach placement at Haven House, they had locked her in a windowless room for two months. Sometimes, the Council would 'interview' her twice in one day, others they would leave her alone for almost a week, while at morning services the rest of the commune were warned about the influence of those who might disrupt communication with the Watchers. All because Shaun had mentioned to her father that he was worried about her. When she came out, so thin that Shaun could count her ribs, she thanked him for helping her to reconnect with her Brothers. Until that moment, he had really thought he was doing the best for her.

"No," he said, looking out of the window, "not really."

There was a bang, distant but loud. Shaun whirled in his seat. The old couple outside were chatting and smoking as though nothing had happened, and Sabina was still drying mugs behind the counter.

"That was a car backfiring," said Shaun to himself.

Popescu raised an eyebrow at him.

"Wasn't it?" said Shaun.

The sharp cracking sound had ripped through the background noise of Castleton Boulevard. Anastasia moved quickly towards the front of the roof. She peered down into the street. She could see nothing obviously amiss, but there was a small group of people clustered at the corner, one of the men pointing towards the flats across the road. The arrangement of pointing hands, the slant of lamp posts, the angle of parked vehicles, a bicycle stand, struck Anastasia as somehow reminiscent of Uccello's The Battle At San Romano, and she raised her phone to photograph the scene. In the delay before the image was captured, the door to the lobby of the block of flats crashed open and a woman flailed out, stumbling, right into the centre of the photograph.

It was her neighbour, Valerie.

Valerie's arm was oddly positioned. It wrapped her in an awkward self-embrace, the hand clutching at her shoulder. The woman was shouting, her voice projecting with shrill clarity, even if her words made little sense. It was as though she was declaiming an absurdist poem.

"Pop, Stop, Can, Man, Run, Gun," she yelled with urgency, pushing on, twirling, toppling a boy with a tricycle, tipping his cargo to the ground, scattering his papers to the wind.

Into this scene, announcing its arrival with a tinny peal of 'Remember You're a Womble', came the ice cream van, a confection of lurid yellow overlaid with giant cones, and phallic flakes, and 'hundreds and thousands' the size of tennis balls. The collision proceeded with grim inevitability. The dervish Valerie met the ice cream van. The impact spun the woman over in an involuntary cartwheel before she flopped heavily to the ground, a repertory Cleopatra clutching an asp to her breast for her final scene. As people rushed to Valerie's assistance, ruining the tableau, Anastasia decided to take a closer look at the commotion herself.

Dropping quickly down the ladder, and out onto the street, Anastasia crossed to the edge of the small crowd of onlookers. A young man was crouching down beside Valerie, the centre of all attention, asking her if she could say anything. Another man shouted, "Put her in the recovery position!", whilst a woman screamed, "Don't move her an inch, she might have broken her back!" Anastasia was less interested in Valerie, who was now overacting being dead, than in the boy with the tricycle, who had broken away from the crowd and was chasing the papers billowing down the street. They looked like a large collection of photographs. One tumbled her way, and Anastasia reached down a hand to pluck it up. It was a contact sheet, with a series of a dozen portrait shots of children.

The photographs had a curious air about them, as if they came from another time and place. But it was one child's expression that held Anastasia's attention, a girl bearing a close resemblance to little Gracie from the flats whom Anastasia had been sketching for her triptych. She realised at once that all her previous sketches of the girl had been wrong. She had rendered the girl too classically, as too Roman, when she ought to have been Byzantine. These images somehow exaggerated the slant of the cheekbones, orientalised the eyes, melding a Slavic broadness with a hint of Asia Minor. Yes, that was the look she needed to create. Turning the sheet over, and as if to confirm these thoughts, Anastasia saw that the information, presumably from the photographer's studio, was rendered in an unfamiliar language.

As the ambulance and the police car arrived in a squeal of sirens and a strobing pulse of blue lights, Anastasia slipped back into her studio, picked up her sketch book, and began to record Valerie Manning's curtain call.

Popescu shifted his rook across a couple of ranks. Shaun's queen was pinned between the rook and a knight.

"Looks like I've killed your queen," said the old man, smiling.

A bell rang as the doors burst open. A girl ran into the centre of the room, breathing heavily. Sweat glued her purple hair to her face. *Laura Greenwood*, thought Shaun, *number eight, opposite Mr Popescu's*.

"That nosey bitch from number twelve just got hit by an ice cream van," she said. "I think she might be dead."

Nobody moved. Laura looked at each of the customers in turn. They looked back at her.

"Why are you only wearing one shoe?" said Shaun.

Laura glared at him.

"Call a fucking ambulance!"

Sabina was already at the phone. The few other customers turned back to their conversations, and Laura was left standing in the middle of the room, tugging at the edge of her t-shirt.

"I think we can both agree that I won this round," Popescu said, extending his hand.

CHAPTER FIVE

Mister Pop's flat smelt different, not very nice at all, and Gracie wrinkled up her nose as she shuffled inside. His old smiling face hovered over her like a genie's.

"Good to see you too, little one," he remarked as she stomped into the lounge and flopped onto her special armchair. "There is a dark cloud over you today, yes? Your mother – Sarah – she told me all about your great adventure the other day. Why would you run away from your own school? You know it is not allowed, very risky to be wandering about on your own without a grown up. They seem to think that this is my fault, putting dangerous ideas into your head. Sarah says if there is any more trouble like this one, I will have to stop letting you come to see me."

"I wasn't wandering around on my own. I met a grown-up and he watched out for me."

"Oh? And how did you know that he was really watching out for you? He could have been an evil man."

"He wasn't evil. He was a clown."

"A clown?" Mister Pop repeated falteringly.

"Yes." Gracie dragged herself off the chair again and trudged towards the kitchen in search of some socată. When she reached the doorway, however, she forgot completely about drinks and even about her dark cloud.

"Mister Pop!" she shrieked. "Why is your kitchen all broken up?"

"Ah," his rough voice lingered in the other room. "I left the front door open yesterday, and somebody – a very bad, bad person – came inside and smashed a lot of my things."

"A bad person?" she repeated breathlessly.

The idea that anybody would try to hurt her neighbour was unthinkable. As she backed out of the kitchen and turned to look at Mister Pop he suddenly seemed so frail and gentle, no good at killing dragons and no good at keeping bad people out of his home. Why would anybody want to hurt him? He was only an old man who had never done anything to anyone. In a burst of fear and love she ran to her ancient friend and hugged as much of his body as she could fit into her arms.

"Why did they come here? Why do they want to break your things?"

He had frozen when she touched him, and only now did his hands rest lightly on her shoulders like careful birds. A sigh lifted his tummy and let it down again.

"There are many evil people in the world, little one." His voice was heavy and gruffer than normal, like he was trying to keep something down in his throat. "And they do evil things. Who knows why? I think even they don't know, sometimes."

He was just mumbling silly words now. Gracie squeezed him tighter. "You sound so sad," she mumbled into his thick grey jumper. "Did they make you sad?"

"Yes," he replied as he held her at arm's length and peered down at her. There was a faraway look in his eyes that disappeared slowly as he focused on Gracie's face. "But I am not hurt. I am very lucky. Let us drink socată and you can tell me all about the other day."

A cold wind had risen from the capricious north, sweeping through springtime Skegness and chilling Bobby to the marrow. The little gas fireplace in the back office of the Coin Fountain arcade was barely sufficient to warm the place during the best of times and it was woefully inadequate now. Bobby had Marcus requisition a number of space heaters and disperse them throughout the office. Bobby wasn't convinced they helped much, even turned up to their full output.

Sure, they warmed the place up but... it was almost too comfortable.

"Marcus," he bellowed, prone in the comfort of his enveloping couch, "do you think I'm becoming a shut-in?"

"I think you were already a shut-in. Now you're just a shut-in with a nicer office," Marcus replied from the kitchenette where he was ostensibly making coffee. "When's the last time you went to your flat?"

Bobby mulled the question over for a while.

"I had a New Year's party there," he yelled.

"That was two years ago, Bobby, and I'm less than three metres away from you, so the screaming isn't necessary, alright?" Marcus said through the door.

"Oh," Bobby said at a more normal volume.

His phone vibrated.

"Looks like we have our first visitors, my man," He said to Marcus. "Which button do I push to activate the camera? And tell me I didn't just hear you mutter 'old man' under your breath."

Marcus grinned and showed him how to activate the camera from his phone.

"Ah, the long, inept arm of the law, DS Young and DC Castell," Marcus said. "Perhaps it's best if I step into the pantry."

"Every time I start to despair of you, young blood, you redeem yourself," Bobby said. "Listen closely. I'll want your considered insight after they leave."

Marcus threw him a salute and disappeared into the kitchen.

Bobby levered himself off the sofa, snapped the crease back into his cashmere blend trousers, and smoothed the wrinkles in his French blue silk shirt. In his experience, cops hated expensively dressed adversaries. His boots alone cost more than either of this pair made in a month and he looked forward to showing them off. He cordially despised both of them and making petty little gestures was part of the game he played.

He let them wait a few minutes more while he poured himself three fingers of Glenmorangie and then sauntered to the door, glass in hand.

"Who is it?" he called through the door in an old woman's falsetto.

"You know who it is, Bobby," replied Castell. "You can see us through the camera you think you hid so well. Now let us in before Katie gets irritated. She skipped lunch and you know what she's like when she hasn't eaten."

Bobby opened the door with alacrity.

"Young, Castell," he greeted them as they stepped inside.

"Jesus, Baron. It's like a blast furnace in here. How can you stand it?" asked Young by way of greeting.

Bobby shrugged. "I'm always cold lately. It's the absence of a good woman to take care of me, I think. The position's open if

115

you're looking to make a move, my beautiful Detective Sergeant Young," Bobby replied. She hated it when he flirted with her.

"Have you really not eaten, gorgeous? I have some biscuits or I could even stretch to making you a sandwich, if you'd like. The thought of you in discomfort pains me, Katie. Did I ever tell you I used to date a Katie? She broke my heart, but then they all do, eventually, don't they, Katie?"

DS Young didn't rise to it.

"You've made some improvements in here, Baron," she said.

"It's refreshing to see someone appreciate a man's efforts. What say we ditch the Cro-Magnon in the room and find a fine restaurant to discuss my good taste? I know a great Italian in town."

Bobby raised an eyebrow and was gratified to see Young at least pretend to consider the offer.

"Wow, the pizza and bullshit offer is tempting," said Young.

Bobby shrugged.

"It's a nice little Italian, my dear. None of your tourist crap."

"That's enough, Baron," Castell said. "This is business."

"I'm bored with business, you graceless baboon," Bobby said. "Can't you see I'm busy talking with Katie? Go write some reports or some other fucking thing that makes your existence seem worthwhile."

"Is that why you divested your interest in the gym? Because you were bored with it?" Young abruptly asked. "That doesn't sound like you, Bobby."

A lesser man might have missed a beat. Bobby wasn't a lesser man.

"They don't hand out those CID promotions for nothing, do they?" Bobby asked. "Is that what this is about? The gym?" Bobby laughed. "Why didn't you just call? Not that I'm displeased to see you. Or to see Katie, anyway. Seriously, how about that Italian? If you want to talk about that wretched gym I'll tell you all about it."

"Tell me all about where Lewis Marshall is, too, and you've got a deal, Baron," Young said.

This time Bobby missed a beat.

"And this Marcus fella that I hear has risen to prominence. Give me the rundown on him and you and I will make a grand night of it in old Skegness," she said.

Castell smirked, making Bobby narrow his eyes.

"Get out. Both of you. Get out now before I lose my patience. Your jobs...fuck that...your *lives* are at my sufferance. Leave while I let you leave," Bobby said.

"We could run him in for threatening behaviour and half a dozen public order offences right now," said Castell. "Say 'fuck' one more time, Bobby. I dare you."

Young laid a hand on Castell's arm, silencing him, and neither said a further word as they left the office.

Bobby poured another whiskey and threw it back. Poured another and waited for his nerves to settle. There was a leak in his organisation and Young knew it. She had someone on the inside feeding her information. It had to be one of Marcus' people.

"It's not one of mine, boss," Marcus said from the kitchen doorway.

"One of my old-timers, then? Someone jealous of your promotion? Only one or two names come to mind and none of them seem the sort to stab me in the back. If they'd wanted promotion they would have spoken up," Bobby said.

"Really only leaves one option, doesn't it?" Marcus said. "We have spies in our midst."

"The police? Laughable. Most can't find their arses with both hands."

"I didn't say anything about the police."

"That leaves...."

"A legitimate rival."

Marcus gave him a look, one Bobby knew well.

"A rival operation?" said Bobby.

"Not of the home-grown variety," said Marcus. "You heard the name Ion Dalca?"

"Not often."

"I'm hearing it a lot these days."

"But that's just the people-trafficking crowd. Do I need to worry about some foreigners whose empire extends to smuggling potato-pickers and ugly prostitutes into the country?"

"You don't need to worry about anything. That's my job."

Bobby gave an involuntary shiver.

"Shit. It's freezing in here. What are we going to do, young brother?"

"Do? We're going to do that voodoo that you do so well, Baron."

And he went back into the kitchen, whistling an old Ella Fitzgerald tune he shouldn't have known, searching for a coffee press that may or may not have been there.

Valerie's heart monitor bleeped to itself in the near silence of the ICU. Shaun was uneasy about leaving the flats, but Valerie had no relatives that he knew of. He had told the receptionist that he was her nephew.

"I'm sorry," he said, wondering if she could hear him.

The nurses had cleaned her up, but there was little they could do about the bruising on her face and arms, the grazes on her skin. Shaun ran his hand through his hair. He hadn't showered for a couple of days, and it was thick with grease. Patches of stubble were beginning to appear on his cheeks.

"The police came yesterday," he said, "they wanted to see the CCTV footage. The external cameras were next to useless. Maybe you'll be able to tell them what happened when you get better."

It seemed like the right thing to say.

"Mr Popescu said you'd been to see him. This is going to sound weird, but I think he knew what was going to happen."

A nurse came into the cubicle. She spotted Shaun too late, and jumped, almost daintily.

"Sorry," she said, in a Polish accent, "I've just come to feed Mrs Manning."

"I'm her nephew."

"Right." The nurse stood for a moment, taking in the heavy, grey skin under Shaun's eyes, the food stains on his hoodie. "Visiting time isn't until six," she said.

"I work evenings," Shaun lied.

The nurse made a small, satisfied noise. She attached a large syringe to the tube in Valerie's nose and pushed the plunger slowly. The clear fluid inside bubbled and disappeared into the darkness. Smiling, the nurse turned on one heel and went to leave. Shaun looked at the ceiling as she swished through the curtains and walked back along the ICU.

"That was my fault too," Shaun said when he was sure the nurse was out of earshot. "I should never have told you about the gun. Things are starting to fall apart, Valerie..."

Two pairs of sensible shoes pattered towards Valerie's cubicle. The curtains swung back, and the nurse who had just left stepped through with another, older nurse.

"Sir," said the older woman, "visiting time isn't until six. I'm afraid we can't have people just wandering into the ICU whenever they feel like it."

"I work evenings," Shaun said, "I just wanted to see my aunt."

"Mrs Manning needs her rest, sir. You'll have to come back another time. Within visiting hours."

Shaun looked from the older woman to the younger and back again. He saw that it would be no good to argue with them.

"All right," he said, "okay."

As he walked away he heard laughter.

"You're right, Marta. He was a strange one."

"Is Bau-bau real?" Gracie demanded as they cupped the hot mugs in their hands, settling into their armchairs. "Are you sure he looks like a man?"

"Yes. I told you," said Mr Pop. "He can look like any man, but he is a bad one."

"But is he *real*?"

The old man nodded with a strange half-smile.

"Mister Pop," she lowered her voice to a timid whisper. "*I've seen him*. He was at the classroom door, and Miss Long was going to answer it, and she'd been telling me off so I had to put my name on the red band with the naughty children, and he *came for me* just like you said he would, and, and..." Her eyes were overflowing as she stammered out the words that she could only tell to Mister Pop, because only he would believe her. "And so I ran away, and they were all angry with me and nobody blamed Bau-bau. And I ran to the pier and the nice clown looked after me, and I haven't seen Bau-bau again but I'm frightened. What if he comes back for me?"

119

The old man sat and thought for a little while, and his face got more and more solemn. "And what did Bau-bau look like?" he asked finally.

"Harry," she breathed. "He looked like Harry."

"And who is Harry?"

"My care worker. The one who brought me to live with Sarah and Arthur and Laura."

"I thought that you didn't remember anything about your old home."

"I remember Harry," she said, "because he brought me here."

There was a long silence, and Mister Pop stared at her with an intensity that made her think fleetingly of Sarah and Arthur. He wore the same expression of deep concern. Then quite suddenly it was gone, and he leaned forwards to look her steadily in the eye.

"There was once a young girl I knew, a lot like you. Cristina. Very much like you. And she thought that Bau-bau was coming to get her as well. She was so afraid that he would take her to the forests of the Other Realm and leave her there. She was an orphan just like you. She did not remember anything about when she was very young. It frightened her that she did not remember. There was something in the way, which stopped her from knowing."

"And did Bau-bau come for her?"

"No. Instead she found something that she did not believe at first. Bau-bau was not chasing her at all. He did not need to."

"Why?"

"There was a reason that she did not remember her childhood," the old man said solemnly. "It was because she did not have one. From birth the only life she had known before was the life of the Other Realm, before she was brought to our world by Bau-bau."

"Wait!" cried Gracie. "But if Bau-bau brought her here from the Other Realm then she wasn't a person at all. She was a fairy?"

"Yes," said Mister Pop, "a fairy who had nothing to fear from Bau-bau."

"How did she find out?"

"I told her." He touched his finger to his nose. "This old Romanian can tell you a thing or two about fairies. I know what to look for in a fairy."

Gracie sat and thought about this for a few minutes. "Harry brought me to Sarah and Arthur. I always thought he was bringing me from Haven House. Do you think – Bau-bau was just coming to see me? Do you think he was maybe not chasing me after all?"

"I don't think he wanted to frighten you, little one."

A bubble of joy swelled up in Gracie's chest. She was safe. She had always been safe. Then she asked, with a great mixture of excitement and sudden anxiety, "Will you tell me more about the Other Realm? Is it really as frightening as you said?"

"Well, I don't know that it is truly *frightening*," he mused, "but it is a place with many secrets and many impossible things, hidden away from prying human folk like myself. I have heard that the fairies are crafty and cunning, but they are also very happy where they are. They do not have to follow rules like you and I. Fairies do not go to school, and they do not go to work. They are free. And that is why no fairy will ever feel at home in our world, with the humans. They are too wild for the way we live. Wild and dangerous."

"Wild and dangerous," she echoed in awe. "And if fairies are real does that mean there are other magic things? Like dragons?"

"And mind-readers," he smiled, "I should know."

"Why should you know?"

"You are far too young to have heard of Marku the Magnificent. That was my stage name, once. I was one of the many misfits who turned their natural peculiarities into amusements for an audience." Gracie frowned, not understanding, and his grin got wider and warmer. "I joined Circus Romero for a brief spell."

"You joined the circus? Doing what?"

"Telling people what they were thinking."

"What am I thinking? Right now?"

"I do not think I would be able to read the mind of a young fairy." He glanced at the front door. "Is it time that you were going home? Your foster parents have had enough to worry about over the past few days, I should think."

"I don't want to go back," she protested, "I want to hear more about the Other Realm. Tell me about the forests, and all the fairy children that run around there and don't have to go to school. Tell me about the children in the forests!"

Mister Pop flinched as if she had slapped him really hard. His watery eyes blinked in such surprise and fear that she wondered what on earth she could have done wrong. He looked so small and sad.

"No, little one," he growled with his voice and his eyes suddenly full of fire. "Children should stay away from the forests. Has nobody told you the story of Hansel and Gretel? Bad things can happen in there."

"But," Gracie argued, confused, "you said that fairy children come from the forests. And they get to do whatever they want. It sounds lovely. If I'm a fairy then the forests won't hurt me, will they?"

But Mister Pop didn't want to talk about it anymore. He stood up and turned away from her, his shoulders hunching up around his ears like he was trying to shield himself with them, and he leaned heavily on the back of his armchair. Slowly, looking like he would fall right over with each step, he made his way to the window and looked out of it while he breathed heavily. Gracie slipped down from her chair and began to tiptoe towards the door, thinking she should perhaps go home after all. She did not want to make Mister Pop ill by upsetting him so much.

"Oi!" Mister Pop shouted, and Gracie jumped. But he was calling out of the window to somebody else. "What are you doing rummaging around in other peoples' waste?"

"Hello, Mr Popescu!" somebody called back. Gracie recognised the voice – it was the artist lady who was always looking for something odd in a plastic bag or a bin to take a photo of or steal for her statues.

"Get out of my rubbish bags!" he yelled, and he had never sounded so scary. He was twisting up like an old tree or a monster, his body knotted with rage. Gracie felt almost as frightened of him as she had of Bau-bau before.

"Bye, Mister Pop," she mumbled, barely loudly enough for him to hear before she tore from the room.

Back at the flats, Shaun checked his mailbox and found an official looking envelope. *Two letters in two days*, he thought, unlocking the door. As he walked down the stairs, he turned it over

122

and read: 'Ketch, Beadle and Lamb, criminal and civil law." His father had found him.

Shaun didn't bother to turn the light on. Navigating by the glow of the CCTV monitor, he made his way to the desk and placed the letter from his father next to an opened envelope. He picked this up and slid the folded paper from inside.

Shaun,

We know you must be unhappy, cut off from the love of our all seeing guides among the stars. Remember that they still care for you, and it is not too late to return to the warmth of their embrace. There are many here at Starhaven, too, who are worried about you, and hope that you will return to the teaching of the Brotherhood, just as Sky has.

We live in exciting times, brother, and the council are revealing new wisdom almost daily. The universal equinox is approaching – surely you should be with us as we lead mankind into a new age of spiritual glory among the stars.

We cannot guess why you left Starhaven, but the loss of a dear brother hurt us more than the loss of the car and the money. As humans, we all carry negative energy, but just as the father lovingly forgives his erring child, when you come home, all will be forgotten. We are certain this letter will find you; the council have provided means to extend their loving protection, even to those who no longer live among us. If you return, no harm will come to you.

Your brother,

David

Shaun slipped the letter back into its envelope. He had read it three times since yesterday, and as he looked around the dark basement it was hard to accept that this was where he belonged. He remembered lying under the heavens the comfortable weight of Sky's head on his chest, looking up at the stars and knowing, that there was a plan for them both mapped out in their splendour. People cared about him at Starhaven. Perhaps there had been real love there too - more than he had felt since his mother died.

He took a spliff from the ashtray and lit it. Hot, heavy air sank into his lungs. He exhaled, and watched the grey smoke curl in the light of the CCTV monitor.

Before he went to the hospital, he had watched Mr and Mrs Greenwood file out of the door, dressed for the warm weather with Gracie trailing behind in her sunhat. Mr Popescu left about half an hour later, heading for Sammy's.

There were three CCTV cameras in the block. Shaun cycled through the black and white screens. In the lift, his eyes drew geometric patterns in the textured wall. He pictured a triangle with himself at one corner, his father and the brotherhood occupying the others. Divided by equidistant lines, the corners were linked, but could never meet.

He hit a button on his keyboard and the screen split into four. The lift, the foyer, the entrance and the car park were all quiet. He imagined that he was the block of flats. The cameras were his eyes. He could feel the rumble of the lift, the tug of doors opening and closing. He thought of number twelve, and felt the dull ache of its emptiness. He would put up cameras in every corridor. He would see everything and look down on the flats like the Watchers looking down on the Earth. He imagined connecting to all the CCTV cameras in the world. He would see Mr Popescu, the Brotherhood, his father, and he would see how they were all linked through him. He would see where Valerie fitted, lying in her hospital bed; how she connected to the body on the beach. It would all be part of a much bigger pattern. Everything would, and it would all be beautiful.

A woman was walking along the path. Shaun hit a button and returned to one screen; Sabina reached the buzzer. She came to the flats sometimes to smoke with him. When his intercom failed to ring, he wondered who she was here to see. She waited for a minute or two, then turned around and started to walk back toward the road. After a few steps she stopped, then strode back towards the door. This time, Shaun's intercom did buzz. He walked over and picked up the receiver.

"Hi Sabina," he said.

"Hey Shaun," Sabina's voice crackled in the speaker.

Shaun hit the button, and the door clicked open. A few moments later, Sabina was standing in his living room. Shaun wished he hadn't let her in. He liked his flat to be tidy; it was one of the few things he felt he could be proud of. He'd just been so busy. Sabina was good enough to pretend she hadn't noticed the mess and the gloom.

"I wanted to see Popescu," she said.

"He's not here," Shaun replied, walking back over to the desk.

"It doesn't matter really," she said "I just wanted to ask him a few questions."

"Questions?"

"Are you okay, Shaun? You haven't been to Sammy's for a few days."

"I'm fine," Shaun said. "Look, I think you should be careful around Mr Popescu."

"Is that what this is about?" Sabina asked. She was standing next to the desk now. "Have you and Popescu had some sort of disagreement?"

Shaun took a deep breath.

"I think he might have had something to do with what happened to Valerie."

"The woman who got hit by the ice cream van? Popescu was in the cafe with you, Shaun."

"Yeah, but there was this bang, and -"

"The car back-firing?"

"And Mr Popescu didn't even..." Shaun stopped. Now that he came to explain it, his theory sounded weak. "I just think you need to be careful, okay?"

"I always am," Sabina smiled again. A sad, sympathetic sort of smile. "It was a road accident, Shaun. It could have happened to anybody."

"No, it couldn't. Something scared her. And it's not just her. There was that body on the beach, and that guy who came into the café. They're all linked somehow. I need to make sure the people here are safe."

"So you've just been sitting at this desk?"

"I can see everything from here," Shaun explained.

Sabina looked around her.

"Let's get this place tidied up a bit," she said. "Then I'll make some tea, and you can step away from that screen and talk to me, okay?"

Without waiting for Shaun to reply, she walked over to the light switch. The room's squalor was exposed under the electric light. Sabina picked up the waste-paper bin, scooped up a couple of takeaway tins, then reached for the open envelope.

"Do you need this?" she asked.

Shaun flinched as she lifted it.

"That's mine," he said.

Sabina looked at the envelope.

"Just give it back!" Shaun said, too harshly and too suddenly.

Sabina frowned.

"Shaun, are you in some kind of trouble?"

"What?"

"You need to talk to someone."

"I'm fine. Please. Give me the letter."

"I just want to help you," Sabina said, taking the letter out of the envelope.

"No!"

Shaun jumped to his feet and ripped the letter from Sabina's grasp.

"Just fuck off!" he said, "Leave me alone."

The two stood silently. Shaun's vision was starting to blur. Sabina looked at him, standing in his small flat among dirty plates and crumpled T-shirts, shaking like a frightened child.

"Okay," she said, handing him the envelope. "I'm sorry, it's none of my business. If you decide you want to talk – about anything – give me a call, yeah?"

Shaun nodded.

"I'm going to go," said Sabina, "Goodbye, Shaun."

She turned around and left, closing the door behind her. Shaun put the letter back in the envelope and slumped back into the chair. On the screen, Sabina walked away.

The key painting was complete. Anastasia was standing on a small stepladder to inspect the two metre high board. Two figures were repeated in varying styles on the panel. One was a saint, mainly depicted in the eastern Orthodox style, sometimes Greek or Russian, sometimes Coptic or Syrian. The other was an angel or cherub, who took a number of forms, from the delicate Slavic romantic manner, to stylised Manga, via Renaissance classicism. Anastasia observed the picture with some satisfaction. Popescu had been the perfect model for her purpose. His dark, heavy lidded eyes moved disconcertingly between iron will and other-worldly contemplation. There was a hint of physical frailty about him that was of the present, yet there was something in his posture, his composure, that suggested power, determination, and the capacity for concealment and deceit.

The angel was the child, Gracie, an interpretation filtered through and tempered by the photograph of her doppelganger. Anastasia perceived a capricious malevolence in the girl's physical perfection. The images showed a face of impeccable beauty, but the figure was placed in clothes, or in settings that implied contamination. She was seated, serene, in rags, on a billionaire's superyacht, playing with a shotgun; or hovering, smiling, over the rusting, rat infested ferris wheel at the ghost city of Pripyat.

It was time to complete the other panels of the triptych. These, too, would feature Anastasia's Skegness neighbours, but mostly obliquely. The broken thespian, Valerie, was a current preoccupation. The artist had tried etching on glass, but that rendered the road accident too delicately beautiful when she'd intended overblown and hammily operatic. Perhaps it was time to go for heavy duty methods.

She moved away from the painting studio area with its pool of natural light, and went round the L shape of the workshop into the harshly lit hazard zone. There was no facility here for casting molten metal, but other than such specialist skills, Anastasia had all the tools and materials to hand to cut sheet metal, glass, acrylic polymers and wood. She had oxy-acetylene for heat cutting and molding, toxic chemical baths for distressing materials, and an array of industry standard power tools, benches and vices. Valerie, Anastasia decided, would be made of chemically corroded acrylic with some decorative flame scorching. But it must wait. A taxi was hooting its presence out on the street. Anastasia had an appointment with a fowl specialist.

"Alford?" said the taxi driver. "Not much call for Alford. Full of foreigners these days."

"Is it?" said Anastasia. "I didn't know it was that exciting."

"Portuguese, Ukrainians, all sorts. Hang on to your bag, that's all I can say," said the taxi driver, nodding at Anastasia in the rear view mirror. She glanced down at her bag, a large sports holdall. It contained a seagull wrapped in polythene on a bed of ice packs.

Tim was sitting behind the till, glancing at a magazine he had concealed on the shelf under the counter, when a woman in a pink, towelling dressing-gown opened the door of the shop with difficulty and stumbled inside. She had something that might have been money clenched in her hand. She staggered round the shop, and came eventually to the drinks aisle. She wobbled as she studied the prices on the bottles, and glanced every so often at the notes in her hand.

Tim placed his magazine in his secret compartment, tip-toed out from behind the counter, and went to find Mr McNair in the store-room.

"Er, Mr McNair. There's a woman just come in who looks like she might be drunk, or a nutter," said Tim.

Mr McNair frowned.

"And what do you expect me to do about it?"

"Could I carry on in here, while you mind the till, until she goes away?"

"Why? If she starts to make trouble, you are much more equal to the task of dealing with her than I am. Don't be such a softie, lad."

"Right. No, Mr McNair."

"Why don't you get whatever it is she seems to want off the shelf for her, take her money, and then gently escort her off the premises? There. Job's a good un."

"Yes, Mr McNair."

Tim tip-toed back into the shop. The woman had moved. She had picked up a wire basket and was filling it with packets of jelly: lime, lemon, strawberry, raspberry, and blackcurrant. Every flavour except, for some reason, orange. The packets of orange jelly she knocked onto the floor.

She wobbled towards the counter, and put the basket down.

"I'll just put this here for now," she said to the un-staffed counter-position, and wobbled back to the aisle with the cooking ingredients, picking up two more baskets as she went.

As the woman was taking down boxes of sponge fingers, tins of custard powder, and tubs of hundreds-and-thousands, two policemen came in. One went to the chiller cabinet, and began to select sandwiches, pasties, and pork pies. The other went to the serve-yourself coffee machine. One of them glanced at Tim, the other at the woman in the damp, towelling dressing gown. The second one walked over and tapped the first on the arm, and nodded towards the woman.

The policemen put their purchases down, and watched, with arms folded, as the woman put baskets two and three down on the counter, picked up a fourth, and began to fill it with bottles of British sherry.

"The Lord spake unto me, and said, 'Maketh thee a nice big trifle for tea. Know ye surely what day this be. On this day, ye should strive to atone for thy back-sliding and for thy sins'," she said, to someone Tim couldn't see. The woman continued until the basket was so full of the brown bottles that she could hardly get her fingers between the glass and the carrying-handles. As she wobbled and struggled back to the counter, Tim wondered what had happened to the money she had been carrying, and whether that moment would be a good time to just go out the back and start running.

The woman glanced up at Tim.

"Timothy Frances Gillespie Walker! What are you doing here?"

She dropped the basket, and then crunched her nonchalant, wobbling way over the resulting shards of glass in what Tim then realised were pale blue, bare feet. Little swirls of blood made the spreading pool of dark liquid on the floor even darker.

Tim cursed himself for freezing just before the moment when one of the policemen grabbed him. Both generations of the Walker family were then subjected to an interrogation. Mrs Walker ignored the policeman's questions.

"I have failed in my duties as a mother. I'm a miserable sinner," she wailed, and started to cry. All Tim caught from his policeman was something about, "anything on you which might injure me or you, or which you know you shouldn't have..." The next thing Tim knew, the policeman was laughing loudly as he examined a document which Tim then realised was his fake driving licence.

"You're nicked, sonny, for possession of a forged document." The other policeman looked at his watch, made frantic notes, looked disdainfully down at Mrs Walker's feet, and called someone about an ambulance.

"You're this lad's mother?" said Mr McNair, whose presence Tim had not noticed.

"Of course I'm his mother. He was born at precisely ten to nine in the morning, just as I was about to have breakfast. It's his fifteenth birthday today."

Mr McNair put out a hand towards the wall to steady himself.

"Well at least the name and date of birth are in order," said one policeman, holding up the licence.

"Why aren't you in school, my lad?" asked the other policeman, as he unclipped his handcuffs from his utility-belt. Tim started shivering. He felt sick. He was supposed to be driving Laura to her interview in the van in twenty minutes.

Streaks of cloud crossed the sky above. Gracie played alone on swings and slides in the cold green fields below. Saturday meant an outdoors day, a day for family and fun, and on this particular Saturday her foster parents had chosen Tower Gardens. Why they had decided to drag Gracie out to a pitiful climbing frame when she could be exploring the fairground just over by the promenade was beyond her. Nibbling on their cheese sandwiches at a picnic bench, they kept a vague eye on their foster child as they attempted to talk some sense into their eldest daughter.

"It might sound very appealing right now, Laura," said Arthur Greenwood firmly, "but moving out is a big step, a big responsibility. Your pay will barely cover your rent – and you can't possibly believe you would be happy working in a meat factory, of all places. Do you want to come home from Holman and Sons every day stinking of tripe?"

"It's an office job, dad. It's a step up. My boyfriend's picking me up any minute to take me there."

"Boyfriend?" said Sarah. "Since when?"

"Why don't you want to study for a few more years?" suggested Arthur. "Set yourself on a much better path, aim for a real career?"

"I've been doing that forever! I'm sick of it." Laura shot Gracie a look which did not go unnoticed. "And I'm sick of being at home."

"Laura," her mother hissed, picking up on the implication immediately. "Have a little consideration."

"She doesn't!"

"She's seven years old," Arthur interjected, "and she's going through a tough time. It's hard enough getting her to accept us without all this unnecessary aggravation." He placed extra emphasis on those last two words, and it was too much for Laura. Folding her arms sharply across her chest, she turned her scowling face away from him. "Don't give me that attitude, young lady. This is only proof that you're not ready to look after yourself. Not by a long shot."

Gracie swung. The beach was close enough to smell the brine and the sand. She could hear almost every exchanged word across that picnic table. Laura didn't want Gracie, not one bit, and Sarah and Arthur were upset about her, and nobody had even asked her why she was being difficult and why she didn't want to fit in. Nobody knew the truth that she was a fairy, and that fairies didn't fit in anywhere except for the Other Realm.

Nearby to the swings and slides was a small copse of trees – nowhere near enough to get lost in, but good for a short stroll. As Gracie leapt from the swing and scurried towards the grove, a rush of exhilaration overwhelmed her. She was struck by the thought that perhaps here she could find a gap like Mister Pop had talked about, a gap in the world that would take her to the Other Realm. After all, he had said that only fairies and Bau-bau could get to the magical forest. If she really was a fairy she ought to be able to find a way into that secret world by herself. She could finally go to her real home, and find her real family, and she would belong somewhere and not have to go to school.

Pausing at the edge of the copse, Gracie glanced back to the picnic bench. Her tummy did a little flip, half nervous and half excited. Bau-bau – Harry – was striding across the grass towards her foster family. He was wearing a scarf too, and he raised a hand to her in greeting.

Gracie was about to take a step towards him. She wanted to explain why she had run away before, and why she wasn't afraid of him any longer. Questions about the Other Realm flooded through her mind. Could Bau-bau help her to find the way back? Was it even possible to come back once you had been put into the human world?

"Harry," Sarah said in a voice that made the care worker turn away from the girl immediately.

Gracie hesitated, then decided it would be best to take a walk in the trees after all. Sarah and Arthur did not seem overjoyed to be meeting Harry. In fact, they seemed very angry and upset about something even though they were keeping their voices down. Gracie caught fragments of sentences like 'doesn't remember' and 'neighbour informed us', and words like 'repressed' and 'trauma' and 'explanation'. The rest was a tangle of language, but all the while Harry was beginning to turn pale and the smile was dying on his lips.

Turning away into the short stretch of woods, Gracie plodded along thinking that she would talk to Harry afterwards, when he had finished his serious talk with her pretend parents. She had not got very far when her foot landed on top of something oddly supple, and there was a sharp human cry of pain directly below her.

"Oh!" Gracie cried as she jumped away from the sound.

There was a man – or what looked very much like a man – lurking in the roots of a tree where the earth had been hollowed out beneath it. He was sucking his finger and glaring sullenly at her. He wasn't an old man, far from it, but he was grubby and worn out like a picture book tramp.

A dozen possibilities sprang to Gracie's mind. Another Bau-bau? A fairy, or some other creature? His sour expression didn't fit with her ideas about what a fairy should be like. Mister Pop had told her there might be all sorts of mythical and magical things besides fairies and dragons. Like mind-readers. Which one of them was this man? Did the strange marking on the back of his hand have anything to do with it? It looked like an eye with a hawkish brow overshadowing it, and a curling line underneath. Gracie pointed to it.

"What's that? Does it help you get to the Other Realm?"

"Eh?" the man replied.

"Are you a fairy?"

"What? No."

He had an Accent, like Mr Pop.

"Then what are you?" said Gracie. "What does your mark mean?"

Still glowering up at her, he rubbed his hand self-consciously. "The Eye of Horus. It is a symbol to ward evil away," he explained with an odd glint in his dark eyes. "It represents sacrifice and restoration."

Gracie didn't know what half of those words were, but she wasn't about to say so.

"Why are you hiding there?"

"Rather," he retorted, "why are you running around here?"

"I'm just looking about," she answered defiantly. "I'm waiting to talk to my Bau-bau."

The piercing look that the man suddenly gave her sent her hopping away from him. His surprise was evident.

"Where did you hear that name?" he growled in a voice that suddenly sounded like a threat.

"From Mister Pop. He lives across the hall from me. He tells me stories."

"Does he?" the stranger nodded with a slow, thoughtful malice. "Does he?"

"Do you know about Bau-bau too?"

"Yes. I know of him."

"Did you know that he takes away naughty children and puts a fairy there instead?"

"I did."

"Do you believe it?" she whispered urgently, moving closer despite her wariness of the stranger. "Do you think he's real? Do

133

you really believe he takes children away to the forest, and they're never seen again?"

The man was studying her with such a careful and steady gaze that she had to stop herself from talking.

"Yes," he replied after a long silence, "I believe in that forest." He smiled but it was not a happy smile. "I have been there."

Creeping nearer, Gracie could barely conceal a smile, her eyes glimmering with intense excitement. "Would you believe me if I told you that – that Bau-bau had already brought me out of the forest and into this world?"

"What?"

"Mister Pop said so," she hissed, "he told me the truth. And now I know why I don't like it here, and why I don't remember about my real mummy and daddy, and why I used to feel so scared of Harry."

"Harry?"

"My care worker," she waved in the general direction of the picnic benches. "He brought me here from Haven House. He gave me to Sarah and Arthur. But he never told me where I came from, I think because then I might want to go back to the Other Realm. But now I know, and I do want to go back. I'm a fairy and I belong in the forest, the biggest forest, where all the fairies and the dragons and the mind-readers are."

There was a long pause. "Yes," the stranger breathed at last, "you do remind me of her. I can see why he would care for you." He shook his head. "Your Mister Pop told you that you belong in this forest, this Other Realm? He made you believe that you are a fairy?"

"I suppose he did. It's true, anyway."

"Child," said the man gravely, "did he never tell you that forests are very dangerous places?"

"I – I don't know. He said once that bad things happen to children in the forests. But – but I'm not a child, I'm a fairy. So it's different. I belong in the forest, don't I?"

"That old man hides many secrets in his own forests," the man snarled as his hands coiled into fists. "Many little secrets, with little hands and little feet and little minds of their own. All gone now. They had no care workers. Only stern men who would lead them away, into the darkness. Into the big forest."

"But – only Bau-bau carries children off to the forests!" Gracie protested in a sudden fear that she was losing hold of what she knew. "Mister Pop isn't a Bau-bau as well, is he?"

"There are many monsters who can spirit the little ones away. People are not to be trusted. Especially people like your Popesc – Mister Pop." He frowned. "Did the old man ever tell you that you should trust him?"

"No," Gracie realised.

"No," he echoed. "You trusted him because you are fond of him."

"But Mister Pop cares about me. He does. He has tried to help me, always. And what about you, anyway?" she bit back desperately. "What if you are the one who's lying? What if you are a wicked wizard or a dragon or a Bau-bau after all?"

"I am not asking you to trust me. I am only asking you *not* to trust *him*. He is an evil man, little one. You cannot fall under his spell. You cannot go the way that the other children did."

Gracie regarded the mark on his hand again.

"Are you a fairy who has come to warn me? Will you take me home with you?"

The man hesitated. "You can't come home," he said, "Not until the evil is undone, and our revenge is taken on the one who caused it. Not until all of Mister Pop's little secrets are resting peacefully again." He stared hard at her, as though trying to see something other than herself. "You do look so alike," he murmured. "What is your name?"

"Gracie. Greenwood."

"My name is Mihai."

"That sounds like a fairy name."

Sarah Greenwood's voice floated towards them from the park. "Gracie! Time to go!"

"I have to go," said Gracie.

"Remember what I told you about your Mister Pop," said Mihai. "Don't trust him. Don't believe anything he tries to tell you."

Where are you, Popescu?
Sabina thought better on her feet. Ever since she was little, if something was troubling her, she walked. With so many things

troubling Sabina today, it was no wonder she was too restless to practise her act. Her conversation with Shaun was imprinted in her mind as she walked along the promenade. Shaun was suspicious about Popescu, but she couldn't quite understand why.

She looked up, where the sun would be if there weren't so many clouds, and thought it must be around midday. The beginning of her shift at the café was still hours away. Sabina slowed her pace, usually fast, and then stretched her arms, coming to a stop. She tilted her head backwards, in the same way she did to swallow a sword, feeling the wind on her face. She looked around, to see where she was.

Home. Sabina was flabbergasted. Ever since her arrival to Skegness she had dutifully avoided the North End and, suddenly, there she was.

"There you are, love. Two ways to go: forward or back," said Sabina. She had already started to turn backwards when she changed her mind. *Forward! That's the one direction we have in life, so that's the way I'm going.*

She could see the ferris wheel of a small fairground. The smell of the sea, of rotting seaweed and urine hung in the air. Beyond the North End, the road turned inland and the beach gave way to grassy dunes. Sabina used to play there as a girl, running with her arms open, so she could touch the tall knife-sharp grass.

Her eyes kept looking for the blackness of the scorched ground but found only the grey coldness of the tarmac. A car park now occupied the grounds of her home. She closed her eyes, trying to imagine the place how it once was, in all its splendour.

And then she saw him, sitting on a bench by the car park, where the circus and all its people once stood: Popescu.

She walked toward him, casting a shadow over him.

"Hello," she said and he looked up at her.

"Good afternoon."

"Do you know who I am?" she asked.

He moved to the side, making space for Sabina to sit down.

"I suppose the waitress from the café is not the answer you are looking for?"

Sabina shook her head.

"You are Rózsi's girl," he said. He spoke in the same way he moved: slowly and deliberately. "I recognised you a while ago, but not at first. You were quite young, then, but you look very much like your mother. Different colouring, that's all. When I saw you talking to the clown – Mungo, is it? – I knew." He looked away from Sabina, into the horizon. "Good woman, your mother. A pity."

She sat beside him.

"But nobody knows," said Sabina. Popescu looked at her inquisitively. "I mean, nobody knows that you survived," she said.

"Don't they? I don't know anyone who would care," said Popescu. "I didn't see the point of sitting through questions I couldn't answer, or facing the overwhelming attention of the press."

Sabina looked at the old man sitting down in his dark, simple suit. She thought he belonged in a painting, immersed in thoughts as he was.

"Somebody should paint you," she said and he looked befuddled. "You just look so, I don't know, paintable, somehow."

He smiled and shook his head.

"I don't think I'd make a very good painting. Too clichéd. Anyway, what happened to you?" he asked suddenly, "after the fire, with your parents... gone?"

"They sent me to London, to live with my dad's aunt," Sabina grimaced at the memory of her great-aunt. "That didn't last. I took to the streets, doing three-card monte for pittance. I'd waitress sometimes too. And then I met Elijah."

"Boyfriend?"

"No, knife-thrower. The great Eli," she bowed flamboyantly. "I became his assistant and we travelled together, performing." Sabina smiled, remembering dear Elijah's wrinkled face. "He was truly great."

"Did he pass?"

"No, retired. Parkinson's. The day of his last performance was one of the scariest days of my life," she chuckled.

"How did you end up back here?"

"When Elijah was diagnosed, he decided to perform one last time before he retired for good, and he wanted his last performance to be here. His first performance was in Skegness, you see. Then, I don't know, I decided to stay. It's as good a place as any, and it's the only home I know." She looked at him and smiled. "So here I am. What about you, why did you stay?"

"The same reason you did, I suppose. Where would I go?"

"Why did you leave Romania?"

"It was bad there. Ceausescu was in power. Entire villages were destroyed and the people relocated; there were energy shortages, shortages of everything; the people were hungry. There was brutality and murder, the people were afraid. People were dying. So many children abandoned." He looked very old suddenly. "And then there was the fire."

"Fire?"

"Yes, in my hometown. A terrible thing, fire. It was my job to clean up, to deal with the remains. The bodies... I just had to get out of there, after that. Just leave, you understand?" Sabina nodded. She wanted to say something that would make him feel better but she knew there was nothing to be said about it.

"Did you come here performing? To England, I mean."

"No, that came later. I was a police officer back home."

"From police officer to mentalist."

"It's a very similar skill set," he said, a little twinkle in his eye. "Observation, judgement of character. And liars. Both have to be good liars. When I came to England I needed to do something, find work, you know. I loved the circ as a boy, you know. The people were welcoming, and they didn't mind I was a foreigner."

"And they don't ask a lot of questions."

"True."

"I wanted to reinvent myself after Romania, thus was born Marku, the Magnificent. It didn't matter that my skills as a conjurer and mind-reader were few; the circus is all about showmanship. And I found out I could put on quite a show," he chuckled.

"This used to be a glorious place," said Sabina, waving a hand towards what was now a car park.

"You should let the past lie, live for the now. Only ghosts live in the past." He got up and placed a gentle but firm hand on Sabina's shoulder. "Take my advice, draga." He walked a few steps and turned back. "Come visit me someday."

Sabina sat there with silly and unexpected tears in her eyes. Draga, dear, was what her mother called her. She wondered how

Shaun could suspect such a nice and open man like Popescu of anything. But then again, mentalists always knew how to tell people just what they want to hear.

Holman and Sons was a meat processing and packaging factory. The entrance was hidden from the road by high hedges, and the factory itself was a series of low rise sheds tucked away in woodland on the edge of the village. The isolated location meant that visceral waste could be sluiced away daily without too many complaints from fussy neighbours. The main entrance was an unassuming place, like the lobby of a Royal Mail sorting office, with a small hatch and a bell to press.

Anastasia pushed the button and waited, studying various hygiene inspection certificates hanging in frames on the pale blue wall. A voice called through the hatch, "Is that Mrs Boty?"

"Anastasia Boty," said Anastasia, "here to meet the manager."

"Tony!" yelled the voice, "Your artist's here!" Moments later a door opened and a man walked out, talking into a mobile phone.

"Yeah, I'm on it," said the man, ending the call. He extended a hand. "I'm Tony Holman."

"Very good of you to meet me," said Anastasia. "I know you're a busy man. Quite a name in these parts,"

"What?" said Holman, "You're probably thinking of my father. He leads the UKIP group on the council. But as it happens, I am a bit pressured. Staff problems."

"I've come a long way," said Anastasia.

Tony placed a hand on Anastasia's forearm.

"Don't think I've forgotten about you, love. I'm meant to be interviewing a new girl for the office but she's running late. But, look, I can get one of the workers to walk you round, tell you what we do."

Tony led Anastasia down a short corridor and out into a busy yard where a refrigerated lorry was backing into a loading bay. The smell of flesh, detectable in the car park, grew stronger, more cloyingly insistent here in the heart of the complex. They passed through a doorframe hung with heavy rubber strips and into a locker room. Tony unlocked the largest locker and took out a white coat, what looked like a white shower cap, and some overshoes.

139

"Put these on and scrub your hands in the basin over there. I'll get one of the guys to look after you."

Anastasia did as she was told, whilst Tony departed. He did not reappear. A younger man came along, a slight bespectacled figure also in white, complete with the bonnet.

"Mr Holman asked me to show you the factory," said the man. "My name is Vassil. You are an artist?"

"Yes," said Anastasia. "I would be interested to look around, but actually I have a problem I need help with."

"Mr Holman was very specific about what I should do, where I should take you," said Vassil. "If you don't mind, I will walk you around. I can answer your questions as we go. If there's anything I don't know, I can probably find someone who does."

The first stop on the tour was the abattoir.

"We process birds here," said Vassil. "Chickens, turkeys, sometimes smaller runs of things like guinea fowl. We don't have an on-site abattoir for mammals."

"This is kind of what I'm interested in," said Anastasia. "The bag I left in the locker room? It contains a seagull."

"If it's in the bag I guess it's already dead," said Vassil. "You don't need an abattoir."

"I need the gull's skeleton. I've tried speeding up decomposition, but that just creates a mess," said Anastasia. "Can you help me to separate bird from skeleton?"

"Decomposition is a natural process following death," said Vassil. "It can occur at different speeds, depending upon a range of environmental factors. Heat, humidity, soil, vegetation, light, entomological activity, the variables are many."

"You sound very knowledgeable, Vassil," said Anastasia. "Do you need to know all this in order to process chickens?"

"You need to know very little to process chickens," said Vassil. "I studied biological sciences in Bulgaria."

"You have a biology degree?" said Anastasia.

"I have a masters, yes," said Vassil. "But I am here to earn enough money to study in this country. I want to become a forensic entomologist. Britain is at the forefront of this field of research and practice."

"So what is forensic - what was it?" said Anastasia.

"Forensic entomology," said Vassil. "My interest is in bugs. More particularly, the part played by insects in decomposition of human and animal remains. It is an increasingly important specialism in forensic science."

"CSI stuff?" said Anastasia, "That's fascinating. You're exactly the man I need."

"Probably not, but I'll do my best," said Vassil. "Now, over there's the plucking bay, but that's not so interesting. We go to the cleaning bay. It's messy in there, so stay behind the yellow line on the floor. We have to walk through a disinfectant bath on the way in and on the way out. It's slippy, so hold the handrail. Just do what I do."

Messy? Understatement, thought Anastasia as they entered the cleaning bay next to the abattoir. The killing room had been relatively bloodless, but the cleaning room was awash with fowlish viscera.

"What are they doing?" said Anastasia indicating a line of women. They were standing at a sloping stainless steel counter seemingly tearing birds' innards to bits, flicking some into a sloping steel gulley, and scooping others into funnels.

"Sorting offal from general animal matter," said Vassil. "If it's legal to put it into the human food chain, we use it. Other bits go for pet food. Very little is actually thrown away. This is a very efficient industry."

"Can I take a photo?" asked Anastasia.

"I don't think so," said Vassil. "I mean, I can ask Mr Holman, but I'm not sure the workers here would be happy."

"What's the problem?" said Anastasia.

"They don't like visitors at the best of times," said Vassil. "You say you're an artist, which is such an unlikely story that I believe you. But many people here don't speak good English. They fear the authorities. You could be anyone. Revenue and Customs. The Border Agency."

"Okay, I won't take pictures," said Anastasia. "But why are they so worried? They're here legally?"

"Yes, in this factory," said Vassil. "But we hear stories. We live amongst people who've overstayed visas, people run by gangmasters, people who owe money. Fear is not irrational."

Walking through the disinfectant bath brought Vassil and Anastasia out into a butchery unit, where birds were dressed, or jointed, and assessed for quality.

"Is this what you want done to your gull?" said Vassil.

"Absolutely not. I need the skeleton intact," said Anastasia.

"A bird is an organism, not a mechanical device, it's not just flesh and feathers draped over a skeletal frame," said Vassil. "Even with natural decomposition a skeleton's likely to fall apart. Many joints require functioning connective tissue to hold them in place."

"But we see animal skeletons in natural history museums," said Anastasia. "There must be a method."

"There are techniques that can be used to simulate intactness," said Vassil. "Is that a word, in English?"

"Don't ask me," said Anastasia. "But I get your meaning. You can't help me."

"I can look at your gull," said Vassil, "If that's what you want. I can advise you about what is possible."

Back in the locker room at the end of the tour, Anastasia pulled the polythene wrapped bird from the bag. "It was in the freezer, but I've defrosted it," she said.

Vassil crouched down next to the bird, but his gaze was directed upwards, at Anastasia. "Miss Boty, if this gull is so important to your art, apply your imagination, not hungry bugs or corrosive substances. I can help you to get at the bones beneath, but that's all they'll be. Bones, bleached, pocked, held together with glue and wire."

"I hear you, Vassil," said Anastasia. "But give me your phone number anyway. And here's my card."

"I'll take you back to reception," said Vassil.

"No, wait," said Anastasia. "There's something else you might be able to help with." Anastasia pulled a file from her messenger bag, and handed Vassil the set of photographs.

"Children?" said Vassil. "These are old pictures, I think."

"On the other side," said Anastasia. "The writing. Can you read it?"

"OK," said Vassil, turning the paper over. "Yes, this is Romanian."

"Can you tell me what it says?" said Anastasia.

"I'm Bulgarian," said Vassil, "But I can read Romanian. Russian, too. This is a list of names."

"Names? Of these children, do you think?" said Anastasia.

"Probably," said Vassil. "Why do you need to know?"

"That girl there," said Anastasia pointing to one of the images, "she might be the twin of a little girl I've been painting recently."

"I doubt it. From this date, she'd be more like my age now," said Vassil.

"It's just that the likeness is so striking," said Anastasia. "It's made me curious."

"OK," said Vassil. "So look, the stamp at the top, 'Departamentul de Sanatate', you can probably guess what that says. Romanian's a heavily Latinate language. Sana, health?"

"So, Department of Health," said Anastasia. "Right. And all the rest are names?"

"No," said Vassil, "The words at the top say that these are children from an orphanage in Mangalia. This is from 1989."

"Mihaela Balan," said Anastasia, running a finger down the list, "These are the names, right? Marius Moldoveanu, Cristina Bog..."

"Bogdanescu," said Vassil, "Cristina Bogdanescu, Cosmin Croitoru, Mihai Radu, Dorin Fieraru." Vassil stopped. He looked up at Anastasia. "Does any of this mean anything to you?"

Bobby pulled his Jaguar into the deserted car park adjacent to a row of chalets bordering the Sandilands beach. Bobby opened his door and stepped out of the Jag. He stared blankly at the only other vehicle in the park before turning his gaze on Marcus.

"Not especially subtle, are they?" he asked.

"It's meant to intimidate, I think," Marcus replied.

"I don't think I feel like being intimidated today," Bobby said.

He walked some distance away from the car and stood comparing the mammoth black chrome-covered Mercedes SUV with his own vehicle. Then, with malicious deliberation, he took his keys and gouged a wide fissure in the Merc's paint from the rear bumper to the hood.

"Why, Bobby?" Marcus asked.

"Because it offends me. That Jag was given to me by old man O'Grady on the occasion of his retirement. It speaks of tradition, of class, of all that is great about this country. This German toy offends me. The way I was summoned here offends me."

"You weren't summoned. This is simply a meeting between you and Mr Dalca. A meeting of equals."

"Equals? *Mr* Dalca? Some jumped up fucking Eastern Bloc gangbanger? Your toadying to them offends me. I marked the car because I can. I don't expect you to understand, but you want to be careful I don't start thinking that you need to be marked, too."

"I'm your man, Bobby," Marcus protested. "You wanted this meeting so I set it up, just like you asked."

Bobby turned his back on the man and contemplated the sea. Sandilands was and always had been a half-hearted seaside resort where none had been wanted. There was the road, less than a dozen houses, the brick chalets, the wide featureless beach and the sea. Bobby had always loved the North Sea, especially at dusk. He found its immensity calming.

"You carrying?" Bobby asked without turning.

"No," said Marcus. "Didn't have time to find a clean weapon."

"There's a .45 in the Jag if you want it."

"I thought the plan was to walk away."

"Plans gang aft agley, according to the man."

"Say again, Baron?"

"Forget it. Let's take a leisurely walk down the strand. It won't do to seem over eager," Bobby said.

He strolled ahead of Marcus.

"Ever been out here before?" Bobby asked without waiting for an answer. "These beach huts have been here since the sixties. I think they have a certain charm in a beat-to-hell kind of way."

Marcus grunted.

"Pity that no one looks after them. A few were burned to the ground last season," Bobby rambled, noting likely ambush points and, more importantly, escape routes.

"Our guests from the East," Bobby muttered, nodding toward one of the more intact huts, the glow of an electric light emanating from its windows. The light was just bright enough to signal the

144

Romanians' presence but dim enough to keep Bobby from seeing anything useful. Smart boys.

"Keep your mouth shut and eyes open, Marcus," Bobby said, trudging toward the little building.

The chalet really was little more than a hut, and a flimsy one at that. Bobby knocked lightly on the doorframe so the structure wouldn't collapse. The door was instantly opened by a large, heavyset man in a cheap suit and cheaper shoes who grunted at Bobby and Marcus to enter. Bobby found another reason to be offended.

"Son," he said to the mook, "you may not know one fucking word of English but when you see me you better smile and nod for all you're worth. You understand that well enough?"

The man spat on Bobby's shoes.

"I see," said Bobby.

Bobby's left hand shot out and caught the man's windpipe in a crushing grip. He squeezed hard and the man's mouth gaped as he fought for air. A three inch triangular K-Bar ditch knife appeared in Bobby's right hand. He angled it past the man's teeth to the back of his tongue.

"You've the necessary equipment for speech, it seems. Some sloppy dental work, to be sure, but you'll forget all about that in a moment. Should we take his tongue back to show the lads or feed it to the gulls, Marcus?"

"Bobby...."

"Make a decision, man. This bastard's about to choke to death."

"I think you should let Emil go," a thickly accented Eastern European said from within the dimly lit hut.

"Which I will, as soon as he's learned a valuable lesson."

"I will undertake to teach my own men lessons of value as I choose, Mr. Bobby," said the voice. "My gratitude for your releasing him, please."

"As a token of good faith, I suppose," Bobby snarled.

"So that my men can be persuaded not to kill you," the voice said.

"Fair enough," Bobby replied. "Here he is."

Bobby laid the blade on the man's tongue and simultaneously shoved him away while jerking the knife from his mouth, ripping the tongue wide open from root to tip. The screaming was horrific. Bobby had once heard a goat scream exactly like that as it was cut open, an abiding memory from his one trip to his ancestral Haitian homeland.

"Fucker," said the voice.

"He'll heal," Bobby shrugged.

The voice rattled off something in what Bobby supposed was Romanian for "stop screaming or I'll give you something to scream about" because the screaming did, in fact, stop. He must have also been instructed to bugger off as, after shooting Bobby a glare of pure hatred, he started tacking back toward the car park.

"That was ill done, Mr. Bobby. Yours is an evil nature," said the voice.

"Christ, it was just a scratch. I've had worse shaving. Now, how about turning on a fucking light and we talk business."

"As you wish."

The little electric lamp was turned up to its full output, revealing approximately what Bobby expected: a single, dingy room littered with broken furniture, a couple of chairs that might possibly support the weight of a man, a truly ancient linoleum table, two men in very bad suits and one man in a suit that would have been passable a decade ago.

"My name is Dalca," said the man in marginally better men's attire. "This is Henric, Skender and... that is Emil's blood all over the floor."

"I don't think anyone's about to lose their beach hut deposit over a little spilt blood," said Bobby.

"Please listen, Mr. Bobby, as your understanding will expedite matters," Dalca said.

Bobby nodded.

"Good. It is my business to help my countrymen to relocate here. To find them housing, employment in their chosen trades, and ensure access to basic services. Do you understand, Mr. Bobby?"

"Seems fairly straightforward, so far," Bobby replied.

"Perhaps not as straightforward as it might first appear, Mr. Bobby," Dalca said with a faint smile. "You see, Mr. Bobby, you present a substantial obstacle to the success of my efforts."

"Me?" Bobby asked, genuinely perplexed. "Why should I care if a bunch of pug uglies emigrate to Blighty? Someone has to collect the rubbish and clean the sewers."

"I'm afraid you misunderstand, Mr. Bobby," Dalca replied evenly. "The employment of which I speak is largely under your so-called protection. You extort money from my business partners."

"Extort is a dirty word," said Bobby.

"Nonetheless, this is not acceptable and will not be tolerated."

"'Will not'?" Bobby grinned. "Listen to the big man talk."

Dalca was unfazed.

"We will provide you a comprehensive list of all enterprises you are required to release but, in truth, I can think of no single business you will be allowed to keep. I understand this is unsettling news to you."

"Indeed," Bobby said.

"Henric, please get Mr. Bobby a drink," Dalca ordered and one of the men handed him a flask of what smelled like raw alcohol.

"Tuica, Mr. Bobby," Dalca elaborated. "A kind of plum brandy. I regret we have nothing else at hand."

"Why start regretting things now?" asked Bobby as he tilted the flask back.

"May I offer a suggestion, Mr. Bobby, that you would do well to adopt?" Dalca asked.

"Offer away, my Romanian replacement," Bobby replied.

"Your existence here is soon to become very...the word eludes me..."

"Fucked?" Bobby supplied.

"Untenable, is the word I wanted. "Fucked", is, as I understand the word, also applicable. Perhaps it is time that you retire and leave Skegness. I have it on excellent authority that lucrative positions are available to you as private security. Positions at which, after witnessing your admonition of my young colleague, I'm sure which you would excel."

"You're telling me to get out of town," Bobby said.

"I'm telling you, Mr. Bobby, that I have no personal dislike of you. In some respects, I am not without sympathy, however, I will not allow you to obstruct me."

For a man in a suit with lapels out to the shoulders, the man made a compelling case, Bobby thought as he opened his awareness to encompass even the most minute details of the room. Something was missing and it was something so glaringly obvious he knew he wouldn't have time to see it until later. If there was a later.

"You've shown me surprising consideration, Dalca. You're a gentleman and that's very rare. I salute you, sir," Bobby said sincerely.

Dalca accepted the compliment with a gracious nod of his head.

"I, on the other hand, am a soulless, heartless bastard who would happily feed your mother, sister, brother, wife, and any other loved ones you might have to feral dogs if I thought it might wipe that sanctimonious look from your soon to be horribly disfigured face."

Dalca's expression of alarmed confusion was too much for Bobby. He threw his head back and roared with laughter. There were layers of comedy here. He only hoped he lived long enough to fully appreciate them.

With a reckless disregard for his own physical wellbeing, Bobby launched his entire body at the man, catching him in the chest with a lowered shoulder and wrapping him in brutal rib-crushing bearhug that, for a moment, put them face to face. A moment for Dalca to witness the depths of Bobby's unrestrained madness and a moment for Bobby, consumed in the glory of violence, to sink his teeth into the skin just under Dalca's right eye socket and rip at the flesh of his of his cheek. He spat a mouthful of Dalca's face and blood at his feet.

Dalca screamed in horror. Bobby howled in joy. The Romanian goons seemed on the cusp of running, until Bobby saw what was missing and faltered.

"Marcus?"

The brutality of the beating the two men inflicted on Bobby reflected their earlier fear. He had unmanned them and that required redress.

"Marcus!"

But Marcus was gone, leaving Bobby with Henric and Skender, all fists, knees and cheap steel toecaps.

"Marcus! Where the fuck are -?"

"Who is Marcus?" spat one of them, planting kick in Bobby's gut.

"Fugging gill 'im!" moaned the almost tongueless Emil through a mouthful of blood. "Tage him to 'olman's an' grin' 'im up into fugging mincemea'!"

But they probably wouldn't kill him. They were lackeys and murder was irrevocable. Lackeys didn't make irrevocable decisions. They would wait for Dalca and, Bobby thought with grim humour, Dalca wasn't likely to say anything recognisable for some time.

So Bobby buried himself deep in his breaking body and waited for the blackness to take him. It would come soon enough and when—or if—it released him, maybe Marcus would be there to explain his betrayal. God help him if he wasn't.

Contrary to popular opinion, Mungo wasn't homeless. Lincolnshire County Council had provided him with a flat twelve years ago, after the fire.

The flat wasn't much, a mere one-room studio but it was certainly better than kipping on his bench. He had done that a few times, mostly by accident, and every time he'd awoken to find Spitfire perched on his chest leaving a mess and several moulting feathers.

Mungo was heading to his flat now, staggering along the moonlit promenade with his polka dot briefcase in one hand and his dinner in the other. He had been to First Plaice for a cone of chips and battered bits. The staff in the chip shop knew him well so the chips were heavily outflanked by the battered bits. *Perfection*, thought Mungo. Less perfect was Mungo's lack of a third hand to wield the little wooden fork that accompanied his cone but Mungo would not go without food for want of limbs so he stuck his face in the paper cone like a horse with a muzzle.

Why stand on ceremony? Mungo considered. *I'm long past that. Besides, the Promenade is a ghost town tonight. Just the stars for company.*

As Mungo filled his mouth and lungs with the heavenly musk of salt and vinegar, he found himself passing Sammy's Cafe where Sabina worked. She mentioned that Popescu played chess in the cafe. Would Popescu be there now? Would Sabina be there with Popescu, toasting the memory of Ringmaster Romero with a mug of hot chocolate? Or had she yet to confront the old man? Perhaps she buried the photos after Mungo's scornful comments, which he now sorely regretted.

The tableau inside the cafe reminded him of an Edward Hopper painting. A warm glow emanated from within, lighting up the cafe like a beacon in a black sea. Each customer sat alone, their backs turned to the glass windows, disregarding not just the dark night but the outside world in its entirety. They reserved their attention solely for the warm beverages over which they huddled so tightly, hunch-backed and withdrawn.

"You must be Mungo!"

A voice spoke from the darkness. Mungo jumped and scrunched his paper cone in shock.

"Who – who goes there?"

A man was leaning against the base of a billboard advertising the Skegness Illuminations six months ahead of schedule. Ironically, the billboard was anything but illuminated and the man would have been completely hidden in shadow were it not for the tiny glow of his cigarette.

"You have me at a disadvantage," Mungo replied. "You are...?"

"Mihai," the man replied with a strong accent. "I am looking for a man."

"We're all looking for someone."

"A man I used to know back in Romania. Perhaps you can help me."

Mungo sighed. "I can't help anyone, including myself. Good night."

He started to leave but the man, Mihai, swiftly tossed his cigarette and skipped out of the shadows, blocking Mungo's path.

"No, I think you *can* help me, *clovn*."

"How?"

Mungo saw Mihai for the first time. He wore a smirk on his face and had mirthful green eyes. A third blue eye was tattooed on the back of his hand.

"I need to find Popescu."

"Popescu?"

"Sabina knows Popescu. You know Sabina. Perhaps you know Popescu too? Sabina tells me all three of you were in the circus together."

"I don't know what you are talking about."

Mihai's smirk faded. "I think you do. Is Popescu coming any time soon? Sabina tells me he visits the cafe often."

So the man wasn't just lurking in the shadows, Mungo realised. *He was spying on the cafe. He was waiting.*

"Please. I'm just trying to get home." Mungo tried to step past Mihai but his way was blocked once more.

"I will ask again."

"Ask. I don't know."

Mihai slapped the cone of chips out of Mungo's hands and it disappeared into the night. Mungo held up his polka dot briefcase in defence and the Romanian shoved hard against it. Mungo toppled backwards and the briefcase burst open, its contents spilling everywhere.

Mihai paused. "What *is* all this shit?"

Mungo lay dazed on the ground surrounded by circus memorabilia: spare red noses, juggling clubs, his make-up kit, an oversized bowtie, a squirting flower, a rubber chicken, spinning plates, a diabolo, a plastic trout, several spotty hankies, a bunch of fake flowers and so much more. The man scanned the items in confusion but Mungo only had eyes for one item: his clown horn.

Mungo grabbed it with both hands and squeezed.

HONK! HONK! HONK!

"Stop that!" Mihai snapped and launched a kick at Mungo's midriff. Mungo barely felt it – he had ample padding after years of feasting on Skegness' deep-fried smorgasbord. Instead he focussed all of his efforts on the horn. He kept squeezing.

HONK! HONK! HONK!

"I said stop!"

151

Mihai reached into the back of his jeans and pulled out a pistol. The sight was so alarming that Mungo dropped the horn and raised his white gloves in surrender. Mungo stared into the barrel of the gun.

"Clovn, this is your last -"

Mihai never reached the end of his sentence. There was movement in the cafe windows, shifting shapes silhouetted in the bright interior lights. Several faces were pressed up against the glass peering out. A customer approached the door.

Mihai scowled. He stuffed the weapon back into his jeans and pointed his finger at Mungo. "I will see you again." And with that, the man scarpered, vanishing into the night.

Mungo lay frozen in fear amidst his circus paraphernalia but there was no time to rest. The door of Sammy's Snacks was open.

"Mungo?"

No, Mungo thought. *This Big Top is crowded enough. No more people.*

And so he scrambled to his feet, hastily gathering his belongings and shoved them back into his briefcase. He snapped the clasps shut as best he could and fled into the night, following the same trajectory as both his attacker and his unfortunate cone of chips.

"What the hell was that about?" Nell asked, stepping out to look along the promenade.

"I don't know," said Sabina. "That was definitely Mungo, but the other guy..."

Nell's phone rang. She stared at the number on her screen. She held up her finger to Sabina. "Yes?"

"The arcade?" She glanced at the clock on the wall. "Maybe eleven?" She hung up without another word and reached behind the counter for her bag.

"Who was that?" Sabina asked.

"Bobby Thomas."

"I've heard about that Bobby character. Never met him."

"Good," Nell said shortly. "Let's keep it that way." She glanced at Sabina. "Are you okay to lock up for me? I've got to go."

"You need to be careful."

"I am being careful," said Nell. "As careful as you."

"What does that mean?" Sabina asked.

"I came to your show last week. You left with some guy?"

"I can't take a man home?"

"Not when dead bodies keep showing up, no."

"He wasn't going to kill me."

"You're right. Maybe he just wanted to make a coat out of your skin."

"Puh-lease."

"'It rubs the lotion on its skin or else it gets the hose again.'"

Sabina snorted. "First of all, that's disgusting."

"I'm just saying, it happens."

"It really doesn't. Secondly, my house is full of extremely sharp swords that I actually know how to use."

"He knows where you live now."

"So does that brute who was in here last week."

"Actually," Nell said, "I think Lewis is dead."

"What?"

"Maybe. Bobby's his boss. Was. I don't know."

"You're an idiot," said Sabina.

"I know."

"Be careful, idiot."

Nell jogged all the way to the arcade. The weather had been balmy today, and the number of people she passed this late were a testament to how a little sun could feel like a holiday. In summer, this part of the city might have seen its share of the action, but tonight, the only place lit up was the lap dancing club between Lumley Rd and Temple Gardens.

The Coin Fountain arcade itself was closed and looked especially dingy in the yellow glow of the streetlights. Nell stopped at the front door. It was dark inside, and Bobby had told her to come to his office around back.

She paused when she reached his door, gingerly pressing an ear against it. Nothing. It was either too thick to hear through, or Bobby was alone. Nell took a moment to say a brief prayer and knocked. There was a buzzer, and as she waited for a response, she thought about pushing it. No. If he wasn't listening for her, tough shit. She glanced up at the camera mounted in the eaves. Nell

153

resisted the urge to give it a little wave. Cheekiness like that played well in the movies, but in spite of what Sabina might think, she really was trying to be careful.

She knocked again, a little louder, and her phone buzzed. She pulled it out and looked at the text from Bobby.

Unlocked.

She pushed the door open. Thomas's office was at complete odds with the alleyway. The oriental carpet was lush, and looked new, and the couch Bobby was currently bleeding all over was covered in gorgeous black leather. He even had a potted ficus behind his desk that looked remarkably well cared for. He might look like hell had spit him back with some serious chunks removed, but he sure knew how to decorate.

Nell stared at the man in front of her. Cashmere sweater. Polished brown boots. "You look like you got shoved face first through a meat grinder."

He grimaced with what might have been a smile, his bloody lips turning it into a ghastly parody. Holding his thumb and forefinger a few centimetres apart, he nodded as if to say *this close.*

Nell pulled the door closed behind her.

CHAPTER SIX

Bobby's office was dark when Nell awoke. The desk lamp glowed, but without windows, time stood still. She lifted her head off the desk and stared around blearily.

"Good morning, sunshine," Bobby said. He had propped himself up on one elbow and was staring at her.

She rubbed her eyes and surreptitiously tried to wipe dried drool off her cheek.

"What the hell?"

"You fell asleep."

She stared at him. "No."

Bobby laughed. "You have a better explanation?"

"I fell asleep?"

"You fell asleep."

"Here?"

"All evidence points to yes."

Nell narrowed her eyes. "Did you drug me?"

"Why would I do that?" Bobby asked.

"I don't know," Nell said. "But since I can't imagine another excuse for this scenario..."

"You assume drugs."

"I'm a cautious woman. I wouldn't just doze off."

"You were tired," Bobby shrugged, his face twisting with pain as he moved his shoulder. "I needed more help than either of us anticipated."

"You tried to bite a man's face off," Nell said softly. The details of last night were foggy, but that confession remained at the forefront of her brain. She'd spent hours trying to undo the damage a few enthusiastic men could do to a body. He was right; she had been tired.

"He deserved it."

Bobby's voice had an edge to it. Last night, it had been fuzzy, hazy with the pain. Now the adrenaline was gone. He had to be hurting, and a man in pain was dangerous.

Bobby levered himself carefully into a sitting position.

"Do you trust me?" he said.

"Should I?"

"And yet here you are, at nearly," he checked his watch, miraculously undamaged during the events of the previous evening, "Seven am. You didn't leave last night when I told you what happened."

"What would you have done to me if I'd tried?" she asked.

"Maybe nothing."

"I don't believe you."

"You think I would have hurt you if you'd tried to run? In my condition?"

Nell nodded.

"I think you command an army, Bobby." A look passed across his face; she couldn't tell if it was anger or regret. "You could hurt me," she said.

"And yet you came anyway," he said.

"Yes."

"Because you are, and I quote, 'a cautious woman'?"

She looked at Bobby. His clothes were stiff with blood. His left eye had practically swollen shut, and his knuckles were bruised.

"No, because I'm a smart one."

He cocked his head. "How do you figure?"

"You're dangerous."

"Yes."

Nell glared at him and held up a hand.

"You're dangerous, Bobby. You're probably unhinged, in fact, and if I were the cautious woman I thought I was, I would have..."

"What? Called the police?"

She folded her hands primly in her lap.

"I would have stabbed you in the eye with a screwdriver while you were sleeping."

He burst out laughing.

"A girl after my own heart! Nothing ties up loose ends quite like a well-aimed projectile, eh?"

"The thing is," Nell continued, "I am not a loose end."

"No?"

"Neither are you, even if you seem to be doing your damnedest to make yourself expendable," she said. "A month ago, you were a respected business owner. You had power and the cooperation of the community. The fear of what you were capable of was enough to secure a comfortable retirement."

"You think I'm old enough to retire?"

"I think you're old enough to be thinking about retirement, and instead, you've fallen into some murdery sinkhole."

"Murdery? Is that a technical term?" He pushed himself off the couch with a groan.

"I don't know. Why don't we ask Lewis?" she asked, standing as he made his way slowly toward the door leading further into the building.

He paused with his hand on the doorknob.

"You best watch yourself," he said. "I'm not the only one with a horse in this race."

"You actually think there'll be a winner here?"

"Maybe not. But there will be losers." Bobby patted the sideboard as he opened the door. "Get yourself a cup of coffee before you go."

She stared at the machine as he limped out and shut the door behind him. Nell grabbed her backpack from the floor by the desk and walked over to check it out. She traced her fingers across the silver Jura logo.

"Of course he has a three thousand dollar coffee maker," she smiled to herself.

Her finger hovered over the buttons. As she was about to select a double shot espresso, she heard Bobby's voice raised in anger. "You're a fucking twat, that's what you are."

The sound of a second man's voice was nearly enough to send her scrambling to hide under Bobby's desk.

"You're overreacting, Bobby. I didn't have anything to do with that."

A door slammed.

"Like hell you didn't," Bobby said. "You're a fucking snake."

"I'd stepped out to check that Dalca didn't have more men coming up our arses is all."

"And yet, when his men decided to use me as a punching bag, you were nowhere to be found. You didn't have my back," Bobby continued, "which means you were worse than useless."

"Who do you think brought your sorry arse back here last night?" the man argued. "Who do you think kept them from killing you?"

"You and I both know they weren't about to kill me. Not when the police still have two unsolved murders and a hard-on for placing the blame on me," Bobby said.

"Well, I don't know what to tell you, man."

"Show some goddamned respect, to start with," Bobby snarled. "I have no problem grinding your ass up and selling it as hamburger if you don't make this right."

"I have a plan," the man said.

"I'm sure you do."

"Dalca could have killed you, but he didn't. Someone's keeping him on a tight leash. Might be our chance to point this whole damned investigation in his direction."

"I've gotta piss," said Bobby, "and if it doesn't hit your shoes, I'm going to be severely disappointed."

Nell held her breath. When she could no longer hear the sound of the other man, she made quietly for the back door. She jiggled the knob, but it was locked and the key taken. She doubled back and out through the arcade.

The arcade was dark, but the light from the windows at the front allowed her to weave through the games. When she reached the door, she saw the locks were much the same as those in Sammy's; for fire safety purposes, they could be opened from the inside without a key.

She flipped them as quickly as she could and shoved the door open, slamming into a familiar chest. Nell looked up at DC Castell.

"What the hell?" The woman standing just behind Castell reached out and grabbed hold of Nell's sleeve before Nell could register the presence of two additional uniformed officers.

"Good morning, Ms. Harrison," said Castell.

The seagulls hovered in the early morning sky above the pier. Mungo had never seen so many. They floated slowly in circles above his usual spot, the air teeming with them. From a distance the birds looked like a mushroom-cloud. That would make his bench the drop-zone.

158

Below the seagulls, a crowd gathered around his bench. Mungo limped over.

The crowd parted, murmuring whispers amongst themselves, some casting Mungo looks of sympathy and confusion.

What Mungo saw made his heart stop: his bench had been burnt to the ground. His bench!

His trusty ship was a charred wreckage of scorched, blackened wood, like the remnants of a bonfire. There was a symbol etched on the pier boards at the foot of the carcass, right where his floppy hat would normally sit waiting for coins. It was an eye sketched in the soot, the same eye that had been tattooed on the hand of the man, Mihai, who threatened him the night before.

Then Mungo understood. The seagulls were waiting for him but not to taunt or attack. They were paying their respects. Their cawing cacophony was a lament for that which was lost. Indeed, that bench was the finest companion Mungo had these past twelve years. It was where his Third Life had begun. It had been his saviour.

After the circus fire, he had meandered his way through the Skegness off-licenses in a cider-fuelled stupor. He had awoken on this bench at noon the next day, a tidy pile of coins in the hat by his feet. A new way of life had been given to him.

Now it was ash. Just like the circus. Mungo was only too aware that his Third Life had ended in the same manner as his Second – in flames.

The crowd around the bench debated the symbol in the soot. Some thought it was a hieroglyphic, others said it was the mark of a cult. One person claimed it was viral marketing for the news series of Big Brother.

Mungo shook his head.

"This is a warning."

"No! It is a review!"

Mungo dropped his head. *Please no, not him.*

The Punchman strode through the crowd and stopped at Mungo's side, his customary grin etched upon his face. Mungo had never stood this close to the puppeteer before. He was overwhelmed by the pungent musk of oiled hair, which even Mungo's spongy red nose was failing to filter out.

"Your fans are losing interest!" the Punchman jested, slapping Mungo on the back. "They ran out of coins so now they throw matches!"

Mungo stared into the ashes and tried to block out the taunts.

"Can't you see what has happened?" The Punchman raised his voice for the benefit of the crowd. "Mungo has burnt down his own bench! He must have passed out in a drunken mess, whilst holding a fag!"

Mungo felt a thudding in his head. He hadn't smoked since he was fifteen and his father had caught him with a cigarette. That beating was enough to stop him ever lighting up again but he was too busy grinding his teeth to point that out. He clenched his fists so tight he could feel his nails through the material of his gloves.

"Ask yourselves," the Punchman addressed the crowd. "Why do you keep giving coins to this clown? He is a danger to all of you. The drunken fool could have burnt down the whole pier! Don't fuel his habits and certainly don't pity him."

The crowd listened. A few mouths hung open in either shock or realisation. There was some nodding too. They had been won over. Mungo's eyes filled with angry tears, as he continued to stare into the ash.

"Don't take my word for it!" continued the Punchman. "Let's ask the gang!"

At that, he raised his hands. The Punchman was wearing the Doctor and the Constable puppets from his Punch and Judy show ensemble.

"What do you think, Constable?" he asked the puppet. He changed his voice before replying: "Well, well, well, this appears to be a case of self-inflicted arson by a self-inflicted arse!"

This raised a few smiles. In an instant, the crowd became an audience and obediently shuffled closer. Now there was a show to watch and the people of Skegness liked nothing better.

"Doctor? What is your diagnosis?" the puppeteer turned to his other hand. "I prescribe a shower, first and foremost. Perhaps they should call him *Dungo* Joey!"

There were sniggers this time. The Punchman, for all his flaws, knew how to work an audience. He deftly switched between puppets, slipping his hands in and out of his pockets. It was a seamless transition, as quick and perfected as a pit-stop tyre change.

He held up Jack Ketch the Hangman. "I sentence him to an early retirement from the pier. Go hang somewhere else!"

Next came the Crocodile. "And make it snappy!" An old line but the audience rippled with laughter.

Mungo's heart raced. His temples throbbed dully. He could feel himself turning a nasty shade of puce under his white face-paint.

Please make him stop. Please.

But then –

"I'VE GOT A BETTER IDEA!"

Oh no. Of course Mr Punch had to make an appearance. The ever-grinning, violent madman was now held up on the puppeteer's left hand and the Punchman was using the swazzle to provide the puppet's trademark voice. But that wasn't the worst of it. On the Punchman's right hand sat the clown puppet, Joey. *This can't be good.*

"LET'S TURN THAT CLOWN UPSIDE DOWN!"

The puppeteer unleashed his Mr Punch puppet on the Joey the Clown puppet. Mr Punch brandished his slapstick and was thrashing the clown full throttle.

CLACK. CLACK. CLACK.

Mungo felt each blow reverberate in his pounding head. His breathing quickened. Above in the skies, the seagulls were agitated, swirling faster and faster.

CLACK. CLACK.

The audience hooted and applauded the beating. Mungo scrunched up his face even tighter than his fists, desperately trying to block out the sound.

"THAT'S THE WAY TO DO IT!"

Mungo's temperature rose – a long dormant volcano. He tried to hold back but he couldn't. He was his father's son after all.

CLACK.

Then came the detestable line. It was the Punchman's trademark closing line but also his father's line whenever he had finished with Mungo's step-mother.

"DON'T WORRY BOYS AND GIRLS," the Punchman shrieked through the swazzle. *"HE HAD IT COMING! HE HAD IT COMING FOR A LONG, LONG –"*

Mungo snapped. He turned and smacked the Punchman in the face.

The Punchman dropped instantly, like a puppet cut from its strings. Mungo's fist had bashed the swazzle into his front teeth and the puppeteer bled freely from his mouth. He lay still.

"No, *you* had it coming," muttered Mungo as he made his exit through the stunned crowd.

While the uniformed officers and the detective sergeant – Young, Castell had called her – went inside, DC Castell stood with Nell on the pavement.

"I didn't expect to find you here this morning," he said eventually.

"That makes two of us," Nell said.

"Pretty early for a game of Whack-a-Mole, isn't it?"

"Would you believe 'walk of shame'?"

Castell took in her rumpled clothes.

"Do you know why *we're* here?" he said.

"Pinball fanatics?"

Nell knew flippancy was not an ideal strategy, but she was exhausted.

Castell glanced up. Nell could hear Young as she came back through the arcade.

"...if you do not mention when questioned something which you later rely on in court. Anything you do say may be given in evidence."

Nell watched Young put Bobby into the car. She caught his eye through the window; he shook his head slightly and winked at her.

"What's he under arrest for?" said Nell.

"Murder," said Castell. "Not so funny anymore, is it?"

Nell glanced down the road. Beyond the clock tower, an ambulance was parked up on the pavement, not far from the pier.

"What happened there?"

"Fight." He flipped open his notebook. "I'm going to need to take a statement."

"Right here, right now?"

He took a longer look at her stained clothes and pale face.

"Skegness police station. One hour."

Nell turned to go. She felt a tug and turned to see Castell holding onto a strap of her backpack.

"I think I'll hang onto that, if you don't mind."

"And if I do?"

"Do what?"

"Mind."

"Then there's still room in there with Thomas."

Nell glanced at Bobby. Handcuffed and locked in the back of a car made him seem, if possible, even more dangerous. She grabbed her key out of the front pocket and headed for home.

The kitchen had been trashed. Mr Popescu had swept away the splintered wood and restacked the dented tins of carrots and peas, but the cupboard doors had been ripped from their hinges, and the top drawer was off its runners. The old man had offered no explanation, and Shaun didn't ask for one. Not while Gracie sat in that huge armchair, sticking her tongue out in concentration as she drew something in Crayola and listened to Popescu tell his stories.

"The king realised that the rags he now wore were the robes of a coward, his punishment for sacrificing his kingdom to Balaur to save his own life," said Popescu. "The king curled up on the cave floor and wept himself to sleep."

Shaun tested the action on the new cupboard door. There was something satisfying about the way it arced on its hinges. Before starting on the next one, he took a sip of the old man's crappy tea. If he closed his eyes he could almost pretend he was standing in this kitchen for the first time, in a world that had not been filled with corpses and guns.

As he worked, Shaun listened in to the old man's fairy tale. Popescu was an enthusiastic storyteller. He did not recite, he performed. The king had become a beggar in a fishing village, begging for coins in the market-place.

"One day," Popescu said, "a young woman came to the market place, as beautiful as Ileana Cosânzeana herself. By now the beggar's face had been weathered from living out of doors, and he had almost forgotten the life he had before. But this woman, he knew her. As a child she had filled the castle with laughter. His shame stung like an old wound reopened."

Shaun listened as Popescu switched between the woman and the beggar; the woman was sure she recognised the man, but he refuted her. He was just a poor old beggar, he said, he did not have the nobility of a king, but eventually she forced him to concede that he had at least lived in the city, and, like her, had just escaped with his life.

While Mr Popescu was engaged in his story telling, Shaun took the opportunity to check out the bottom drawer. Looking over his shoulder to make sure Gracie was still busy with her crayons, he slid it open. It was empty.

"Why didn't he tell her he was the king?" Gracie asked.

"Because sometimes, when you fail the people you love, you wish you could be somebody else," said Popescu.

There was a long pause.

"Carry on with the story, Mr Pop," said Gracie.

"Sorry little one," Popescu replied. "The woman gave the beggar a few small coins, and although he was ashamed to do so, he took them, for he was so hungry."

Shaun lifted the cutlery drawer back onto its runner and thought about the missing gun. He had been certain a shot had been fired when Valerie had had her accident. *I guess Popescu knows that too now,* he thought.

"Before long, the whole town knew that the beggar had come from that once-happy city, and crowds would gather to hear the story of how it was lost to the great dragon. And the young woman? Three times she came to hear the tale of her homeland, and three times she wept."

Unsure of what he should do, Shaun took another mouthful of his tea. He had not noticed it before, but the clock was about three inches off-centre above the oven. A nail hole marked where it should have hung. Shaun stepped carefully across the kitchen and lifted the clock from the wall. There was a dirty impact crater behind it, a lump of metal buried at its centre.

It was a bullet.

"The first time she heard the story," Popescu continued, "her tears pooled in the palm of her hand and were transformed into a silver compass. She gave it to the beggar."

Shaun knew he should go to the police, but he was afraid of what they might find.

"The next time, her tears resolved into a beautiful crystal," said Popescu, "which held within it a brilliant white light. The beggar accepted this gift, and hid it in the darkness of his rags."

A police background check might reveal Shaun's time in the Brotherhood, they might even find out about the car and the money he stole when he left. He risked everything. Worse, it would prove the one thing that the Brotherhood and his father agreed on – that he could not survive on his own. Slowly, he packed his tools back into their boxes and listened to the rest of the old man's story.

"She listened to the tale one last time," said Popescu, "and her tears were turned into a silver knife studded with one white jewel. When she handed it to him, the beggar gazed at it in awe and dread. Was this a sign? Did the gods expect him to defeat Balaur with this, the smallest of weapons?"

"Finished," said Shaun, walking into the living room with his holdall rattling on his shoulder.

Gracie stopped drawing, and looked up at him. A small stack of pictures sat on the arm of the chair. The one on the top was a man in a black jacket. There was a blue eye drawn on his hand. His tattoo might have moved, his broken mouth transformed into a smiling red line, but there was no mistaking him; Gracie was drawing dead men.

"I like this one," he said, lifting the picture. "Who is it?"

"Um..." The little girl studied the picture as though she had never seen it before. "I think he knows Mr Pop."

The old man looked up.

"Gracie," he said, calmly, and Shaun noticed the deliberate nature of the old man's calmness, "where did you see this man?"

"He was in the forest," she said. "He said bad things happen to children in the forest."

"What forest?" the old man asked.

"The fairy forest, silly," she responded.

The two men looked at each other, for a moment the invisible wall between them dissolved. Neither knew quite what to ask next.

The sound of a door knocking across the landing saved them the trouble.

"It's Harry!" the girl gasped. She looked at Shaun, then at Popescu. "I don't want to go..."

"Go on Gracie," said Mr Popescu, "I'll tell the end of the story another day. It's time to go home."

"That's not my home," Gracie said, sulking. She got up out of the armchair, gathered up her drawings, and walked towards the door.

Making him wait for a couple of hours in a holding cell was a trick, but Bobby knew all about tricks. He'd built a life on them.

The trick was meant to make him more susceptible to questioning by putting him in a state of unreasoning anxiety. First, the shock of the arrest. High drama, a show of power to put him in his place. Next, processing in the custody suite. Intimidation through bureaucracy. And, finally, a holding cell where he was forgotten. The real artists sometimes included a police officer who wandered by the cell and expressed mild surprise it was inhabited.

It was, admittedly, a good trick and tended to work even on those aware of it. One moment you were going about your life with criminal joi de vivre, hopes and dreams more or less intact. The next you were utterly alone, contemplating life in a windowless, concrete box.

Chances were you'd be willing to say almost anything to get out of that box, even if it was only to get into a better box. Bobby, however, knew a counter.

He went to sleep.

When a uniformed officer came to take him for questioning, he found all six feet, five inches of Bobby sprawled across the cot, head hanging off one end, his feet hanging off the other, snoring loud enough to be heard through the cinderblock walls. The officer had to shake him with substantial force to wake him.

He rose, feeling refreshed and, if not quite at peak operating levels, at least capable of dealing with Young and Castell. His body hurt, and a quick look in the metal mirror bolted to the cell wall confirmed he looked moderately gruesome, but that might work to his advantage. He splashed some cold water on his face and slipped on his shoes. They'd taken his belt and shoelaces at the custody suite. He hitched up his trousers and waved to the officer to lead on.

This wasn't his first visit to this station and little had changed. The fluorescent lighting was still too bright, the concrete walls were still painted a faded yellow, and the smell of industrial cleaner still failed to cover the underlying stench of human misery common to all places where people were imprisoned. The officers talked too loud and laughed too hard at jokes they'd heard hundreds of times. Police stations always reminded him that even coppers were human, if only marginally.

The officer led him to the interview room and left him there without saying a word. Bobby was grateful for the man's silence and mentally wished him well in his crime fighting career. Then he wondered if he was on the take and, if he wasn't, when he would be. A man that could keep his mouth shut was invaluable.

The room was a standard questioning room: grey painted walls, table, four chairs, and a camera mounted in the corner between the wall and ceiling.

Bobby deliberately sat in a chair on the questioners' side of the table—with his back to the camera— put his feet up on the table, and closed his eyes. He was reconciled to the fact that he would be kept the full legal twenty-four hours.

The door opened and an unfamiliar young man entered. He was clearly not a police officer, thought Bobby. His suit and shoes were high quality and he was carrying an expensive leather briefcase. His haircut was of the variety that cost more than any hat that would cover it and his aftershave was a subtle statement of class. Intense green eyes assessed Bobby.

"Mr Thomas?" he said perfunctorily. "My name is Campbell. David Campbell. From Becker, Beadle, and Lamb. I'm your solicitor."

This was a bit of luck, Bobby thought. He hadn't known he had a solicitor. Things were already looking up.

"I recommend you sit on the other side of the table, Mr Thomas. The police are not in a whimsical state at the moment. In fact, I think you'll find them to be quite the opposite," Campbell said.

Bobby looked at the man in consideration and then moved to the other side of the table.

"Thank you, Mr Thomas. Now, if I may, I'd like to briefly state the relevant details of your case."

Bobby nodded.

"You have been arrested for suspicion of the murder of one Lewis Marshall and suspicion of the murder of one Dorin Fieraru. The police are in possession of both bodies. Mr Marshall was a known associate of yours and there are witnesses that can testify that you were the last person to see him alive. Mr Fieraru was a migrant worker with no known affiliation with you or with any of your enterprises. There are witnesses to an argument between you and Mr Fieraru on Monday, 27th of last month in Tower Gardens. Mr Fieraru's body was found two days later on the beach."

This was news to Bobby. The police had an extra body and clearly needed to pin it on someone. Bobby was convenient. Still, they couldn't prove a damn thing. He decided to let it go for now. He nodded at Campbell again.

"Mr Thomas, is there some reason you're not speaking? It's critically important you take these accusations seriously."

"What would you like me to say, Mr Campbell? That I'm innocent? Right. Here goes. I'm innocent."

"Yes, Mr Thomas, I believe you are," replied Campbell. "DS Young and DC Castell, however, do not share that belief. They are convinced of your guilt. Can I ask, do you know of Ion Dalca?"

Bobby's silence was clearly the only answer Campbell needed.

"And is there any link, any link at all between Fieraru and Dalca?" asked Campbell. He grunted at Bobby's lack of response. "You must not answer any questions that implicate yourself in these matters. You understand?"

"I do," said Bobby.

"Excellent. Do you have any questions for me?"

"Yes. One," Bobby replied. "Who hired you?"

For the first time, Campbell's composure faltered. "Why, you did, Mr Thomas. Not me, personally, but my firm is on retainer."

"Of course," Bobby covered. "I didn't know you handled criminal matters, is all."

He knew he'd never put Campbell's firm on retainer. The only solicitor he employed was in Nottingham and handled his ever-shifting property portfolio.

"Ah, I see. You were surprised that I was here and had already spoken with the police," Campbell said. "The firm's senior partner gave me my instructions this morning. It would be inappropriate for me to speculate as to how he knew you had been arrested."

"Good enough. Where are the inquisitors?"

"They extended me the courtesy of speaking with you before questioning. I will notify them that we are finished."

He left the room to fetch Young and Castell, leaving Bobby momentarily alone to consider his thoughts.

He was fucked.

Who was this Fieraru character? He'd known both Young and Castell a long time. Neither would manufacture evidence. Would they? And something wasn't right about Campbell either, Bobby decided. As much as it pained him to admit it, Bobby was small fry. Criminal lawyers on retainer? The magical appearance of a young, uber-professsional legal eagle had not put Bobby's mind at ease.

Campbell returned with Young and Castell. They both looked at him with a faint disgust that hadn't been there before. In their eyes he was a murderer and nothing would change that. They were apparently his enemies now.

The questioning was bad. Much worse than Bobby had anticipated. Ever mindful of the camera and the audio recorder, Bobby stuck with simple, straightforward answers or simply refused to reply. It went on for hours until he lost all sense of time. The fever he had been battling began to return, adding a surreal quality to the interview.

He snapped. Castell was waving pictures of the bodies in his face and Bobby snatched them out of his hand in a blur. He was almost finished shredding them before Young recovered enough to stop him.

"Jesus, Bobby," she gasped.

He glared at her. "What?" he asked.

"You're...fast," Young replied.

"Spry for an old man, eh?"

She was on the cusp of answering when Castell blurted, "Oh, hell, it wasn't that fast. We've been in this room too damn long. Let's take a break. He's not going anywhere."

Campbell piped up, "I must protest, Detective Constable. My client is obviously unwell. His injuries are causing him significant physical discomfort, undoubtedly caused by forcing him to sit here for hour upon hour. He also appears to be feverish, which is likely to be the result of this interrogation."

"I don't care if he bursts into flames," growled Castell. "His private nurse can put him back together after we're done with him."

"Constable," Young warned, glancing meaningfully at the camera.

Castell glared malevolently at his boss, but said nothing.

Bobby was fascinated. The look Castell shot Young had been pure evil.

Young turned to Campbell. "You are correct, Mr Campbell. It seems Mr Thomas is, indeed, unwell. He can return to his cell until his discharge is processed. He will not be formally charged at this time. I estimate his discharge will be ready roughly twenty four hours from the time he was booked."

"Detective Sergeant, my client is ill and needs medical attention."

"We can have the police doctor come down to him."

Campbell shook his head.

"I suggest you arrange for immediate discharge or I will see both you and Detective Constable Castell charged with assault and negligent abuse."

"Are you threatening us, Mr Campbell?"

"Not at all. Perhaps, it would be better if I discussed this with the detective inspector."

"DI Scott has far better things to do with her time than listen to false allegations and flimflammery."

Campbell took a mobile from his pocket.

"I could call Vivienne and ask her."

Young suddenly seemed strangely unsure of herself.

"Immediate discharge," she muttered. "Right, I'll see to it. In the meantime, back to his cell."

"I'll walk you out," Campbell said to Young and, with a nod to Bobby, followed the sergeant out of the room.

Bobby and Castell walked back to the cells in silence. Bobby walked in and flopped onto the bed.

Castell hesitated in the doorway.

"It's not like you, Bobby."

"What's not?"

"This. Something isn't right," said Castell.

"No," Bobby said, "nothing is right. I thought it was, but I was wrong."

"People get hurt when you're wrong, Bobby."

Castell closed the cell door. Bobby lay on the bed with his back to the wall and wondered if Castell was right.

"He's not, you know," Marcus said, right behind him.

"You're not the most credible source on people not getting hurt," Bobby said.

"Of course I am. Think of all the people I haven't hurt yet," Marcus laughed.

"Where have you been?" Bobby asked. "The wheels are starting to come off."

"I've been around. Minding the store while you make eyes at the lady paramedic. Whispering in ears. Pointing people in the right direction. The things you can't be bothered to do."

"You're better at that sort of thing than I am."

"And you're better at...what exactly?"

"Public relations."

"Point taken."

"She did a nice job fixing you up. You must have enjoyed that. I would have."

"Leave her alone, Marcus. I mean it."

"I do what I want, Baron."

"No, you do as I fucking say or I'll make you suffer," Bobby said.

When there was no reply Bobby turned his head to face the breeze block wall and saw that Marcus was gone. Good. He was in no shape to argue with him. He turned on his side once more and closed his eyes, shaking with fever.

Gracie stepped out into the corridor, leaving the door to the Greenwood's flat ajar behind her. Mister Pop's door no longer looked welcoming. Instead the spyhole seemed to peer at Gracie as she stole down the corridor.

She could still hear Sarah and Arthur's voices, openly talking about Harry, and about Gracie, and most of all about what on earth they were going to do. Ever since Tower Gardens she had not been allowed to see her old care worker. She had never got the chance to talk to him about the Other Realm, to tell him that she was safe from him.

Mihai's warnings still stuck in her head as clearly as if he were hissing into her ear: 'People are not to be trusted. You can never tell what they might be hiding.'

Were Sarah and Arthur Greenwood working to keep her away from her Bau-bau? Did they plan to trap her in the human world forever? Gracie wasn't willing to wait around to find out. She was going to figure out a way to get to the Other Realm whether they wanted her to or not.

She was going home.

Outside, the street wasn't very busy, but it wasn't empty either. Gracie felt eyes on her as she scuttled across the road and halted on the far pavement, wondering where to go.

"Are you lost?" a tall male figure asked as it bent over her.

Gracie flinched away. "No. I'm going to my mummy," she replied defiantly – only half a lie, really. When she found her way to the Other Realm her fairy mother would surely be waiting.

"Where is she?" the stranger pressed.

Without a second thought she pointed at the building right next to them – the place where the strange lady took all of her rubbish and dead things. If she could only escape from this interfering adult, there would surely be a corner of the studio to hide in until night, and she could easily slip away unnoticed in the dark.

"She's waiting for me," Gracie explained before turning tail and running at top speed towards the building. With this assurance the man did not follow her, but went once again about his own business.

The red-haired rubbish lady was standing at the front door of her workshop, but she wasn't looking at Gracie. Her neck bent forwards, she was deep in conversation with an olive-skinned man, their backs to the street. His heavy brows were furrowed as he spoke in the same low accent as Mister Pop and Mihai.

Skirting widely around the distracted pair, Gracie noticed the side door of the studio at the end of the alleyway. It stood open. For now, it was best just to get out of sight, Gracie decided.

She had only been inside the workshop a few seconds when the door closed behind her of its own accord. A lock clicked into place; the rubbish lady must be leaving. Abruptly Gracie's pulse was thrumming in her ears. Could she open the door from the inside? No, she couldn't. For a moment she closed her eyes and saw rushing darkness. Her breathing echoed.

"Can't scare me," she hushed herself, "can't scare me."

What was the worst that could happen? The rubbish lady would come back tomorrow and Gracie could sneak out again. Tower Gardens would still be there. Haven House would still be there. She would be hungry tonight, but what did that matter when soon she would be in the Other Realm?

More calmly she began to investigate the room once more. Papers, sketchbooks and photographs littered the tables, illuminated by the large windows and skylight above. This was only one half of the studio. Around the corner heavy looking tools hung from the walls, and white statues huddled like gossiping women. There were big metal tubes stacked in a corner, and huge containers with odd names on them. Goggles and gloves sat on the work surfaces. It was another world, and Gracie wasn't sure that she liked it. What did the rubbish lady do with all of these things?

A board twice her height caught the girl's attention. The images jumped out at her, drawing her closer, until she was craning her neck to take in the towering panel.

"Mister Pop."

She reached out to touch the ethereal character. He had been painted over and over again, always the same and always a little different. It was him, unmistakably: his dark powerful gaze and the hook of his nose, the wrinkles in his skin. He looked very old, yet somehow very strong. There was something in the way that he stared down at his small counterparts that sent a little shiver up Gracie's spine. Who was he looking at, time and time again? She peered closer at the other repeated image; it was a child. Herself, only more beautiful, like a baby angel. She frowned. A sinister twist had been added to each of these pictures too. What did it mean? Was it a warning about Mister Pop?

A rustling, scraping sound behind her made Gracie jump and spin about. Was the rubbish lady back so soon? Where could she hide? Glancing wildly about, she scampered under a work table and curled up against the wall.

It wasn't the lady's legs that stepped through the side door and into the workshop. There were two pairs of men's dark trousers, moving from a cautious creep into a slow shuffle, as their owners confirmed that nobody was in. The bitter smell of cigarette smoke wafted down towards Gracie's nose.

"I cannot understand this, Skender," came a gruff voice in a familiar accent. Another Mihai! This one sounded surprised. "The place does not look like police, no? Why are all these things here?" The speaker's feet moved towards the white statues. Gracie could see more of him now, his hand gesturing in confusion.

His partner paced the small L-shaped space. When he spoke, it was in a slightly different accent. "It is a cover, maybe? If yes, it is very clever."

"Have a better look. Dalca said she asked about photographs. Look there." The papers on the table opposite Gracie whispered against each other as the men rifled through them. "Nothing. Look around the corner."

The smoking man left the table and ventured over to the vats and cylinders, then to the work surface where various bottles and tools sat in disarray.

"Dalca is not happy right now," he remarked sourly, "we had better make him happy, Henric. Give it a proper look and no missing any clues. Remember what happened to Emil. Nasty."

"You seen Dalca lately too?"

"Yeah, I saw him. That bastard bit his face up good."

The man with the Romanian accent, Henric, became more serious, lowering his voice even though they were alone.

"The black man is mad," said Henric.

"Thinks he knows better than Dalca," replied Skender. "Thinks he can take him on. He won't live for much longer."

"No?"

"No." Shrugging to the room at large, the man dropped his cigarette and stood on it indolently. The red glow had not quite gone out.

"Idiot!" Henric hissed. "She will know we were here! Pick it up!"

With a snort of contempt, the smoker bent to retrieve his cigarette stub – and something clunked to the floor beside him, leaking fluid all across the linoleum. Gracie was astonished to see light spring up from the cigarette and out over the surface of the puddle, blue and yellow flames lunging towards the ceiling.

"Futu-i curul lui!" yelled Henric as the smoker, Skender, leapt backwards from the fire. "Put it out!"

The stacked tubes in the corner scattered loudly as the man collided with them. "What with?" he cried. "What with?"

But the Romanian was pointing madly at the cylinders, the whites of his eyes showing horribly. Gracie was peeking out as far as she dared; they didn't even see her small spying face, they were so fixated on the spinning containers. Backing away with increasing speed, they banged the workshop's door behind them as they fled, and she was finally left alone in the flat again.

Gracie crouched still. The yellow flame was merging into orange, fiercer and brighter, so bright that it hurt to look. She ought to follow the men out, no matter who got hold of her once she emerged. Even if she had to go back to the Greenwoods.

Edging out from under the table, she began to back away from a cylinder that was rolling towards her, and the swift arm of fire that followed it. As though in slow motion she watched those amber tongues of flame licking at the air, licking at the cylinder as it came to a gradual halt at her feet.

On her bare skin she vaguely felt a sensation of cool droplets, like rain falling from the ceiling.

Anastasia picked a path through the play area of The Sand Castle. Insolent gulls stood on tables spotted and streaked with the abstract expressionism of their guano. A colony of diseased pigeons pecked manically at a polystyrene take-away box. A suggestion of furred mammals slinked in the shadows. Anastasia made a mental note to return with her sketchbook.

Inside the building was a hangar-like space to warehouse everything that was sub-prime about the English seaside. No one theme dominated the design. Jamaican beach bar pastiches sat on Balmoral plaid carpets. One corner was devoted to a Parisian cafe-bar mood, with bentwood chairs and a few signs on the wall announcing random foodstuffs - *beurre, pastis, pain, choucroute, croque monsieur*. The scent of stale beer hung in the air, and in the distance a vacuum cleaner wheezed across the tartan floor. Anastasia could see only one customer, sitting at a table near a mural of a Venetian gondola. She realised that she had come prepared to identify Vassil by his blood spattered meat factory overalls and white mob cap. The long haired young man in double denim and cowboy boots might well be her Bulgarian would-be forensic entomologist.

"Vassil?" said Anastasia as she approached.

"Miss Boty," said Vassil, laying down his copy of The i, and standing formally, hand outstretched.

"Ana, please. Can I get you a drink?"

"Thank you, but I have a coffee here," said Vassil.

He looked up and clicked his fingers in the direction of a woman who was laying tables. The woman heeded the imperative instantly, walking swiftly towards their table.

"I wouldn't try that in a Skegness pub on a Saturday night," said Anastasia.

"Nor would I," said Vassil, smiling. "She is Ukrainian."

Green tea ordered, Vassil turned to the matter which had led him to call the number on Anastasia's card. "It is very good of you to see me, Ana. I know you must be busy."

"If I can help you, I will," said Anastasia, "but you may be over-estimating the power I have."

"My friend, Troyan," said Vassil. "We share a flat. He also works at the factory."

"If it's a legal problem you'd be better off going to the Citizens Advice Bureau," said Anastasia. "There must be one here."

"But we are not citizens," said Vassil. "In any case, this is an artistic matter."

"Go on," said Anastasia.

"Troyan is an artist. I believe he is good, but I am no judge of these things. I have some of his work with me, if you would like to see it."

"I don't want to disappoint you, but I'm unlikely to buy anything," said Anastasia.

The waitress returned with a small tray bearing a teapot, a cup and saucer, a small milk jug, and a bowl filled with pre-packed sugar portions.

"Milk with green tea?" said Anastasia, raising her eyebrows. The waitress shrugged, left the tray on the table, and walked away. Anastasia bowed her head in the direction of the teapot and sniffed. Tentatively she poured the brew into her cup.

"It is green," said Vassil.

"It's peppermint," said Anastasia. "It'll have to do. So, your artist friend wants to sell his work."

"No," said Vassil, holding up his hands, palms forward. "Troyan wants to know how to meet local artists. He says that everywhere in the world there is an art scene, but he can't find it in Skegness. I thought you would know."

Anastasia took a tentative sip of her peppermint infusion. "I'm really not the person to ask about the Lincolnshire art scene, if there is one," said Anastasia. "I'm based in London normally, but I needed some headspace for the work I'm making now. The London contemporary art world is crazy at the moment. There's silly money flowing though the galleries. Much of it's Russian money. Oligarchs indulging their beauty queen girlfriends' pretensions to culture. Not that I'm knocking it. A Russian guy, Kaletsky, bought half my last show."

"I worked in a Russian restaurant in Cyprus before their banks crashed," said Vassil. "I saw it firsthand. I don't know where the money comes from, but they certainly like to spend it."

"OK, let's see your friend's work," said Anastasia. Vassil nodded, and pulled a clunky laptop from his messenger bag. It took time to boot up.

"Troyan has no space to work here, but you can see a selection on his website," said Vassil. With this he turned the laptop around so that Anastasia could see the screen. "I can translate it for you, but it's the pictures that matter, I think?"

"These are large canvasses?" said Anastasia.

"Yes," said Vassil, "Troyan said that you wouldn't like them. He knows that painting is unfashionable in Britain."

"I paint," said Anastasia. "I'm increasingly drawn to painting. That's one of the reasons why I came here to work. The east coast light. It's not a pretty light. It's cold and clear and unflinching." She scrolled through the images on the screen.

"Troyan's English isn't so good," said Vassil. "But he doesn't want to lose touch with artists while he is here."

"Troyan's work is interesting," said Anastasia. "It's confident, distinctive. Troyan has an eye."

"You can help him?" said Vassil.

"I'll ask around," said Anastasia. "There's probably a scene in Lincoln. There's a university there. But I'd be interested to talk to Troyan."

"You would?" said Vassil, tucking a stray lock of hair back behind his ear.

"I'm not a political artist," said Anastasia, "but the rise of the Russian billionaire art collector has given me a philosophical focus. Perhaps Troyan would understand this?"

"He's not Russian, and if he was rich he wouldn't be working in a meat factory," said Vassil.

"There's something about the aesthetic of Orthodox religious art, and the cultural primacy of the soul," said Anastasia, "that seems at odds with the acquisitiveness and vulgarity of the Russian international super-rich. I'm trying to explore that dichotomy in my work."

"I understand your words, Ana," said Vassil, "but I'm not sure I understand your meaning? Rich people are rich people, and some are vulgar in their tastes. Are Russians any different from rich Americans, or rich Germans, or rich Chinese?"

"Well," said Anastasia, "I think perhaps they are. The rich Chinese buy European and American luxury brands, but they don't buy western art. They are connoisseurs of their own culture. They have an acute appreciation of quality. Russians collect in the same way that rich bankers used to blow their bonuses on a Damian Hirst. They're dazzled by fame."

"They're sentimental, too," said Vassil. "At the restaurant in Cyprus, after the vodka and champanski started to flow, there would always be tears, and the singing of Russian laments."

"And Bulgarians?" said Anastasia, "Are you like this, too?"

"You have to understand, Ana," said Vassil, "things in our countries have changed, and keep changing, since the end of the Soviet Union."

"I've been to Sofia," said Anastasia, "Prague, Sarajevo. It looks to me as if everything is just becoming bog standard European. Starbucks, Costa Coffee, Zara, Carrefour."

"That's true, but it's superficial," said Vassil. "We don't know what we want, yet. We want BMWs, and Swiss watches, and Italian shoes, but we also want our religion, our language, our culture. Are we to look west, or east?"

"What do you want, Vassil?" said Anastasia.

"I want to study the things here that I can't learn in my country," said Vassil. "But then I want to go home and be a scientist, marry my girlfriend, play in my rock band. We work hard, but we have our dreams."

"Call your friend, Vassil," said Anastasia. "Tell him to meet us at my studio. It won't be the Skegness art scene, but I'm happy to show him what I do."

They scraped back their chairs and stood, Vassil snapping his fingers once more. The Ukrainian woman was nearby. She rested a pile of folded paper napkins on a table, jotted something down on the bill, and walked over to present it to Vassil.

"You are from Ukraine, yes?" said Vassil.

"You know I am," she said.

"Katya, tell this lady, Anastasia, what your profession is," said Vassil.

"I'm a waitress," said Katya.

"She's a physics teacher," said Vassil to Anastasia. "I believe you have a shortage of qualified physics teachers in Britain. But we scientists pluck chickens and serve drinks for you, because you don't want our knowledge."

Mr Culpepper, the general manager of the Sand Castle, cleared his throat, Sabina's cue to nod and smile.

"I'm not sure why they want a fire act at their party," he said. "They're accountants, for heaven's sake! But, if they want it, we, the Sand Castle will be delighted to provide, for we pride ourselves..."

Sabina's attention drifted again. Mr Culpepper had the kind of voice that caused one's attention to wander.

"Where should we do it?" said Mr Culpepper.

"Do what?" Sabina was startled. For the first time it seemed she had missed something important.

"The fire breathing. You brought your gear, I trust," said Mr Culpepper, looking anything but trusting. Sabina nodded, pointing at the bag by her feet. "Excellent, excellent. It is not that I don't trust your capabilities, dear girl, but you only swallowed swords for us, you never breathed fire. And everything must be just perfect because here in the Sand -"

"Outside, by the picnic area, will be just fine. There's nothing flammable nearby and the wind is not too strong right now," said Sabina, interrupting what looked like it would be another long and dull speech.

They stepped outside and she started removing the needed objects from her bag: a bottle of water, a cloth, a large towel, a flask, a lighter, and a torch. She tied her hair and removed her jacket, placing it in her empty bag. She did all this to the sound of Michael Culpepper's voice. She placed the towel on the floor, poured some water onto the cloth, and lit the torch – he was still talking. It was her turn to clear her throat.

"If you could stand over there," she pointed, "I'm ready." He walked to the indicated location and folded his arms, waiting.

"In case something goes wrong, like the wind turns or something, use that towel to put the fire out," said Sabina.

"What could possibly catch fire out here?"

"Me."

Sabina opened the flask, inhaled deeply, filling her lungs, and put some of the fuel in her mouth. She raised her arm, putting the torch in front of her, looked up at about forty-five degrees, and blew a spray of fuel into the flames.

The fire-breathing act was both unnerving and exhilarating for Sabina. After Circus Romero had burned, she became terrified of fire. Learning to perform with fire, to control it, and play with it for the delight of an audience was her way to deal with that fear. She could make fire dance, transfer it from one torch to another using her tongue or fingers, extinguish it with an expert move of her mouth. However, this did not deceive her. Fire was powerful and, like people, tricky.

Fire breathing always wowed the crowds. It was beautiful and impressive to see the flames growing and slithering away from the performer's mouth. It was like watching a mythical bird taking flight. Today, the flames rose wildly up the sky, impossibly high and far. It was like watching a dragon, rather than a bird, rise.

Behind the flames Sabina had produced, almost at the same time, an explosion lifted up from a rooftop across the way.

"Oh, Jesus!" said Anastasia breaking into a run as they rounded the corner into Castleton Boulevard.

"What is it?" said Vassil.

A cloud of acrid black smoke scudded around some buildings half way down the street.

"Get back everyone!"

This was Shaun, the young caretaker from the flats. A piercing crack rent the air, accompanied by the first lick of flame to exit the building. Everyone ran, as, in a black rolling boil, the roof was lifted off the workshop on a pillow of fire.

The explosion transfixed Anastasia. She stood, as others backed off or ran for cover. Was the conflagration in her studio in some way pleasing? She began to walk in a slow, unhurried manner towards the flames. Shaun placed himself in front of her, urging Anastasia to stop. It was as if she did not see him. He wrapped his arms tightly around Anastasia, tugging her away from the burning building.

For a moment, Sabina just stood there, incapable of understanding what she was seeing. Then realisation dawned upon her. A building not far away was aflame. She wiped her mouth with the wet cloth, removing any trace of fuel. She put the fire out with her mouth, tossed the extinguished torch on the ground, and started to run. Like twelve years ago, Sabina was running with all her strength towards the roaring, raging fire.

Sabina's heart was pounding to the rhythm of sirens. The buildings were but a blur of bricks, paint, and peeling posters as she fled down Castleton Boulevard.

She halted to a show of lights and sounds. There were people gathered around the building. They were pointing, chatting and moving about in a mix of nervousness and excitement, trying to get a glimpse of...of what? *Why is tragedy always a spectacle?* Sabina wondered, looking around. The blue lights of the police cars and fire engine cast eerie shadows all around. Everything looked raw and primitive, somehow. Even the people. There were neighbours, passers-by, a tourist or two, the police, and the fire engine. Sabina noticed some familiar faces among the many gathered around the building. Shaun was there with that artist woman and so was Marku. Marku, Popescu, whatever.

Popescu looked like a Madame Tussauds statue, only it was the statue of an old shrivelled thing, whose life has become too heavy to bear, like an ancient Atlas, holding the world on his shoulders. Above all, he looked as Sabina felt: haunted.

She walked towards the old man, and gently put her hand on his shoulder. He didn't have to turn to know whose hand that was.

"History repeats itself once again, draga."

He turned to face her, his eyes the holes of a mask.

"It is like the circus," said Sabina.

He nodded, sad, tired and old.

"That too."

"And the fire in your hometown, in Romania," she said.

"It was an orphanage," said Popescu. These four little words carried all the sadness in the world with them, all of that old man's sadness.

"Orphanages in Romania..."

She was not quite sure how to continue. She was sad, afraid, and cold. She became acutely aware that her jacket was in her bag back at the Sand Castle.

"I mean, they are not very good places, are they?" she said. "Orphanages in general, but in Romania, I mean, you read stories."

"No. Not very good places at all," he said. "They are places where unwanted children were put to be forgotten. Nobody cared about them. And if that was not enough..."

Popescu buried his face on his hands. Sabina stood by his side, waiting patiently, and wishing again there was something she could say to make him feel better.

After a few moments, he lowered his hands and lifted his head.

"As the local captain of police, I was called there. The fire services were slow, no, they were beyond slow arriving at the scene. The roads were all broken. By the time they finally arrived, it was all over. They were all dead. All of them. Dead."

His hands were balled up into fists, and he was clenching them so hard his knuckles were white.

Movement caught Sabina's eyes. Firemen exited the building. Sabina's eyes widened with horror. *There were people inside! They are carrying the bodies out!*

"They are only mannequins," said Popescu.

Sabina looked again and realised he was right. Dummies. They all looked the same and they all looked like the artist woman. She wondered why anybody would make several mannequins of herself. She concluded that maybe she didn't understand art.

The fire fighters brought out another figure. Only this one was smaller. Popescu collapsed to the ground as Sabina realised size was not the only difference: this was a real body. A child's body.

She crouched by the old man, to try to help him up, and heard him mutter a name.

"Who is Cristina?"

"Cristina Bogdanescu. A girl I knew..." said Popescu, and that was all he said.

She looked around, helpless and grieving. She could feel death around her, as palpable as the tarmac she was still crouching on. Her eyes stopped on a figure standing at the top of the road by the promenade, watching it all. Mihai. Something about his stillness, about the way he stood there, reminded her of a vulture.

CHAPTER SEVEN

Bobby lay in the darkness, trying to piece together not only where he was, but who he was. He was critically ill, he was certain of that. Given time, he would probably heal, but he was just as certain that wasn't an option. Remnants of his fever dream lingered. Marcus calling him "Sergeant" in a city he had never visited. It wasn't important. Dreams were always strange. What was important was that he was in a world of trouble and he needed to get his head straight.

He remembered the police releasing him to his solicitor. Campbell wanted to take Bobby to the hospital after he'd been released but Bobby overruled him and Campbell had been oddly compliant. Instead, he'd driven him back to his office at the arcade and left him with a warning that the police would be watching him closely and that he was to be "whiter than white", a phrase that made Bobby laugh in spite of his pain. Campbell almost blushed, but his eyes held a warning that Bobby couldn't overlook. Campbell knew more than he let on and was a strong ally. Bobby needed every ally he could muster right now.

A quick check of his mobile revealed it was almost three in the morning. He must have fallen asleep right after Campbell left. He'd lost almost twelve hours since his release; twelve very valuable hours. He needed to move.

He peeled his sweat soaked body off his couch and decided a trip to his flat was unavoidable. He needed a long shower, fresh clothes, and more cash than he kept in his office. There were also a handful of other things he needed to collect. A plan was starting to form in his mind and if he had to leave Skegness, he damn sure wasn't going to leave it empty handed.

His office had been turned over, but it was nothing he hadn't expected. Half the cash in his wall safe was gone which meant it had likely been the police. Pros would have taken it all. They had fewer forms to fill out.

The floor safe under his desk was untouched. He emptied its various contents, except for a flat, black subcompact 9mm pistol, into a small duffel bag. The pistol he stuffed into the back of his trousers. He cursed himself for not getting a holster for the weapon.

He'd have no one to blame but himself if he blew half his arse off before he got to his flat.

He shrugged on his heavy overcoat and made for the door, moving fast. He was suddenly gripped with worry. He needed to find Marcus. If he didn't, the killing would start and he couldn't be certain he could stop it. He'd seen Marcus level entire cities in the old days....and where the fuck did that thought come from? He'd never seen any such thing.

No matter. More crazy fever thoughts. One thing at a time.

By the time he was down the stairs and on the street he was close to running and had to force himself to slow down. A black man streaking down the high street at top speed tended to draw attention.

A hand grasped his forearm and jerked him to a complete stop.

"Oh, for fuck's sake!" he shouted when he saw who it was.

"Dalca requires your presence, Mr Thomas," said one of the thugs. Henric. Bobby remembered the face and the cheap shoes. He'd got a good look at both while they were beating him in that Sandilands beach hut.

"We have a car for your convenience," said Henric. He gestured toward a black Merc parked across the street that might as well have had "Rent-A-Killer" painted in dripping vermillion on the side panels.

"Does he require the removal of the rest of his face? I'd be happy to oblige, but at the moment I'm in a bit of a rush, dead man," Bobby spat.

The man seemed a bit put out.

"Right, English isn't your first language so I'll try to convey this as simply as possible," said Bobby. "You're already dead for putting your hands on me whilst I'm walking. I'd choke you to death with that hand you've so unfortunately attached to my forearm but, not only am I crunched for time, I'm being trailed by those two police officers in front of my shop who seem so obsessively fascinated by nothing in particular. Killing police officers, as you may or may not know my dead friend, is a much more complicated endeavour than killing worthless cunts like you. so piss off!"

Smart man, Bobby thought, as he watched him retreat at a full gallop. He appreciated a man who valued saving his life over saving face. Unlike Dalca, Bobby laughed to himself.

It was a shame Marcus wasn't around for that joke. But, of course, that wasn't true. Marcus was almost always around.

"Marcus?" Bobby called softly. "We need to talk, sunshine. I'm afraid I'm dying here and I'd like to get a few things sorted before I go. I'm bleeding inside and I think it's bad. What's the score, boy-o? Pax?"

"You're not dying, you damn fool. Yeah, you're bleeding and beat all to Hell, but you're not dying. Even if you were, there are ways around that," came a response from the shadows.

"How the fuck would you know?" Bobby asked. "If I say I'm dying, then I expect you to goddamn well agree with me. Now get out here so I can see you."

"Careful about taking His name, brother. Don't want to call attention to yourself. Not after all this time."

"My patience, Marcus. You're trying it."

"Remember the Falklands, Bobby? Remember a certain nurse that tended to you in the hospital? You've always had a soft spot for the Florence Nightingales of the world. Especially when it's the same one over and over."

"Leave her alone, Marcus."

"Leave her alone? I'm the one who's been watching out for her while you wander around with your head up your arse."

"Where are you, Marcus?"

"Not here, brother, but I'll get what you need from your flat and meet you on the beach. You're right in one thing, we have a lot of to sort out and Nell is only part of it. Now, lose the coppers or slam their heads together. We've got trouble waiting on us."

"Don't we always?" Bobby sighed.

Anastasia scrutinised the police interview room as Detective Sergeant Young spoke. She noted the scuffed blond wood table, like something from a 1980s IKEA catalogue. The obsolete recording equipment with its peeling labels. The vertical strip blinds, the bleak lighting. Anastasia had covered her pad with sketches of details, prominent amongst them DS Young's hands with their gnawed fingernails.

"That's not an answer, Miss Boty," said Young.

"It's the only answer I have," says Anastasia, eying Young whilst holding up a pencil to measure the proportions of her face.

"You say you need those dangerous materials for your work," said Young. "Maybe. My question is why you chose to store them in an insecure workshop on a residential street."

"If the siting of my workshop is an issue," said Anastasia, resuming her sketch, "it's perhaps a question for the council. They issued the safety certificate after they inspected the premises."

"How did a child get in there?" said Young.

"I'd like to know how she got in, too," said Anastasia. "If she wanted to see my work I'd have shown her."

"Why was it so easy for Grace to start the fire?" said Young.

"Wrong question," said Anastasia. "She couldn't have caused that fire. To make those gas cylinders unsafe, to put dangerous substances in contact with one another, that would have taken a lot of strength. You'd need to move things. Heavy things. Those gas cylinders? I can scarcely move them without help."

"You're saying there was someone else in there? Someone who escaped?" said Young.

"The child didn't start that fire, I'm certain of that," said Anastasia.

"But someone did," said Young, looking pointedly at Anastasia. Anastasia maintained the eye contact.

"Why would anyone enter your workshop, move things about?" said the male DC.

"You tell me," said Anastasia. "I came here to get away from the madness of London, to make my art without distractions. Since I've been here I've seen more violence, more death, than I've seen before in my life. A man murdered, his mutilated body left for anyone to see. A woman shot in my apartment block..."

"What makes you think she was shot?" said Young.

"It's what everyone's saying," said Anastasia. "I was in my studio. I heard it. Now a blameless little girl is dead. This place is a bloody war zone!"

Anastasia was trembling as she left the police station. Holding a pencil in the interview room, sketching randomly, had helped to control her emotions, but now, alone and about to return to Castleton Boulevard, the full scale of recent events hit her. An icy wind drove in from the North Sea, whipping her hair viciously across her face. Rain fell, yet Anastasia barely noticed it. Her coat, unbuttoned, flapped heavily around her legs, her drenched dress clinging tight to her thin form.

Close to the corner of Castleton Boulevard a slight figure fell into step with her.

"Anastasia," said Shaun, "Come with me." He led her into the flats and down into his own space. She went with him silently, assenting to his gentle concern. He put a mug of tea in front of her, and she gripped it tightly with two shivering hands.

The bell sounded, and Shaun went to the door. Anastasia looked about her. The small flat, sparsely furnished at the best of times, seemed to have been cleared of personal items. Shaun came back, followed by a man in a protective jumpsuit.

"Anastasia Boty?" said the jumpsuit man.

"Yes?" said Anastasia, her eyes, unusually, not fully focused upon anything.

"I'd better explain," said Shaun. "I called the London number on your card when you didn't answer your mobile."

"The police have it," said Anastasia.

"I spoke to your assistant in London," said Shaun. "Told him about the fire. He said he'd handle things. The art salvage team have arrived. They're going to try to save your work."

"My work!" said Anastasia, standing. She dropped the mug down on the table, slopping tea across the stained surface.

"I've had a word with the fire service," said jumpsuit man. "The workshop area is still a crime scene, and they have a forensic investigation to complete. But we can have access to the studio area at the rear. There's still a roof there, and the fire engineer said it was structurally sound. My colleagues are in there now, making an assessment of what might be saved."

"I want to see," said Anastasia.

A small huddle of people were still standing at the police tape, trying to get a better look at the scene of the tragedy. One of them broke away as Anastasia approached.

"Are you OK, Ana?" said Vassil. "I was so worried about you."

"I've been with the police," said Anastasia.

"Me, too," said Vassil. "Troyan is here, as well. I thought as he is an artist he might be able to help you. He says paintings are more resilient than people think."

The scene in the studio was bleak. The greater part of the building, where the workshop had been, was charred wood, melted plastic, twisted metal, blackened concrete. Much of the roof had gone, and a light mist of rain fell, diluting the pungent chemical odour of the firefighting foams used to kill the blaze.

The rear of the building, where it turned the corner of the 'L' shaped floor plan, retained a roof, and most of the windows. Sprinklers had automatically activated when the fire began, drenching the space. Anastasia lifted a sodden sketchbook from a table. It had the weight and texture of a saturated sponge.

"It's not as bad as it looks," said jumpsuit man. "I'm Si, and my colleagues here, Francesca and Rob can restore quite a lot of this stuff."

"Are you sure?" said Anastasia doubtfully.

"Speed matters now," said Francesca. "If you could help us to sort the papers, the canvases, photographs, we can bag them separately, and get them into the van."

"Then what?" said Shaun.

"They're stored at the optimum temperature for preservation while we transport them up to York," said Francesca. "At the labs there we'll dry them out in whatever way will produce the best results."

"Can I help?" said Vassil. "I'm a biochemist."

"The science bit goes on at the lab," said Si. "But we can use another pair of hands."

Anastasia seemed to re-energise at the sight of her studio. "We've two artists here. If we divide into two teams to sort the stuff according to the main medium used, that'll speed things. Maybe you could work with Troyan, Shaun? He can identify what I've used. Vassil, come with me."

190

At the far wall stood the completed triptych. Under the harsh salvage lighting the destruction was clear. Smoke damage obscured some of the most delicate sections, especially those featuring the dead child. Anastasia lifted the hem of her dress to dab it on the grey misting, and it changed at her touch to an effect like a crackle glaze. Gracie's beauty was revealed again, but under a patina of what looked like coats of decayed antique varnish.

"It has been destroyed," said Vassil.

"No," said Anastasia, excitedly, ripping at the skirt of her dress. "And look!" She pointed at the largest of the Popescu icon figures. His raised hand was now disfigured by a stigmata in the form of a puncture.

Vassil looked at the hole in the canvas, then down on the floor. "The bullet! It is still here!" He bent to pick something up.

"That's not a bullet," said Si. "The holes and pocks were made by the force of exploding gas cylinders."

Anastasia worked quietly, dabbing gently at the smoked panel with cloth torn from her dress, stepping back occasionally to gauge the effect. Vassil brought panels, books and boxes forward for the artist's approval, before taking them to the salvagers for packing.

"I was so worried about you, Ana," said Vassil. "An artist should not endure such things. Such ugliness."

"Prettiness is mere decoration," said Anastasia, tearing off more of her dress. "Art deals with truth. That's not always comfortable."

"But you must be shocked," said Vassil. "As a woman..."

"As a person," said Anastasia, "I am very shocked. Appalled, distressed. A little girl died here. A little girl I knew. I observed her closely, not just for my sketches, but because she was extraordinary. I recognised something about her. She didn't accept the world as other people see it; she made it her own. She would have been an artist."

"I know it is tragic," said Vassil. "But no one would want to kill a child in this way? They must have wanted to kill you."

"That's ridiculous," said Anastasia. "Anyway, what makes you say 'they'? The police haven't said anything to you, have they?"

"No. It's probably nothing," said Vassil.

"What?" said Anastasia, putting down her scrunched cloth on a damp table and turning to face Vassil. Shaun, working nearby, twisted around a little the better to hear their conversation.

"Troyan asked me if you would help him, that is true," said Vassil. "But I called you yesterday because I was made to do it."

"Made to?" said Anastasia.

"Your visit to our factory," said Vassil. "It unsettled people."

"You told me," said Anastasia. "Those women thought I was from the Home Office."

"They don't matter," said Vassil. "There are other people. People who don't like strangers. People with much to hide. Bad people."

"What's that got to do with me?" said Anastasia.

"I was, instructed," said Vassil. "I had no choice. They said I was to meet you somewhere in town. Not the factory, not here. To find out more about you, to see if you were who you said you were."

"You told me at the Sand Castle you'd googled me," said Anastasia. "Why didn't they just do that."

"I don't know," said Vassil. "And I was happy you agreed to meet me. I pack meat all day, with people I wouldn't mix with back home. Uneducated people, criminals, even. A conversation with a cultured woman, a woman like you..."

Anastasia returned her gaze to the painting, and resumed her cloth dabbing, her back turned to Vassil. His face reddening, Vassil took his dismissal and returned to his task of sorting papers.

Tim cried on his first day at secondary school. His foster mother had gone to the charity shop to buy his school uniform without measuring him, and his blazer, shirt, and trousers were all too small. The shoes had been too small as well, but he had worn his own, instead. The shirt he could deal with by leaving the top two buttons undone, and his elasticated tie held the collar together. The trousers, similarly, he could leave unfastened, and let his belt hold them up, but the blazer had ripped up the back when he was involved in a tussle with a boy who kept calling him a "retard". Tim had not known whether to use his superiority in size and strength to turn his enemy into mincemeat, or to try to appeal to one of the teachers to protect him.

He hated being in such a confined space with so many people and so much noise. Adults he had always found susceptible to bribery or deception. These screaming children seemed utterly incorruptible. They were too full of reckless hate to allow him to negotiate with them. By lunchtime, he had had as much as he could take. He didn't go to the dinner hall. He found an unlocked stockroom, sat down on a pile of A4 paper, and cried. He cried for the whole dinner hour. He would have cried longer if he had had more time.

The lessons did not absorb him. They were just so easy. Most of the children did not seem to understand what the teacher was saying. Tim presumed they were being deliberately awkward. Miss Dixon, the English teacher, was the most irritating. She kept asking, "Are you all right, Tim?"

The one thing that kept him going was the prospect of meeting Laura. He had arranged to meet her at the school gate. Laura had texted him some days ago about her job interview. She said Holman's liked her, and wanted to take her on, but she had missed the part of the job advert which said that candidates had to provide their own transport. She didn't have a car, nor any ready means of obtaining one. She had asked Holman's if they would give her the contract so that she could get a loan, but they said no, a car was a pre-requisite for the job. Tim had a surprise for Laura. It was in the right-hand inside pocket of his blazer. He checked regularly to make sure it was still there. In fact, it was two surprises.

He stopped looking at the clock. He realised that the best place to sit was as close to the teacher as possible. Some of the teachers seemed to like him. Talking to the teacher was the best way to pass the time. Eventually, the hour hand crawled round to three, and he was allowed out.

The school gate was blocked by women with buggies, women with fake tans, women with long, dangly earrings, women making exaggerated remarks about certificates or pictures being presented by ugly children. Tim navigated his way through them, got to a spot far enough away from the school to let him feel like himself again, and scanned for a sight of Laura. She was late.

He saw a red-haired goth in a black overcoat waiting at a pelican crossing, and his heart leapt. It wasn't her. This goth was shorter than Laura, and quite plainly pregnant.

The crowd of mothers and children had dispersed, and Tim was starting to feel foolish as well as bored and lonely. Then he saw Laura.

"*Hello, Tim,*" said Tim, to himself. Laura said nothing. He could hardly tell whether she had noticed him. He couldn't speak. There was a long pause.

"There's something I need to tell you," said Laura, without looking at him.

"What?"

"I can't see you anymore."

"What?"

"I can't see anybody. I can't see me getting my life back. Not ever."

"Getting your life back?"

"My sister."

"What?"

"She was burned to death, Tim. You didn't know?"

Tim felt the rip in the back of his blazer gaping open.

"I've got the money for your car."

"What? I said that my sister was burned to death. Is there some part of that you didn't understand?"

Tim fumbled in his pocket for the envelope. He opened it. He reached for Laura's hand. She let him count the money into the palm of her hand. It came to two thousand eight hundred pounds.

"That's for you, for your car, so you can get the job at Holman's."

"This doesn't mean anything, you idiot. I don't want your play money that you printed off the internet."

"I earned that money."

"It doesn't make any difference. I'm not taking it."

"Why?" Tim looked at Laura. He thought she might be weakening.

"Where did you get this money?"

"Where do you think? I earned it. Every penny."

"Why don't you spend it on toys and sweeties for yourself?"

"Because I want to spend it on you. I don't need anything. You need a car." Tim nodded at the money. "That's a car. That's your car, Laura."

"No," said Laura.

"Yes."

"Yes. All right then. I'll pay you back."

"I don't want you to pay me back."

"I pay you back, otherwise it's no deal."

"All right." Tim handed the envelope to Laura. Laura grabbed Tim's wrist with one hand, and crushed his fingers around the envelope with the other. "There. I've paid you back. Now we're even." She looked him in the eye.

There was a long pause. Tim fidgeted with the other thing he had in his pocket. "There's something else I want to give you, Laura."

"Tim, I think you have given me enough for one day."

"It's important."

"I don't want anything else, thank you. I think anything else would be pushing it."

"That's not all the money I had saved up."

"Good for you. You'll go far."

"With the rest of it, I bought this." Tim took the little box out of his pocket, and opened it. Laura's eyes widened.

"Oh, no," said Laura. Tim knelt down.

"Laura."

"No, no, no. Stop it, for fuck's sake! This just isn't happening."

Laura ran away. He stood up.

He walked home, but he could not get in because the locks had been changed. He cried all the way back to his foster home. Nobody noticed the split in the back of his blazer.

Shaun sat in Sammy's Snacks, among the sausage sandwiches and stainless steel teapots, so he could think clearly. Whatever evil had killed Gracie was not confined to Castleton Boulevard. It permeated Skegness, and there was nothing he could do. It taunted him.

He shook his head and placed the knight back on its starting position. He had been moving it around the board since he got back

195

from Anastasia's studio, jotting down co-ordinates in a notebook and periodically striking them out and starting again. Each neat line was another failure.

A man in a well-cut suit stepped into Shaun's field of vision and sat down at the other side of the table. Shaun retreated back into his chair.

"You do know chess usually needs two people, right?" the man asked.

Shaun hesitated a moment before answering. "It's called the Knight's Journey," he said, "You have to visit every square on the board without landing in the same place twice."

"Can you solve it?" the man asked.

"No," Shaun shrugged, glancing at his notebook.

"Sometimes, Shaun, if you want to win, you need to change the rules."

As he spoke, the man lifted the knight and placed it on the square to its immediate right.

"Much easier," he said.

"Who are you?" asked Shaun.

The man took a business card from his top pocket. "Name's David Campbell. I'm with Becker, Beadle and Lamb."

Shaun looked at the young man sat opposite him. Apart from the fact that David's stubble was a deliberate statement and his dark hair was swept neatly to one side, there was some resemblance between the two men. Maybe that was what his father wanted in a son – crisp white shirts and tie-clips.

"Drink?" David asked.

He pushed the glass of Coke across the table, before taking a sip of his coffee.

"Your father wants you to come home, Shaun," he continued. "I heard a little girl died in some warehouse fire the other day. This isn't a healthy environment for somebody of your... sensitivity, shall we say?"

"They need me here," Shaun said.

"Need you? You're a handyman, Shaun. They can get somebody else to unblock the toilets. And besides, there are plenty of leaky taps in Kensington. I daresay your father might have slightly loftier ambitions for you. Eventually."

196

"You don't understand. The flats are in danger, somebody needs to protect them."

David shook his head.

"Listen to yourself. You're not well. It can't have been easy." David's tone was more sympathetic now. "Coming out here on your own after you left those UFO people. When your dad told me about you, I wondered why you didn't go back to London in the first place."

Shaun shrugged.

"I was a kid when I went away," he said, "I needed to work out who I was as an adult."

"So why here?"

"My mum used to bring me here sometimes. After the divorce."

"There's no shame in going to your family for help, you know? Like you said, you need a chance to find yourself. Skegness isn't a great place to do that now. Anybody can see it's not doing you any good. When was the last time you slept?"

Shaun had to admit, he was tired. His eyes were glazed with a thick lens of water. He rubbed them with the heel of his hand and took a long drink from his glass.

"It's all right," said David. "You don't need to be here. You should be somewhere safe, with people who care about you. It's all taken care of, Shaun. First-class ticket and everything."

Shaun nodded uncertainly. Already, his burden felt a little lighter.

"I'm staying at the Lyndsay Guesthouse, on Scarborough Avenue," David said. "Look, your train isn't 'til half five. I can pick you up around five to and run you to the station. That gives you a couple of hours to do whatever you need to do, yeah?"

Maybe this was for the best – had he really thought he could protect anybody? Shaun knew one thing for certain: he needed to rest.

"Could you..." he started, "could you keep an eye on the flats while you're here?"

"Yes. Not a problem." David got up to leave. "Five o'clock. Make sure you're ready."

Slowly, Shaun packed away the chess set and carried it back to the counter.

"Are you okay, Shaun?" Sabina asked him.

There was so much he needed to tell her, and it all came out at once: "Popescu's not who he says he is. He's got some sort of secret. He -"

"I know," Sabina interrupted him.

"You know?" Shaun hadn't been expecting this

"Back when he was in Romania, there was a fire at an orphanage. Can you blame him if he doesn't like to talk about it?"

"He's dangerous, Sabina. He's got a gun. And he knows the man from the beach - Gracie saw him."

"Gracie's dead, Shaun," she said, kindly. "I need to deal with this queue, and you should go home and rest. I'll come and check on you later, okay?"

Shaun sighed and tore a page out of his notebook.

"Just have this," he said, passing it to her, "It's everything I've been able to work out."

Sabina put the notepaper with the receipts in the till. She didn't even look at it.

"Just be safe," he said.

"I always am," she replied.

Nell checked her watch for the third time.

"Do you have somewhere more important to be?" DC Castell asked.

Nell studied the photos spread out on the table in front of him. Three people dead in the last month. Castell looked exhausted. It was the second time she'd been called to the police station since he had discovered her at the Coin Fountain arcade, and she had nothing new to tell him.

"I'm going to be late to work," she finally replied.

He loosened his tie and cracked his neck. "Ms. Harrison, I'm not sure you appreciate the gravity of the situation -"

"You're joking, right?" Nell said, her hand reaching out for the picture of the child who had died in the fire. "My aunt has spent the last two days trying to hold it together while she helps Sarah

198

Greenwood plan a funeral for a seven year old. She hasn't slept."
She glared at Castell. "Rachel...well, she even called my mother."

He checked his notes. "Her sister?"

"Yes."

"She probably needed someone to talk to."

Nell shook her head. "They aren't close."

"Tragedy often makes us re-evaluate our relationships," he replied.

"You think I don't know that?"

Castell began gathering the crime scene photos up.

"No, of course you do."

"Did you know my uncle?" Nell asked after a minute.

"Your uncle?"

"He owned Sammy's. Died of cancer about ten years ago."

"I remember when he married your aunt and brought her back here." He looked down at his folder. "It seemed like a big deal at the time. Marrying a Yank."

Castell seemed embarrassed, but Nell just nodded. "When my uncle was dying, Rachel called my mother three times. Once, to tell her about the diagnosis, once to say he had died."

"What was the third time?" Castell asked.

"She called in the middle of the night. We thought he'd died."

"But he hadn't?"

"Rachel was just overwhelmed. Lonely. She wanted my mother to come visit." Nell leaned forward. "You know what? We didn't even come for the funeral." She paused, pushing her hair behind her ears. "So when you tell me I don't understand how serious this is – Rachel hasn't shared more than polite conversation with my mother in a decade. This week, she's called her twice."

"I see," Castell said.

"Do you?" Nell asked, standing. "Do you? Look, if I could help, I would." She looked down at Castell and sighed. "Did you know Gracie Greenwood?"

He shook his head. "Not before I got the call."

"It must have been awful."

After a moment, Castell met her eyes. "I can't seem to forget the smell."

"I meant for her," Nell said quietly. She picked up her bag and let herself out of the room.

It took Shaun about half an hour to walk home along the promenade, and as he watched the grey sea beat against the dirty sand he wondered how he had ever thought this place was welcoming. There were ships on the horizon, full of people going home. When he reached the flats, Harry stood outside.

"You shouldn't be here," Shaun said, walking down the driveway. "The Greenwoods won't want to see you."

"And what about me?" Harry replied, "I worked with that little girl for almost her whole life. Am I not allowed to grieve?"

Shaun couldn't say why, but something about the man made him feel uneasy.

"Anyway," said Harry, "I'm not here for them. I came to see you."

Shaun knew he should go. He was supposed to be leaving all of this behind.

"What do you want?" he asked.

"I just want to talk," Harry said, rolling up his sleeve and revealing a Nazca spider tattooed on his arm.

"You're from the Brotherhood?"

Harry nodded. "I've been keeping an eye on you, Shaun. It's why I'm here."

"I thought the only Brothers who weren't at Starhaven were the ones in the Outreach Centres?"

"And one of those is Haven House. We cared for Gracie. But me? Let's just say we have other sorts of missionary too."

"You're a Watchers' Eye," Shaun said.

Harry nodded. Shaun had heard the phrase at Starhaven, whispered between council members. There were rumours, but most people assumed they were a metaphor.

"The Watchers want me to bring you home," said Harry.

"I am going home," Shaun said, "to my father."

"What good would that do you?" said Harry. "You've seen how bad things are here – the world is out of balance, Shaun. The equinox is coming, and when it does, you should be with the people

200

who care about you. Who love you, even. Is that really your father and his lawyers?"

The last word was filled with venom. Shaun still suspected that his father only wanted him home to keep him from embarrassing the firm. He wasn't sure he could bear living in that big house, with a father who was distant even when they were in the same room. He could be working in the sunshine with his Brothers. Not just fixing cupboards, but actually *making* things. He could chant at the Orionids, surrounded by people who knew his name, who wanted to know how he was. He could hold Sky again, and one day maybe the Watchers *would* come. He still had doubts, but his brothers could get rid of those. Shaun knew what he had to do.

He didn't even need to pack.

Mihai was standing in the bathroom door of Sabina's flat when she got home from her afternoon shift. He stared, nothing of a vulture today, but a predator nonetheless.

"How...?" she started, but then she remembered. "The spare door key."

"I just want to talk," said Mihai. He spoke gently, the way one would to a scared child, turning his palms up in front of his body. He walked towards her very slowly and repeated, "Just talk."

Then he kissed her.

She felt her muscles relax in his arms, his lips slowly brushing against hers, then his tongue finding hers. Everything disappeared for a moment, only to come crashing down on her. Sabina placed her hand on his chest and pushed him away, disentangling herself from his embrace as quickly as she had succumbed to it. She was tired and confused.

"You said you wanted to talk," said Sabina.

"Yes, we need to talk. I need to talk." He took hold of her shoulders and looked into her eyes. "You see, the fire means I have to talk. I have no other choice, I have to act now."

"Let go," she said, but he did not loosen his grip. "Mihai, you are hurting me, can you hear me?"

He released her at once.

"I'm sorry, Sabina, I never meant to hurt you."

"It's okay."

He pulled out a chair and sat. Sabina stared at him for a moment and then she sat opposite him. Mihai looked as if he was struggling to concentrate. His mouth kept moving but no sound came out of it.

"You were talking about a fire?"

"Yes, but that is not where it starts," he said.

His accent was stronger than she remembered. She ventured a guess.

"Popescu?"

He nodded. "I came to this country for him, to find him. I had to pay some bad men to get here. Gangsters. I did things I'm not proud of but I had to find him, no matter the cost. I spent every penny in this. It is my mission, what I live for."

"You live to find Popescu?"

He nodded again.

"I came with Dorin, but then they killed him. He is dead now, Dorin."

"Dorin? Was that the man on the beach?"

He nodded.

"You came all the way here for Popescu, you and Dorin," said Sabina. Mihai had said he was looking for his brother but he was really looking for Popescu. Her brain was working hard to fit all the pieces together. *None of this makes sense*, she thought, *except...* "You were in the orphanage, weren't you, the one that caught fire?"

"So, you know about the orphanage?" His eyes were slits now. "No matter. Yes, Dorin and I both were there. That's why we came to find Popescu. Now Dorin is dead and the police are looking for me. This is not the way things were supposed to be."

"Things rarely are the way they are supposed to be," said Sabina.

"You are right. I should know this by now." He shifted his weight on the chair. "What did Popescu tell you about the orphanage, about the fire?"

"Not much," said Sabina, trying to remember Popescu's words. "He said he was called there because of the fire. He was the captain of the police. There was nothing he could do, though. The fire had killed them all."

"Nu! No!"

His shout was so visceral and unexpected that it jolted her to tears.

Mihai's expression was still filled with rage but his voice was gentle as he spoke.

"Sabina, I'm sorry, don't cry. I didn't mean to scare you. But his lies anger me. All he told you are lies. The only children in the orphanage when it was *torched* were already dead. He is the father of lies."

"I thought that was the Devil," said Sabina, wiping her cheeks with the back of her hands.

Mihai nodded vigorously. "He is." He got up and walked to the window. "Things were bad in Romania with Ceausescu; they were bad after him as well. His regime had fallen and Western scrutiny was upon us. Suddenly, they cared." He turned to face her, a twisted smile on his lips. "The authorities, where they still existed, were cleaning up the mess. Popescu and his men were sent to the orphanage. So, they came. They found the place in ruins. The scent of death was everywhere. The angel of death did not bother leaving, he set up residency right among us."

He crossed the short distance between them and dropped to his chair. She wondered if she had ever seen such sadness outside of a mirror.

"I'm so sorry, Mihai," said Sabina, and she reached for his hand. He patted her and pulled his hands back, placing them under the table.

"The carers had abandoned the children weeks before. Over a hundred had died of hunger and illness before Popescu even arrived. The living, malnourished and ill, were taken out. Popescu's men torched the building as they left."

"Taken out," Sabina repeated, a shiver running down her spine. Her voice mirrored the sorrow in his. "Taken where?"

"To the woods."

"The woods," she repeated.

"The woods."

She looked up as he laid his hand on the table. This time, it held a gun.

"Don't worry about it," said Mihai.

The mind is a funny thing. As Sabina saw the gun, her first thought was of Mr Culpepper. She started laughing as hysteria took her over, thinking about what he would say if he were here to see her now: "Here, in the Sand Castle, we do not get involved in hostage situations. The members of our staff do not know people with guns."

Mihai's arms were around her, the gun within her grasp. She hadn't even noticed him getting up. He was speaking to her; his voice was calm, soothing. Whatever he was saying, she couldn't understand, he was saying it in Romanian.

"Why haven't you taken your revenge?" she asked.

He kissed her head and returned to his chair.

"I need a confession; I need to hear him say the words. He has to know what he has done, the harm he has caused. I want him to know that he will suffer for it, that *I* will make him pay for his crime. You understand this, don't you, dragostea mea?"

This Sabina understood. My beloved. *The man is demented,* she thought, *he doesn't even know me properly. And he's waving a gun around!* She could feel hysteria making its way back.

"This is too much," she said.

"Yes," he agreed. He placed the gun on the table, and leaned towards Sabina. "And then there was that woman."

"What woman? Valerie?"

"I didn't mean to shoot at her. I didn't mean to shoot. But she startled me in that devil's kitchen. I was looking for proof. She had no business being there."

Sabina stared at the black hole that was the barrel of the gun. So many times she wished she had died in the fire with her parents, only to realise now that she hadn't meant it, not really. *I want to live,* she thought.

"It was an accident," said Sabina. It was her turn to speak softly. "Everyone can see that. She shouldn't have been there."

Mihai relaxed his grip on the gun, then removed his hand altogether, reaching for Sabina. She let him take her hands and smiled at him.

"Popescu needs to pay, his crime was unspeakable. You need to tell the authorities, here or in Romania, they -"

Mihai let go of her hands and shook his head slowly. His face was a mask as he laid his hand on the gun.

Nell was a few minutes late for the evening shift, and her aunt's new summer hire glared at her. Nell grabbed an apron and replaced the teenager at the till.

"It's been crazy," Katherine said, pushing her hair out of her eyes. "I'd stay to help with this-" she gestured at the line, "but I tutor. And I'm late."

Nell nodded absently. "I'm sorry."

"Whatever," Katherine said, tossing her apron in the hamper and waving to a kid waiting by the door.

Nell grunted and turned her full attention to her customers. It seemed like everyone was still talking about the fire. The atmosphere had been tense all week; even the unusually bright spring weather hadn't proved a distraction. After her husband was killed, Nell had discovered that people preferred to flock together like this in grief. It felt safer to gossip, to cry, to question what kind of God would allow such a thing to happen.

Since most of their regulars knew that Rachel and Sarah were close, Nell assumed this burst of business was partially fuelled by survivor's guilt and partially by a desire to be close to someone directly affected by the tragedy. Nell had lost count of how many had offered their sympathies. She'd told each well-wisher she would pass on their kind words, because that's what they wanted to hear, but she hadn't actually done it. Maybe she would, at some point, when it wasn't so raw. When Rachel started sleeping again, or when she stopped coming home with trash bags full of children's clothes.

The flat was filled with those white bags. The Greenwoods had wanted to throw away Gracie's things, but Rachel had offered to take them instead. It was a smart move. Nell had donated all of Brian's clothes the weekend after the chaplain notified her of his death. It had been unbearable to come home to his shoes by the door, to have his coat hanging in the closet. One night, she'd got out of bed and filled bags just like the ones upstairs. She had been waiting at the door when the Salvation Army opened at nine.

It was six months before she'd actually regretted it though. By then, she'd given away more than just clothes. She'd sold the rugs they'd bought together before they were married, the lawnmower Brian had insisted on for their postage stamp backyard, the matching mountain bikes her brothers had given them as a wedding present. Nell had tossed what she couldn't sell, then moved into a cheap efficiency studio in a motel across town.

Eventually though, after the first wave of grief had burned itself out, Nell had been sick about it. Her mother-in-law hated her. His whole family felt betrayed that she hadn't offered them the opportunity to take mementos. Her own mother had simply settled into a grating rhythm of "I told you so." *Your marriage was a mistake. You were too young. You threw away your education, and for what? What have you got to show for it now?* Gracie Greenwood's bags taunted her anew.

Skegness had been such a relief after all that. Over the past few months, her life had even begun to take shape again. Rachel gave Nell space without shutting her out, and Sabina had proved to be a nice distraction, with those swords and her own mostly healed scars. A distraction; that was what Nell needed. A night out on the town, some drink, some company.

She dug in her backpack for her phone. She dialled Sabina's flat, and on the third ring, it picked up. She heard a muffled thump, then silence.

"Sabina?"

After a moment, she could hear a man's voice speaking, although it didn't sound like English.

"Hello?"

Nell looked at her phone. The call had been disconnected. She hit redial, but this time, it went straight to voicemail. She left a message telling Sabina to call her right back, but by closing time, Sabina still hadn't returned her call.

Nell dragged herself upstairs, already resigned to a different night on the town. She threw on shorts and a tee shirt and laced up her running shoes before she could decide that a bottle of wine was an easier way to get through the evening.

Mungo journeyed into the Underworld like Odysseus, Aeneas and Dante before him. The Underworld went by a different name in

Skegness and that name was the funfair. But as with the eternal inferno, there was nothing fun or fair about it.

Mungo had turned to the drink after losing his bench and his thirst worsened upon hearing about Gracie, the sweet girl he had shared donuts with. Now, here he was, bundling through the vestibule of damnation with a mostly empty canister of Wonky Donkey super-strength cider. He had nothing left to lose. Immediately, his senses were bombarded with the screams and burning lights of the Outer Circles. The demons took much amusement in the drunken clown, howling and cackling at his drunken delirium. Little imps pointed and tittered, red toffee apples smeared around their cherub cheeks. The bigger demons, hooded like the Grim Reaper himself, spun Mungo round and round then shoved him to the ground.

Lying on his back, he saw feathered harpies wheeling overhead in the black starless sky where the rides did not reach. *Oh, the rides!* Such nefarious abominations. They bore names like Waltzer and Sky Swat and Tumble Bug and The Tea Cups but the cider helped Mungo see their true form. These contraptions were instruments of torture.

The damned were shackled into the mechanisms, closed and locked with the finality of an Iron Maiden. The contraptions would then come to life, inflicting torment on their prisoners with a never-ending assault of spins and loops and drops and ricochets until each victim regurgitated the contents of their stomachs.

Some wore demonic grins, airbrushed on like tribal markings, taking the guise of crude cartoon characters, but these were a facade, worn like a Halloween mask. Under those bright, sprayed colours were sinister hollow eyes and a hunger for Skegness souls. The Haunted House wore the thinnest disguise, with the Devil himself looming out of the front like the bow of a great ship. 'Abandon all hope, ye who enter here,' he roared through tinny speakers. Mungo had given up hope long ago.

The closest thing Mungo had to a guide was the bottle in his hands. *Cider is my Virgil,* he told himself before draining the contents. It gave him the strength he needed to scramble to his feet and hurtle through the remaining Circles, catching glimpses of sin despite trying to shield his eyes. The Second Circle contained the lustful, fornicating atop wheelie bins round the back of the carousel. The Third Circle held the gluttons, gorging themselves on burgers of unspecified meat. Then he was at the Seventh Circle, a place of violence, where demons fought over penny-machines in the arcade, punching and kicking and biting.

Finally, he reached the Innermost Circle of Hell, a place reserved for frauds and traitors and the most fiendish of sinners. A place reserved for him.

The structure in front of him read Marley's House of Mirrors.

It was time to face judgement. Mungo entered.

Drunk, Mungo lost the entrance immediately and staggered back and forth, bouncing off the labyrinthine corridors of mirrors like a pinball. It was as if he had stumbled into an Escher painting.

Whilst the mirrors distorted his reflection, the cider had been distorting his mind. He whirled around in a daze, surrounded by unfathomable numbers of clowns in all shapes and sizes, but sharing the same green wig and red nose and unforgiving staring eyes.

Mungo had come here for this judgement and welcomed the burning pain it caused. He was driven to his knees under the weight of their eyes. The clowns spun faster and faster like a zoetrope and he thought his sanity would crumble.

Then everything stopped.

Mungo took a deep breath and looked forward. He saw a new Mungo. This one was a young Mungo and it was no reflection either. The Young Mungo was laying out a large towel. *Oh no, please.* Mungo knew what played out before his eyes. He was watching the night of the circus fire.

"Please, I wanted punishing, not reminding," he wept.

"That *is* your punishment," the other Mungos said together.

Mungo watched his younger self. He could have been in the stalls watching the rest of Circus Romero perform their dress rehearsal but instead he was backstage helping prepare the fire breathing equipment. He was different back then, always looking for a way to help, never wanting Ringmaster Romero to think he took the circus for granted. After all, Romero had saved him from his–

"Father!" Mungo and Young Mungo said in unison, becoming one. The mirror did not lie. Mungo's father had been there on the night of the fire. Mungo watched his father approach, swinging his infamous cane.

"Joseph," said his father, shaking his head in disgust. "So this is where you've been hiding all these years. Just a stone's throw from home."

Mungo swallowed. Somehow he managed to find his voice and mumbled, "That was no home."

"You ungrateful little shit! I thought you were dead. Instead, you were prancing around in costume and make-up like a nancy boy. You're coming home with me and then I am going to take that Ringmaster to court for kidnapping young boys."

"Don't you dare!" said Mungo. "Romero is -"

"Is what?"

"More of a father to me than you ever were."

His father swung the cane and smacked Mungo across the temple. Blots of pain burst into his vision.

"More of a father? *I* brought you up properly. Made you smart. Made you tough."

"I didn't deserve what you did," said Mungo, looking at the cane.

"You needed toughening up."

"And my step-mother? Did she need... toughening up?"

His father stared at him, as if that were obvious.

"She was *useless*, Joseph. She wasn't a patch on your mother. But what could I do? What could I do when you dragged out half her innards in your chubby little fist? You're lucky that you had your mother's eyes or I might have smothered you with a pillow on the delivery table."

The cane struck Mungo again.

"Please," the young Mungo begged.

"Ungrateful little shit! You killed my love but I kept you, didn't I? And how did you thank me? You ran off to join the circus."

The cane struck Mungo hard across the nose.

Mungo mumbled through the blood that streamed from his nose.

"What was that, boy? Speak up if you're going to say something!"

Mungo's hand came down on a can, small, hard and rectangular.

"You always were a sniveller," his father snarled.

"Go to hell," said Mungo.

His father had just enough time to narrow his eyes.

"What?"

Mungo squeezed the bottle of lighter fuel as hard as he could, spraying it across his father's chest. His father looked down at his dripping jacket and gave a derisive snort of amusement.

"Go to hell, dad!"

Mungo thumbed the wheel of the lighter he held in his hand and watched as the man who had once broken his step-mother's jaw burst into flames.

His triumph was short-lived. His father staggered into the canvas wall of the Big Top and so began the circus fire. There was panic and screaming and failed attempts at rescue but Mungo was too afraid to help. He ran and ran, never looking back. He couldn't save his troupe, his friends or his surrogate family.

"Please, no more," wailed Mungo at the mirror. "No more."

At that, the mirrors started spinning once more. Flames and wings, revolving faster and faster round his head. Mungo covered his ears to block out the burning and the cawing but it was no use so he screamed for mercy until he thought his head might split open. Then he collapsed, tumbling down into a dark pit of dust, chip papers and discarded lollipop sticks.

The weather was still pleasant even though the sun had dropped below the horizon. Nell ran down Castleton, passing the police station before cutting right onto North Parade to the Scarborough Esplanade. As she headed toward the water, she saw a few young couples taking advantage of the relative privacy, but by the time she passed the pier, the beach was hers. Sandcastles had been abandoned to the encroaching tide, and the donkeys were gone for the night.

The only sound was her breath and a soft splash every time her feet struck the water. Nell was so intent on following the curve of the tide that she almost fell over Bobby Thomas. He was sifting through beach debris on his hands and knees. He had clearly been at it for a while. His pants were stiff with sand and he had thrown his suit jacket aside. Nell could see he the gun shoved into his waistband.

She stumbled to a stop as the light from his torch swung into her eyes. His hand reached for his weapon.

"Bobby! It's Nell," she called, hands going up instinctively.

"What do you want?" he growled.

"What do I...?" She gestured at the empty beach. "I'm having a goddamned tea party. Bobby. What does it look like?"

Bobby glanced around, clearly flustered.

"It's here. I know he's left it here. I just have to find it." He lunged at her, grabbing her arm and squeezing it tightly. "Help me look."

His face was damp with sweat.

"You look like shit." She pried his fingers from her arm. "I bet some of your stitches have come out. And you must be getting sand in everything! Those wounds have to stay clean, Bobby."

He thrust the torch at her. "We have to find it. Tonight."

"What the hell are you talking about?"

"Marcus is going to kill you," he hissed, his breath hot on her face.

"Can you back up a sec?" Nell asked. "What's going on?" He stood close enough that she could feel the heat radiating off his body. "Bobby?"

"Just...help me." He sounded exhausted. Nell wondered what infections might have developed since she'd last checked him over.

"Okay. Can you tell me what we're looking for?" She flicked the light across the empty sand.

Bobby dropped back to his knees too quickly and lost his balance, grabbing at her legs to right himself. Nell glanced up to gauge how far they were from the road when she saw two men by the iron railings separating the beach from the street. She knew they were armed. By the positions of their arms, the shape of their jackets, the way they held themselves, she knew they were armed.

"Uh, Bobby?" she murmured, switching off the light. "Were you expecting anyone?"

He looked up, and she pointed toward the figures.

"Fucking Henric and that shit-eating dog who's always hangin' on him. I'll fucking kill them."

Bobby had his gun in his hand but didn't have the energy to stand though. Nell crouched down and put a hand on his shoulder. He was shivering.

"They haven't seen us yet. What if we just try and stay very still?"

"They'll go away?"

She hesitated. "Yes."

"And if they don't?"

Nell squeezed his arm nervously. Bobby needed a doctor; he sure as hell wasn't going to be able to make a break for it if things went south here.

"I kill them," he said softly, answering his own question.

CHAPTER EIGHT

A cold bucket of water struck Mungo in the face. He had spent the night in Marley's House of Mirrors.

"Gah!"

"Wake up mate," said the attendant. "This isn't a B&B."

"But I ordered the Full English," said Mungo.

The attendant barked with laughter.

"I will give you five minutes then I'm calling the police."

Mungo blinked around with bleary eyes. The House of Mirrors had lost much of its charm in the light of day, which streamed through the open fire exit. The labyrinthine complex of mirrors was now just a corrugated iron shed with a few planes of glass drilled to the walls.

Then he froze. He found himself looking into one mirror he had not seen the night before. This mirror was more terrifying then any of them. The glass was smooth, devoid of any distortion. Mungo was face to face with his own true self.

The water had washed off his clown make-up and Mungo saw his face clearly for the first time in years. Wrinkles cut across his face like battle-scars. His nose was peppered with burst blood vessels almost as red as his fake nose and his eyes were redder still, bloodshot, swollen. His wig had dropped off and Mungo saw his own grey hair which receded up his forehead as if fleeing the erosion of his weathered face.

"You have grown old behind that make-up, Mungo," he said to himself.

But he still had some time and he would use it well. He could never make amends for the circus fire but perhaps there was some good he could do with the days he had left. There were people who needed him, people who needed his help, people who looked for him for strength and support that he had been unwilling to offer.

"Sabina."

"Have you got a home to go to?" said the attendant, leaning against the doorframe of the exit.

Mungo nodded.

"Homes to go to. Souls to save. Wars to fight."

The attendant scowled.

Mungo reached into his briefcase and pulled out his white clown make-up. If he was going to war then he would need some war-paint. He walked out, leaving the mirrors empty.

It was a cold morning on the promenade and Mungo's breath plumed out in front of him, as if he were a dragon. He certainly had fire in his belly.

To the right of Mungo was the usual row of chippies, greasy spoons and seafront shops but they were all deserted. The locals were at home and the tourists were nursing hangovers in their B&Bs. To the left of Mungo lay the sea, which stretched off into the starkly lit horizon. The sun took its time rising, casting fresh light over the lapping waves and turning them into molten gold. The wind turbines punctuated the vista, lining the horizon like sentinels.

Looking at the windmills reminded Mungo that Sabina had once compared Mungo to Don Quixote and he certainly felt like the delusional knight now: awkward, past his prime and engaged in a task beyond his capacity.

But he was sober and that counted for a lot. Well, technically he was hungover but at least that was heading in the right direction. Mungo was determined to see his task through. This was his Fourth Life. He was done being a victim, a performer, a slob. In this life, he would be a hero.

"I'm coming, Sabina."

Skegness was his La Mancha. Mungo rode on.

Sebastian paced the small room in Anastasia's Skegness flat with the air of a recently captured macaque suddenly confined to a laboratory cage. It seemed a long way from his natural habitat.

"We need to play this carefully, Ana," said Sebastian. "You see this..." He held up a copy of The Daily Mail, the headline 'Death of an Angel' over a photograph of the dead child.

"They're sick," said Anastasia.

"They're offering you a hundred thousand pounds for an exclusive," said Sebastian.

"I won't talk to the press," said Anastasia. "Not for any amount of money."

"We are talking to the media, darling," said Sebastian. "Just not these tabloid vultures."

"So why did you bring these rags with you?" said Anastasia. "I feel grubby just being in the same room as this stuff."

Sebastian gathered the bundle of papers together and put them down on the coffee table. On the top was The Sun. How they had got hold of one of her sketches of Gracie was a mystery Anastasia did not care to contemplate.

"I've shielded you from the reptiles, Ana," said Sebastian. "In any case, the blood money they're offering would kill off your career in an instant. But they will pursue you until they get something. Without you this is a one-day wonder, a photogenic child who dies in a fire. Sad face, move on."

"So why feed the frenzy?" said Anastasia.

"You are the story, darling," said Sebastian. "That's why the Mail wants you so badly. Look at their photo spread." He turned through a few pages and held the paper out to Anastasia. "You with David Tennant. You with Kate Moss. You with Boris. Celebrity, politics, dead babies, what more could they possibly want?"

"It was a charity fundraiser," said Anastasia.

"For Children In Need," said Sebastian. "The headlines just write themselves."

"So what do you want me to do?" said Anastasia.

"Three interviews," said Sebastian.

"No way," said Anastasia.

"Hear me out, Ana, darling," said Sebastian. "They won't all happen at once."

"I'm not talking to the tabloids," said Anastasia.

"No," said Sebastian, "You're not. You're talking to the Financial Times. It'll be about your work. They'll ask about this sorry business with the fire, and the child, of course, but it will be sympathetic."

"I'm not sure," said Anastasia. "Talking to any newspaper looks bad in these circumstances."

"The red tops want you," said Sebastian. "You talk to the FT, and it gives you control."

"You said three interviews," said Anastasia. "That's a lot."

"Wall Street Journal," said Sebastian, "and Vogue."

"You are not serious," said Anastasia. "Vogue? They'll dress me in Dior and Jimmy Choos. How the hell is that going to help?"

"Sit down, Ana," said Sebastian. He put his hands on her shoulders, pushed her gently down onto the sofa. He sat on a low chair, facing her, leaning forward. "I have thought this through. In your interests."

"You can't bully me, Seb," said Anastasia.

"I wouldn't even try," said Sebastian. "But there is a problem. You are an artist. You have a big show coming up. Much of the work for it has been damaged in a crime scene where a little girl lost her life."

"I intend to find out why," said Anastasia.

"That's for the police to do," said Sebastian. "The point is, this business has raised your profile. People are interested in your work."

"You surely don't think I'm going to use that child's death as a marketing tool?" said Anastasia.

"The centrepiece of your show is a triptych in which the child features prominently, don't forget," said Sebastian. "We can get a million for that now."

"Jesus, no," said Anastasia. "And what would the papers make of that?"

"The triptych will be at the centre of the gallery," said Sebastian, "but there'll be a little sign up. NFS."

"Thank God for that," said Anastasia.

"It's not for sale," said Sebastian, "because I've already sold it. The owner will loan the work for the duration of the show. There will be no public price tag."

"Nobody pays that kind of money for my work," said Anastasia.

"They do now," said Sebastian, "look." He pulled out a copy of the FT's glossy magazine 'How To Spend It'. "The Aesthete feature, Viktor Kaletsky."

Anastasia scanned the article. It was a full page feature on a Russian billionaire. His favourite island, his signature cologne, his prized art collection. "That's one of mine," she said. "From the Zoroastrian studies."

"How many times have I told you? Kaletsky is a serious collector," said Sebastian. "He's an influential taste-maker in his circles. The FT, WSJ interviews will speak directly to those people. The Vogue interview will be some months down the line. That'll position you nicely with the oligarchs' WAGs."

"You're a bastard, Sebastian," said Anastasia.

"I'm your bastard, Ana," said Sebastian "No one wanted a child to die, or for you to get caught up in this stuff. But face facts, darling. You've just gone from respected mid-ranking British contemporary artist to global hot property. The decimal point has just moved on your prices. If Damian Hirst was the artist of choice for millionaire bankers ten years back, you are now the name to watch on the billionaire scene."

Mungo arrived at Castleton Boulevard to see a car pull away from outside Sabina's flat.

Sabina was driving and did not look happy. Popescu rode shotgun and looked equally distraught. The source of their displeasure was clear. Mihai sat in the back-seat with his gun levelled at Mungo's fellow circus survivors.

"Stop!" yelled Mungo and ran after the car, shouting and shaking his gloved fist. It was a futile effort. He was never going to catch up with a moving vehicle, especially in clown shoes. He had a better chance of flying after Spitfire the seagull.

"Now what?"

Mungo decided to head upstairs to Sabina's flat above McNair's Convenience Store. Perhaps he would find an indication of where Mihai might be taking them. The door was wide open so he let himself in. There was no sign of a struggle. He found two mugs of untouched tea which suggested that Sabina was entertaining Mihai up until the moment of the kidnapping. Mihai had gained her trust. He was a manipulative snake.

"Speaking of which..."

Whilst he was here, Mungo decided to arm himself with all the tricks and terrors of Sabina's performance arsenal. He filled his spotted briefcase with her daggers, her fire-breathing gear and the handcuffs from her escape-artist routine. Regrettably, he had to leave the sword she frequently swallowed because it was too long to conceal. He suspected the Lincolnshire police would not take kindly to a clown strolling around Skegness, armed like a samurai. Never mind, Mungo found a weapon even more lethal than Sabina's sword.

He picked it up with both hands and smiled.

"Easy, Foc," he said as he lifted the Ursini's viper out of its glass case. "You know, I am going to rename you Sancho. You riding with me?"

The old Mungo would have wallowed in defeat, but he was a clown on a mission and his next move was an obvious one.

"All roads lead to Sammy's," he told himself. "Where the Nighthawks roost."

Anastasia watched her agent drive off. She knew he was right about one thing. She was making the best work she had ever made; and that work was indivisible from the circumstances in which it had been created. That included the girl, Gracie, the old man, Popescu, and the conflagration in her studio. What Anastasia hadn't shared with Sebastian was the suspicion that she was not herself a hapless victim, but the target of the crime in which the child had perished.

Artists work through intuition, sensibility and instinct, not cold, forensic reason. Anastasia spread the newspapers out on the floor, and stood in the centre, scanning them for an understanding of what had happened, and why. She moved to the small dining table, and covered it with a large piece of paper. Picking up a pencil, Anastasia began to draw. She drew Gracie as a Slavic princess, Popescu as a monk. She sketched in other figures: the body on the beach, the clown, the actress lying in the road, the quiet caretaker constantly looking over his shoulder. Chicken processing workers wrenching the guts from birds still warm from the sheds. Birds? Of course. Seagulls everywhere, they had to be part of all this. Firefighters, too, and police officers, paramedics busily going about their duties. Anastasia stepped back. What was missing? She added incidental figures; waitresses, assistants from the corner shop, the kid with the bicycle. Anastasia had created the outline of a latter-day Hieronymus Bosch, or a damnation painting from the younger Brueghel, an unsettling mixture of the mundane and the grotesque.

But where did she fit in? Was she another figure on the edges, or ought she to position herself at the centre?

The newspapers spread out across the floor suggested a different story. They had two principal actors - the child and the artist - and their roles were clearly distinguished. The child, plainly, was innocence; the artist a champagne drinking metropolitan. She was, in tabloid land, guilty as sin. Anastasia knew in her gut that this was not the story at all. She gathered up the papers and dumped them in the recycling bin; all except the How To Spend It magazine.

Kaletsky. Anastasia took the profile over to the table and added the sleek billionaire to her sketch, his Patek Philippe just visible below the handmade cuff that emerged from the bespoke Savile Row suit. Anastasia's current work was influenced by Orthodox religious iconography. Popescu was Romanian. Kaletsky was Russian. The workers at the meat factory were Bulgarian, Romanian, Ukrainian. The poor, dead girl was almost identical to the child in a photograph of a 20th Century Romanian orphanage. Could there be some thread binding these things together?

Anastasia left her flat and walked up to Popescu's door. She rang the bell, but there was no answer. Anastasia looked around her with irritation. Down on street level, in the convenience store there were signs in the window, advertisements for services in Roman and Cyrillic script. Instant Money Transfer. Lebara Phone Cards. Anastasia pulled out her phone and called the number for Vassil, the Bulgarian scientist and meat packer.

Sabina worked at Sammy's cafe where Popescu played chess daily. Both would have friends there. Sabina often mentioned an American waitress, Nell. Mungo knew that Popescu played against a young lad. Maybe they could offer some suggestions as to where Sabina had been taken. If not, perhaps they knew something about Mihai. After all, Mihai had attacked Mungo right outside of Sammy's. Had the Romanian thug been hanging around the cafe during the day? He intended to find out.

Mungo booted open the door of Sammy's like a gunslinger entering a saloon. The effect was less dramatic than he had hoped. Sammy's was empty.

Of course, realised Mungo. It was Sunday and Sammy's was closed. Should be closed...

"You must be Mungo," said an American voice. Mungo jumped. A woman appeared from behind the counter. If she was surprised at this auguste apparition walking through her cafe door then she hid it well.

"Sabina speaks highly of you," said Nell.

"It is Sabina that I wanted to talk to you about," explained Mungo, ignoring her bedraggled appearance and the bloody cloth in her hands. "She has been kidnapped by a Romanian thug."

"What?" Nell said. "How do you know this?"

"I saw them driving off together just now. The thug was pointing a gun at Sabina, as well as an old man called Popescu, a former friend of ours."

"It could be Mihai," said Nell. "Sabina said he was Romanian."

"Yes," said Mungo. "He said he knew Popescu back in Romania."

"It's like Skegness is hosting a Romanians Reunited festival," said a hidden voice.

Another person sat up in one of the booths where he had been lying, previously concealed by the table. It was a bloody and bruised black man. He was covered in sand. He was big and terrifying and glared at the clown. Mungo almost turned and ran right there and then.

"Who's this?" asked the black man.

"Reinforcements, Bobby," Nell said with obviously forced cheer.

"Is that so?"

Bobby was pale and hurt. This explained Nell's bloody cloth. She was fixing him up. It also explained why he sagged towards the seat, although some of that might be due to the bottle of whiskey in his hand.

"Bobby, this is a friend of Sabina's. She was just kidnapped by a man called Mihai. He might be one of Dalca's men."

Bobby groaned and lay back down.

"The only reinforcement I need is Marcus and when I find him we're burning this cesspool to the ground," Bobby shouted. "And I don't need any goddamn clowns following me around!"

Mungo walked over.

"Christ," said Nell. "You both stink of alcohol. First things first, I'm going to fix us some coffee. We could all do with some."

And off she went to the kitchen. That was how Mungo found himself alone in a booth opposite Bobby. He gulped. Bobby nursed the bottle and appraised his new companion. After a few moments of this eyeballing, Bobby jerked forward and Mungo yelped. Bobby laughed, clearly pleased by the reaction he had caused.

"Why *are* you dressed like a clown?"

"Because I am a clown," Mungo answered honestly enough. "Why are you covered in sand?"

Bobby glared at Mungo, as if deciding whether to answer.

"I was looking for something on the beach," he said.

"Did you find it?" asked Mungo.

"Nope."

"What did you lose?"

"My mind."

Mungo nodded. "I know the feeling."

"You're definitely a clown," said Bobby. "Have a drink. Helps numb the pain. If you even feel it anymore, that is."

He offered the clown the bottle he'd been working on. Mungo didn't touch it.

"Romanian gangsters are looking for me," explained Bobby. "They might know this Mihai bloke of yours. I took the liberty of chewing off the ringleader's face but he didn't see it as an improvement. He is after me. Perhaps Nell too."

He took another swig from the bottle.

"We spent the night on the beach, hiding from his men. It goes against my nature to hide but I had to think of Nell." His face twisted. "No more though, clown, no more. I won't spend another night like that. If they want a fight then I will save them the trouble of looking for one. I will go to them."

Bobby slammed his fist on the table. "Are you scared of me?" asked Bobby, leaning forward.

Mungo nodded.

"I have hurt people, clown," Bobby growled. "You should prepare yourself for that eventuality if you want your friend back. This is war. Nell and I cannot have a soft, flabby clown getting in

221

the way. Are you prepared to hurt people? Are you prepared to kill?"

Mungo leant forward to meet Bobby's challenge. "I killed seventy-nine people and twelve animals, including my father."

That was met with silence. Bobby raised his eyebrows. "You killed your father?"

"I set him on fire."

A scrape and a hiss drew Bobby's attention to Mungo's briefcase. Mungo casually draped an arm over it and looked at the ceiling.

"Strange clown, you have something in that case that I don't want to know about. Keep it to yourself."

"Coffee!" announced Nell, returning from the kitchen and slamming down a pot of thick black tar. "Drink up gents. We need you both sober for whatever comes next." She snatched the bottle from Bobby's hands.

"And what's coming? asked Mungo.

"Death, of course, Mungo," Bobby replied. "The question is on what scale."

Mungo drank the coffee – black, bitter, brutal – and felt good. For the first time in twelve years, he was part of a troupe.

"I found these in the cash register," Nell said, waving a sheaf of loose paper in front of their faces. "Looks like gibberish but Popescu's name is all over them. Do they mean anything to you?"

Bobby snatched them out of her hand. Nell and Mungo watched as Bobby went through the pages one by one.

"Your friend is in a great deal of trouble," he eventually said.

"Do you know where she is?" said Mungo.

Bobby nodded. "Dalca probably has her at a meat packing factory in Alford. That's where they take all the meat for the grinder. We need to get to my flat and get you two kitted out."

"Kitted out?"

"That's right," Bobby said from his prone position. "Welcome, private, to the Independent Auxiliary Angelic Horde of Skegness. First standing order, avoid Nell's coffee at all costs. It's terrible."

Sabina glanced at the rear-view mirror and her eyes met Mihai's.

"It will all be over soon," said Mihai. "Just drive."

His words were as reassuring as the gun at her back.

"Pull up over there," said Mihai, pointing at the gates of a factory, next to some woodland.

"What is this place?" Sabina asked as she brought the car to a stop.

"It's a meat packing factory. I know this guy. He won't mind me using the space."

"Use it for what?"

He handed her a key.

"Go open the gates."

As she unlocked the gates, she realised the place was deserted. *Who would be here on a Sunday, anyway? Only us.*

Sabina got back into the car and drove as directed to a storage shed attached to the rear of the factory. She parked up in the shadow of the boxy metal building. They walked in through the high sliding doors. Sabina, then Popescu, then Mihai bringing up the rear.

In the shed, packaging and non-meat goods competed for space with pallets, crates and cardboard boxes galore.

Mihai pushed the old man to a corner, causing Popescu to fall and hit his head on a crate. A trail of blood was visible on Popescu's forehead. Sabina started running to Popescu, to make sure he was all right. Mihai, perhaps misinterpreting the move as an attempt to escape, clobbered her over the head with the grip of his gun. She heard Mihai saying something about not wanting to hurt her as darkness clouded over her and Mihai began to drag her across the dirty floor.

Bobby pulled his Jag on to the pavement, right in front of Sammy's, sending a frog-shaped litter bin flying. He vaulted out of the car and started shouting orders.

"Both of you get in. Nell, you're driving and grab that bottle of whiskey. We'll need it."

The clown looked confused. He wished he had time to sympathise, but it was his damn girl they were off to save.

"Get in the fucking car, clown!" he screamed.

Clowns, Bobby reflected, knew how to take orders with alacrity if this one was a typical example of the breed.

"Weapons, Bobby?" said Nell, looking at the open bag on the back seat. "Did you get enough weapons?"

"Nell, love, before we're done you'll think sawn-off shotguns are for dealing with difficult customers," Bobby grinned.

Sabina's head started to hurt. Every time she tried to move, both her head and her wrists burned with pain. *I'm going to die*, Sabina thought as she blinked again and opened her eyes.

Her head hurt everywhere, not just where Mihai had hit it. She was sitting on her side, propped against a crate, her wrists bound on the back with handcuffs. Her vision was blurred and she was thirsty, and for a scary moment, she couldn't remember what her own name was.

Popescu sat opposite her, his hands tied together in front of him with some rope. He rocked himself back-and-forth and she could see three of him. Sabina blinked a couple of times, and Popescu came into focus. She could see his mouth moving but it took her some minutes to understand what he was saying.

"Once upon a time, once upon a time, once-," said Popescu, over and over again.

Once upon a time, thought Sabina, *that is how it begins. But how does it end?*

"Good, you woke up. And just in time, too. I feared you would miss it," said Mihai from the other side of the shed.

He was cutting some of the boxes into pieces, a pile of cut cardboard by his feet. He looked focused, clear-headed, and scarier than anything Sabina had ever seen. There was a determination in him, a kind of fervour that overtakes some men when they are about to do something really horrible and yet think it is the right thing, the only thing to do.

"You see Sabina, we are going to play a game."

"I'm in no mood for games," she mumbled thickly.

"This place isn't an orphanage, and the woods are nothing like home, but it will have to do," said Mihai. He turned to stare at Popescu, fixing him with a glare of total hatred. "You will pay for your crimes, monstru. Judgement day is finally upon us, and you will pay. First, you will confess, then, well, then the fun starts. What I've lost...what you've taken from me. You will pay."

Popescu had stopped muttering and lifted his head.

"You don't understand," Popescu started, "I didn't know what was going on."

"Lies. You all knew. You just left us to rot and pretended not to know."

"No," he insisted. "If I had known they were to be transferred to a place suspected of being involved in such dark matters."

"Dark matters?" sneered Mihai.

Popescu muttered something.

"What?"

"Bau-bau."

"What's Bau-bau?" said Sabina.

"Fucking joke," bellowed Mihai, dashed over and cracked his fist over the top of Popescu's head.

Popescu cried. It was a weak sound, a child's mewling.

"Transplant organs for rich foreigners," the old man whined. "Brits, Germans, Americans, French."

"Lies! Nonsense!"

"Please," said Sabina. "He's an old man. He's hurt."

"But maybe it was for the best," whispered Popescu. "The conditions these children lived under." Popescu paused, slowly shaking his head in sadness and distress. "I didn't know what to do, I was so young. He wanted to get them, Bau-bau, he wanted to harm the children. He thought they had been naughty, so he was going to get them." He turned to look at Sabina. "I wanted to help them, Cristina, you understand that don't you? Tell me you understand."

Cristina? Sabina nodded anyways. That seemed to sooth the old man. He continued his twisted tale.

"I was trying to help you, I didn't realise. The winter. I didn't account for it, the cold was too harsh, and they were too weak."

"Too weak." Mihai shook his head in disbelief. "You marched us into the woods, in our T-shirts and pants. To that circle of trees..."

225

"I should have thought," said Popescu. "All I could think was that I needed to get them to safety, away from him. I just didn't realise it was so cold. I wanted to save them."

Mihai's laughter echoed in the shed, interrupting Sabina's slow thought process.

"You expect me to believe that you were trying to help us? You really did lose your mind, old man," said Mihai and then put a cigarette between his lips and lit it.

Popescu turned to Sabina again. "You know I'd never let them hurt you, Gracie. I won't let him get you."

Now I'm Gracie? thought Sabina. *Great! I'm stuck with two lunatics, one doesn't even know who I am anymore and the other wants to see the world burn.*

"It's time," said Mihai. He walked to Popescu and dragged him to his feet. "We are going into the woods, you and I, and we'll have our game, the end game." He started to walk towards the woods, pulling Popescu by the rope. "Oh! I was almost forgetting."

He turned, looked around the shed, and then he threw the lit cigarette in the pile of cut cardboard boxes. They began to smoulder and burn almost instantly.

He exited the shed with Popescu, locking Sabina in the gloom.

As the fire took hold, Sabina wondered if she would die in the same way her parents and little Gracie had died. She remembered a phrase she heard somewhere – in my end is my beginning – and hoped that would be true of her. *I could be like the phoenix of the tales, or the X-men, and rise from the ashes.* For a moment, she didn't move, waiting for something to happen. *In fairy tales someone always come to rescue the princess,* Sabina thought, *but I'm no princess and no one is coming.* She started to twist her wrists, trying to get free from the cuffs.

She was coughing and her eyes were tearing up but still she fought to get free. She thought of every trick in her father's repertoire, trying to find one that could save her. Moments from her circus life flashed past her eyes, a merry-go-round of memories. In one of them, Ringmaster Romero sat on a stool reading a book. Sabina could see the cover of the paperback, and the title that read *As I lay dying*. She had never asked him how it ended.

"Jesus, Bobby! Stop waving that thing around," Nell said, grinding his car into third gear.

She looked both ways before making a right turn, her concentration spilt between the agitated man armed with a brutal looking sap beside her, and remembering which side of the road she needed to end up on.

"You ever driven before?" Mungo asked. He had refused to put a seat belt on, and every time Nell checked the rear view mirror, he was fidgeting from one window to the other.

"On this side of the road? No." The car coughed and lurched as she tried to force the gear without depressing the clutch. "Not a stick, either."

Bobby laughed at that and made a crude gesture for Mungo's benefit. The clown let out a sharp bark from the backseat. Nell glanced back and saw he was actually laughing.

Nell forced herself to take a deep breath. She was starting to wish she could afford to leave them on the side of the road. "Do you two idiots actually have a plan, or are we going to rescue Sabina using your razor sharp wit?" Nell held up her phone to check the map. "Shit. I missed the turn."

She threw the wipers on, slammed them off again, then found the turn signal just before throwing Mungo across the backseat with a wide u-turn. "I can't believe this is the crack rescue team Sabina's relying on."

"What could we accomplish if we knew we could not fail?" Mungo asked from where he'd been crushed against the door.

"Did you just quote Eleanor Roosevelt at me?" she asked.

"It was on a box of tea."

"By the smell, it's hard to believe you drink anything besides scrumpy," Bobby said. "It's going to be impossible to get the scent of failure out of the leather, you know."

"Can't be any harder than the blood you usually have to scrub out," Mungo said.

Bobby tensed, twisting in his seat to glare at the smaller man.

"By all means," Nell said, "antagonise the man with the weapons."

"He started it."

"And I'll finish it too," Bobby replied, casually stuffing the sap in his jacket pocket and drawing a 9mm pistol.

"Bobby." Nell reached out, her hand hovering just above his arm. "Put it down," she said. "With our luck, you'll kill the clown."

"How do you make a dead clown float?" Bobby asked.

"Add some coke and two scoops of ice cream?" Mungo replied.

"I was going to say 'take your foot off his head', but your thing works too."

"Shut up the pair of you," Nell said, "unless you want to die in this car."

"The clown needs to learn respect," Bobby replied, though the gun was back in his lap.

Mungo sighed.

"Nothing kills the spirit of a new day like charging into battle with a psychotic gangster at your back."

"Unless the clown has untapped experience in search and rescue or neutralizing threats using deadly force," Nell said grimly, "perhaps he should stop treating the psychotic gangster like a bear to be poked."

"Or a lion to be tamed," Bobby cracked his neck. "Which one's more likely to bite someone's face off?"

Nell clenched the steering wheel. "Don't want to know."

"Who was he again?" Mungo was back at Bobby's shoulder, their squabble apparently forgotten. "The man whose face you ate."

"Man that owns this meat packing plant, or at least he's the money behind it."

"I once sawed a woman in half," Mungo bragged.

"Oh?" Bobby glanced at him. "Where'd you hide the pieces?"

Mungo chuckled.

"That's a good one. I'll have to remember that."

Bobby just stared at him blankly. The clown eased back in his seat.

"How much further is it?"

"A couple of miles," Nell said, checking her phone again.

"How many cops does it take to throw a man down the stairs?" Mungo said to fill the silence.

Bobby snorted. "None. He fell."

"How many cop jokes are there?"

"Mungo!" Nell snapped.

The clown answered himself. "Just two. The rest are true."

"Could you just look at those notes Shaun left again?" Nell asked. "All we have to go on right now is your word that you saw Sabina and Popescu get into a car."

"The man with the tattoo was forcing them in."

"Sabina knows Mihai," Nell argued. "Maybe she wanted to go."

She didn't really believe it though. Sabina would have called by now.

"What about the gun?" Mungo said, squinting at Shaun's cramped scribbles.

"Sabina told me Pop used to be on the police force. Before he was in the circus."

"Pull in here." Bobby grabbed at the wheel and spun them hard to the left.

Nell dropped her phone and shoved his arm away. "What the hell!"

"We need to take the back road in."

"Then fucking tell me that!" She swatted him away angrily when he reached out again.

"Relax," Bobby said. His breathing was shallow again, but he still radiated an eerie calm.

"I have two friends," she said softly. "And one of them is missing. When we get her back, I'll relax."

"If," Bobby corrected her. "If we get her back."

Nell slammed her foot onto the brake. Holman's meat packing plant was visible up ahead. It was surrounded on three sides by a fence topped with barbed wire. On the fourth, it backed up to a forest.

"What are you doing?" Mungo demanded. He looked down at the oversized shoes he still wore. "We can't climb the fence here."

She stared at him, then at the man beside her. "Before we go any further, I just want you to understand," she said in a measured tone, "that 'if' is not an option here."

"She might already be dead," Bobby said.

"She's not," Mungo replied, patting the briefcase on his lap nervously.

Bobby laughed coldly. "Men like this, they don't take hostages. They wrap up loose ends. Luckily for you, Dalca likes games. If this Mihai is his man, we may still have time to save the bitch."

Nell stared at the 9mm. For months after his death, she'd been haunted by how her husband must have looked at the end, a pistol pressed to his temple. To think of Sabina the same way, tied up and tortured – it was unbearable.

"If we aren't in time?"

"We burn it to the ground," Bobby said. He looked at Mungo for confirmation, and the clown nodded hesitantly. Nell just brushed her hand across her eyes and started the car again.

When they reached the factory entrance, the gate stood open. Nell pulled in past the empty gatehouse and parked in the shadow of the plant.

"What now?" she asked. "We still have no plan to speak off, and this place is huge. She could be anywhere."

Mungo opened the car door and grabbed his briefcase. He stared up at the blank windows. Holman & Sons wasn't just one factory building but a densely packed complex of warehouses, steel sheds and admin buildings.

"Not many people working on a Sunday," he said.

"No shit," Bobby said.

"Maybe we should split up," Mungo suggested.

"Good luck on your own," Bobby replied. Mungo held his coat open. He'd shoved two of Sabina's daggers into his belt. Bobby rolled his eyes and turned to Nell. "What've you got?" She pulled her knife out. He stared at it, then up at her. "Are you kidding me?"

She shrugged and slipped on her backpack of medical equipment.

"I know how to use it," she said.

Bobby rubbed the sweat off his head.

"You two know these men. They're going to have guns!"

"I don't know how to shoot," Mungo said.

"I do." Nell told him. "If I have to." She pocketed her blade and turned to the clown. "We'll circle the building. You go that way. Bobby and I will go this."

"You get the armed back up?" said Mungo, with a sideways jerk of his head towards Bobby.

"You want him?" said Nell.

"Hell, no," said Mungo. "What if we don't see signs of Sabina?"

"Come back to the car," Nell said. Mungo clutched his bag nervously, and she reached out and patted his arm. "Be careful."

His mouth twitched. "I thought you might tell me not to be a hero."

"Isn't that why you're here?" Nell asked.

Mungo threw back his shoulders. "To tilting at windmills," he saluted grimly, raising his hand in farewell.

Vassil came at once. As Anastasia emerged from the kitchen holding two small espresso cups, she found Vassil standing over her drawing, scrutinising it with care.

"This is a strange picture, Ana," said Vassil.

"It helps me to think," said Anastasia. "That's why I need to talk to you. Help me to work out what is going on."

"Why do you think I know anything?" said Vassil.

"For a start," said Anastasia, "you told me you were - what was the word you used? - *instructed* to meet me away from my studio on the day of the fire. Who instructed you?"

"My English is not so good," said Vassil. "Maybe 'instructed' was a poor choice of word."

"Your English is better than mine," said Anastasia, "So answer the question."

"I don't know where the instruction came from," said Vassil. He sipped his coffee. "I would tell you if I did. You have to understand how things work here."

"Enlighten me," said Anastasia.

"I have been here since January," said Vassil. "Almost everyone at Holman's either came in January, or they got legal employment this year. It is not an accident that we are nearly all from EU accession countries."

231

"Cut to the point," said Anastasia. "Someone told you to get me away from my studio when the fire started."

"You think I sat in my house in Stara Zagora and thought, OK, I'll go to Skegness and try to get a job?" said Vassil. "I'd never heard of Lincolnshire. No. It's a matter of middle men, moving people, moving goods, taking a skim off the top here, or a cut from the bottom there. The meat we pack, the people doing the packing, we were all traded in some way. If we want to keep our jobs we accept that."

"Sorry, Vassil," said Anastasia, "but that's a load of shit. You can go anywhere in the EU, work anywhere. You speak perfect English, you have a science degree. So tell me - what's your real role, and why did someone want me out of my studio on the day it was torched?"

"It's true, I'm not just a meat packer," said Vassil. "I'm numerate and I speak many languages. I assist with administration at the factory. They need me for that, because the factory is more than it seems. It fits into a more complex set of business interests. Some of these are probably not legal."

"You're telling me Holman's is a criminal enterprise," said Anastasia.

"No," said Vassil, "it is what it is. But it is also more than that. When I handle invoices I can see it. Meat comes in as one thing, it goes out as another. It might come in as Romanian, and go out to Holland as British. And those invoices, they often relate to bigger sums of money than the amount of meat going in or out would justify."

"What does that mean?" said Anastasia.

"We might send out fifty pallets of meat, but get paid for eighty," said Vassil. "Once the money's in the company bank account, it's clean, and the invoices match the balance sheet."

"Money laundering," said Anastasia. "So where does the money come from?"

"I don't know. Sometimes it's in very small denomination bills, like a lot of loose change," said Vassil.

"And what's your cut?" said Anastasia.

"I get to sit in an office instead of pulling out chicken viscera," said Vassil. "I'm not supposed to notice this stuff. But I see it, and I

232

see the men who turn up at the factory. They are the same people who recruited us from home, the same people who own our lodgings, they are people we dare not cross."

"So you know who instructed you," said Anastasia.

"I know who gave me the message, the suggestion," said Vassil. "But they'll be a middle man, to a middle man, to a middle man. Where the suggestion started, I cannot say."

"Then take me back to the meat factory," said Anastasia. "I want to meet those people."

"I cannot do that," said Vassil.

"I'm instructing you now," said Anastasia.

"It is a very bad idea, Ana," said Vassil. "You do not know these people."

"They attacked me, Vassil," said Anastasia, "and they killed a child. It feels bloody personal. And you're coming with me."

CHAPTER NINE

As Mungo headed counter-clockwise round the building, Nell followed the limping gangster clockwise through the light woodland that bordered the factory.

"That clown's a dead man," Bobby said.

"At least he's trying."

"He's got no business being here, and you know it. Best we can hope for is he provides a diversion. Might buy your friend some time."

Nell shook her head. "I just don't understand how she got caught up in this."

"Could say the same about you," Bobby said. "No good reason for you to be up to your neck in this shit. And yet here you are, nursemaid to a murdering son of a bitch."

"Sabina's my friend."

"Most people would've called the police by now."

"What makes you think I didn't?"

"I know Castell and Young. If you'd called them, they'd be here already, white fucking horse and all."

He stumbled, and Nell reached out to catch him. His face was chalky, but he pushed her away.

"You sent Lewis to me, remember?" she said. "You got me into this mess."

"I didn't send him. But, yeah, whatever, all the more reason to let me die."

He held up a hand, and they paused at the corner of the building. In front of them, the car park stretched toward the trees.

There was movement at the edge of the woods.

"Did you see that?" said Nell.

Bobby nodded.

"Two people. Men."

"One of them was Mr Popescu," she said.

She strained to get a better look. Whoever was with the old man was small – maybe small enough to be Sabina. Nell couldn't tell from this distance, not with the soft shadows of the trees obscuring her sight.

Mungo charged round the side of the meat factory.

"Hold on Sabina," he panted. "I'm coming."

He turned the corner and froze. There was a storage shed annexed onto the side of the factory and it was engulfed in flames.

Mungo's chest tightened immediately. *I should have seen this coming.* Fire seemed to cut in and out of his life like a predator that had developed a taste for his misery. The circus, his bench, poor little Gracie – it was only fitting that the flames returned for an encore as Mungo prepared for his final bow.

The flames were taunting him, bombarding him with waves of heat. He heard voices amidst the roaring flames. His father, Punch, Mihai.

You ungrateful little shit.

She had it coming.

Clovn!

Mungo found himself taking a step back.

No! He would retreat no further. Sabina was in there and needed help. He tilted at the flames, clutched his briefcase like a shield and charged into the fire.

"Sabina, hold on!"

Mungo burst through the smouldering door of the storage shed and was met with a thundercloud of thick black smog. It filled his lungs within seconds. Mungo whooped and spluttered trying to expel the relentless fumes as he staggered blindly into the shed.

"Sabina? Where are you?" he tried to shout but the smoke reduced his voice to a hoarse whisper.

And then he saw it. There was a chair placed in the middle of the room. An *empty* chair. A pair of unlocked handcuffs had been discarded underneath.

That's my girl, smiled Mungo.

It appeared Sabina could take care of herself after all. She didn't need a knight in shining armour and she certainly didn't need Mungo. He was right all along – nobody needed a sad old clown.

A loud crash signalled the collapse of the storage shed entrance through which Mungo had entered. Immediately, the flames rose up even higher, towering above him like a hungry leviathan. He realised he would not be leaving the shed. The flames would claim him. However, Mungo felt no despair at the thought – he only felt relief that Sabina was okay.

It was finally time for Mungo to rest. He took a seat in the chair that had previously contained the girl he was trying to save. It wasn't as comfy as his old bench but it would do.

He closed his eyes.

Bobby coughed, wiping blood from the corner of his mouth. "So how come you didn't let me die?"

"Later!" Nell hissed, trying to keep track of two figure crossing in into the woods.

"I might be dead later."

"Then it won't matter, will it?"

Bobby shook his head. "No way to talk to a dying man."

"Then don't die."

"So, if I live through this, you'll answer my question?" he asked.

"Why do you even care?"

"Information is everything in my business."

"Fine." Nell pulled her knife out of her pocket and flipped the blade out as they made their way slowly forward to intercept. "If we survive, I will."

"Not if. When," piped up Marcus suddenly.

Bobby startled at the voice, missed a step, and very nearly pitched face first into the ground. He reached a break in the trees and pushed through them before answering.

"I thought I left you behind," he said irritably.

"Me?" said Nell, confused.

"Not the important bit," Marcus replied.

"I twisted my knee, damnit. It's already starting to swell."

"Stop your whinging and take a look at the cars parked in front of the building. Any strike you as familiar?"

"What cars?"

"Look, brother."

Bobby went to the very edge of the trees and squinted in the direction of the factory. Vehicles clustered around a loading bay at the rear of the factory.

"Not especially likely that there'd be two of those knocking around Skegness, is it?" Bobby asked needlessly.

"Two of what?" said Nell.

"It's the spinning chrome wheels that give it away," Marcus replied.

Bobby snorted a laugh. It was Dalca's black Mercedes SUV.

"I'm strangely unsurprised to find him here, Marcus."

"Marcus?" said Nell.

Bobby looked at Nell as though seeing her for the first time.

"Right, my medical friend, this is where we part ways," he announced to Nell.

"What?"

Bobby gestured with his pistol.

"Your Romanian went that way into the woods. Use cover as it presents itself. Go find your friend."

"What the hell?" she said. "You came to help me!"

"Go take care of your business," said Bobby. "It's nothing to do with me. I have my own matters to attend to."

"Since when?"

He almost missed the look of betrayal that flashed across her face, it was so brief. With a sharp nod to Nell, he turned his back on her.

"Jerk," she muttered and trotted off into the woods.

Let them sort their own fucking problems, thought Bobby. *I've plenty of my own.*

"That's my boy," said Marcus. "About time you got your priorities square."

"So...plan?"

"Why bother? You wouldn't stick to one," Marcus said. "Dalca's in there somewhere. If you can refrain from picking a fight with the mouth breathers between us and him, you have a chance of getting the jump on him."

"If I'd known you were this useful in a noncorporeal state, I'd have taken an axe to you long ago, brother," Bobby said.

"That's not funny, Bobby," Marcus replied hotly and perhaps a little nervously. "Say you're just fucking around. I mean it. Say you're just joking, Bobby."

But Bobby stayed silent. He'd lied enough for one day.

"Hello Mungo."

Mungo opened his eyes and found Gracie standing in front of him.

"Gracie?" said Mungo, dazed and confused. "What are you doing here?"

"I died," she said.

"I know. I was very sorry to hear that. Does it hurt?"

The little girl shrugged.

"Am I dead?" he asked.

"Not yet. Sabina still needs your help."

A scream cut through the membrane of consciousness, and through their conversation, like a knife.

"Sabina! Where is she?"

"In the meat factory," said Gracie. "There is a door back there which joins the factory to this storage shed."

"There is?"

"Yes. You spotted it when you first walked in."

"Very well. I must go to her."

Gracie nodded. "Good luck, Mungo. Break a leg."

"We don't say that in the circus."

"Well then, knock 'em dead."

"That's boxing."

"God speed?"

"I think that's astronauts."

Gracie crossed her arms. "So what do you say in the circus?"

Mungo smiled, remembering. "Don't forget your nose."

"Well, you better not forget it then." Mungo watched in amazement as the little girl opened her fist to reveal his red clown nose. She leant forward and placed it on his face.

"How do I look?" Mungo asked.

"Like Mungo Joey."

"That's my name."

"Now," said Gracie, swinging her hand towards Mungo's face. "WAKE UP!"

SM –

239

– ACK!

Mungo jerked awake. Gracie was gone. The heat, the smog, the deafening flames were all back and more intense than ever. Mungo wasted no time. He ran through the billowing smog, searching for the connecting door. The inferno roared, closing in from all sides.

"Sabina! I'm coming!"

Mungo ran into the door and almost knocked himself out. He grabbed the metal handle, which burnt his hand in spite of his white gloves, and pulled with all his might.

Locked!

No! Wait, hold on... Mungo pushed the door instead. It swung open. *Victory!*

Mungo dived through and slammed the heavy metal door behind him. There was instant silence, coolness, brightness. Mungo slid to his knees, sucking in clean air and savouring his new environment. He had swapped the dark, burning pyre of the storage shed for the clinical, chrome sanctuary of the factory.

But then he heard Sabina scream again.

"So much for sanctuary," he muttered.

Mungo followed the sounds of Sabina's cries and found her in the middle of the factory floor, down among the work benches, processing units and spike-filled grinding vats. Sabina was cowering under the blows of a wooden broomstick swung by an unsavoury looking thug. Mungo was reminded of his least favourite pier attraction.

"I told you to stay down," growled the thug, before drawing on the cigarette in the corner of his mouth. His arm was bleeding. Evidently, Sabina had fought back. "You will stay here until the boss arrives. Dalca will want to talk to you. He likes to deal with trespassers personally."

Mungo slowly began to sneak towards Sabina's attacker but a firm hand grabbed his shoulder and spun him around. Mungo was faced with a second thug who grinned devilishly and casually held a handgun in his other hand.

"Cornel," the second thug called to the man who had been beating Sabina. "Looks like we have another trespasser."

"Bring him over here, Skender," replied the first thug. "I have plenty of stick for the both of them."

Mungo panicked and squeezed the flower on his chequered waistcoat. The flower squirted Skender in the chest. The thug looked down at his damp shirt and scowled. He was not impressed and retaliated by smacking Mungo in the face with the butt of his handgun. Mungo crumpled.

Skender patted Mungo down for weapons and found the throwing knives in the clown's belt which Mungo had borrowed from Sabina's flat.

I forgot I had those, thought Mungo miserably, as Skender tossed them aside. The thug then dragged Mungo across the factory floor and dumped him on top of Sabina, where Cornel could watch them both.

Skender looked like he was about to say something then stopped and sniffed.

"Is that smoke I can smell?" He glared at Mungo. "Did you start a fire in there?"

"The boss is not going to be happy," said Cornell.

"Then we'll toss them back into their fire and they can die sobbing like that little girl," said Skender.

"How do you know about that?" asked Mungo.

"Who do you think started the fucking fire?" Skender said with a smirk.

"You're a fucking bastard, Skender," Cornel chuckled.

Mungo met Sabina's gaze, seeing a hardness and a desire for vengeance that matched his own. An impromptu plan appeared in his mind.

"Please," said Mungo. "There is money in my briefcase. Take it and let us go."

Skender and Cornel exchanged a glance. Cornel shrugged.

"Take a look," he told Skender.

Skender strolled back over to the briefcase where Mungo had dropped it.

"Clown, if you are lying," said Skender, "we will put your hands in the meat grinder."

Mungo watched expectantly as Skender unclasped the suitcase.

"What the hell is this?" shouted Skender, pulling out the plastic trout. "Clown, I warned you –"

But then Sancho sprang into action. Sabina's Ursini's viper had spent the day being bumped around in Mungo's suitcase and was currently at the end of its patience. Upon seeing the light of day, Sancho was ready to unleash all of its grumpiness on whichever target was in closest proximity, which in this case was the unfortunate Skender. Sancho shot out of the briefcase like a coiled spring and sank its fangs into Skender's neck.

Skender howled and fell backwards, distracting Cornel for just enough time for Mungo to sweep his legs out from under him and jump on top of him. But Cornel was strong and rolled on top of Mungo, his hands around Mungo's neck and ash from his cigarette falling down into Mungo's face. Mungo felt himself choking but suddenly – *CLACK!* – Cornel's grip loosened. Sabina had whacked Cornel with his own stick and successfully knocked him out.

Judy knocks out Punch, noted Mungo. *A much more satisfying end to the show.*

"Are you –?" began Sabina but suddenly the wooden stick was shot out of her hands.

Mungo and Sabina turned to see Skender staggering towards them. He moaned, disorientated, the pistol wavering in his hand. He had thrown off Sancho the snake but the venom was now coursing through his veins. Mungo supposed it was a miracle that he was still conscious, let alone standing, but bloody-mindedness and rage were driving him forward step by tortured step.

"You!"

Skender tried shooting again but he could barely lift his arm. The bullet missed Mungo by two metres. *Though still a little too close for comfort*, thought Mungo, standing in front of Sabina to keep her safe.

"Kill you trespass," mumbled Skender nonsensically, his throat swollen. "You start fire... Hit Cornel... Snake... Kill you... Plastic fish... Shoot you..." He edged closer and fired the gun again. He missed but his aim was improving. "I make you suffer... You, you, squirted water!"

"That isn't water," said Mungo.

He snatched the cigarette from the unconscious Cornel's mouth and flicked it onto Skender's chest. The embers in the cigarette ignited the clear liquid on Skender's chest. It was the lighter fluid from Sabina's fire-breathing kit. Skender shrieked thickly as his torso burst into flames. He dropped the gun and staggered to one of the big meat-grinder vats. Mungo had no idea why. Perhaps Skender's addled mind thought that it would be full of water. In either case, Skender dived in voluntarily and landed on the sharp-studded wheels. They were not switched on but they were lethal all the same. Skender gave a final squeak of surprise and pain and then fell silent, only his legs poking out of the top of the vat.

"That's the way to do it," said Mungo.

Bobby skirted the factory, rather than head straight towards the cars by the loading bay.

"In through the rear," said Marcus. "Strike from behind. That door, there."

With Marcus navigating, he swept swiftly across the gravel to the indicated door.

Marcus was suddenly a snake's hiss in his ear. "Guards!"

"Where?"

An elbow came crashing down between Bobby's shoulder blades, answering his question and knocking the wind from his lungs.

Bobby went down, rolled, and came up with a fist that slammed Henric's ugly jaw shut, biting the end off the gorilla's cigarette.

The other guard was on Bobby now and flight was no longer an option. Bobby half-recognised the man.

"Muvvafugger!" the man growled as he charged.

"Ah, Emil," said Bobby and brought up the pistol.

The man was too fast and too strong for Bobby and slapped the pistol from his hand before backhanding him with utter savagery. Bobby rolled with the blow, dug deep for the lead-weighted sap in his pocket but did not have time to pull it free. Emil vented his anger with a combination punch that Bobby only partially blocked and, for the first time in memory, Bobby was truly scared

"Circle to the left, Baron," Marcus instructed. "He wants to throw a left to your head. Circle hard. If he catches you with a left hook he'll kill you, Bobby. He wants to throw a left so much he's going to do it without an opening. Circle hard and cool him with the sap."

Bobby was mildly surprised he actually had the sap in his hand. That Marcus thought he was in any shape to use it was even more surprising. He could taste blood boiling up from his stomach and the edges of his vision were turning dark red. He was going to die.

"Circle left. Hard!" Marcus screamed again.

With a sudden, intense hatred for Marcus and his fucking screaming, Bobby toppled to the left, twisting his body as he fell. He felt the displaced air of a killing haymaker rush over him and lashed out blindly with the sap, connecting with something that caused a man to howl like an animal.

"Fugg!"

"You bust his ribs, Baron," Marcus said with something like awe. "I thought you were dead and you broke his ribs."

"I am dead," Bobby said.

Henric had now recovered and he pummelled Bobby from behind with a flurry of devastating body shots.

There was the unmistakeable sound of a pistol hammer being cocked. Henric backed up and gave Bobby a knowing grin. Emil, almost bent over, had his .38 revolver aimed at Bobby's face.

"I am dead," Bobby repeated.

"Nod yed," Emil mumbled.

"Not yet," agreed Henric, taking Bobby's sap from his hand.

The cab driver negotiated the quiet Lincolnshire roads like a man pursued by bandits. He hurtled across roundabouts, failed to slow at junctions, and cut corners in a squeal of brakes.

"Are you licensed to drive this?" said Anastasia, involuntarily leaning into a bend. The man jabbed a finger towards the laminated card mounted above the rear view mirror. Anastasia saw that it had been issued by the correct authorities, and whilst she accepted that the man had every right to be called Mohammed Shafique, it was difficult to see a clear resemblance between the lean, dark haired man in the photograph, and the taciturn, pink fleshed, balding Scot at the wheel.

Vassil, in the front passenger seat, said not a word on the journey. His pale face and rigid demeanour may have been a response to 'Shafique's' driving, but Anastasia suspected that it was not. Nor did she care. She was on a mission.

The cab pulled into the driveway of Holman's and Sons.

"There is smoke," said Vassil pointing at the dark grey wisps in the sky behind the factory.

"Stubble burning?" suggested Shafique.

"Is that allowed anymore?" said Anastasia.

The cabbie cruised round to the rear of the factory. Men in boiler suits were loading pallets into a van. A monstrously over-sized black SUV was parked up by it.

"Here's your fare," said Anastasia, holding up a small clutch of notes to their driver. "If you wait for us - wait for up to an hour - here's your tip." With this, she held up another, larger bunch of notes. He reached out for it, but Anastasia pulled away. "Wait for us."

"Aye," said the cabbie, "Lay-by down the road. One hour. I'll need a deposit. To cover a no-show."

"Fair enough," said Anastasia. "But I've got your name and number."

"One hour. From now."

Anastasia got out of the cab. Vassil, beside her, was alert and tense.

"Busy for a Sunday," said Anastasia.

"Stock is moved around the clock according to demand," said Vassil. "I don't know really. I don't work Sundays."

"Where do you suggest we start?" said Anastasia.

"By getting back in the taxi and leaving this place," said Vassil.

"You know why I'm here," said Anastasia. "I'm going nowhere until we get some answers."

"There are no answers here, Ana," said Vassil. "Only questions."

"I owe Gracie Greenwood and her parents," said Anastasia. "The police don't have a clue."

"And what evidence can you get?" said Vassil. "These guys come and go. If they think they're in trouble here, they move on."

"So I'm supposed to shrug my shoulders, go back to London?" said Anastasia.

"Yes," said Vassil. "You should do that."

"You know, you sound just like my agent," said Anastasia. "He said exactly the same thing. That's why he's a money man, and I'm an artist."

The men in boiler suits began to winch down the hatch on the loading bay.

"Those men by the big Mercedes. No, don't let them see you. They are dangerous."

"They must be who I'm looking for, then," said Anastasia, turning to face the men. "Perhaps you'd like to do the introductions?"

"I don't like this," said Vassil. "They shouldn't be here today."

None of the men wore blood spattered white overalls, nor the boiler suits sported by the loading crew. One man, casually dressed, went back into the factory. The other approached the workers' entrance where Anastasia and Vassil stood. He wore a suit and an air of superiority. He had a scar across his face, livid and recent.

"De ce ai adus-o aici, Vassil?" said the scar man.

"Dalca, ea m-a făcut s-o fac'," said Vassil.

"Madame," the scar man turned to Anastasia, "we are closed. Next time you must have an appointment. This is a food factory. There are rules of hygiene."

"Which don't apply to you," said Anastasia.

Scar man narrowed his eyes.

"Mr Dalca," said Vassil, "May I introduce you to Miss Anastasia Boty. She is an artist."

Dalca the scar man bowed slightly, and reached for Anastasia's hand. His grip was merciless. He could break an artist's fingers.

"Enchanté," he said. "As you are here, please come through to the office."

"We can talk here," said Anastasia. "Vassil, is this the man I need to talk with?"

"You do not need to talk with anyone, Ana," said Vassil. "Please, you should go now."

"Mr Dalca," said Anastasia, "Are you the man who instructed Vassil to get me out of the way on the day my studio was burned down?"

"Yes. I knew I'd seen you before," said Dalca. "The artist who let a little girl burn to death in Skegness. You were on television."

"Answer my question," said Anastasia.

"You are the one who needs to answer questions," said Dalca. "That's what the police say."

"Dalca didn't tell me to do it, Ana" said Vassil. "It's like I told you before. People didn't trust you, coming to the factory, asking to look around, everyone thought you were from the Border Agency."

"Madame, this is a business. We trade in meat. We have no concern with artists, or pyromaniacs, for that matter. You are a sick woman, I think."

"You can't say anything I haven't read in the papers already," said Anastasia. "The fact is, this factory is a cover for criminal activity, and someone here wanted to scare me off."

Then Anastasia saw the two men coming round the building. One, pumped up, a stub of cigarette seemingly welded to his lips, was dressed like a pimp from a cheap TV movie. The other, dressed in dark jeans and a hooded top, looked to be in some pain. Between them, they supported the crumpled figure of a third man. Was he alive or were they carrying yet another corpse?

"What do you want us to do with him?" shouted one of the men. "It's the Black Baron."

"Fucking scum!" said Dalca, almost amused. "Where did you find him?" He shook his head. "Put him in the car."

"Your car?" said the pimp.

"There is sheeting down."

Dalca turned back to Anastasia.

"Can't you see," this time addressing his words directly to Anastasia, "we have work to do here?"

The hoodie-wearing man lifted the boot of the black Mercedes and the two of them tossed the figure they had been carrying, living or dead, into the boot of a big black vehicle.

The two men sauntered back over. A pistol hung casually in the hooded one's hand. The pimp one – he had thrown himself into the role so thoroughly, he was practically kitsch - dropped his cigarette and executed an impressive display of projectile expectoration. The phlegm bomb hit the tarmac close to Anastasia's booted foot. She did not flinch.

"Henric is a simple man," said Dalca. "But he is loyal and obedient. Isn't he, Vassil?"

"I don't know him," said Vassil. "This has been a mistake."

Dalca breathed deeply and looked at Anastasia.

"You don't like what the newspapers are writing about you," he said, "but you believe what they write about us. That we are all gypsies and criminals."

"Don't twist my words," said Anastasia. "Holman's is a racket, whatever the nationality of the people involved. I want to know how I got caught up in all this, and above all I want to find whoever was responsible for murdering that child."

Henric gave a look; cocky, insolent. Anastasia knew what it signified.

"So you did it," said Anastasia, staring at him.

As though in response, as though the guilt might also spread to him by mere proximity, Emil gave a minimalist shake of the head.

"Be very careful what you say, Madame," said Dalca. "If you upset them, who knows what they will do."

"We know what they've done," said Anastasia. "But who gave the order? Was that you?"

Henric, his face a mask of boredom, pulled a packet of cigarettes from his pocket, followed by a knife. He held them loosely in his hands, as though balancing up which of the items he was to use.

"Nu-i face rău, Dalca!" said Vassil.

Dalca turned slightly to face his colleagues, giving a barely perceptible nod of the head. Henric responded at once. Slowly he moved towards Vassil, bullet-shaped head dipped like a snorting bull. Perspiration stains were visible on the Beer Venom T shirt Vassil was wearing under the denim jacket. He took a step back. Henric struck out with one rapid move. He grabbed hold of Vassil's long hair at the nape of his neck, locking his victim helplessly. He raised his other hand, the one with the knife, and drew the blade gently along Vassil's warm throat until the tip was just below the scientist's chin.

"Let him go now," said Anastasia. "He's done nothing. I made him bring me here. He didn't want to."

"If he was a man," said Dalca, "he'd have kept you away from here, and if he wasn't a fool he'd have kept his mouth shut."

"I saw frightened people when I came here before," said Anastasia. "I didn't need Vassil to tell me this place was dodgy. Just now, what were you all doing? Legitimate goods going out in a van. But what were you were loading into the van? I bet that didn't have an export license."

"What kind of stupid bitch are you?" said Dalca. "You know nothing."

"I know plenty," said Anastasia, "But I need to know the truth. About Gracie Greenwood's death."

Dalca took a few steps towards Anastasia, and stood, aggressively close. His face, with its scars, its open pores, the veined eyes, the bulbous nose, the cauliflower ears, struck Anastasia as fascinatingly singular. In other circumstances she'd have sketched him on the spot.

Dalca opened his spittle flecked mouth. His teeth were surprisingly good, despite the foul breath. He spoke. "You would not learn your lesson when you had the chance," said Dalca.

As he said this, the phone in Anastasia's hand began to ring.

Mungo and Sabina exited the factory by a side-door and collapsed onto the ground. The storage shed still burned behind the factory but with waning ferocity, as if its bloodlust had faded now that its prey had escaped.

Sabina was in bad shape. She was bloodied and bruised and those were just the visible injuries. Mungo himself was no better. His nose – his real nose – had been broken by the butt of Skender's handgun and his lungs were clogged with smoke, like an overstuffed vacuum bag.

"I didn't think you would come," said Sabina. "Why did you?"

Mungo hacked up more smoke before replying.

"These past twelve years, you have never given up on me. It was time to return the favour."

Sabina squeezed his hand. "I always knew there was a knight in shining armour under that clown suit. I'm sorry you got dragged into this mess."

"No, I should be apologising to you. All this time, I have been trying to put the circus behind me but that was selfish. I should have been there for you long before today."

"I know why you wanted to forget," said Sabina. "We lost our home, our livelihood, our family –"

"Sabina," said Mungo

" – and it hurts to remember all of that. I shouldn't have forced you -"

"Sabina, I started the fire."

She stopped and stared at him. A grave silence fell on both circus survivors, as if the world was holding its breath. Sabina's face appeared to be searching for an expression. Her mouth twisted into a dozen different shapes as she formed and unformed potential responses on her lips. All the while, Mungo was aware that Sabina held Skender's handgun.

Eventually, her shoulders drooped and the world exhaled.

"I know Mungo," she said. "I have always known."

"You did?"

"I saw it all. I was only sixteen at the time so I was too scared to intervene but I heard the things your father said to you. I would have torched the bastard too."

"But why did you never say anything?"

"I saw what your guilt did to you. If you knew that I knew, I feared you might do something rash, like taking a long walk off a short pier."

Mungo remained quiet.

"Besides," continued Sabina, "if you knew that I knew you would never be able to look me in the eye again. You would push me away even more."

"But why would you want to be around me? I cost us everything.""

Sabina wiped a tear from her eye.

"Someone had to be there to keep an eye on you. Who do you think kept your hat overflowing with coins? A drunken layabout clown is not as entertaining as you might think."

"But why? I didn't deserve your grace."

"You watched your father die," said Sabina. "I was not about to do the same."

The silence returned.

Mungo puzzled over that one.

"What do you mean by that?"

"Do you remember my mother, Rózsi?"

"Yes, I remember. Rózsi and I were very close once upon a time."

"More than close, as I hear it."

That was true enough, thought Mungo. They had had a fleeting romance in his early days of the circus.

"It was a long time before she met your father, Thoros the magician," Mungo said. "And besides, our relationship only concerns your mother and me."

"Wrong on all three counts," Sabina said. "It wasn't that long before she met Thoros, in fact there was quite a bit of overlap. Thoros wasn't my father and your relationship with my mother is very much my concern."

"Are you saying what I think you're saying?"

"Yes," Sabina said. "My mother told me on my sixteenth birthday, a few months before the fire. It was why I could never give up on you."

Mungo was speechless, his mouth hanging open like the plastic trout in his briefcase.

Nell slowed as she neared the clearing. She'd been following the sound of Mihai's one-sided conversation for nearly fifteen minutes, and everything she'd heard urged caution. Although she'd never met him, she had no doubt the man she was spying on was the one Sabina and Mungo had described. Unfortunately, it was obvious now from Nell's position in the bushes off the path that Sabina wasn't with him.

She could see Popescu, however; the old man's hands were tied behind his back. Mihai had used the sleeves of Pop's shirt to wrench his arms back. From the way it hung, Nell suspected at least one of his arms was out of its socket.

"What, you senile bastard?" Mihai was saying. "Are you crying? You think you deserve mercy?"

Mihai shoved Popescu to the ground and kicked him in the jaw.

"You know what happens when you cry?" He kicked him again. "Do you? Do you remember?"

Popescu coughed. He spat a tooth out, his chin tucked to his chest.

"Te rog, oprește-te. Please."

"Du-te la naiba!" Mihai grabbed him by the throat and shook him. "No one's coming for you. No one ever comes, do they?"

Popescu shook his head weakly.

"I tried to help."

Mihai laughed. Nell had to dig her nails into the bark of the tree to keep from rushing at the man.

"How? By taking us to the woods, children who hadn't eaten? Who could barely walk? My brother – do you remember him? He was tied just like this." Mihai tugged Popescu's arms and the man groaned. "With his own clothes, they bound him. With a sheet if they thought he deserved it, and all because he was strong. Because the pills didn't make him quiet."

"I didn't know..."

"You knew," Mihai said. "All those children. Ceaușescu's children."

He studied the man in front of him.

"You must have your own. I've done my reading; I know the laws now. The five children required in each family, the police who checked every woman to be sure they bore more than they possibly could feed."

Grabbing his collar, he pulled Popescu to his feet.

"Maybe you sent yours to die too? For all you know, I could be more than a devil sent to punish you – I could be your own son.

Wouldn't that be a twist?" He backhanded Popescu and sent him crashing back into the trees.

"Those children, starved and beaten, ignored, touched. I hope you dream about us every night."

Popescu was so close Nell could almost touch him. He was shaking, the fresh blood swelling out of the cuts across his lips. She froze as Mihai's gaze drifted from his victim to her.

"Who's this now?" he asked, covering the distance to her hiding spot in three long strides.

Nell's hand was already on her knife. As he grabbed for her, she slid through his arms and slashed up, the blade just nicking his skin where his jacket rode up. She darted left. Popescu hadn't moved. She said a silent prayer that Mungo and Bobby were having better luck and turned her concentration to the man in front of her.

"I don't want to hurt you," she said.

Nell kept the knife grasped loosely in her right hand, but held the empty one up, palm open.

Mihai stopped beside Popescu, nudging him with his foot. Popescu groaned.

"You're interrupting," said Mihai.

"He doesn't deserve this," said Nell.

"What do you know? Have you ever watched a girl die, tied to the rails of her crib?" Mihai asked. "Did you know a baby will stop crying if she's left alone long enough? That a whole room full of children who are dying of starvation will just sit silently and wait for death?"

He took a step toward her, but she held her ground, her hand tightening reflexively around her little blade.

"Where I grew up, that was the death we prayed for."

His hands were shaking, but his gaze was steady and surprisingly clear.

"Better that than to be bound and left alone for hours, a blanket thrown over you as a punishment for daring to ask for water."

He glanced at Popescu.

"I used to unwrap my brother from those sheets. Do you know," he looked back at her. "His skin came away with the cloth. His body was just an open wound, and you think this man, this măgar who took us on a death march in the dead of winter, he doesn't deserve to know how that felt?"

"No," Nell said. "I don't."

Mihai stared at her.

"You think you're tough enough to stop me? That knife will only kill me if you dig deep."

"I'm not here to kill you."

"No?" He seemed surprised. "I would have thought you'd want revenge."

"Revenge?" said Nell.

Mihai shrugged.

"Maybe you weren't the friend Sabina thought you were."

Nell felt her throat close. Without the tattoo and the rough stubble on his chin, she might have mistaken Mihai for a narrow-shouldered teenager if she'd passed him on the street. His expression, though, was one of a man who lived only to inflict the pain he'd been carrying all his life on others.

He pulled out his pistol. She sprinted forward and rammed her shoulder into him, forcing his shot wide. Mihai brought the butt of the gun around and slammed it in her face, and she fell back, stumbling over Popescu. The second shot rang in her ears

As they heard the gunshot fired from the woods, Mungo and Sabina ducked out of instinct. Immediately, they looked at each other and reached the same conclusion.

"Popescu!"

Sabina dragged Mungo to his feet.

"We've got to help him."

"Very well, my girl," he said. "Let's put the circus troupe back together."

Anastasia saw the name on the screen of her mobile.

"Sebastian! You idiot."

"Ana, darling," Anastasia's agent's voice on speakerphone addressed the assembly in the meat factory yard. Dalca stepped back a fraction. Emil looked up. Henric eased his grip a little on Vassil's hair.

"Not a good time, Seb," said Anastasia.

"Au contraire," said Sebastian. "This is an excellent time."

"Believe me," said Anastasia, "it's not. I'm in a meat factory with a bunch of crooks, and one of them's got a knife to my friend's throat."

"Very droll, Ana, always the artist's surreal sense of humour," said Sebastian. "Guess who I've got with me? And he's absolutely dying to talk to you."

"This is no bloody joke," said Anastasia.

"No, it isn't, darling," said Sebastian. "It's absolutely marvellous. Dinner at The Ivy, next Thursday. We're celebrating."

"Give me the phone!" said Dalca. Emil reached out and snatched the phone from Anastasia's hand.

"Cine esti tu?" These words were issued in a commanding manner from Anastasia's telephone in Emil's hands.

"What the hell?" said Anastasia.

The voice, most certainly not that of Sebastian, continued to bark commands at Dalca.

"Who are you, Russian?" said Dalca.

"My name is Viktor Kaletsky," said the voice.

"That means nothing to me," said Dalca. "But I have the woman, the artist. What is she worth to you?"

"You still haven't answered my questions," said Kaletsky. "Your protectors. Who are they?"

"Why should I tell you anything?" said Dalca.

"Perhaps you'd prefer to speak to my friend in Bucharest?" said Kaletsky. "Tristan Tzara."

"Tzara?" said Dalca. "No."

Dalca had frozen at the mention of Tristan Tzara, Emil and Henric looked at one another in bewilderment.

"Miss Boty," came the Russian voice from the telephone, "Tell me, are you in difficulty? We know where you are. We can be with you very quickly."

"Mr Kaletsky," said Anastasia, "I have no idea what is happening here, but Dalca and his men are armed and reckless. They killed a child. I have no doubt that they would kill anyone without a second thought."

"Tzara," said Dalca once more.

"Tristan Tzara," said Kaletsky, "is a brother to me. More to the point, he is not foolish, like you. I have instructed one of my people to call him immediately. Would you like to speak to Tzara?"

"No," said Dalca, his voice stronger. "Pune jos cuțitul. Stai în spate!"

Emil lowered the knife slowly, and released his grip on Vassil's hair.

"At last your brain is working," said Kaletsky. "Now, Miss Boty. Why are you in such a place? What do you want with these men?"

"Robert said you bought my triptych," said Anastasia, "the girl, the angel on the central panel..."

"I have heard the news," said Kaletsky. "It is sacrilege. To desecrate beauty, art. You believe this Dalca killed the child? Why would he do that?"

"That's what I'm trying to find out. Why he gave the instruction to destroy my work," said Anastasia. "There must be justice for Gracie Greenwood. And I want these men to leave me alone."

Dalca gestured to his men to move away from Anastasia and Vassil. They did so with surly insolence, shuffling backwards. They gazed at their weapons as if willing the objects to countermand the instructions of their boss. Emil begrudgingly gave Anastasia's phone back to her.

"Dalca." Kaletsky's voice was low and steady, its menace icy. "Why did you kill the child?"

"I did not kill her, Mr Kaletsky," said Dalca. "The child was just unlucky. We needed to frighten the woman, the artist. She was asking too many questions. "

"And you did not ask enough questions," Kaletsky said. "You are in England. The European Union. Tzara's money must now be clean, not rinsed with blood, as in the old days."

"This has nothing to do with Tzara," said Dalca, "Nothing. It was a question of business. She was in the way."

"Miss Boty, or the child?" said Kaletsky. "It does not matter. Miss Boty wants justice. I am her patron. I will see that she gets it."

"She wants justice, does she?"

In one swift move Dalca reached out a hand, seized Emil's pistol, and put the gun to Henric's head. Henric's execution was instant. Vassil staggered from the sound and the sudden ending of a man's life.

"Emil," said Dalca, "you know what to do."

"Sgender?" the man lisped.

"Skender, of course."

With that he passed the gun back to Emil, and gestured towards the factory with an upward flick of his chin. Emil headed to the nearest door.

"The two men who killed the girl have paid," said Dalca. "Justice."

Anastasia took a step towards Dalca, and the lifeless body of his henchman. "How dare you speak of justice?" she said. "You killed a man before my eyes. This is barbaric."

Vassil reached out a hand towards Anastasia, seizing her elbow.

"Ana, do not provoke them further. You know the truth now. That must be enough."

"Your friend," Kaletsky's voice declared, "he is right about one thing. These men will not face English justice. The important question now is your safety. You must go, Miss Boty. My helicopter is in the air. Get to the city, and you will be taken to safety."

"Go," said Vassil, "Please."

"If you go after her, you are all finished. You understand?" said Kaletsky.

"Da," said Dalca.

"Miss Boty," said Kaletsky, "you can be assured that no harm will come to you if you leave now. You have my word, and that of Tristan Tzara."

"I am grateful, Mr Kaletsky," said Anastasia, "but I still don't understand why any of this happened."

"Keep the line open," said Kaletsky, "and leave. My people are investigating this matter. We have connections all over Europe. You will have your answers soon."

"Go, woman," said Dalca. "You have been lucky this time."

Anastasia stepped away, but did not dare turn her back to the scene. She looked at Dalca, a bundle of steroidal aggression, at Henric, a slumped carcass with a nimbus of blood.

Mungo and Sabina followed the sounds of gunfire deep into the woods, pushing their way through the thick trees. The two circus survivors brushed the branches aside with increasing desperation before finally bursting out into a wide circle of trees.

Mungo struggled to immediately interpret the tableau he had stumbled upon. At first glance, it looked like Mihai was reaching out for Popescu, as if he were offering his hand as a gesture of friendship. But then Mungo's eyes adjusted to the light, allowing him to see the truth of the scene. Popescu was a broken man, knelt on the floor, with a crooked jaw and one arm hanging limply by his side. Mihai's arm was not reaching out towards Popescu in friendship – it was pointing a gun at the old man.

The third person in the clearing was –

"Nell!"

Sabina rushed over to Nell who knelt beside Popescu in Mihai's firing arc.

The two friends embraced and Sabina touched the red and recent mark on Nell's face but Nell immediately brushed her aside began to check Sabina's injuries. Mungo crossed into the clearing behind Popescu. Popescu turned his head at Mungo's appearance.

"Mungo. It has been a long time," he said.

"Hello Marku."

"Marku?" snarked Mihai.

Popescu sighed weakly.

"Marku was just a chance to escape from myself for a while." Popescu nodded towards Mihai. "But the past has now caught up with me."

At this, Mihai spat at Popescu and addressed Mungo.

"*Clovn*, this bastard deserves death for what he did. Him and all the others."

Mungo took a step towards Mihai.

"You don't have to live like that. Living in the past. Live off hatred and fear."

"Stay out of this, *clovn*!"

"No, listen to me," said Mungo. "I know about this. I have been running from my past for a long time and you have been holding on to yours. That's not life."

Mungo's voice trembled as he thought back over the past twelve years, rotting on his bench.

"But this man deserves to die," Mihai said. "You don't know what he did!"

Mungo shook his head.

"It doesn't matter. I suffered in the past. Perhaps not like you, but I had revenge on my tormentor. I watched him die at my own hand and, believe me, it brought me no satisfaction. In fact it cost me everything."

He glanced briefly at Sabina.

"Well, almost everything."

Popescu spoke. "Listen to the clown, Mihai. We are only here on this earth for a brief spell, take it from an old man. I am truly sorry for what I did. I tried to help the children as best I could. I wished them no harm back then and I wish you no harm now."

Mihai stared back through bloodshot, teary eyes.

Nell's head snapped up at the sound of a safety catch being released. Mihai raised the gun, but Mungo was already there, running at Mihai and shoving Popescu aside. A shot went off, and someone screamed. It might have been Sabina. Nell didn't have time to look before the second shot rang out.

Nell didn't wait to see which of them he planned to shoot next. She had failed to disarm him before but there was even more at stake now. She grabbed a chunk of old bark off the ground and threw it hard. Her angle was wrong, but it knocked him off-guard long enough for her to scramble to her feet. She swung a right hook at Mihai. It was graceless and telegraphed for any fighter to read. A wiser and stronger man like Bobby could have taken advantage of her panicked delivery and rolled with it, but Mihai had spent his formative years malnourished, and his bone development and reflexes reflected it even if his musculature did not. As she felt the explosive crack beneath her fist, she heard his gun go off again.

This time, it was Mungo who screamed. He fell to the ground, hand pressed against his chest, fingers already damp with blood.

Nell slammed her foot into the side of Mihai's knee and he crumpled. Nell snatched the gun from where it lay on the earth and re-engaged the safety. Mihai lay trembling, weeping.

Popescu had dragged himself over to Mungo. Nell nudged him aside and knelt down.

"Hey, Mungo," she murmured. Her own pulse pounded in her ears, but she allowed her training to take over. "Are you with me?"

He groaned. Nell snatched some gloves and a small pair of scissors from the front pocket of her backpack that she was still wearing.

"I'm going to cut your shirt away so I can see where the bullet entered. Sabina?"

"Yes?"

"I need you to come find the gauze pads in my bag. I'm going to need them right away."

Sabina moved slowly toward them, her eyes trained on Mungo.

"Is he dying?"

"Sabina," Nell said, "I need your help right now. I know you've been through a lot, but you can do this."

She kept her eyes on the fabric as she carefully snipped around the spot where Mungo was struggling to keep pressure on the wound.

"Mungo, how are you doing? Can you tell me how you feel?"

"Like somebody fucking shot me," he whispered.

Popescu had begun rocking back and forth. Nell got the feeling he was praying, although she couldn't hear half of what left his lips. She glanced over her shoulder, but Mihai was no longer there. Crawled away. Gone.

She took the pads from Sabina and tried to remain focused on her patient.

"Okay, Mungo, I'm going to move your hand now."

She gently pried his fingers away and slipped the gauze in place. "The good news is it looks like the bullet went through higher, in the shoulder, and not the chest."

"The bad news?" he asked, as Nell checked his pulse.

"You got shot in the middle of nowhere."

"Oh," he tried to nod. "Of course."

"And Mihai's disappeared," Nell said, glancing around the clearing.

"Does he have the gun?"

"Not anymore. It's over."

"No," said Popescu, shaking his head gently. "It's never over. The circus doesn't stop here."

The clown winced.

"I can hear a helicopter," said Mungo. "Is that a bad sign?"

Nell looked up at the trees around them.

The noise burst upon the factory seconds before the helicopter itself, swooping low and then rising up again to circle overhead.

"Ana, darling?" Sebastian's voice issued from the phone in Anastasia's hand.

"Did you hear that?" said Anastasia.

"It's Kaletsky's helicopter," said Sebastian. "No distance at all from Cambridge."

"Is Kaletsky still there?" said Anastasia.

"I am," said Kaletsky. "My men cannot land where you are, but they can take out the gangsters who are threatening you if they have to."

"Vassil," said Anastasia, "are you coming?"

Vassil took a step towards her, but Dalca blocked his path.

"You work for me," said Dalca to Vassil. "You're going nowhere. I have just lost one man to please your girlfriend. You will do his job now."

With this Dalca used the toe of his boot to nudge Henric's inert form.

Vassil gazed across at Anastasia. His face had the opacity of a man resigned to his fate. He shook his head slightly. He lowered his gaze. For an instant.

"Dalca," shouted Anastasia. "I have an army on my side. Let Vassil leave with me."

At that the helicopter dipped again, its rotors slicing powerfully through the air overhead. Two shots rang out, popping the heavy duty tyres of a refrigerated lorry by the loading bay as easily as balloons.

Emil emerged from the factory, a grim look on his face.

"Sgender is dead," he shouted over the helicopter. "Gornel doo. There is a fire on far side of fagdory."

Dalca frowned.

"What?"

Emil leaned to speak into Dalca's ear.

Eventually, Dalca turned his gaze back to Anastasia, a coldness in his eyes.

"Just go. We have things to do here."

Pushing Vassil roughly in the back, he released the young Bulgarian to Anastasia's care. Vassil ran towards her, and together they backed out of the car park and sprinted down the lane towards the waiting taxi.

"What the fuck's going on here?" said the Scotsman, as they climbed into his cab. "Did you see that? Like Apocalypse fucking Now! Are the Americans about to napalm the fens?"

"Not the Americans this time," said Anastasia. "The Russians."

"Jesus Christ," said Shafique, "and I thought the Cold War was over."

Nell nudged Sabina with her elbow.

"I have another set of gloves in my bag. Can you put those on?"

Sabina fumbled in the pocket and pulled them out.

"Okay. You're going to come over here and put pressure on the wound for me."

"I don't think I can do this," Sabina said. Her hands were shaking.

"You can," Nell said.

She pulled her own gloves off and bundled them up. Reaching into her bag, she pulled out a HeatReady blanket and wrapped it around her friend with an awkward hug.

"I need to get help."

"What about Mihai?" Mungo wheezed.

Nell pulled off her sweatshirt and tucked it around his torso. She ran her hands over his legs, but he didn't seem to be losing heat as fast as he could have been.

She glanced around.

"I don't know. I don't think he can get far in the shape he's in."

"What if he comes back?"

Nell held out the gun. "Would you feel better if I left this with you?"

"Definitely," Mungo said. "Sabina, take the gun."

Nell looked down at her little circus of three – all sharp edges and illusion, they were. Three broken and battered performers. She rested a hand on Sabina's shoulder.

"I'll be back. As soon as I know help is on the way, I promise."

Before she could think of another reason to delay, Nell took off, phone in hand. When she'd followed Mihai in, it had taken at least ten minutes, but at full speed, even with her knee twinging, she made it back to the parking lot in less than half the time.

She reached the end of the path and paused. It was quiet here, on this strip of dirt, and a part of her just wanted to sit down at the border between the horror behind her and the reality ahead. Instead, she dialled 999 as she tried to catch her breath.

She didn't relish the idea of explaining away the opportunities she'd had before this to call the police instead of trying to Nancy Drew this goddamned disaster, but Sabina was alive. That's what mattered. That and getting a certain pain-in-the-ass DC out here to sort this shit out.

The sound of a door slamming across the parking lot made her pick up her pace. "Bobby?" she called. "That you?"

"I'm afraid not," came the loud reply.

Outside the large rear doors of the factory stood a black Mercedes SUV. Tracks in the dirt and gravel suggested other vehicles had been here recently. There was a broad patch of blood nearby, already becoming one with the dusty ground.

Two men stood by the boot of the SUV. One of them had a face that was scarred and stitched up and it occurred to her that this must be the person Bobby had gone looking for. And apparently not found. Beside Dalca, a younger man in hoodie and jeans stood with one hand on his ribs, the other holding a pistol.

Nell heard a voice on the other end of the line pick up.

"Emergency – what service do you require?"

"Ambulance and police..." Nell managed before Dalca stepped forward and smacked the phone out of her hand.

"You're with Bobby Thomas then?"

"No."

"Don't lie to me. I've had a very bad day." The smile that crossed his face was an ugly one. "Haven't I, Emil?"

Emil spat on the ground. It was more blood than spit.

"Fugging terrible."

"Don't know what you think you're doing," Dalca continued, "but this is private property, and I have plenty of room back here for a meddling friend of Bobby's."

He held up his key fob and the boot levered open behind him.

Behind them, in the back of the SUV, a bundle of white plastic sheeting shifted and parted. Bobby, more blood and bruise than man, pushed himself up into a sitting position, levelled the gun in his hand, and shot Dalca in the back before the man even noticed him. Emil spun around, gun in hand and Bobby put bullet in his skull.

"Thought I'd kill myself if I had to listen to them fuck around much longer," Bobby said, heaving himself out.

He examined his torn pants and the bloody ruin that was his shirt, then grabbed Dalca's legs with a groan. "Give me a hand with this?"

She kept her gaze focused just above the carnage. "Bobby..."

"No need to be squeamish. It's nothing that didn't need to be done," he said, heaving the body up into the boot himself, then turning to throw Emil in as well. Bobby picked up Dalca's keys.

"Guess it's about time I got out of town though."

"You've killed them."

It couldn't be that simple though. A single shot and a man became meat? There had to be a moment in between that stretched on and allowed the possibility of redemption, of survival.

Bobby shrugged. "Not your problem."

"How do you figure?"

She swallowed, tasting bile. There was no undoing any of it. There was only surviving.

He dropped a hand on her shoulder and squeezed it tightly.

"Because I'm telling you not to make it your problem. They were bad men," he said, giving her a little shake. "This is no less than they deserved."

"You're a bad man too."

Bobby regarded himself and his injuries and then the keys to the SUV.

"No less than I deserve either."

He bent down to retrieve her phone. He held it up to his ear for a moment, then tossed it to her.

"Sounds like it's for you."

She wrapped her fingers around the phone and pushed it against her ear.

"Ma'am? Are you still there?"

Nell watched the Merc peel out of the lot.

"I'm here."

CHAPTER TEN

Nell leaned against the wall by Sammy's and unwrapped her sandwich. She had saved her last break of the day for Sabina's show, and it felt good to stand in the sunshine and watch her friend perform on the wide green space on the pavement across the road. She still wasn't sure how Sabina managed to get a sword all the way down her throat, although she'd had the mechanics of it explained to her several times. To Nell, every time looked like magic.

"Nice day, isn't it?"

Nell twitched in surprise, then nodded as Castell settled in next to her. On the grass, Sabina extracted her python from its secured box.

"It's a great day," she said as she watched Sabina gently wrap her pet around her neck.

So much trust. Even after everything that had happened, Sabina bounced back. If anything, her life was better – new act, new father, fewer hours serving snacks to the summer crowd. Disaster seemed to have a way of making her friend thrive.

Nell envied it. She still woke multiple times a night, sheets tangled tightly around her. After a few weeks of it, she'd broken down and bought makeup to cover the bruised circles under her eyes and the narrowing of her cheeks when her appetite didn't return. She'd even dug out an almost empty bottle of prescription anti-anxiety pills and returned it to the front pocket of her backpack for easier access.

She had thrown herself into work to numb her brain and seek out exhaustion. She'd even picked up Sabina's extra shifts. The last day off she'd taken was Gracie Greenwood's funeral. She and Rachel had closed up shop and joined what felt like the whole town in remembering the little girl.

Nell caught sight of a face in the crowd. The older Greenwood girl had been coming by Sammy's more frequently this spring, often in the company of the skinny kid who used to work at McNair's.

Castell followed her line of sight across the street. He took in the whole scene, illuminated as it was by the great breaths of fire Sabina blew toward the crowd.

267

"Your friend seems to have made a remarkable recovery," he said.

"Sabina's tough," Nell said.

"And her father?"

She nodded. "He was lucky."

"He might not have survived the shooting if you hadn't been there."

Nell looked away from the show. She could feel her chest tightening, and if she didn't take a pill soon, it would balloon into a panic attack.

"If you don't mind, I'm going to wash up before I get back to work."

"Nell." He grabbed her arm and she pulled roughly away. "I'm sorry," he said and took a step back, his hands falling to his sides. Across the road, the crowd let out a roar. Sabina was coming to the big finish.

"I'm just trying to help," he said.

"I'm fine," said Nell.

"Are you?" he asked. "Because, frankly, you look like hell."

"Thanks."

"I just meant we're...concerned."

"We?"

"Your aunt. Sabina also said something to me when I was in last week. Whatever it is that's eating you up, it shows."

"I've had the flu," she lied. "That's all."

"I hope not. Wouldn't want Rachel in trouble with the health inspectors. She might stop giving me free chips."

"It's allergies." He looked unconvinced. Nell could feel her pulse in her fingertips. "Look," she rooted around in her bag and grabbed her pills, carefully keeping her hand wrapped around the label. "These keep me from sneezing in your free food."

She popped one under her tongue. He put out his hand for the bottle, but she tossed it back in her bag, a few papers fluttering to the ground as she did.

Castell knelt down to retrieve them. He glanced up at her, but Nell kept her expression blank. Gracie Greenwood with wings sprouting out of the back of her school uniform. Razvan Popescu, cheek resting on his hand as he stared at the chessboard in front of him. A sketch of a truck and a bicycle and a woman sprawled across the pavement, her arm jutting out at a terribly familiar angle.

"Did you draw these?" he asked.

"I bought them." She looked down at the crumpled papers. "The artist is back in London now."

"Yes, I know." He stood and smoothed them out, handing her the sheets to return to her bag. "You like her work?"

"I guess. I've only seen what's online."

"But you liked these enough to buy them," he said, studying her face.

"They're just copies. She was raising money for the Greenwoods, and I wanted to contribute." She shrugged. The aftertaste of the pill was bitter, but it should erase the tightness so she could go back to work.

"But you carry them with you," he pointed out.

"Sometimes."

Castell handed her a business card. She ran her thumb over the embossed type.

"Another friend of yours?"

"Actually, yes. He specialises in PTSD. Totally confidential. Whatever it is you won't tell me, maybe you can tell him." She stared down at the card. "I helped Rachel get an appointment for you Thursday."

"Oh really?" She had a right to the prickle of anger but it was gone as quickly as it came. In its place was an almost forgotten feeling lapping its way around the edges of her sharp, broken bits.

"Can't lose my access to free food," he said solemnly. "Not on my salary."

She tucked the card into her pocket. "Better watch out. Word might get around that you're going soft."

"I just hate to see good go to waste," he said, turning to go.

"Richard?"

"Hmm?"

"Thanks for your..." she trailed off uncertainly. "For interfering."

He smiled. "Sure."

Nell gestured across the street.

"If we hurry, we can catch the end of Sabina's show."

"I thought you were late for your shift."

"I am," she said. "But the finale's worth it."

Mungo found Popescu at the end of the pier staring out to sea. Popescu looked up as he arrived.

"Hello Mungo," said the old Romanian.

"Joseph, please."

"Joseph then."

"Mungo is resting in peace with Marku the Magnificent these days."

"I'm sorry to hear that," said Popescu. "That clown saved my life."

Joseph smiled. "He saved mine too, once upon a time, but I wallowed in those clown clothes long after they stopped fitting. This is a new life."

"So no putting the circus troupe back together? We could do a Circus Romero tribute act in memory of our fallen comrades. Doctor Delirium has been calling, inviting us to join his circus. Did you know they give the audience 3D glasses nowadays?"

"I heard," Joseph sighed. "I let the Doctor's calls go to voicemail. I have retired from clowning."

"I'm sorry to hear that. You were one of the best."

"I was taught by the best," said Joseph. "But I lost my nose in that meat factory. It might have rolled under one of the machines or perhaps it has been sat in an evidence bag these past few months. Either way, I'm taking it as a sign. Mungo is gone."

The two old men stood in thoughtful silence, watching the seagulls wheeling in the sky and the wind turbines turning out at sea. Eventually, Popescu nodded towards the brown paper bag in Joseph's hand.

"What's in the bag?"

"Donuts."

"I thought Sabina had you on a diet?"

"She certainly does," laughed Joseph. "Five portions of fruit and veg a day, no takeaways, no processed fats and no sugar."

"You better hide those donuts then, my friend. Her act will finish soon."

"It's okay, they're not for me."

"No? Well, the diet appears to be working."

"A lot of that is giving up the alcohol. Wonky Donkey has a lot of calories."

"I imagine that was a hard habit to kick. Are you going to Alcoholics Anonymous? The Twelve Steps and so on?"

"No, I was never an alcoholic, just a drunk," said Joseph. "I follow the One Step programme."

"Oh?"

"If I take one step out of line then Sabina will saw me in half!"

Popescu laughed.

"So, your bench is gone, your nose is lost and Mungo Joey has passed away. What will you do now, Joseph?"

"This is the fourth time I have started over. Or fifth time, I've lost count. I want to use this life to be a good father to Sabina. I need to make up for lost time. I don't know the first thing about parenthood but my own father showed me how *not* to behave."

"I imagine that is half the battle," said Popescu. "You'll find your feet, even if you can't find your nose. What else will you do?"

Joseph looked thoughtful.

"I'm going to help people. Young people, especially. Considering what happened to me as a child, and what happened to Gracie, I want to make sure that children have a voice."

"How?"

"Not sure yet. Give me time."

Popescu smiled.

"You know, I used to tell Gracie fairy tales from Romania."

"I met Gracie very briefly, once upon a time," said Joseph. "She had just run away from school."

"That certainly sounds like her."

"We spent all afternoon talking and eating donuts on my bench until the police arrived to take her home. She told me a story then."

"What story?"

"Something about a king who became a beggar because he was too cowardly to defend his people. His Kingdom was set aflame by a monster -"

"Balaur the dragon," said Popescu.

271

"That was it," said Joseph. "It was a wonderful story and she told it well. She never told me how it ends."

Popescu sighed. "No, Gracie never heard the ending either." His voice shook and it took the old man some time to compose himself. "I will tell you the ending now. After all, an unfinished story is a terrible matter."

"I would love to hear it."

"So, the king had fled and only the maiden knew who he was and the tears she cried at his stories became remarkable gifts. But then, after many years, the smell of the burning Kingdom and its subjects finally faded from Balaur's nostrils and he detected a new smell. It was the smell of the king and the maiden who had both survived its merciless attack. Balaur was furious and set out to destroy those who had escaped its annihilation.

"Balaur found the maiden first, collecting berries in the woods for the beggar. Balaur seized her in its scimitar talons and took her to its cave. However, Balaur did not kill the maiden immediately, instead hoping to use her as bait to draw out the other survivor.

"Word of the maiden's capture spread through the village. When the beggar heard this ill news, he became enraged and, in his rage, became a brave man, and remembered who he had once been.

"The King also remembered the three gifts, formed from the tears of the maiden. He used the silver compass to find the dragon's cave, he used the crystal to light his way to where the maiden was tied up with rope and he used the little silver knife to cut her bonds.

"The moment she was free, Balaur descended from the shadowy roof of the cave, roaring with its fiery breath. The beggar stood between the maiden and the flames, prepared to sacrifice himself for his loyal subject. The flames burn away the beggar's clothes, revealing the garments of the King underneath. The garments flashed bright and white and blinded the dragon. All six of Balaur's eyes went dark and the three heads thrashed around, bumping and biting each other in confusion. The Dragon fled in blind panic. It was never heard from again."

Joseph nodded.

"This king?" he said.

"Yes?"

"I kind of like him."

"Me too," said Popescu, patting Joseph on the back.

"What happens next?" asked Joseph. "Do the king and the maiden live happily ever after?"

Popescu simply shrugged. "It is not known. That is all that has ever been told."

"I thought an unfinished story was a terrible matter?"

"Oh, very much so," said the Romanian. "But we must finish this story ourselves. The ending can be whatever we choose." At that, Popescu turned away from the sea. "It was good talking to you, Joseph. I'm off for a stroll along the promenade. Fancy joining me?"

"I said I would wait for Sabina. She should finish her performance soon."

"Very well. Until we meet again then."

They shook hands and the old man left Joseph alone with the sea.

Joseph thought on the old man's words while he waited for another old friend.

Here he comes now.

Spitfire the seagull, landed at the side of the pier, dirty, emaciated and grouchy as ever. Spitfire appraised Joseph with one malevolent eye, whilst his other was crusted shut with gunk. The seagull might have cawed to express its hostility but its beak appeared to be occupied with a blood-red toffee apple.

"We meet again," Joseph said to the bird. "We were enemies when I was Mungo but perhaps we can be friends now that I am Joseph."

Spitfire ruffled his matted feathers suspiciously, not yet advancing any closer.

"I've brought you some donuts as a peace-offering, although you appear to have found some lunch already." Joseph nodded towards the toffee-apple skewered in the bird's beak.

However, Spitfire then hopped closer and Joseph realised the red shape in its mouth wasn't a toffee apple. It was his old clown nose. Joseph's mouth dropped open in surprise and Spitfire mirrored this gesture, letting the red clown nose fall next to the bag of donuts.

"Where did you find this?" asked Joseph, picking it up in amazement. The shape, the texture, it all felt very familiar in the palm of his hand. It was definitely his nose.

Spitfire simply cawed, their business now successfully concluded, and dived into the sugary bag of donuts, gorging itself in a feeding frenzy. Joseph decided to let the seagull enjoy its lunch. He bid farewell to the sea and took his leave.

The Authors

Yasmin Ali has mainly written on politics and social policy, but turned recently to writing fiction. She has published two short stories in anthologies (links below), one a piece of crime fiction, the other a tale of a politician caught up in a sex and drugs scandal. She has also written drama for theatre and for radio. Yasmin is a member of the Tindal Street Fiction Group (www.tindalstreetfictiongroup.com), and is completing a novel. She blogs at yasminali.org .

A Southerner displaced, **Sue Barsby** is a full time communications officer, as well as a writer, knitter, conker fetishist, grammar nerd, and caffeine appreciator. Having sold books for ten years, reviewed them for a range of magazines for 17 years and read them for many more years than that, she thought it was high time that she sat down and wrote a book. Her short stories are beginning to see the light of day in journals and websites and she is currently working on a novel set in 1930s variety theatre. She blogs about books – reading and writing them – at Books from Basford and can be found on Twitter at @Basfordian.

Luke Beddow studied English and Creative Writing at Birmingham City University, where he was awarded the 'Jim Crace Award for Creative Writing' for *Megiddo Junction*, a collection of poetry he compiled as a final year project. He worked in learning support roles in West Midlands secondary schools before qualifying as a teacher of English. He lives in north Birmingham, and can be seen reading at open mic nights in the city. His blog, undertheinfluence88.blogspot.co.uk, contains book reviews and sundry other things.

Danielle Bentley graduated from the University of Birmingham last year with a BA Hons in English Literature and Drama. She has performed her work at university and Birmingham writers events, and acted in several theatre productions. As well as dabbling in journalism and film, Danielle has recently written a WW1 screenplay and has plans to produce it herself. She is currently working on the novel she started during JuNoWriMo.

Simon Fairbanks studied MA English Literature at the University of Birmingham and has been a member of the Birmingham Writers' Group since 2011. His story, The Monster That Stares Back, appears in the Darker Times Anthology Volume One and he won the Belper Arts Festival Short Story Competition in 2013 for his entry, The Tick Tock Man. Simon's first fantasy novel, The Sheriff, was released in March 2014. The Sheriff was later chosen as one of ten novels to be launched at the One Big Book Launch in London. Simon was announced as winner of the Ten To One writing competition in March 2014.

Jason Holloway is an award-winning non-fiction writer, editor, marketer, and business executive in the non-profit, public, and private sectors. He has held a variety of positions with some of the most storied publishing houses in Washington, DC, including Congressional Quarterly and American Psychological Association Books. Ernst & Young named him to its annual Forty Under Forty. He is currently Principal of Holloway & Associates, LLC, which provides a broad cross-section of consulting services with a particular emphasis on non-traditional revenue generation. Jason holds an MBA with a Finance concentration from Drexel University's LeBow School of Business.

Maria Mankin has published six books with Pilgrim Press and has contributed to several anthologies. She's one of ten authors involved in Circ, an innovative collaborative novel published by Pigeon Park Press. She's currently working on a series of children's books about the animals of Tanzania, as well as a collaborative mystery novel. She also has a successful literary review blog, Books, j'adore, published weekly. When she's not writing, she takes great joy in exploring best practice for engaging young readers both in and out of the classroom. She lives in California with her husband.

William Thirsk-Gaskill was born in Leeds in 1967. After working as a research chemist and IT consultant, in 2010 he began to study creative writing with the Open University. Since then, he has published poetry and short stories, and become a regular contributor to spoken word events from Manchester to York. His last publication is a novella, called 'Escape Kit', which was one of the winners of the Grist 2013 chapbook competition, and was also short listed for a Saboteur Award. During the 2013 Ilkley Literature Festival, he helped to carry one of Simon Armitage's socks for 47 miles around the Yorkshire Dales in a charitable cause. William's poem, 'Eleven Colours of Loneliness', won the Wakefield Post Code prize in the 2014 Red Open Poetry competition.

Giselle Thompson has always wanted to write, but instead she went to medical school. She now works part time, with one day per week free to write. She studied creative writing with the Open University, and has been a regular contributor to the Telegraph Creative Writing Group, an on-line writing group where writers submit short stories, and learn from others' critique. Giselle will be publishing an anthology of short stories 'A Receiver of Stolen Words'. Her work in progress, 'Doughty', is set in the dynamic city of Birmingham, during its Victorian glory days, and features a coroner, some dark deeds in the workhouse, and a housekeeper with a secret past. Giselle's blog is at chateauxenespagne.com and she's on Twitter @GiselleThompsn.

Livia Akstein Vioto studied History at the University of São Paulo, thus becoming a well of useless information, at least according to her father. Although she is currently unpublished, several of her plays were performed by the now extinct O Circo theatre company, where she also tried her hand at acting and directing. She writes from sunny Brazil, just under the Tropic of Capricorn, where she also works as a translator and copy-editor. You can find her blogging at labyrinthandmirrors.wordpress.com.